IF THE FATES ALLOW

MARYSA STEVENS

CHAPTER 1

ALICE

First, I ate the head because I hated to see its little beady eyes staring at me. I had to eat it in at least two bites, otherwise the gelatin stuck to my teeth, and I played a tongue war with my molars.

Clearing his throat, my colleague Patrick leaned against my cubicle, intently watching my jaw work. "I've always found it disturbing that you decapitate the bear," he said. Without blinking, I pulled out another cinnamon gummy bear from my desk drawer and chewed off the head, staring straight at Patrick. He grimaced. "Why don't you eat the whole thing at once?"

I shrugged. "We all have our quirks."

"Some more than others." He walked backward to his cubicle behind mine, sitting down at his office chair, and spinning back to face me. "What's this early-ass meeting about?"

"Hell if I know," I replied, intent on consuming my next victim.

Patrick snorted. "Bullshit. You always know everything around here."

I tucked my candy bag back in the desk drawer, before a mirror check for any pesky lingering red candy in my teeth. "Not today; it was last minute."

"I swear if he tells us we have to organize another team-building 5K race, I'll quit."

"And he didn't even run in it," I whispered. "I'm still freaked out by him watching the three of us go around and around the high school track."

Our small team in the Department of City Planning was one step above answering calls from concerned citizens complaining about the lack of trees in Phoenix—an argument never worth having with someone delusional—but our jobs were well below anything that brought about meaningful change. Our boss, Devin, wore ill-fitting khakis and always smelled like his overly greasy breakfast. He managed an annual six-figure budget to bring ancient documents into the twenty-first century. Basically, our roles involved a lot of scanning. It was only a matter of time before a robot took our jobs.

It wasn't world-changing work, but it was satisfactory; it was a job that brought a means to an end, and I was completely and totally fine with that. I didn't need to do something on a grander scale. Every community needed worker bees, and I was happy to be one. I stayed behind the scenes, letting others with an important life purpose take center stage.

"Probably an announcement of the promotion," said Bethany, who had been eavesdropping nearby, although she was still embroiled in a face-off with Patrick after she stole the credit for a big win last fall. They had worked together on a new digital filing system that saved the department ten grand a year, and they both wanted to be the teacher's pet. Ultimately, Bethany was given the gold star, and I still didn't know if it was fair or not. Patrick had been so hurt he instructed me, as his designated work wife, to not speak more than ten words to her per week until she admitted the truth. That was six months ago.

Patrick winked at me. "We all know who's getting that promotion. Don't we, Alice?"

I rolled my eyes. It was obvious Devin favored me, but not in a gross, inappropriate way. I was a bit of an Excel wizard from obsessively watching YouTube tutorials for the past decade. He often pulled me into projects above my pay grade that didn't earn me a bonus—*yay for being a government employee!*—but did make him look good to his bosses.

I bit down on my lip, holding back a smile. Maybe Patrick was right, and today I'd finally be recognized for going above and beyond.

"It should be *me* since I implemented DigiVault," Bethany argued. "But Devin thinks I'm a dumb blond."

"'DigiVault' is still a stupid fucking name," Patrick muttered under his breath.

To cover for Patrick's insult, I retorted, "The only one who calls you a dumb blond is yourself, Bethany."

"Word quota!" Patrick raised his hand to cut me off, eliciting a stuck-out tongue from Bethany. He ignored this and continued his hell-bent crusade to make the case for why I was a shoo-in for the promotion. "But you did project manage the online tool that saved the call center hundreds of calls a year."

"Yes, saving the city of Phoenix one angry phone call at a time," I said with faux bravado.

"Innovative," Bethany replied with equal sarcasm, but her smile faded. She and Patrick had their issue, but I didn't want to choose sides, even if she made off-handed rude comments. I got the sense she was continuing to find what role she played in life. Was she the villain or the dumb blond subject to everyone's jokes?

Despite Patrick's confidence in me, I questioned whether I wanted the promotion. A promotion would mean more work and expectations to answer emails on vacation. I was satisfied getting through each day and going home without having to take my work with me. The job was a paycheck. It was fine here, I had no real complaints. It was never my intended plan to be here for so many years, but sometimes life didn't go to plan.

I fiddled with the geode my sister mailed me from Madagascar; I repurposed it as a paperweight on my desk. I kept the note she sent me buried under my candy drawer.

If you crack this rock open, you might find something spectacular on the inside.

Every time I read her words, it reminded me of my apathetic attitude that masked my disappointment about not yet having found my true calling in life. The note had been crumbled into a paper ball a dozen times, but I could never find it in myself to throw it away. She cared about me, and I was exceptionally bitter about that.

In college, my favorite class was on historic preservation. I dreamed of a career in a public department that designed and fostered more vibrant communities with history at the heart. But those jobs were secured for individuals with backgrounds in architecture or engineering. In the shitty post-grad recession, I settled for this job and never left.

According to my sister, who held a Ph.D. in geology, my Bachelor of Arts in Anthropology was merely a degree in puppetry. She wouldn't have knocked it so hard if I had gone to grad school, but her doctorate degree had her nose too high in the air. Truthfully, she was an obnoxious, self-centered person, and it was best we were separated by a few layers of earth as she was mining for fossils or whatever. However, I had something my rock-hunting sister did not: a boyfriend with an MBA from Harvard who was going to make us filthy rich.

"Alice, grab your laptop," Devin shouted. "Mine's got the blue screen of death."

Lips pursed, I stifled a groan and quickly retrieved my computer. In the conference room, I connected it to the HDMI cable and logged in.

I'd seen four-year-olds work on a laptop better than Devin, and his incompetence was what put me on the spot to be his driving horse to begin with. Still, I couldn't help myself. "Want me to lead?" I volunteered.

"If you could pull up SharePoint, I can maneuver from there," he said, hovering over my shoulder. His breath smelled like an egg breakfast sandwich, and I forced myself to breathe through my mouth to fend off disgust. "You can sit now."

Patrick pulled a chair out for me next to him, and I watched the projector warm up as it connected to my computer. Devin muttered to himself and moved the mouse around, clicking the folders for the sake of clicking them. I wanted to offer advice to help him find what he was looking for, but it was best for everyone to continue the ruse that he was our competent, all-knowing leader.

"There, it looks like that's it." He opened the folder for next quarter's projections and launched into a monotonous speech about more cost-cutting measures and fiscal stewardship. On the next document, a large photo of my face appeared. I cocked my head to the side, certain it was me, but also...it wasn't. My skin was too smooth. The whites of my eyes were too bright. Not a stray strand of dirty-blond frizz in sight.

"Whoa, it's Alice, but like, with a good skin care regimen," Bethany said. Patrick gave her a dirty look and subtly flipped her off. "It looks like a headshot for a marketing ad on a city bus."

"I am pleased to announce that our own Alice Woods will be promoted next quarter to serve as the Assistant to the Executive Director of Leads—the Director of Leads, of course, being me." Devin's extremely wide smile revealed his back molars, and a pit formed in my stomach. The room was silent, except for the sound of Devin jangling his keys and coins in his pant pockets. He rocked back and forth on his feet, waiting for someone else to speak.

Speechless. I should be grateful for a promotion, but this one felt like a giant slap in the face. I wasn't truly being promoted or given any leadership role. Was I even getting a pay bump? My title was changing to ensure Devin could keep me as his personal assistant. My chest felt hot, like a rocket warming up ready to blast off.

When no one spoke, Devin shifted nervously. "Well? Everyone say congratulations!"

Bethany chuckled and grinned tightly, like her cheeks were forced into position with tape. She gave me a passive-aggressive handshake, squeezing tight enough to make my middle finger pop. Patrick attempted a round of applause that came out like a delicately subdued golf clap, the kind reserved for the player when their ball falls in the sand trap and they still need encouragement for hitting it in the first place. *"Think of all the people who wished they could be playing golf. At least you're here!"* a spectator would say with two thumbs up.

"An email from human resources will be sent to you shortly with your new employee agreement and your raise." Devin made a show of finger guns. "Don't spend it all in one stop at Forever 21. I'll hold on to your computer until IT fixes mine."

The heat in my chest roared to a full wildfire as I forced a smile. I was closed in, trapped, and ready to claw at the walls. In my periphery, Patrick nodded toward Devin and mouthed, *"What a jerk."*

After tuning out the rest of the meeting, cringing at the sound of Devin's voice, I walked to my desk, forcing myself to keep my head high. Patrick huddled at my side and whispered, "Are you screwed or *fucking* screwed?"

I closed my eyes and nodded my head. "My promotion is the job I've already been doing, but now Devin can officially fire me if I don't do his personal assistant work."

"At least you got a raise."

I texted my boyfriend Mark to tell him I had news, then opened the email from HR that showed my new employee agreement, and the raise Devin had made such a show of: a whole extra sixty bucks a month. *Before* taxes.

Patrick's nose scrunched and he backed away slowly. "That sucks."

The three of us—Patrick, Bethany, and me—made a good team, even if two-thirds didn't get along with the remaining holdout. We worked hard and made Devin look good to his supervisor. We each found our niches and stuck to what we were good at. Unfortunately for me, Devin liked that I could move my way around a spreadsheet with the speed of an Olympic swimmer, and recently assigned me projects that bordered on personal. He wanted a spreadsheet for everything: how much he spent on lunch every day, his favorite new song on Pandora radio, the height and weight of every player on the German national basketball team.

He called us his "small but mighty team," and the way he always said "small" made me feel a sense of generational rage. He called us lowly workers straight to our faces, and we had to accept it. I endured this for years, letting it simmer and simmer. And now it boiled at a dragon-breathing-fire level.

"By the way, Miss Assistant *to* the Director of Leads," Bethany paused for dramatic effect. I looked around my desk for something sharp I could throw at her. "What was with the AI photo of you?"

"*That's* what it was!" I snapped my fingers. I couldn't place why the photo of me was so unsettling; I had assumed Devin had just taken my headshot and ran filters on it to death until he was satisfied. AI made more sense. "That's so creepy, right?"

"I wonder what *I* would look like in AI," Patrick mused.

"Still ugly," Bethany sang.

"If we're handing out insults," Patrick geared up, "fix that bleach-blond job before you get confused for a desperate buckle bunny chasing the bull riders at the rodeo. Oh wait, you already are."

"You're jealous because you're not their type—"

"—that *you* know of," Patrick barked back. Bethany stopped talking after that.

Devin kept my computer while he waited for his to work again, which gave me time to get my head together. He could keep it for the day for all I cared. I wasn't an idiot who kept personal information on my corporate computer. I didn't even use our free Microsoft subscription to update my off-the-clock spreadsheets for trivial things like ranking flavors in candy, cakes, and drinks, cinnamon being top and peppermint my least favorite.

My self-taught expertise in Excel was a pathetic, lackluster topic of conversation between Mark and me. He had an MBA from Harvard, as if I could go one day without remembering that he and his start-up bros came up with their million-dollar idea over beers and pizza at the famous Pinocchio's. It's why they named their investment firm Jiminy Cricket, completely unoriginal and surprisingly not eligible for a plagiarism lawsuit. They chased the dream that someday they'd quit working for the man and be self-employed.

I called Mark again and leaned over my desk, tucking my face away from my colleagues to whisper over the phone.

"Sup, babe? Gotta be quick."

"I sort of got a promotion," I squeaked.

"Awesome, so awesome."

I frowned at his response and continued anyway, not hiding the disdain in my voice. "It's to be Devin's assistant."

"That's great, really great."

Mark didn't understand. He didn't even hear me, I could have told him a taxi ran over me and he'd mutter the same mechanical responses.

"I won't be home until super late," he said, voice muffled by the sound of fingers typing furiously across a keyboard. "Have a few drinks with your buds to celebrate."

"My *buds*?"

"Yeah, whoever. Sorry, babe—got to go." He hung up faster than I could make sense of the conversation.

In moments like this I wasn't sure why I was still with Mark, probably for the same reasons I was still in this job. They were both simply *there*.

We met at a bar in typical fashion. He approached me, said something flattering I don't remember, maybe about my face or was it my ass? I fell for his hook and shortly after he asked me to move in with him, which was an ideal situation, since my old roommate, Barbara, had become a self-taught mycologist who grew fungi in the dark corners of our house.

My relationship was turning out to be like the rest of my life: dry, apathetic, uninspiring.

We were roommates with the occasional hurried intimacy, which always concluded with him working on his after-hours stock portfolio. We didn't argue; we didn't even get into heated discussions over sports or politics. The last time we had a date night weeks ago, he spent the dinner responding to urgent emails that made me wonder if there was even a distinction between "urgent" and "non-urgent."

But even after eight months together, it wasn't love. At least not the kind of love I saw my parents still had after forty years. He was too enamored with his finance job and get-rich-quick-schemes. He'd write a love poem to cryptocurrency before doing a romantic gesture for me. Still, he had a way of making things happen, so the thought of a comfortable life with a substantial financial cushion kept me hanging on.

Patrick chuckled under his breath when my phone pinged, laughing at his own joke. He texted me an AI image of Devin as a Roman emperor watching his gladiators fight to the death. I shook my head in playful comradery, opening the browser on my phone to pass the time as I waited for my computer to be returned. I created an AI image of Devin riding a tricycle with a group of plastic sex robots, a crown on his head made from hot dogs and nose strips. I downloaded the image and texted it to Patrick, struggling to contain my laughter.

"I want in on the secret," Bethany said, popping her head up over the cubicle. I gasped, holding a hand over my mouth as my heart rate kicked it up a notch.

"Jesus, you can't startle me like that," I said. "And it's nothing for you to see." She would one-hundred percent rat us out; it would be the best day of her life. All things considered, despite the drama between her and Patrick, I *liked* Bethany; she was a sharp-tongued snake who looked like a fifties pinup. I wanted her to find another job—not just so she'd leave us alone with some of the nonsense she spewed, but because she deserved to be respected and use her skills somewhere else. She was whip-smart and detail oriented, traits I admired.

"Pipe down, nugget," Patrick said, mindlessly clicking and scrolling through files. Most of our work was divided into two sections: pulling data and research to respond to public inquiries and complaints, and scanning the endless amounts of decades-old documents into digital files. He whistled at me and raised his arms. "But tell me what's so funny."

"Check your phone," I said, and pulled up a word game app. "Sorry, I can't help you work right now. My computer is otherwise occupied."

"Yeah, must be rough," Patrick scoffed. "Anyways, I didn't get anything from you in a text."

"It's a large image. It'll take a while to come through." I pulled up our conversation and texted him as we waited.

Alice: You and Bethany should totally hate-fuck.

Patrick: I'm gay.

Alice: Oh right, I forgot.

Patrick: And now that image will live in my brain forever. Thank you so much.

Alice: You know I love you…

Patrick looked up at his computer at the alert of a ping and set his phone down. I fidgeted, anxious to get mine back so I could get to work. I distracted myself with a Blow Pop from my stale Halloween candy collection, spinning around in a circle sucking on the lollipop.

"Patrick, is my tongue blue?"

I opened my camera selfie facing to see a terrifying double chin. God, that was not a good angle. Is that what Mark saw when he went down on me? Is that why he never offered? I stuck my tongue out and snapped a picture, sending it to Patrick. **It looks like I blew a Smurf,** I typed. I immediately heard the notification on his phone.

"Well, you got that one quickly. Here, let me show you the image since it's taking the Pony Expressway to get to you."

I turned my chair around and came abruptly face-to-face with Devin. I had been too engrossed with my texts to hear his noisy pockets as he sauntered up next to me. His neck was splotchy. Ears fire engine red. And his breath sounded like someone who used a CPAP machine when sleeping.

"My office. *Now.*" He stormed off and I glanced at Patrick, who looked pale and sickened. Bethany smiled so genuinely her cheeks glowed from the happy hormone.

"What's—what's going on?" I asked.

Patrick rolled his office chair to the other side of his desk, revealing his computer screen. Open on his email app was the AI image of Devin dressed like a motorcycle king surrounded by his posse of sex dolls. Hot dogs on his head and a cowbell around his neck. Holding a flag that said, "Horndog King of Arizona."

Patrick gulped and opened his mouth to tell me what Bethany couldn't wait to interrupt with: "You didn't send that as a text. You emailed that image to the entire list serve of city employees. All 33,000."

CHAPTER 2

SILAS

I would have donated a kidney on the spot if it had kept me on that beach for one more day. Five days wasn't even close to enough time spent smelling the salty breeze and feeling soft sand under my feet. And if it wasn't for a few job interviews, I would have spent every minute here by myself.

Fall in southern California was like a mild summer peaking at eighty degrees. It thawed my bones enough for me to feel them again. Hell, I could even wiggle my toes without requiring two layers of thick wool socks and insulated boots. And the endorphins from the sunshine were almost too much to handle; the first day here, I felt manic, like I could run straight across the state from San Diego to Sacramento.

The sun warmed my back as I laid prone on a beach towel courtesy of the hotel's cabana service. The cushioned lounger and umbrella were a holding space so I could store my bag and lay in the sand soaking up the direct sun all day. Drowning in the UVA rays was the *only* thing on my to-do list this week.

Preaching mental and physical health to my patients was easy. I knew exactly what to say and do to help them in life-threatening situations and prolong their lives. But lately, taking care of my own mind and body was a foreign concept. Escaping to California twice a year wasn't enough to keep me healthy long-term, but it was enough for now. To get me through another few months in Tidings, the frozen hellscape I had called home for almost four years.

Fuck, I *really* needed a life.

And that's what I hoped this week would do—give me that jumpstart I needed to finally take my life back. Back home, I had unfinished business to take care of, but I'd be out of there soon.

"Excuse me, sir?" I cracked open an eye to a blurry shadowed figure standing above me holding a tray. "Would you like another spritzer? It's your last day here; maybe go big this time."

"Glen, you've been trying to get me drunk on this beach for two years," I said, sitting up to face the helpful waiter with whom I'd developed a rapport, despite his frequent attempts to get me to "live a little." I swallowed the last bit of ice in my cup and handed it to him. "Just a refill on the mint water is fine, please."

I reapplied sunscreen and noticed that even with the sun protection, my skin had shifted from vampire white to a more natural, lively tone. I started taking this bi-annual trip three years ago and now I had it down to a disciplined science.

Rule number one: always travel alone. Occasionally, I'd check the dating apps to meet a girl and see where things went. Every so often, those casual date nights turned into flings understood by both parties as no strings attached.

But not this trip. I had important meetings that

required all my focus. Besides, I didn't have the desire or even self-esteem for a fling this time. Every ounce of my energy was being poured into rescuing myself from the lowest I'd ever been.

Rule number two: consume as much vitamin D as possible. I was outside from the first ray of light in the morning until the sun vanished over the Pacific Ocean each evening.

Seasonal affective disorder was a real fucking bitch. Believe me, I was the expert. In Tidings, the summer months were far too short, especially this year when the first snow fell in early autumn. The day I woke up and had to pull out my wool socks, I nearly punched a hole through my bedroom wall. Now, in November, enjoying the California sunshine felt so good it was positively sinful.

Glen handed me two full cups, one of mint water and one of the house spritzer I didn't ask for.

"Maybe one day you'll use the comfortable cabana bed instead of laying on the crusty sand."

"I'm not here for shade, my dude." I tucked my sunscreen in my backpack and pulled out a couple bucks for a tip. I squinted into the sun with my hand over my eyes as I reached up to hand Glen the cash. "You, however, look like you could use some sunscreen; you're as tanned as a horse's hide."

"Doesn't fit my vibe, bro."

"Skin cancer by twenty-five?"

"I'm a California surfer; the tan skin goes with the shaggy hair."

"You have red hair; you're significantly more likely to develop melanoma."

"Ok Dad," he said, pocketing the tip. "Maybe this'll be

the year I finally visit you. My mom's still mad that I haven't taken her to the Christmas market in Cambria."

I scoffed. "Tidings is not for winter novices, but if you make it, hit me up." I hadn't told Glen I wasn't planning on being there much longer.

I didn't even tell my family. No one knew the real reason why I was in California. Not yet.

My phone buzzed in my backpack, and I grabbed it immediately, anxious for an update from my interview yesterday, only to see a missed call from my sister. That was a call I could ignore for another day until it was time to deal with her in person again.

Not five seconds after I sent her to voicemail, my phone pinged.

Dagny: When you get back, we need to talk.

Silas: Are you at work or studying?

Dagny: Neither. Getting ready to go on a date.

Silas: With who?

Dagny: A wealthy foreign prince.

I rolled my eyes so hard I knew she could see it even thousands of miles away. There must be a link to early mortality rates for siblings with younger sisters. She'd send me to an early grave and snap her gum watching my casket go six feet under. I fumbled the screen between my thumbs, debating what to write back.

For a moment, I thought about telling my sister about what I was doing in California—the *real* truth, not the excuse of my bi-annual sun trip to thaw out from the dismal weather back home. But the fewer people who knew I was interviewing for other jobs, the better it was for me. I couldn't deal with the pressure and long faces, the *we'd really hate to see you go* sentiments. It needed to be on my terms.

Dagny: Miss your stupid face.

I convinced my little sister to join me in Tidings after she graduated with her biology degree last year. I made a deal she could live with me and focus on studying for the MCAT. She had a rough break-up, so running away to the ends of the earth worked for her, but she insisted on paying her own way. She picked up a job at a restaurant and lived with two roommates. It seemed like, despite her assurances that she was focused, there was far more partying than studying. I had the social awareness of a lake trout, so it was possible there was some underground shithole for partygoers even in Tidings.

Silas: Love you, Dags.

I tossed my phone back in my bag and stored my belongings in the personal safe assigned to my cabana. I jogged toward the ocean and dove in on the crest of a wave. At the surface, I took a sharp, shallow breath and tipped my head to the sun. I floated on my back, letting the current bring me back to shore. My lips twitched, smiling on their own. And then I laughed and laughed like a maniac, so drunk on sunshine.

Tomorrow I'd leave for Tidings—but I couldn't wait to call this my home.

CHAPTER 3
ALICE

After the most humiliating dressing down of my life, I collected my belongings from my desk leaving my access badge with the security guard who stood watch as I was escorted from the premises. My block heels galumphed across the hard floors, echoing louder than I'd ever heard before. Blood roared in my ears as everyone in the building stared at me. They watched the biggest fool who had sent the most embarrassing work email walk the plank to her career execution. I could never show my face in this city again.

In the parking lot, the bright Arizona sun burned my eyes like I had walked out of a dark cave into a spotlight. While most of the country enjoyed a crisp fall, early November in Phoenix was still bikini season.

I drove to the townhouse I shared with Mark. He owned the property, but invited me to move in at a discounted rent in exchange for my investment in Jiminy Cricket, LLC.

I thought I would see him more often by sharing the same roof, but he was at the office before I was out of bed, and he'd come home when I was already snoring with a book plopped on my face.

I slapped my steering wheel before I willed myself to grab my phone, texting my boyfriend: **call me urgently.**

I stumbled into the townhouse, dropping my purse on the floor by my feet. I leaned my back against the front door, examining the blank white walls we had never hung pictures on. My phone lit with a news update, and I frowned at a generic nature photo as my background image. I had no pictures of Mark and me together, almost like he was a figment of my imagination. That's how little time we spent together—he was practically a ghost.

He worked more than he did anything else while I was always waiting on him. Waiting for him to come home, to make time for us, to want more from me besides another investment.

A strange numbness overtook me. Despite the day's mortification, I wasn't unhappy... but I wasn't much of anything at all.

I was numb and frozen in place.

Do I sit on the couch? Lay prone on the floor with a pillow over my head? Do I change my hair color? Job hunt?

My phone vibrated in my hand.

Patrick: Proof of life?

Alice: I'm fine.

Patrick: You're definitely not.

Alice: Everything will be fine.

Patrick: Please brace yourself.

He followed up with a news link to the international

gossip website we often perused together at the office. It captured everything from politicians getting caught with their pants around their ankles, to the latest pop star and her new mystery man, to average people going viral overnight.

But me—I had gone viral within two hours.

The email, along with the AI image of my face doctored by Devin—*how the hell did that get around?*—was on the splash page.

<u>Arizona city employee axed for sending SALACIOUS AI image of her boss to ALL city employees!</u>

My breathing intensified, short and fast, never getting enough air to my lungs.

Like a ticking bomb that had finally detonated, my phone blew up with notifications: emails, texts, calls, social media messages from friends, people I hadn't talked to in years. A torrent spilled through—and yet, nothing from Mark. He always had his phone on him; it was practically his third arm. If he couldn't support me through this, there wouldn't be a future with us.

Think, Alice, my stern inner voice reprimanded. *What should I do? Call a lawyer? Olivia Pope?*

I needed money, fast. I opened the financial app Mark set me up with to check on my investments, holding my breath for good news. Instead, I was faced with a lot of red numbers. It was a risky move to make such a significant investment, but Mark assured me that it was common for the markets to fluctuate, and with the novelty of cryptocurrency, it may take more time for trends to appear. Each time I asked him when we'd see a payoff, he'd give me the same casual reassurance.

"Soon, babe, your retirement will triple, and we'll both be multimillionaires."

I logged into Instagram, hastily deactivating my profile but not before I saw notifications of unread messages and a dozen message requests.

Only a couple hours ago, I lost my job and now someone got a payday by cashing in my stupid mistake, letting the whole fucking world know I didn't know how to properly send a message to the right person.

Idiot.

The doorbell rang and I flinched. I felt the unnerving sense that on the other side was a man with a camera and a hundred questions. Wasn't that what happened when people went viral for stupid shit? I peeked through the side window to find a man holding a manila envelope. I opened it enough to peek one eye through the gap in the door.

"Hello, can I help you?" I asked.

"Alice Woods?"

"Yes?"

"You're being served," replied the man in a neutral voice.

"Served what?"

"I don't know ma'am. I'm just the courier." He passed me the envelope with my name and address printed on a sticker, but no return address. "Have a good day ma'am."

I ripped open the envelope and pulled out an eviction notice from Mark. The notice specified that I had twenty-four hours to leave the premises, and anything left behind would be discarded at my own cost. Mark hadn't insisted on a lease, and I paid him my half of the rent each month through a payment app. Legally speaking, I was simply a roommate without any tenant rights—a squatter, really.

I called Mark and again it went to voicemail. I texted him a series of scathing messages: *You coward! At least have the balls to say it to my face.*

I slammed the door shut and chucked my phone at the wall, leaving a black mark on the crisp white paint. *Fuck.* I picked it up off the ground—not busted, thankfully. I called the one person I felt like I could trust at that moment.

"Girl, are you okay?" Patrick whispered, the sound of wind whipping past him on the other line like he stepped outside to take my call. "Everyone is talking about it. It's on TikTok!"

I crouched in the corner, burying my head between my legs. "P–Pat—" I struggled to grasp air, never mind finding words.

"Do you need me to call someone?"

I waved away the question with my hand, even though he couldn't see me. Gesticulating felt easier than speaking. "*No.* I, um—I need a place to stay for a night or two. I know you can't risk being seen with me and I don't want to put a lot of pressure on you. But I'm being evicted."

"What? Don't you live with your boyfriend?"

"He owns the townhouse. He sent a fucking courier to evict me. He couldn't even text me."

He let out a low, incredulous whistle. "That was suspiciously fast."

"Yeah. Almost like he was waiting for something to happen to get me out." Mark had gotten my investment for his company and kicked me to the curb. I didn't see the signs in front of me that he was *this* much of a jerk. Or maybe I did—the blank walls in our "home" seemed obvious to me now—and just didn't want to admit it. That phone holster on his hip should have given it away.

I was jobless, homeless, and now a card-carrying member of the publicly humiliated club. *If it isn't the conse-quences of your own actions,* my older sister's voice rang through my head. God, she would be insufferable as soon as she heard about this.

How did I mistakenly send what I thought was a text as an email on my work account to the entire list? I closed my eyes and ran through the scenario again: I had pulled up the image, hit share and selected the text thread with Patrick...

Unless—I opened my eyes, digging deep for a breath. My chest felt tight as I searched through my phone, selecting a photo, then walked through the process again. The most recent app was Outlook. My muscle memory must have turned on and I didn't think it through. How could I be so stupid?

Mere hours ago, I had a job, a home, a boyfriend, colleagues, and friends. A decent reputation. A *promotion*, for fuck's sake. Then, like an incompetent seamstress on her first day, I found myself surrounded by the shredded fabric of my life.

I LAID ON MY STOMACH WITH MY FACE BURIED IN PATRICK'S carpet, which still smelled like regurgitated ground beef and cheese after he got me drunk on cheap beer and cheaper tacos. There may have been a shot of tequila. Or three. He said I could crash in his studio apartment until I figured out what to do next with myself and all my worldly possessions that I carried in two suitcases.

I procrastinated next steps until the early hours of the morning, spending the night staring at Patrick's walls that he had covered with eclectic art prints, and jogging in place while holding my boobs together so they wouldn't slap me in the face. Great tits were all I had left going for me, I feared.

Avoiding my phone and the hundreds of notifications pouring in, I picked at the fibers in the blue shag rug. Eventually, I gave in to temptation and army crawled across the floor to my laptop, scanning the website I typed in hours ago. Debilitating anxiety came over me as I scrolled through the endless list of job postings in the city. I was the laughingstock of the town; how could I ever find another job *here*?

Get out of Arizona, a voice in my head screamed.

"Hey Siri, find me a job off the face of the earth," I slurred into my phone.

I FELL ASLEEP WITH MY NOSE ON THE TAB KEY OF MY OPEN LAPTOP before I woke up to the sounds of literal jingle bells. I knew better, but for some reason I couldn't help but peer out the window, expecting a festive vignette and the source of the sound. But my eyes met a cotton candy blue and pink sunset, desert mountains, and cacti. Nothing that resembled the jingle of any bells anywhere.

Phoenix certainly buzzed with holiday energy, like faux snowy scenes decorated on shop windows. Wreaths hung on palm trees. Soon the city would host a public lighting for a cactus ordained with traditional ornaments. Winters in Phoenix were a far cry from cozy and glittering. The only snow we had was digitally projected onto the side of terra cotta buildings.

"I think I found a job you might be interested in," a feminine robotic voice said, drawing my gaze back to my laptop. I tugged it closer and squinted my blurry eyes at a job posting offering immediate hiring for a front desk clerk at a hotel located in Tidings. Just Tidings. Like Santa or Beyoncé.

I scrolled through more of the location's description.

The self-proclaimed crown jewel of the North American Continental Divide is a small dot somewhere between northern Montana and Canada. No airports and no highways, only a small two-lane road through town and a train called The Klocka Express.

Bells jingled.

That chiming must be a marketing feature on their website. I scrolled through photos of happy people walking downtown with dreamy smiles. Couples holding hands, families laughing in a snow-covered valley.

No way that's real. No one was that happy in the snow.

It looked more picturesque than a movie set; it was a ceramic Christmas village come to life.

I picked up a half-empty bottle of beer from the sofa table, Patrick's or mine, I wasn't sure. I took a swallow and continued to read the website.

Tidings was founded more than one hundred years ago as a popular train station stop on the American railway system for those heading west. Settled and developed by Scandinavian immigrants who largely influenced the culture, food, and life-style of residents then and today.

The juxtaposition of the wintry, frosted pictures on my screen against the view out the window of the dry, hot Sonoran Desert made my head spin. I rubbed my eyes, willing it to make sense.

Patrick said when I applied for any job, he'd vouch for me as a colleague and say our manager had a mental break-down and wasn't reliable. It was a nice offer, but it wouldn't work now that my big oopsie was easily found on Google.

As intriguing as Tidings looked, there was no way I could possibly go for that job. My parents would have me involuntarily admitted to the hospital for a brain scan. I had the same temperature requirements as a lizard. Place me on a scalding rock in the direct line of the sun on a triple-digit day. Anything below seventy degrees and I required a space heater.

I pinched the bridge of my nose. Snow should be my karma. And if those damn bells didn't stop jingling, I'd toss my laptop out Patrick's window. I closed out of the webpage and slammed my computer shut.

No.

I can't do it.

I could not live in a village where there was more snow than dry ground. I could not live in the snow, period. I was not built for it. I'd rather sleep on black concrete in the summer heat. I had to find another option. I searched for the contact for a girl I met through my now ex-boyfriend's friends who sold solar panels door-to-door, which I thought was code for sex work, but was in fact what it said it was. She walked up and down the suburban neighborhoods, knocking on doors and offering products to help save the planet. An honorable job I could get behind.

I opened her contact and typed a message that bordered somewhere between "I'm desperate as fuck" and "exploring new opportunities."

Interrupting my outgoing message was one from an unknown number, with a plus sign and two zeros before its nine other digits. I thought it was my sister calling from wherever in the world she happened to be that day. I never knew someone who liked rocks so much could be insufferably knowledgeable. It was a cute hobby when she was a kid, constantly collecting gemstones and begging my parents for an encyclopedia on sedimentary rocks. Her insatiable thirst for learning about everything added to the family mission, which was to make me feel as useless as stepping stones over the Atlantic Ocean.

I cleared my throat and put on my clearest, most professional voice. If I'm drunk on a weekday afternoon, she'd be on the phone with my parents convincing them to infiltrate my life faster than I could sober up.

"Hello, this is Alice."

"Good tidings, Alice," an unfamiliar peppy voice responded. Definitely not Andrea. "My name is Ginger Jones, and I'm the human resource manager assigned to Evermore Winter Lodge."

"Yes, hello—I mean, er, tidings?" I said, echoing her greeting. I straightened my posture and squinted my eyes, willing sobriety to find its way to me now.

"We saw you were interested in an opportunity to work at the Evermore Lodge in Tidings."

I must be drunker than I thought.

"How did you get my number? I didn't apply."

Ginger responded with some technical babble about my employment profile on the job posting site. "I reviewed your resume and believe your experience would translate well into working directly with customers at the most beautiful lodge nestled in the heart of Tidings." Essentially, I'd be a glorified front desk receptionist, working five days a week checking in guests and managing the maintenance work.

"This is truly an unprecedented opportunity, a once-in-a-lifetime experience," she added in her closing like she was a politician earning my vote. "Tidings caps the number of tourists allowed each year. They earn entry through a lottery system that sells out within hours."

I'd heard this all before. *You can't pass up this opportunity. The payoff will set you up for life. Don't look a gift horse in the mouth.* This wasn't real; it was a fever dream of my subconscious testing me. I would not fall for another scam.

"I'm actually not looking for employment."

"You completed an application and while it's different from your most recent employment work, it's an excellent opportunity to try something new."

My mouth agape, I held the phone to one ear, jamming my thumb in the other in desperation to align my equilibrium.

She continued, "It's a temporary contract for three months. Lodging is provided as you'll be staying on site."

The room spun. Damn tequila.

I couldn't go back in time and change the mistakes I'd made. But I could learn from them, and this was my first test. *Don't fall for the trap, Alice.* "Listen, Nutmeg. First of all, you seem like a nice gal. But I think you better try someone more gullible."

"I'm going to table that nomenclature for now," Ginger said through exasperation, which I could hear through the phone. "You have a background in anthropology. We find that education and your skill set are valuable in a place like Tidings. We have a unique tourism structure and regular visits from out-of-town scientists performing research on our climate and environment. Perhaps you could aid in their investigations."

"I'm not an anthropologist." I sighed.

"Do you not have a degree in anthropology?" she pressed. "You also published a peer-reviewed paper."

"Just because someone mows their own yard does not make them a landscaper."

"What?"

"Never mind," I said, exasperated. "None of this makes sense. It's a multi-level marketing scheme, right? I pay to get involved, and then I convince other people to join me in Tidings, but it's not a real place and we are all waiting for our train ticket to arrive while selling the idea to more people."

A robust, feminine laugh reverberated through the speaker. I held my phone out, watching the seconds tick by until it clocked a full minute. Finally, Ginger reclaimed her wits and turned up the patronizing professional voice. "You are clever, Alice. Your sense of humor will be much appreciated here."

"Only one problem, Spice Girl."

"What's that?"

"I'm *not* coming to work at your hotel." Now more than ever I needed to embrace a healthy dose of skepticism.

"It's not a hotel, it's a *lodge*."

After minutes of Ginger performing her recruiting job duties at the highest level, she almost had me convinced. She put me on the ropes, nearly convincing me this was not an MLM, catfish scam, or a one-way ticket to my own kidnapping. I agreed to review the terms in the next twenty-four hours, but I did not agree to accept the work yet.

This was what I wanted, something to take me so far from here no one would know my name. And this opportunity had fallen right into my lap, something to give me a moment to catch my breath and figure out next steps. I wondered if my sister already knew I was the joke of the southwest. She'd never let me live it down. She'd be insufferable.

If Patrick were home, he'd slap me awake from this glistening snow globe nightmare. He'd probably laugh in my face for getting swindled by a Nigerian prince with a voice changer software, building trust before he pleads for my help to access his locked funds in American banks.

I was the queen of piss-poor decisions, it seemed. Everything sucked. My life could not get any worse. And I still smelled like a tacos.

ONE EYE WAS SQUASHED INTO A PILLOW AS MY LEFT HAND dangled off the couch, while my still-wet hair was crumpled in a messy bun on my head. The sounds of sizzling oil and the clanking of pots and utensils infiltrated my ears. I pawed around for my phone, wedged between couch cushions.

It was about six in the morning, and I had an email notification from Ginger containing the employment contact.

It looked real.

"Fuck." I tossed my phone on the floor and rolled onto my back.

"Morning! Any luck with jobs?" Patrick asked loudly and brightly, his voice carrying over the sound of a blender. He waved me over to have a seat at the kitchen counter.

"Patty Cake, it's barely dawn." I tugged the blanket over my head when Patrick maneuvered himself over me like a parent getting their kid out of bed for school.

"Alice," he said, decrying.

"Did you tsk-tsk me?" I mumbled through the blanket.

I'm never drinking again.

He ripped the blanket off me, dropping it on the floor so I would stop resisting the siren song of bacon frying. I grabbed it on my way to the kitchen draping over my shoulders. I forgot exactly what I was wearing but I was cold enough to know that my nipples would be offensive this early in the morning. When my brain finally rewired itself for me to make coherent sentences, I launched into a truly unbelievable description of the Tidings job.

I caught him up on everything, including the benefits package which included free rent and a stipend for food. He shoved a plate of something too healthy for my hangover in front of me.

"Is this f'acon?" I asked, examining the piece of meat with the wrong texture and color to be pork.

"It's good for you," Patrick took quick sips of his green-brown smoothie, elbow planted on the countertop. "So, let me get this right. A woman named Ginger from a town called Tidings, an actual real-life Christmas village, offered you a paying job and a place to live and all you have to do is fake smile at guests and hand over hotel keys?"

I muttered an agreement as I chewed through a bite of bland egg whites I slathered in ketchup. "Working at a front desk is a means to an end. That end is surviving. I've got nothing left."

"You're going to take it right? Because if you don't, I will."

"I had a nightmare about Tidings. It looked like that old claymation movie with the abominable snowman. What if I get there and it's more of a holiday horror film than a quintessential Christmas town?"

Patrick raised his eyebrows. "At this point, honey, what else have you got to lose?"

"Besides my life? Gee, thanks."

Patrick rolled his eyes and raised his arms in the universal sign for surrender before he pulled a barstool out next to me to take a seat. "You will muddle through."

I bumped him with a friendly nudge of my elbow. "Somehow." And I believed, even for a nanosecond, that it was true.

"Hey, Alice—I'm proud of you." He slung his arm around my shoulders. "You've been through some shit, girl. If anyone deserves a break it's your perfect, carefree Aquarius heart."

If this was my break, why did it feel like a *breaking*? With nothing else to lose after all...

"What if this is a human trafficking scheme?"

"I doubt that. But I dated a guy whose cousin was in the FBI. I'll reach out if I don't hear from you in forty-eight hours." I nodded, maintaining eye contact. "And I really, *really* hope you get laid."

I burst out laughing.

"I'm serious. Pinky promise me you'll keep a lookout for some hot snowmen...or whatever."

I trusted my ex enough to invest all my money in him. Now I was recklessly broke and alone. Who would want tainted trash like me?

"I don't know, Patrick. Getting involved with someone so soon seems like a bad idea. I never thought Mark would dump me and leave me stranded like this. I gave him so much money! I mean, who wouldn't trust a Harvard MBA?"

"The subprime mortgage crisis," he said matter-of-factly, refilling my glass of water and sliding it back across the countertop. "Look, have fun. You don't have to get married." He leaned in closer and lowered his voice. "But you need to get some new lingerie."

I squinted my eyes and pursed my lips.

Patrick refused to be quelled by my accusatory stare. "You left your suitcase lid open on the floor. I saw those cotton Hanes, girl, and that won't cut it."

"You're walking a fine line between inappropriate and helpful."

He closed his fist and playfully bounced it off my jaw. "Go get 'em, Tiger."

"I'm so ill-prepared. I don't have a damn thing to wear for anything below sixty degrees."

Time to trade in the saguaro for the snow.

CHAPTER 4
ALICE

My life was functioning at the efficacy of trying to start a fire in the snow with wet tinder. I neared the end of my twenty-four-hour travel day, concluding with a train ride through a snow-covered valley. Destination?

Tidings.

My new home for the next three months.

If I'd survive was still up in the air. I wasn't confident I'd leave here in one piece.

This is my penance.

Tidings' average high temperature wasn't even my beloved sunbaked Arizona's low. And here I was, sitting in a train car surrounded by excited kids and the smell of peppermint and pine, an unpleasant scent that reminded me of a public restroom cleaner chemical.

The small commuter plane that brought me from Phoenix to a municipal airport landed, and my next instructions were to take the train from the joint train-plane station "through the mountains, into the woods, and around the bend to Tidings."

After using the restroom, I waited for my luggage to appear on the carousel before heading to the on-ramp for the train. To pass the time, I reread messages from my mom and sister urging me to call them. They didn't hint at knowing about my embarrassing viral mishap, but I wasn't ready to face that conversation either.

An alarm blared, announcing that our bags were arriving. I stepped forward, but as I reached for one of my large black suitcases, another hand shot in at the same time. Our fingers tangled awkwardly, and the suitcase tumbled to the ground with a thud.

The source of the other hand, a dark-haired man in a long wool coat, reached down to grab the handle and looked up at me. His hair was disheveled from the beanie he removed from his head. His long sigh and furrowed brows made it clear I'd committed a travel faux pas. I reached for my bag out of his hand. "Sorry about that," I muttered.

I pulled on the handle.

He held firm.

The wheel squeaked across the floor as I tried to inch it closer, but he outpowered me, tucking it snugly against his side.

"*What* are you doing?" he asked.

"This is mine," I said, indignantly, reaching around his side for my bag.

"Please stop," he said in an exasperated tone, like how I'd repeatedly asked my mom to stop asking when I'd be engaged to Mark. *Enough. I've had enough.*

We were deadlocked as its twin bag, black with a blue ribbon, carried down the carousel. I smiled wide, saying, "And that must be yours."

"Is it?" he asked sarcastically.

Or were we flirting? Which was preposterous, because I

looked like a drowned sewer rat and probably still smelled like tequila. When I didn't respond, he took that challenge.

"Okay then," he agreed and removed the other suitcase from the carousel. He squatted and unzipped the bag, flipping the lid over with a thud. "*This* is most certainly not mine," he said, dangling my bra off his pinky finger for the entire damn airport to see.

My chest tightened and I felt a now-familiar wave of anxiety and humiliation that carried to my cheeks. "Put it away," I pleaded in a harsh whisper. I shook my sweaty palms as I croaked, "*Please.*"

His eyebrows furrowed with perplexed concern, eyes boring into mine, before he nodded and delicately tucked my bra back in my suitcase, handling it with far more dignity than TSA agents when they rummaged through my bag and threw away my oversized hair products. With tenderness, he zipped up the suitcase and set it down at my feet. He opened his mouth, then thought against saying something, simply nodding and heading on his way.

THE HUM OF THE TRAIN'S HEAT SYSTEM KICKED ON AND A BLAST OF warm air poured in at my feet. If I could fit, I'd curl up on the floor and have the heat bake me like the frozen turkey I felt like. I wiggled my cold toes in my shoes and shimmied in the chair chasing the heat pouring from the vents.

My bare fingers were numb as I scrolled through my phone, the text from my mom staring daggers at me. I hadn't replied to her incessant calls and texts. Turned out someone *did* share the viral story with her, and, per her seventy-nine texts, she needed to speak with me. It was only fair I explain myself to my parents, and I'd get to it... at some point. She didn't know I was homeless and now single, as tempting as the prospect of my breakup being an early Christmas present for my parents was. I wasn't equipped with the mental fortitude to sit at the dinner table enduring the collective gazes of *we told you so* blended with the disbelief that echoed, *we can't believe you are so dumb.* As a thirty-three-year-old woman, I would sell a kidney before I dropped my problems on my parents. I had an entire generation of angry boomers to prove wrong.

A man with a pinched expression walked past me down the aisle. His thinning comb over and too-thin nose reminded me of Devin and the sight of him nearly sent me ducking for cover under the seat.

It had only been two days since my public disgrace, and I was still rattled. I saw Devin's slimy face everywhere. Shuddering from both the cold and the memory of my former boss' sneering expression, I turned my gaze back to the window, watching the blur of snow whoosh past me.

Like the plane, the train was small with only enough seats for twenty passengers, with space for suitcases stored beneath the train car for each passenger. Ginger wasn't kidding when she said Tidings capped tourists. People could only arrive and depart Tidings by train or helicopter. According to a conversation I overheard between a parent and child on the plane, it wasn't safe enough for planes to land in Tidings due to the sharp mountain peaks, rolling hills, and endless snowstorms.

Fresh garland adorned with red bows was draped across each window, and matching red ribbon decorated the back of each red velvet seat. Curled into the plush material, earbuds tucked snugly in my ears, I blasted my pop playlist to drown out the sounds of Christmas music blaring overhead from the train's speakers. My ideal

Christmas included a beach chair, not a snowplow. An ironic setting: the anti-winter girl headed to Tidings whereas the rest of the passengers were looking for a wonderland of glittering snow and the spirit of the season. Children beamed and bounced on their toes with excitement as parents snapped photos of wide smiles and toothy grins.

Evergreen trees and rolling hills blurred past the speedy train, and the farther we rode, the darker the sky turned, enveloped in a white fog, a promise of snow to come.

"Ma'am, may I interest you in a complimentary brunch?" A crew member pushing a food cart smiled down at me from the aisle. She was a pleasant middle-aged woman wearing a navy-blue wool skirt and a white blouse with a pussy bow tied around her neck. Her long, candy-cane red fingernails contrasted with the enormous emerald ring on her left hand.

"No, thank you," I replied through clenched teeth. "I don't think I could stomach eating anything with this motion."

She smiled broadly and nodded like she'd heard that response a dozen times already. "You will acclimate to it shortly. Before you know it, you'll think you're sitting stationary at a restaurant."

My empty stomach gurgled with nerves and remnants from this morning's hotel coffee. "Maybe some crackers? Or peanuts if you have them?"

She let out a high-pitched giggle. "No stale snacks here, ma'am. Eggs Benedict topped with arugula salad and a cup of pomegranate arils, or a bagel with lox and all the fixings."

"That sounds too fancy for a train meal," I said as she handed a stack of napkins to a passenger behind her and kept the smile plastered to her face. "Have you worked here long?"

"Only a year," she replied, chipper. "I needed something to keep busy since my kids are in school now."

"In Tidings?"

"Yes. A third grader and a seventh grader. Don't blink; they grow up fast," she said as she tossed me a wink. "Have you decided on your meal?"

Eggs didn't sound like a smart meal to eat on a moving train. "I'll go for the bagel and lox, please."

"Sure thing." She crouched at her cart, pulled out a few trays and began assembling my bagel with thin strips of lox, a spoonful of capers, and slices of pickled red onion. "This is your first time to Tidings," she stated.

I nodded and thumbed through my wallet looking for spare cash to tip her. "I got a job at the front desk at the Evermore Winter Lodge. I have no idea what I'm doing but I suppose it can't be too hard."

"You'll find your way quickly," she said, offering a comforting smile. "Tidings is very hospitable."

"Any sage advice for me?"

"Oh, *loads*," she said, thrilled to be asked. "What would you like to drink? Peppermint tea, cinnamon coffee?"

My stomach roiled again at the options. "Water is fine, thank you."

She handed me a water bottle and leaned her elbow on the cart. "Dress warm, don't engage with the moose, and let fate guide you. You're in Tidings for a reason."

She strolled down the aisle and greeted the next person leaving me with a tray of the most beautiful breakfast I'd ever seen and more unanswered questions than I had before.

Before she was too far out of reach, I looked over my

shoulder and tapped on her shoulder. "Excuse me—one more question: if everyone is eating eggs or smoked salmon, why doesn't it stink on this train?" I asked.

"Peppermint," she leaned in and whispered, "it's everywhere."

I took a deep inhale, burning my nose on the sharp mint and pine scent.

A foreboding chill ran down my spine on the exhale.

A COLD BREEZE WAFTED PAST AS A MAN WALKED DOWN THE AISLE, claiming an open seat in the row across from me. I'd kept my head down as much as possible on the journey, paranoid that someone would recognize me. I was old news by internet standards, and it was likely most people wouldn't even place me as that weird email girl who got fired. But crowds made me uncomfortable, something I'd never felt before.

As I peered over the rim of my coffee I had opted for when the kindly crew member made another pass down the aisle, a sense of familiarity hit me as I studied the man. I drank in the languid movements of his fingers as he unbuttoned his black wool coat. He unwound a forest-green scarf from his neck and delicately folded it three perfect times.

It was the man from my suitcase snafu in the airport.

A barrage of people shook his hand or gave him fist bumps as they walked by with their brunch selections. It was his own personal parade route, and he greeted every bystander with a sickeningly sweet smile that held an air of professionalism.

He pulled out a sleek black laptop from his bag and placed it on the seatback table in front of him. The screen lit up with spreadsheets and charts, prompting him to pull a pair of reading glasses out from the inside pocket of his jacket.

I popped on my headphones and pretended to watch something on my phone. Instead, I watched his cursor fly across the screen. The pretty charts hypnotized me. I appreciated a man who was good with complicated numbers and formulas; it was what had initially drawn me to Mark, although I knew now that proficiency was all for show.

I watched the man work for a minute or two at a time before he'd inevitably be interrupted by more people approaching him to say hello as they carried food and drinks, gathered from the front of the train car back to their seats. He smiled politely, but his hands at his side flexed into fists, a telling sign he wanted to get back to work—or to be left the hell alone.

Was he famous or something? Maybe the town's hot, well-liked mayor?

Like a moth to a flame, I continued fixing my eyes on the shifting colors across his screen when an iMessage popped up interrupting his charts and files. And I mean an *iMessage*—the kind that's a very long, intimidating blue bubble, usually not good news. After scrolling and reading, he shut the laptop with a hint of force and let out an exasperated sigh.

He tilted his neck from side to side, a slower, second turn to his left hedged an intentional swift glance at me. Our eyes met and a rush of heat to my cheeks forced my gaze to drop toward my lap—my *very* interesting lap with microfiber pilling I needed to pluck one by one. He gave me a wave and a sly smile, recognition dawning on his face.

He said something, lips moving silently before I pulled an AirPod out of my ear.

"What?" I asked, panicked he had caught me staring.

"I said, 'Make sure you add your name to your suitcase.'"

"You too," I said, then grimaced, realizing I sounded like a fucking dork.

He smiled back in amusement with a flick of warmth in his green eyes.

I shifted my focus back out the window, ignoring everyone else until the train arrived at our destination.

EVENTUALLY I FELL ASLEEP BUT WAS WOKEN UP LATER BY JINGLE bells. I wiped the drool off my chin with the collar of my jacket, silently cursing the incessant chiming; it was a sound that I'd need electrotherapy to remove from my brain after this.

And I'd only just arrived.

At the Klocka Express Station, a group of us first-timers were instructed to wait for a welcome message from a town ambassador. Others, presumably residents including Wool Coat Guy, headed for the nearest exit.

I observed the train station, appreciating the ornate details of the architecture and design. Original hardwood floors, arched ceilings, crystal chandeliers, and a profusion of fresh Christmas trees, garlands, and wreaths adorned the classic train station from one end to the other. I stopped in the center of the room, looked at the ceiling and slowly spun in circles, taking in every square inch. I had never seen anything so beautiful in a traditional, comforting way. The glimmer, the scent of pine and fir, the crackling of the fire-places, and the smell of warmth overwhelmed me so much that tears sprung to my eyes. It was more than enough to poke holes into the anti-Christmas persona I was starting to adopt.

If anyone hadn't already gotten their fill of peppermint-infused hot cocoa, they didn't have to go far. A server offered me a cup as I waited in line like we were going through international customs. Before we exited the train station, a tall Viking-like man in a beige forest ranger uniform and blond man-bun, corralled us first timers into a corner facing a small TV to watch a brief presentation on the customs and regulations in Tidings.

Rule number one, and the most important emphasized by red font and exclamation points: do not approach moose. If you see a moose, slowly back away and go inside a car or building as soon as possible. Especially during mating season, the bulls will be aggressive and charge toward any threat, including humans. I blanched as the TV showed video footage of a man being chased by a moose, his massive antlers poking the man in the ass before the screen faded to black. I looked around at others watching. We all carried the same expression: eyes wide, jaws gaped. No one answered when the ranger asked if anyone had any questions.

"Don't forget to spread good cheer and tidings to all!" he said, his enthusiasm a strange contrast from his otherwise gruff and burly demeanor.

I'll get right on that cheery persona as soon as I can locate a pair of wool mittens, I thought, flexing my nearly-frozen fingers. Even with the heater blowing inside the buildings, my hands and toes felt like ice. I worried I'd never get warm enough here. With my sun-kissed skin and light layers, I looked like I belonged in Tidings as much as a tropical flower planted on the moon.

Near the exit door, a driver sporting a pointy nose and

crimson cheeks flushed from the cold held up a tablet on which my name was written in festive typography. He was shorter than the Viking but even more shockingly, also shorter than my five-foot-five height. Gustav, or Gus as he insisted I call him upon introduction, smiled big and greeted me with a handshake and a slight bow. He guided me to a large black SUV carried on heavy-duty tires sturdy enough to get through feet of fresh snow.

Feet of snow was a foreign concept to me. Other-worldly. I'd only ever seen snow on TV and travel magazines.

"What does snow feel like?" I asked as he loaded my luggage into the trunk.

Gustav giggled in a squeaky little laugh and then I knew why Gus was a completely appropriate nickname. "You've never felt snow, Miss?"

"No." I twisted my hair over one shoulder and shook my head. "I've lived in the southwest my whole life."

"Snow feels like nature instructing you to forget everything else," he said in a wistful tone. "Like in that moment, all that matters is building a snowman, throwing a snowball, or watching it build and build from the comfort of the warm indoors. And it always makes me crave peppermint hot cocoa, which is why I've got this belly here." He patted his stomach in a gesture I found endearing. "Mmmhm. I love that drink."

I rubbed my temples in disbelief at someone waxing poetic about snow. "Or it feels like you're alive trapped in a morgue freezer," I said under my breath. When he lifted the lid on his insulated tumbler, the scent of mint and chocolate punched me in the nose. "Peppermint hot cocoa must be the town's official drink."

His round cheeks flushed pink in confirmation. "And

yes, we do get warmer weather than this. Although sommar might not be what you are used to."

"*Sommar?*" I asked, repeating his pronunciation with the long *O*.

"Uh—yes, like your warmest months. But it's not a typical summer."

I got the impression nothing in Tidings could be described as anything but atypical.

"Gus, can I snag a ride?" a male voice shouted from behind me.

Eyes bright, Gus enthusiastically waved the man over. "Come on in, Dr. Hill."

I turned to find the man I couldn't seem to shake off staring me straight in the face as he approached our vehicle.

Dr. Hill.

"We meet again," he said as he set his identical black suitcase next to mine. The memory of our airport snafu moment made me flush, a lingering feeling of embarrassment I couldn't shake.

"Miss?" Gustav asked, pulling me back to the present. "Are you ready to go? I hope you don't mind Dr. Hill sharing a ride with us. Your stop at the lodge is first, so it won't impact your arrival time."

"Actually, I'll stop there, too," Dr. Hill replied, buckling into the front seat. Gustav held the back door open for me. "I'm meeting the crew for a late dinner."

We set out on our way and after a few minutes, Gustav asked, "What do you think, Miss Woods?" I pressed my face against the window, taking in my first real look at Tidings as we drove through the dark evening, buildings lit up with what must have been millions of lights. I propped my elbow on the door and bit on my thumbnail. It wasn't exactly nature's masterpiece like Gus' poetic speech had implied, and I couldn't feel my toes anymore.

"It's... cold. But pretty in its own way." That was the best I could do.

As we slowed at a yellow light, I snapped a picture of my current view out the window. Even though it was dark outside, I could make out the snowy, tree-covered hills towering over bright streets jam-packed with bustling businesses and people casually going to and fro like they weren't on an Arctic expedition. Downtown Tidings had to be the most secure economy in the world. Each of the dozens of restaurants and bars—where I assumed they served spiked peppermint hot cocoa—small markets, bakeries, and coffee shops, were full of patrons. One restaurant had a line out the door onto the sidewalk. A clothing boutique hosted a sidewalk sale, complete with free peppermint hot cocoa for each customer. The windows were decorated for the holidays, spray painted with snowy scenes or holly and berries.

"I've never seen anyone as excited for Christmastime as this entire town," I said.

"It's not Christmas, or one specific timeframe—it's an everyday spirit," Gustav said sternly, like a parent reminding their teenager about curfew.

"What does *that* mean?"

From my seat in the back, I saw his shoulders bounce in time with his chuckle. "If Tidings brought you here—"

Silas turned around to face me, finishing Gustav's sentence, "—you'll know it at the right time."

CHAPTER 5
SILAS

Gustav parked alongside the curb in front of the lodge. "You'll know it at the right time," we said in harmony. I was so sick of hearing that phrase that I wanted to throat-punch the words. I'd been in Tidings for four years and the persistent serendipitous push was toxic to me. Old-timers like Gus and Ginger were the greatest offenders. I was here and fading away. When would I learn my *why?* I couldn't stay longer to figure it out.

The travel requirements to Tidings of car, plane, and coal-powered train were grueling, especially when I was forced to smile and make shitty small talk with everyone who recognized me. Most were familiar faces from around town or had been patients in the emergency department at some point. They were locals returning from holiday break on the "mainland," the Tidings term for anywhere outside of the town. I pummeled through the barrage of niceties with haste so I could settle into the paperwork I needed to complete and mentally prepare myself for returning to Tidings after a week of thawing out in California.

It was as easy to spot a first timer as it was to find a

snowflake around here. The woman from the airport, train, and Gus' transport was as green as an unripe mango; she traveled alone and was overwhelmed by the culture and weather already.

I caught her reflection in my computer monitor and her eyes were as big as saucers, her nose pinched like she was blocking out a disgusting smell. In the car, she sat in the back and kept to herself while I made small talk with Gus. I told him I went to California to dry out and visit old friends, which was mostly true. I wasn't ready to tell anyone about the plans I was setting into motion. I wasn't sure I was prepared to tell *myself*.

Her scent wafted from the back, carrying a mixture of fresh, sweet floral aromas, reminiscent of the scent after rain. My heart thudded hard, and a warm rush of blood warmed my toes even under a pair of heavy-duty wool socks and my boots.

Before we had wrestled with suitcases at the airport's one carousel, I had already succumbed to that fragrance on the airplane, mistaking it for lingering sunscreen and fresh air on my own skin. It tempted me, like a starving dog drooling over a steak. The train ride had been painful enough, but I tried to avoid it by facing forward, not wanting to get too close to her. Now, in the car, it was unbearable. Her scent overwhelmed me, igniting my blood and making me crave her. Jesus, she had me fucked up. It was an unnecessary distraction as I gathered the strength to return to the smell of Tidings: pine, snow, and diesel.

Yet, she was the first tourist I gave a second look.

I usually steered clear of them because, after my first year in Tidings, I'd learned most single women got clingy, convinced they were living some cheesy small-town romance. That wasn't a fantasy I shared. In fact, my dream was the exact opposite—getting the hell out of here.

But my personal and professional obligations held me back, and I was stuck in survival mode each day. For once, it was nice to see someone who looked as miserable about coming to Tidings as I felt on the inside.

Instead of going inside Fire & Ice, I should have prioritized my sleep before diving into another round of shifts tomorrow, but I'd promised the guys I'd make it tonight. It was rare we were all available, and when our schedules aligned we always took advantage of hanging out outside the sterile hospital walls. I rehearsed my story, ready to omit the truth about my trip to California. Better for them to assume I chased the sun and girls instead of looking for a new job. To my sister and friends, everything was business as usual. My light and nimble personality would shine, and they'd be none the wiser.

I turned back to Gustav, who was still unfastening his seatbelt. "I'm running late. Are you all good?"

"Sure, sure," he said, waving me off. "I'll help the miss get set up."

I hurried out of the car toward the back to the open trunk and grabbed my suitcase. Alice didn't speak much in the car, but I felt her all around me—her scent, her sunshine-baked skin glowed. When she did talk, her voice was raspy, like she'd been awake for two days straight, and that sound made my muscles tense. That rasp was sexy, and it drove me mad. I got away from her as quickly as possible, before I was claustrophobic.

I still hadn't responded to the novel my sister, Dagny, had texted me on the train. I got a migraine from her stubbornness and had popped a painkiller before I flung myself out of the Klocka Express and never looked back. We'd been arguing over when she would take the MCAT for six months. She kept putting it off because she needed to study more, but I knew she was hesitant to commit. I knew she *didn't* want to be a doctor as much as I wanted her to be one. That was another reason why I wouldn't reveal how miserable I was—she'd never follow my path if she knew I was withering away. I often asked myself why I wanted her to be a doctor when I was so miserable myself. But not everyone was like me.

When I exited the airport shuttle, I took a sharp breath of cold air. Fuck, it hurt my face and lungs after my body had gotten used to the balmy California climate. I would have to acclimate quickly.

I walked inside Fire & Ice, the most popular restaurant and bar in Tidings, mainly because it was attached to the lodge that most people stayed at if they weren't in a cabin rental. I made my way back to the regular booth the guys and I always took up, tucking my suitcase between my chair and the wall.

Allan waved maniacally at me from the bar, pointing to his empty beer glass. I gave a nod of my chin and plopped down, finally letting out a breath as I stretched out my long legs that had been bent in a ninety-degree angle for the past twelve hours.

"You look like shit," said Erik with a frown, looking up at me from his seat across the table.

"Better than you, asshole."

"*I* have a newborn. What's your excuse? Getting too old for traveling?"

"Or maybe I was busy all night. Almost missed my flight this morning."

He grunted, tossing an approving smile. "Is that why

you smell like a candle shop? Got a woman still clinging to you?"

"Things a little frosty at home? Need some tips?" Henry asked, and Erik flipped him off, rightfully so. It was a low blow, especially to a new parent. Erik was the only married doc in our group. Most people with families didn't move here and people didn't come to Tidings looking for a nice girl to settle down with. The town had a reputation as magical and cozy. It was also full of slutty behavior. It was a miracle STIs weren't our greatest export.

When my family had asked why I wanted to go to Tidings after residency, I said it was an excellent opportunity as a young emergency medicine doctor to sharpen my skills before going for a more competitive job at a city hospital. The truth was, at the time, I had needed to get as far away from California as possible. The irony was not lost on me now.

By design, residency was hard as hell—competitive and cutthroat. One bad day, one mistake, could impact the rest of your career. I passed residency but I failed in relationships. Going into my third year, I thought I'd graduate with a new job in state and a fiancée; instead, I took a position as far removed from California as possible. And I was single. Dumped. Humiliated.

Lia and I were together for two years until one day I met her at her apartment where she greeted me with a shoebox stuffed with personal items I kept at her place. The ring in my pocket felt like a cement block dragging me to the depths of the ocean. On my walk of shame home, I carried the box with the ring buried in the bottom. I left the box on the sidewalk for some lucky schmuck to find.

I had to disappear. Yeah, I came to Tidings thinking I could screw it out of my system. Until it got old and exhausting. Henry, Allan, and I were each other's wingmen, but I was getting too old for that shit. I wanted to go home, eat ramen and sleep, not feign interest in a bachelorette party amped up on peppermint vodka looking for a story to tell back home.

I wasn't interested in being someone's one-and-done anymore.

Allan brought a fresh pitcher of beer to the table and the guys passed around glasses. I sipped on mine mindlessly, listening to their banter, and nodding when appropriate.

Before I recognized it in a cerebral way, my body told me it hated waking up here every day. Sommar was the only redeeming quality and even then, nine months of miserable snow and ice wasn't worth it.

Tidings chewed you up and spit you out, on her terms —the mystery of fate controlling who was in, who was out. As evidenced by my trip to California for secret job interviews was a massive clusterfuck where nothing went right. I woke up late for my interview despite setting my alarm, then I was locked from the inside of my hotel room like a fucking hostage and had to wait half an hour for maintenance to fix the lock. The interview team told me they'd let me know soon, but the frowns across their faces didn't bode well. My gut feeling was right when I received an email when I got off the plane that all but said, *Thank you for your interest in our hospital but please fuck off.*

I was trapped in Tidings forever.

"You do smell a little girly, Silas." Allan raised his eyebrows with a teasing smirk. He was awkward and a total nerd, but he was a thirsty ladies' man.

What the fuck were they talking about? I only smelled the ever-present combination of peppermint and pine.

"It's pleasant though," Allan added. "Like a flower and dirt. But in a nice, fresh way."

"Dirt? Bro, you're fucking weird," Henry said.

Allan ignored him, which was the most appropriate response to Henry, who overdid it on protein shakes and could use a slap upside the head. But he could read an MRI damn well, and unfortunately seemed to be the only board-certified radiologist in America who wanted to live in Tidings, so we were stuck with him. He loved the snow and the girls, so the lifestyle fit him.

I pulled my shirt up to my nose and inhaled. Fuck, Alice's scent lingered like she had imprinted on me, an aroma of fresh air and warm sunshine.

Before we had that awkward exchange over the suitcase mix-up after the flight, I saw her on the plane. She looked petrified and extremely shy, tucking her head against the window to not make eye contact with anyone. I knew I was an asshole for not helping her with her luggage leaving the car, but that was what Gustav was for anyway. My heart raced and I couldn't breathe around her, like she'd induced a psychosomatic episode in me.

"You'll know it at the right time."

I swallowed the remainder of my drink and slammed the glass on the table.

"Well gentlemen, I've got that health care fair tomorrow before shift. Need to call it a—"

And then chaos swept in, fierce and relentless, like a blizzard crashing through an open window.

CHAPTER 6
ALICE

I buried my head in my arm as a sharp, bitter cold hit my face more brutal than anything I'd felt before. Not even when I got locked in the industrial freezer for two minutes at my high school restaurant job did I feel that pain. I stretched my lips, not as a smile but to check for any movement in my face. My lips were cracked and cold as icicles. Shivering through my long-sleeve shirt and an entirely inappropriate lightweight jacket, I dragged my suitcases down the curb, damaged wheels scraping as loud as a leaf blower.

Outfitted with my duffle bag draped over my left shoulder, my small leather purse on my right side, and one suitcase in each hand, I marched like a mule toward the massive pine door. Lights flickered from the front windows and through the fogged-up glass I could make out people sitting at long tables in the middle of the room and on plush leather chairs against the wall. I bumped my shoulder into the door and gripped the iron handle to open it without free use of both arms.

Gustav had offered to carry my luggage, but I wanted to

do this on my own. Independent woman and all that. I also wanted to turn the hell around and get back in the car and go home.

Shit, it's cold.

Instead, I watched Gustav drive off, along with my fleeing fantasy. I nudged the door open with my shoulder, dragging my well-worn suitcases over the thick sill molding. The wheels picked up snow and chunks of ice accentuating the scraping sound along the floor as I finally pulled everything inside.

The door slammed shut, trapping me inside the warm room, and I let out the kind of holler you do when you're trying to catch a dog that bolted down the street. "It's fucking *cold!*"

The room went silent as everyone's eyes landed on me and the spectacle I dragged in—a single woman hunkered down with two ratty suitcases and gasping for air. I couldn't breathe at this damn elevation. My snow-crusted hair was matted to my forehead. I swiped it out of my eyes with the crook of my elbow. I already hated this place. Any enchantment I had briefly felt at the train station had completely evaporated into the frigid air.

I glanced over the crowd in the busy restaurant and cleared my throat. "Um, hello," I said to no one in particular. "I'm looking for the front desk of the Evermore Winter Lodge."

The room came to a stunned silence, but commotion near the back drew my eye toward a group of men who looked to be in their thirties, with wool coats and scarves draped on the backs of their chairs. The doctor—now familiar and inescapable, it seemed—looked at me with wide eyes like a rabbit being stalked by a coyote.

A man with a stiff blond comb-over pushed his chair

back, the legs scraping against the hardwood floor, and stumbled over a chair leg as he hurried toward me. Endearing, like a puppy. He looked nervous, like maybe he hadn't seen a single new girl in a while. From my observations on the train ride, most of the passengers were affluent families or elderly tourists checking off items on their bucket lists. Not many available young women.

"Hi there—you must be new to Tidings." He extended his hand for a shake. I lowered my eyes, taking in my pack mule status and awkwardly dropped my bags to free my arms.

"Oh, allow me," he added, stepping forward to assist me with my luggage. "The main entrance to the lodge is through *that* door." He pointed to a large steel door at the end of a short hallway in the adjoining room. "The restaurant and lodge share the space, so it looks like one building, but with separate front entrances." He smiled at the confusion that must have been written on my face. "It's okay, most people make that mistake. The main door is easy to miss, especially when it's dark."

"Thank you," I replied with sincerity. "Yes, I'm a new employee at the lodge. I start tomorrow."

He faced his friends at the table in the back. "She moved here, guys," he said loudly. "Not a tourist. She's going to work for Elvin."

"Who is Elvin?" I asked.

"He's the manager of the lodge. You haven't met him yet?"

"I'm afraid not. I've only spoken over the phone to the Human Resources manager, *Coriander*."

His lips tilted and a warm red blush of amusement ran across his puffy cheeks. "Ginger? By the way, what did you say your name was? I'm Allan with two *l*'s and one *n*."

"I didn't give my name yet—and it's nice to meet you, Allan." I gave him a bright smile I was sure sent his nerves into overdrive. I wasn't creeped out by him; he was kind of a cute bumbling, nervous guy, but after Mark, I'd sworn off blonds. "I'm Alice from Arizona."

With a projection loud enough for the whole room to hear him—hell, I'd bet the moose were alerted—Allan let the people at his table know he'd be leaving with me. "I'm going to help Alice here from Arizona get to the lodge."

Through an open door connecting the restaurant to the main lodge entrance, Allan took me to the front desk and then rang a set of literal jingle bells, the exact chiming I heard the other day when I applied for this job and again on the train. Many things in Tidings were turning out to be inescapable, I thought with dismay.

"Elvin!" Allan shouted and I flinched. His shrill tone carried an echo to the back of the room, boomeranging around us. "Alice from Arizona is here."

We stood in uncomfortable silence, exchanging awkward tight-lipped smiles. Allan rang the bells once more when the elusive Elvin failed to appear. I tapped my heels, shifting nervously from side to side. A thin sheen of sweat covered Allan's forehead.

"Allan, I appreciate you helping me, but please don't feel like you need to wait for me."

"Not a problem to wait, Alice from Arizona."

My thin smile morphed into a grimace. "I'm fine waiting alone." After the travel day I had—hell, after the last few days that had rocked my world—I needed to be alone to gather my thoughts and take a deep breath. "Preferably."

Allan's brow furrowed, as if I was someone familiar to him, making me uneasy. I didn't need anyone, especially someone like him who appeared to be missing a filter, recognizing me on day one. Could that stupid story have made it all the way to the internet up here?

Blushing and flustered, he saluted me with a folksy "okie dokie" and heel-toed his way out.

Thirty minutes went by with no sign of Elvin, or any other life appearing at the counter. I dialed the number Ginger called me from, but it went straight to voicemail. Ah—finally, the other shoe that dropped. This wild, mythical daydream of a wintry paradise was indeed a scam. I was catfished all along. *You, stupid, stupid, silly girl.*

My mind raced. Could it be that Tidings wasn't a magical winter wonderland after all? But a cult that recruited fresh blood and sacrificed us to the god of snow? I was trapped in a freaking snow globe with nowhere to go.

"He can't hear very well," a deep, steady voice said from behind me, making me jump. My heart skipped and I pressed a hand to my chest, letting out a small squeak as I spun around. I hesitated, taking in his dimpled smile appearing beneath a layer of winter stubble, the same smile I'd noticed on the train.

My mouth dried and I tried to swallow around a thickness in the back of my throat, but I choked on the saliva pooling in my mouth. I searched for air and swatted a hand against my chest.

"Are you okay?" he asked, concerned.

Hunched over, I held up a hand waving him off. *Totally fine, not dying,* I acted out.

He handed me a bottle of water he grabbed from behind the counter, and I gulped disgustingly loud as I forced the water down my tight throat.

"I choked," I said through a broken breath, desperate to

recover after that embarrassing fumble. *Is it too late to get back on the damn train?*

He pulled his face in, casting a furtive glance in every direction, undoubtedly looking around for an audience. "My apologies. I'll be more cautious next time."

He walked behind the counter, disappearing down a hallway and leaving me alone with my bottle of water and a new level of shame. I peered around the corner, unsure of my next moves. Fatigue from the long day of travel and the events that transpired in the past few days overcame me. I rested my head on the counter, hoping a few seconds of shut-eye could re-energize me.

I jolted when a call came through the phone. The ringer was not a delicate chime, more like a trumpet blast heralding an aggressive emergency alert notification. *That* would be the first thing I'd fix in my new role, after maintaining a reliable customer-friendly seat behind the desk.

Walking behind the doctor was a shorter man, nearly an identical twin to Gustav in height and features. "I told him he needed a buzzer attached to his person, not dainty jingle bells to alert him when he's needed up front," he said.

"The ringer on that phone is anything but dainty," I replied.

"Tradition is very important here," said the quirky, stout man, strolling around the counter and bowing similar to Gustav. He smiled so wide the apples of his cheeks darkened to a cherry red as they held his grin. "I'm Elvin, and you must be the lovely and talented Alice. My sincerest apologies for the wait, my dear." In a gray suit with a red and white striped bow tie and matching handkerchief in his front breast pocket, he was oozing pure holly-jolly joy.

I reached my hand out for a shake, bending slightly in

the knees to greet him at eye level. "It's my pleasure to meet you."

"We are happy to have you, dear. And I see you met the town busybody," Elvin nudged his chin toward the handsome doctor. I took that opportunity to look at him, noticing a piece of wavy brown hair peeking out from under his wool cap. "Silas is too concerned about my hearing, but I get along fine."

Silas tilted his head back, his gaze drifting to the ceiling as he crossed his arms. "It's literally my job to be concerned about you, Elvin." He stepped toward me, and I panicked, fearing another embarrassing choking episode. *Get a grip, Alice. It's just a man, big whoop.*

But his presence was undeniable. Silas extended a hand, his eyes glinting with something unreadable, something that made my pulse quicken. "Maybe we start fresh, Alice from Arizona?" My name lingered in the air, heavy with what could have been nothing—or everything.

I wiped my damp palms across my back pockets before giving him my hand. When we connected, tension skittered from the base of my spine to the back of my neck. He gave me a cocky smile.

Down girl.

"Simply Alice will be fine." His fingers scraped across my palm as we released our hands.

"I don't think there is anything simple about you." Silas' voice was low, a hint of something beneath his words.

Elvin reached for one of my suitcases and tumbled backward at the unexpected weight of the small bag. He wiped his forehead with his handkerchief.

"Sorry, the wheels are broken," I said apologetically. "Or maybe they're frozen."

Silas inserted himself, grabbing the handle. He lifted

both my bags, holding them to his sides like small children that he was carting off the playground under each arm.

"Did you bring the whole damn train with you?" Silas asked, although he showed no signs of exasperation.

"My wardrobe, actually."

"All this and you're wearing that flimsy jacket?"

"I'm from the desert," I reminded him. "This is practically a winter jacket in Phoenix."

Then like something out of a classic Dickens novel, Elvin handed me a vintage brass key. "Well, if you two have it, I'll leave you be. Down the hall to the end, take a right. I'm headed home now."

"Did the internet get fixed?" Silas asked.

Elvin shook his head. "It'll be alright lad. That's why we have our trusted paper system."

"What time do you want me here tomorrow?" I asked. "And am I on shift now, or how does this work if you're not here?" There was still much unknown about this place and the daily tasks required of my job. It seemed straightforward, but I couldn't afford to mess up again.

"We aren't expecting any guests until tomorrow evening. Ginger will be here in the morning. She does all the orientation stuff. Real nice gal. I think you two will be pals."

And with that, the character that was Elvin nodded his head in a farewell gesture and exited the main front door.

"He doesn't live at the lodge?" I turned on my heel back to Silas, who was still not breaking a sweat holding my luggage under his arms as if they were only Trader Joe's bags containing air-fried chips.

"No, he stays at the Reindeer Lodge with all the old-timers. They've all been here for a hundred years. Real set in their ways but hospitable, sometimes to a fault." Silas led the way to the back of the lodge, the smell of vanilla permeating through the hallways, a nice reprieve from the peppermint I'd been invaded by since arriving in Tidings.

"What about the internet?"

"It's been spotty," he said. "They haven't upgraded technology here in a while. After you," Silas said, gesturing to the door at which we had arrived, allowing me to step inside first.

I twisted the brass key in the lock and pushed the door open. When I stepped inside, I released an inappropriate moan, dropping my purse on the floor and covering my mouth. The floor-to-ceiling windows caught my eye first in the warm, atmosphere-rich room. The sky beyond them swayed with colorful ropes of green, blue, and violet. Magical and captivating. The Aurora Borealis was nearly at the tip of my fingers.

Silas gently approached my side, as if I were a skittish cat. He spoke tenderly. "Have you ever seen a celestial phenomenon?"

"Does a roving Russian satellite count?" My response pulled a huff out of him. "I didn't spend much time in Arizona admiring the sky."

"It looks even better when you get away from the city lights."

"Tidings is considered a city?"

"As much of a city as it gets around here. Ask Elvin— he'll tell you it's *too* big." Silas reached out as if to offer me something, but stopped himself, pulling his hand back and tucking it in his front pocket. "Go ahead. Explore your new home."

A cognac leather sofa was perched in front of a white brick hearth that stretched up to the ceiling, containing a fireplace crackling with strong flames, filling the air with a cozy, woody scent. *Who lit the fireplace?* I wondered. Were fireplaces just perpetually lit in Tidings? That sort of random, magical thing seemed entirely plausible in this kind of place.

I flung myself back onto the luxurious couch. My body relaxed for the first time since I'd been fired days ago... although it seemed like an entire year had passed since then.

"Did Elvin start the fire?" I asked.

"It's all gas—just hit the on and off button," Silas said, lifting a remote off the sofa table.

"But it smells and crackles like real wood burning," I said, squinting my eyes at the fireplace, trying to get a closer look.

"Tidings has some cool elements," he shrugged.

From the open living room, I eyed the spacious kitchen —nothing like the cramped kitchenette I'd imagined, the kind you'd expect to find in a Holiday Inn. Instead, it was outfitted with high-end appliances, including an eight-burner stove and a stainless-steel refrigerator. I flung myself off the comfortable couch to poke around and found that the kitchen contained every pot, pan, utensil, and gadget needed in a chef's kitchen. Too bad I didn't cook. In the corner, a basket of fresh fruit rested next to a hot cocoa station, complete with white and dark chocolate peppermint gourmet truffles.

I breezed past Silas as he tip-toed around the room, wary of his place. He propped himself casually against the kitchen cabinets, watching me with a quiet intensity as I dug through the fully-stocked refrigerator like a starving, feral rodent at a backyard buffet. There was no mistaking the way his gaze lingered on me. A knot twisted in my stomach.

"Is it okay that I'm here?" I asked, my tone uncertain.

"What do you mean?"

I wasn't sure myself. "Just the way you're watching me makes me feel..." I trailed off, unsure how to finish. I rubbed my hand over my tight bun hairstyle.

"How do I make you feel, Alice?" His voice was intimate, the bold question carrying a palpable challenge.

"I—I don't know," I stammered, my heart pounding in my chest.

I stepped around him to avoid answering, instead exploring the space by dragging my fingers along the taupe-colored walls, picking up knickknacks off the side tables. And when I opened the bedroom door my knees weakened. A king-sized poster bed, dressed in a white down comforter and a red-and-green quilt, faced a wall of floor-to-ceiling windows. French doors opened to a balcony and covered patio, where an outdoor fireplace crackled, and fur blankets were draped over a small sofa. Maybe there was some appeal to this frigid environment after all, if I got to come home to these decadent furnishings every night.

I peered through the glass door leading to a balcony, looking up at the black sky that drowned in endless stars like a universe tucked inside another universe.

"Go take a look, Arizona," Silas said.

I opened the door, immediately smacked by brutally cold air that stung my face. I pressed the back of my hands to my cheeks as a shooting star went overhead, momentarily taking my mind off the icy pain. "Is this real?"

Silas stepped closer, his hands gripping the balcony railing, fingers flexing as if testing the durability of it. His hands were pink tinged from the cold, the veins running beneath the surface of his skin like taut ropes.

"How long have you lived here?" I asked, attempting to

get to know this stranger whose presence and deep voice were making me feel off-kilter.

Silas started to reply but was interrupted by a vibration in his back pocket. He checked his phone before glancing up at me. "I have to go," he sighed, but lingered as if deciding whether to say more. Our gazes locked, the air between us thick with tension. Then, as if the moment had slipped through his fingers, he straightened, shoving his phone back into his pocket.

"Don't stay out in the cold too long," he added, his eyes meeting mine a final time before he turned and walked away without another word.

THE BATHROOM WAS FULLY EQUIPPED WITH RICH-PEOPLE SHIT, including a massive claw foot bathtub that could probably fit a moose. I flicked on a light switch and a soft red bathed the room from the ceiling lights: heat lamps warming the cold tile floors and the porcelain tub. I drew a steaming bath, more than ready to sink my body under the water and feel a world away from Arizona.

I tossed my phone on the rug next to the clawfoot tub, and as it bounced on the floor, a notification lit up from an unfamiliar name. Bracing myself, I opened the email.

FROM: BUMPER AUSTIN

SUBJECT: Interview regarding your recent viral story

Ms. Woods,

My name is Bumper Austin, and I am a reporter for The Buzz Bulletin, a popular online news site where we strive to tell the full story of one-sided moments that go viral. I recently came across the story of you acciden-

tally sending a lewd A.I.-generated image to all employees of the State of Arizona. It was a silly error, one I'm sure you massively regret now. But I think if we did a quick interview, you could put a face to your name and explain that you're a human who made a dumb mistake, clearing your reputation.

Please email or call me at your earliest convenience.

—BA

My heart raced and my breathing turned shallow. A thousand thoughts went through my mind: *would* this clear my name? How bad was it back in Arizona? And fucking hell, do I really need a lawyer? How serious was this?

I just wanted to be left alone. I had gone to the *ends of the earth* to get away. Secluded in Tidings, nothing outside this community seemed to exist. As Silas said, the Wi-Fi worked sporadically and there was no satellite television. We were isolated and I liked it that way. I *needed* it to be that way.

My anxieties did not fade even as the coldness in my bones drifted away, immersed in the steaming water.

I ruined my own life.

Should I confess to Ginger and Elvin? Did they already know? The thought that worried me the most was what Silas Hill would think if he found out I was fired for being an idiot, dumped, and kicked out of my apartment because I was an embarrassing liability.

I sank deeper into the water, hoping that if I stayed long enough, I could forget everything—just for a little while longer.

CHAPTER 7

SILAS

I typed with one finger, crunching on an apple that had a faint chemical aftertaste on its peel. Fresh produce was hard to come by in the coldest months, so it'd been on the backs of trucks and trains for a month before it made it to the local market. My body was crying for nutrients. Poor sleep and a worse diet were going to send me to the ER as a patient if I didn't get a handle on my health habits soon.

"Dashboard," said Pete, acknowledging the music coming from my phone's speaker. "Nice."

Pete was a recent hire, fresh from nursing school after a career as an Army medic. He had a sleeve of tattoos on both arms and one creeping up beneath the V-neck of his scrub top. To be honest, he scared the shit out of me. Every doctor knew you didn't mess with the nurses, and between him and Imelda, I was a skittish cat.

He hummed the lyrics to the chorus: *"I'm gonna hear the saddest songs and sit alone and wonder how you're making out."*

"I don't think you were born when this song came out," I said, grumpier than I intended. I had two more patient notes to finish, and I didn't need the nurse for the mafia breathing down my neck.

"We played it downrange. Mostly when we missed our warm beds... and something else warm to sink into," he mused, grabbing a chair at the nurses' station behind me.

I harrumphed, holding back a response before this conversation tilted more toward inappropriate. "Bar conversation, Pete, not in the hospital."

In the ER, we worked as a cohesive unit, and I rarely used the office dedicated for the doctor on shift. It was a more casual environment compared to other departments, but I appreciated the chatter and jokes from my colleagues. It helped keep my mind from spinning— except, like now, when I was rushing through patient notes just to get the hell out of there.

Pete rambled about the Army days, and I listened with one ear as I typed. "Before we went after the assholes, we hyped ourselves up with the classics: Metallica, Slipknot, Black Sabbath. Man, miss that shit."

In the reflection of my computer, I saw him spin around in the chair, looking youthful. The tattoos and battle scars covered up the fact he was still a kid at twenty-four or five.

"Maybe you should re-enlist... since you miss that shit."

"Fuck no," he said. "I got something much better here." I eyed him over my shoulder. "Warm bed and all that," he winked.

I rolled my eyes, then turned my focus back to work.

When I signed off on the last patient note, I pushed the chair back and stood, heading toward the communal lockers. I always looked forward to going home after work, but I dreaded layering up with my winter gear, leaving the warmth of the hospital, and stepping into the icy torture chamber outside.

Pete rolled his chair across the floor from one station to another like a pinball. "What's a happy-go-lucky guy like you listening to emo at six in the morning, anyways, doc?"

"I work nightshift in the ER," I said, and the bluntness surprised even me. It was the first time I'd let the mask slip that covered up my outward composure. "Don't think there's anything lucky about that."

"No one forced you to go to medical school."

"Watch it, Nurse Pete."

He lifted his hands in surrender. "Just do what makes you happy, doc. Life's too short."

Instead of going home where I was desperate to be glued to my couch, I drove to the high school for the fourth annual healthcare assembly, an event I created to help grow student interest in the field of medicine. It was always a hit. I brought all the cool shit: X-ray images, stitching kits, needles, and my most badass stories of saving lives. I made medicine look fun, or at least an alluring circus freak show showing off the gadgets and ways we use them to quickly fix trauma wounds or set broken bones.

Everyone mistakenly thought emergency medicine doctors were superheroes with endless energy and extraordinary knowledge of how to save lives. I wasn't here to correct them—today at least.

They didn't need to know the number of energy drinks I consumed weekly, and the sticky wrappers and crumbs in the pockets of my fleece vests often constituted my daily three-square meals.

After I gave a quick lesson on how to place a tourniquet, a student asked what kind of person made a good ER doc.

"Quick thinking, mental fortitude, and a sociopathic craving for adrenaline," was my practiced answer. The last part always earned me a few laughs.

The truth was an unhealthy sense of macabre humor and a devastatingly high dose of self-loathing. Whatever rest I accumulated in California quickly dissipated as I forced a smile and made small talk for hours.

I finally made it home with enough time to snag a couple hours of sleep before my next shift. But first, a non-negotiable skin-burning-level hot shower. I squeezed a dollop of two-for-one shampoo and conditioner into my palm and rubbed it into my scalp, then stood back under the hot water, rinsing the soap out to flow down onto my face, which only intensified the burning in my bloodshot eyes. This routine was easier four years ago, when I was still wet behind the ears as a young, eager doctor.

It felt like my body and mind aged in dog years, seven for each one I gave to emergency medicine. I chose this specialty knowing the sacrifices and commitment it took to be successful, and with my tenacity and craving for the adrenaline rush, I was all in. Well, what a big fucking surprise: years of self-neglect only led to disastrous mental health levels of self-loathing. Now, I understood the high burnout rate and overall unhappiness of my colleagues across the nation. Even in a small town like Tidings, people still got stupid, avoidable injuries. Add the dangers of snow, below-freezing temperatures, ice, and wildlife attacks, and we were a revolving door of blood transfusions and stitches.

I turned the shower off and wrapped a towel around my waist. I wiped the fog off the mirror, my swollen eyes glaring back at me. My dog lay between my feet as I stood at the bathroom sink brushing my teeth, soaking in the warmth from the heated floors. Resting my hands against the edge of the counter, I closed my eyes and imagined the warmth I felt on my skin two days ago in California. A world away from here.

But instead of being transported to the beach with its salty air, a mixture of earthy florals overwhelmed me. I didn't see the beach; I saw Alice's face.

Touring the suite with her last night sent my blood pulsing into overdrive. It didn't help when we entered the bedroom, and that four-poster bed might as well have had a neon vacancy light flashing above it. I faked an emergency and left. Desperation had sizzled inside me, and I couldn't be confined with her in that space any longer.

My phone vibrated on the counter, nearly falling off, disrupting my thoughts of Alice and the empty bed. I reached for it and after reading the message, I should have let it drown in the toilet. The hospital scheduling assistant asked if I could cover extra shifts over the next two weeks. But I didn't really have a choice. If I didn't do it, it was near impossible to find a per diem who could travel to Tidings with short notice, leaving our surgeon to cover the ER where he'd attempt to cut his way around a fever. I replied back with confirmation, then the she-devil herself messaged me.

Ginger: Open up.

Silas: Go away.

Ginger: Got to talk to you about Dagny.

I groaned my way through getting dressed and dragged myself to the front door. Ginger was a friend, but she was also a bit too much, especially on days like today when my patience was waning. But if she wanted to talk to me about something my little sister did, I better listen.

"What's wrong with your face?" Ginger asked as she stomped through my front door, nearly pummeling me to the ground.

I barely had my hand on the doorknob before she barged in. "Technically, this is breaking and entering."

"Oh, go cry." She helped herself to a cup of coffee from the pot I brewed earlier. I didn't even get the first sip.

"You're leaning into the nickname 'Devil's Spawn' today," I said.

She rolled her eyes and handed me a cup of straight black.

"So, Dagny?" I prompted, cutting to the chase.

Ginger was the human resources manager for all the small businesses in Tidings. They were a union that relied on her to manage the business of employees, while the café, boutique, restaurants, and lodge took care of their daily operations. She ran around looking busier than me, but she never complained or even yawned. I couldn't look weak next to her.

"I lied," she said simply, without an ounce of guilt.

I took another sip and closed my eyes. "I don't have time for this crap, Ginger."

"I heard you met our newest temp at the lodge."

"Don't start," I bit back. Another thing about Ginger was that she was always in everyone's business, beyond the scope of her actual job, especially mine. She'd been trying to fix me up with women for years, and it was rather insulting. I was perfectly capable. Frankly, it was none of her fucking business. "I have to get ready for work." I went up the stairs to my room on the second floor, tossing on a scrub top over my long-sleeved shirt and a pair of socks.

She hollered at me from the bottom of the stairs. "She got drunk and asked Siri to find her a job. Very serendipitous, right?" She emphasized that word, *serendipitous*, like I needed to take a hint.

I inwardly groaned and clenched my teeth. The long-standing superstition surrounding Tidings claimed the town only allowed in who it wanted, when it wanted. "It" being the town in some silly, sentient form.

I didn't care for the "magic of Tidings." It was a black hole that sucked people in, trapping them forever. I couldn't say that out loud around the old-timers like Elvin or Ginger without being sneered at and ostracized, making my experience here worse than it already was. I stomped down the stairs finding Ginger leaning against my front door, typing furiously on her cell. "It's a miracle our first meeting wasn't with her in my emergency room being treated for hypothermia," I said curtly.

"Give her some pointers," she said without looking up from her phone.

"Her jacket was as warm as tissue paper. She should have known better before coming here."

"Maybe they don't have snow-appropriate gear in Arizona, Silas." She popped a bubble and smacked her gum as she opened the door. She glanced over her shoulder and gave me a stern look like she was my fucking mother. "Take her shopping."

"I don't have a lot of free time," I said, pausing for dramatic effect with jazz hands, "for shopping." Taking a woman shopping was at the bottom of my list. Hell, I'd rather get my nostrils waxed again like that time Dagny insisted it would make a difference. But Alice... she was a breath of fresh air. Someone I wouldn't mind spending more time around. But the timing was all off; she arrived too late. "You came all the way here to tell me to take the new girl shopping for thermals and a snow-appropriate jacket? Jeez, it must be nice to have a lot of free time."

I sounded angry and defeated, because I was. About a year ago, I had an incident that was a rude awakening, showing me how unsustainable my work-life balance had become. After thirteen straight days, I ended a painful shift, miraculously stumbling into my house before collapsing on the floor. I slept for an entire day before Snøf woke me up with a concerned growl, biting at my shoelaces. The urge to quit and find a job with more support where I wasn't the only backup on top of my regular shifts was overwhelming. But there would be a devastating void in health care access for residents and tourists. I told myself it was selfish to want to leave because of the fucking weather. I could over-come that.

"Well then, save a triage room for her in the ER," she said. I attempted to pull the door shut, and she wedged her foot between the gap. "We're looking out for you. A little attention from a pretty girl wouldn't kill ya." This time she successfully slammed the door in my face, leaving me pissed off and alone.

My dog's whimpers drew my attention to her at the back door. I cracked it open before she squeezed her giant body through to run outside, belly flopping onto the fresh layer of snow. She rolled on her back soaking up snow over her heavily coated fur body. Her tongue flopped around, and her tail wagged. She was so happy here.

At least one of us was.

CHAPTER 8
ALICE

I kicked off the heavy velvet down comforter, untied the robe, and aired out my sticky skin, feeling a comforting breeze across my chest. I reached for my phone on the nightstand to check the time, ensuring I didn't sleep in on my first day at work. I was greeted with a text from Patrick and a missed call from my mom I'd handle later.

Patrick: You safe, or do I need to call the National Guard to find you trapped in someone's snow dungeon?

I messaged Patrick back a proof of life selfie, then fumbled through my clothes to find something appropriate for work. My suitcases were a chaotic jumble, as if I'd grabbed everything I owned and was running from the law. The first part was true; the second, though, felt all too real. Buried underneath the crumbled balls of well-worn black leggings, I found my toiletry bag and the nicest professional outfit I owned. I settled on a pair of caramel-brown wide-leg trousers and a fitted white turtleneck.

I swiped on mascara, brushed blush onto the apples of

my cheeks, and dotted concealer under my eyes and around my nose where dry skin had turned red. If the hot, dry Arizona air had already aged my skin rapidly, the tundra weather would only make it worse.

My sleek bun, tied at the nape of my neck, was the same style I'd worn for years—practical, predictable, and endlessly uncomplicated. It wasn't glamorous or exciting. It was tight, almost painfully so, but it kept every strand in place, every stray thought at bay. This style had become my refuge, a small act of control in a world that often felt too chaotic to navigate.

I waited at the front desk to start work when the door to the lodge's main entrance swung open, and a strikingly beautiful redhead stepped in. She wore a black, floor-length wool coat, fuzzy black earmuffs, and leather gloves that looked like they belonged in the wardrobe of someone who didn't shop on sale.

"Oh my god," I whispered, the words slipping out, "it's a mob wife."

She flicked her red locks over her shoulder and snatched her sunglasses off her face like a very important person would glare at a peasant, revealing hazel eyes with flecks of gold. Freckles scattered across her nose. She gave a half smile, something seductive that made me blush. "Hello, Alice. Welcome to Tidings." She moved behind the desk and brought me in for a tight hug. She smelled like gingerbread cookies, and despite her frosty exterior, her hug was warm and comfortable—a little too on the nose to not be suspicious.

"You must be Cardamom?" I teased. But Ginger was the first person who either didn't handle me with kid gloves or swing to the other side of the spectrum to knock me out.

She seemed authentic, tough, but cared deeply about Tidings and her people. I admired her loyalty.

"I knew I liked you." She couldn't have been older than thirty, but her presence felt like a safe, old soul. "Welcome to Tidings, and to your first day on the clock. I am technically not your boss, but I am the HR manager for all local, small businesses. The owners handle the ins and outs of their enterprises, and I handle employees, payroll, and a million tiny details no one ever sees. Elvin will give you the lay of the land, but heads-up—you'll have to teach yourself the computer software. He's a little old school and not with the times."

"He said the Wi-Fi wasn't working."

"It happens," she shrugged. "I think he appreciates it that way. A bit *too* much if you'd ask me."

Everyone in Tidings had been so friendly, even this ball-busting firecracker of a woman. Yet a heavy storm cloud hung over me, thick and tense, full of secrets and shame, waiting to burst open and flood the room. Surely a highly capable—and a little scary—professional like Ginger had done a simple Google search on me. *But then why did she hire you, you idiot?*

As my thoughts spiraled, I tried to listen as Ginger reiterated the moose safety briefing I heard yesterday, and gave me a few pointers about what to do, not if, but *when*, it entered the lobby. The most important rule was not to leave the door propped open while guests loaded luggage in and out of the building. Remain calm and slowly back down the hallway to either the small staff office or to my suite and then call emergency services. Do not engage with the moose. Very clear directive.

"Any other questions?" she asked, holding her phone up and swiping through notifications.

I needed to confront the elephant—er, moose?—in the room. "Ginger, do you know why I'm here?"

Light reflected from the screen onto the black sunglasses perched on top of her head. She typed furiously on her phone and didn't lift her eyes. "You were qualified, and you said yes."

"I'd never worked in customer service before. Besides, you could train a circus monkey to do this job."

She flicked an eyebrow. "Exactly," she drawled. A *whoosh* sounded from her phone, and she tucked it into the pocket of her wool jacket. "Any more questions?"

"Nothing you said made sense."

She hit the ignore button on her buzzing phone and gave me a pointed look. "Elvin and sometimes the other guys from Reindeer Lodge will be by to help." Her phone buzzed again. It'd been going off most of the time she was with me. "Guests arrive during midday Friday and Saturday, so those will be your busiest times."

"What is the Reindeer Lodge?"

"Technically, it's a small condominium building where many single male Tidings residents live. We call it the old-timers club. They play a lot of pinochle, and perform concerts with string instruments and flutes." Ginger flicked her wrist to read messages buzzing on her smartwatch. "Shoot. I'm running further behind than I thought. But you should be set for now." She pulled her glasses back over her eyes and jolted toward the door. "My number is saved in the house phone, slot two on the speed dial. And if you need Elvin, call for him."

"Do I have his number?" I asked as she bolted for the exit.

"Just ask for him!" Ginger shouted, her back facing me on her way out the door.

The little old man couldn't hear the bells at the desk ten feet away from him, and I'm instructed to—what? Speak him into existence?

Crooning, classic versions of winter songs played throughout the lobby. My mom tried calling me again, likely asking for a brief life update for her annual family holiday newsletter. I sent her to voicemail. I wasn't sure how to explain where I was and what I was doing. I wasn't the prized child like my sister, the famous geologist with her own regular featured column in *National Geographic.* Maybe I'd be an overstated footnote. "Alice is... participating in an Arctic immersive learning experience and owes back taxes."

I fumbled through the day, checking in groups who were graciously patient as I explained it was my first day when I mixed up the keys and somehow caused the computer system to freeze, requiring me to reboot it twice.

When my shift ended at five, a server from the restaurant attached to the lodge's building popped her head in through the connecting swinging door. The name badge clipped to her black sweater read *Dagny,* and she had creamy blond hair and ice-blue eyes. "Hey, new girl. Our pastry chef made cranberry cheesecake." As quickly as she peered in, she ducked back out. I looked around and as Ginger had suggested, I called out for Elvin.

"Uh... hello, Elvin? This is Alice. I'm off my shift." I waited for... something. The phone to ring, maybe. A voice over the speaker. A sign from above. Nothing.

"Okay, I'm leaving now," I called out into the ether. I tip-toed out from behind the desk and before I opened the connecting door, I stopped to turn over my shoulder. "This is Alice. Signing out of her shift today. I was told there's cheesecake." In response, those damn jingle bells chimed.

"Either there's some spooky shit here or I'm losing my mind hearing those." Another chime sounded. "Not funny!" I looked around the room as if someone would pop out from a dark corner shaking a bell.

I hesitated at the swinging door that connected the lobby to the adjoining restaurant. So far, everyone here had been welcoming and warm. Did they not have access to the outside world? Maybe my viral mistake hadn't made it to the Tidings' algorithm yet.

Watching Dagny work was like watching the world's best server combined with the pace of an Olympic speed skater and the efficiency of a surgeon. I'd never seen anyone work so hard. I was envious of her competence; I could never be responsible for bringing people food without tripping over my own two feet, pegging someone in the face with a bowl of mashed potatoes. I was good enough for a simple job, sitting behind a desk and handing out hotel room keys. In my downtime, I played word games on my phone.

Dagny puttered past me, dropping off a menu and sliding a glass of sparkling wine with fresh cranberries toward me. She was attentive to all her customers, a controlled friendliness. I ordered the house special, a roasted guinea hen and root vegetables; lefse, which the menu explained was a thin potato bread topped with warm butter and brown sugar; and water to go with my wine. The meal was delicious, filling and hearty, with intention and purpose to nourish and warm my body.

Dagny untied her apron and sat on the chair across the table from me and stretched her legs to rest her feet on the brown leather booth. She let out a long exhale and helped herself to a sip of water from my glass. "Sorry, that is too friendly for someone you recently met," she said in between deep breaths. "I'm parched."

I held my champagne up in a mock toast. "You work hard; you should have one of these yourself."

"As much as I'd love to imbibe, I have to study tonight. Got to keep the head clear."

I rolled up the lefse and took my first bite, savoring the unique meld of potato, brown sugar, and butter. "You're in college?"

"No, I already graduated. I'm studying for the MCAT actually." She pointed at my mouth as I chewed on the thin, warm bread. "Delicious, right?"

I dusted the flakes from the potato flatbread onto the napkin in my lap. "A future doctor in my presence. I'm honored."

She crinkled her nose and with a dismissive shrug added, "It's a family thing."

I raised my eyebrows and gave her an impressed grin. "Sounds fancy." I thought of Silas—Dr. Hill—and wondered if maybe he thought of me, too. Our cluster of happenstance meetings culminated in a bewildering ending to the evening. Him in my suite, touring my bedroom with me. It was so unexpectedly intimate, a shiver tickled the back of my neck.

Dagny busied herself, running her hands across the lip of the glass, generating a chime-like sound. "How are you liking Tidings?"

"I can't put a finger on it yet. The hotel gig is easy enough, though."

"Lodge," she corrected me.

"Lodge, right. But I got to meet interesting people, and everyone has been super nice." She eyed my uneaten portions, and since I was more than full enough, I pushed the plate toward my new friend. My phone buzzed, disrupting the conversation. With a flimsy glance I hit the button to ignore my mother. Again.

"Boyfriend back home?"

I shook my head and chewed my lip.

She chewed through potatoes and carrots. "Everything okay?"

"Just my nosy mom." I pushed my phone away.

She pitched a smirk that told me she deeply understood. "Anything interesting happen on your first day?"

"I met the town doctor on the first day when I couldn't find Elvin. Silas was on my train back, and then Allan tried to—well, he was trying to be helpful, I guess."

Dagny arched a brow and looked at me with a sly smile. "Let me guess—Allan was hovering?"

"You'd be correct. And then Silas rescued me from Allan's awkward conversation. He helped me get settled in my room."

Dagny's eyes widened.

"*Nothing* happened," I pressed. "He carried my bags for me because they were so heavy and bulky."

"Why would anything happen?"

"Oh—I meant because you looked shocked when I said he came to my room. I didn't want to come off like—oh, gosh, I'm sorry, this is so awkward."

Dagny laughed and waved me off. "He's hard to pin down. Lucia's got him on a leash doing all her dirty work. If not that, then it's the wild bitch."

Whoa.

I wanted to ask clarifying questions, but Dagny's manager hollered for her from across the room about the engagement party celebrating tonight. "Silverware won't roll itself. Thanks for the food."

❄

I'D MADE IT THROUGH THE FIRST DAY ON THE JOB WITHOUT messing things up so badly that I would once again become a viral embarrassment. But it was rough learning the ancient computer system to check in guests. Elvin was of no help; he'd rather write everything down with a pencil on graph paper.

I needed to upgrade my socks—my feet were freezing beneath the desk in my flats, which were as useful as a parka in Phoenix. All I could think about was a scorching hot bath.

The front desk phone rang, this time with a pleasant, generic tone that didn't feel like an emergency alert to a national crisis.

"Thank you for calling the Evermore Winter Lodge. This is Alice speaking. How may I help you?"

Muffled sounds and beeps came through the other end, likely someone calling from the train station. "I'm sorry I can't hear you well, but unfortunately, we are completely booked out this week. I can give you recommendations for rental homes available."

In the background, a door slammed, followed by a cuss word or two. "You there?" a man's voice shouted. "Can you hear me?"

I pulled the phone away from my ear. "Loud and clear, sir."

He shouted, "This is Silas. I—"

"You don't have to shout," I interrupted, "I can hear you fine."

Why was Silas calling me? My mind raced through a million options settling on the one I liked the least, panicking that he was giving me a gentle warning to get out of this town before I brought shame upon his home.

"Sorry. Sometimes the hospital reception is terrible."

"No problem. How can I help you?" If he was looking for a room for a one-night stand, I'd rejoice in telling him again we had no vacancy.

"What are you wearing?"

I flinched. "Excuse me?"

"Shit." He let out a long puff of air. "I meant, are you wearing anything warm?"

"What's happening?"

"The jacket you wore the other day wasn't warm enough. And if you don't have a dead toe yet I'd be surprised."

Was he trying to be helpful or insulting? He wasn't wrong but I figured if I stayed inside this lodge during my time here, I wouldn't have to fork over money I didn't have on winter gear I'd never wear once I left. I hated winter. I hated snow. It would be a miracle if I lived to tell the tales of my three months here. He didn't ask a question, but I fumbled my words, pausing, without a response.

"Can I try this again?" he asked.

"Okay?" The line went dead, and I put the office phone back on the receiver. When it rang, I cleared my throat, attempting to be professional and not rattled by whatever that was. "Thank you for calling Evermore Winter Lodge; this is Alice speaking. How may I help you?

"Hi Alice, this is Silas."

"Yes, hello. How may I help you?" We crossed over into awkward role-playing.

"I noticed you were new to a winter climate, and you might not be prepared clothing-wise." He sounded rehearsed, like he was reading a script for a corny infomercial selling me copper-lined socks. "If you'd like, I could help you get around town to the right clothing stores so that you are safe and comfortable during your stay here." I placed the back of my hand on my cheeks feeling their warmth radiate through my body. That was adorable. And cheesy as all hell.

"I haven't stepped foot outside in two days and I have a space heater that is probably breaking the fire code under the desk."

He chuckled, and even on the phone I could picture a lightness lifting across his face.

"I work until Sunday. If that would work for you?"

I leaned back in the chair and twirled the cord from the receiver around my finger. It'd been a long time since I'd talked on a phone like this. "You're working twenty-four hours?"

"Ha. Yeah. I usually crash pretty hard after that."

"That can't be good for your health."

"Look who's the doctor now," he teased.

"Common sense, I think."

"The same common sense that had you wearing a windbreaker in sub-freezing temperatures?"

"I'm from Arizona," I quipped as he echoed me in a playful tone. We both laughed and I found myself kicking my feet up on the desk and indulging in this moment. "I don't want to take up your time; I can find my way around town. But I appreciate the offer."

My polite rejection was met with a faint throat clearing. "I'm happy to help you."

"What if I need new underwear? Which guy in town do I call for that?" I heard the sound of something dropping and I took a sick pleasure in imagining his jaw on the floor. I was happy to keep up this game in person.

"Okay." He cleared his throat. "Alice, I—" Beeping sounds interrupted him. "I have to go. I'll see you on Sunday afternoon."

"See you," I said to a dead phone line. He hung up before I could get a word out. And I smiled.

Maybe three months here wouldn't be so bad after all.

To prepare for my first excursion outdoors, I wore my warmest shirt—a thin, white turtleneck good enough for the coldest day in Scottsdale, but in Tidings, it was as cozy as a mesh top. I layered a pair of leggings underneath my jeans and two pairs of socks. Silas offered me a ride when he called me at the lodge this morning, but I politely declined and insisted on walking two blocks to the first store on his list. According to the map on my phone, it was eight minutes on foot. I gripped a thermos of hot coffee like a prayer in hopes of transferring heat to my hands.

The sidewalks were cleared from last night's storm. My old tennis shoes crunched on the salt that sparkled under the partial sunny day. Even at mid-morning, the dim sky allowed the street lamps and lights strung along the walkway to glow as bright as an Arizona sunset.

Oversized SUVs and trucks with chunky studded tires or snowmobiles rumbled through the streets. I fought for deep breaths, the cold air like an ice pick stabbing my lungs with each inhale. The sidewalks were full of people going about their daily business, bundled in layers of fleece, fur, and wool, smiling as though it wasn't a health hazard to be in this temperature. Warm lights shone from busy clothing shops, cozy cafes, artisanal bakeries, a bookstore, and so much more I had yet to see. It was a picturesque town and thriving community with an eclectic mix of rosemaling-painted storefront buildings (a term I had Googled to name the designs I kept seeing in Tidings) and charming Bavarian villages.

Finally, I made it to the store, blessed to have only lost one toe to frostbite. I stomped my snow-covered tennis shoes on the welcome mat and shook off the clumps of snow that gathered on my jacket. It wasn't snowing at present, but wind gusts picked up stray flakes from rooftops, dusting my clothes.

Three long months of this torture. Even the occasional bright spots I kept noticing weren't yet enough to help me see this all through rose-colored glasses.

But then I could take my earnings, go back to the land of sun, and defrost my bones. Start over. I had a little more time before I decided if I needed to change my name.

Like every door in Tidings, bells rang when it opened. A full-length mirror met my stare, and I fluffed out my flat hair. My cheeks and the tip of my nose turned poppy-pink, my lips a faded, chapped-red. I smiled and my face lit up in a natural rosy glow. Somehow, I looked pretty as a cold girl.

"Good morning, welcome to Needle & Wool. What can I help you with?" asked the employee as he gave me a long look from top to bottom.

"Everything." I outstretched my arms and twirled. "I'm from Arizona."

"I see." He waved me to follow him to the back of the store where a section was smartly labeled, "Winter Basics."

"I'm Bror. And you are?"

"Alice." I took in the racks of wool sweaters, gloves, hats, scarves, socks, and fleece-lined leggings. "I'm meeting someone here. And I think I'll need one of each." I rubbed my hands across the soft, goose-filled parka before wincing at the price tag.

"It's an investment piece," Bror said. "It snows September through April." He was as tall and broad as the blond Viking man from the train station, but his black hair was cropped short with tiny bangs. He educated me on dressing in layers, when it was appropriate for regular clothes (preferably, long pants, and a sweater, and only when I was inside with proper heating), and always wear a down parka outside. "The official first day of winter is weeks away and the coldest weather won't hit until January when the nighttime lows drop to lower than fifty below zero."

"That can't be survivable."

"Which is why you need to wear the appropriate clothes," Silas said, appearing near the sweaters. "Word of advice. Bundle up and try not to cry because the tears will freeze to your face." Silas flicked through a row of hangers and plucked off a gray sweater, handing it to me.

"It gets to fifty *below* zero? I didn't even know you could measure that."

"We stop counting at minus ten," Silas said. He looked at the sweater in my hands, then dropped his gaze to my feet before he flicked his eyes away. He bit his lower lip and exhaled.

"You two have already met?" Bror asked.

"We shared a ride home from the airport with Gus," Silas said. He meandered around, looking adorably clueless in the women's clothing section, kind of like he'd rather set himself on fire than be here. "She's from Arizona."

"So she wouldn't know any better," Bror replied, dismissively. "But inside I'm hyperventilating over those shoes."

"What's wrong with my shoes?" I scanned my well-loved tennis shoes, not admitting how cold and wet my toes were. They stared at me with blank expressions. Bror leaned on a rack of sweaters and muttered something under his breath about laypeople.

"It's a miracle she hasn't lost a digit yet," Silas said.

"Hello, I'm standing *right here.*"

Silas crossed his arms and continued talking to Bror like I wasn't in the room. "She needs wool socks and boots. Definitely a jacket."

"What about bras?" I said louder than necessary for this space. I wanted Silas' attention on me, and maybe shock was the way to do it. I liked the way he looked at me like I was a mystery, a puzzle needing to be solved. "My nipples feel like ice. Any fur-lined bras?"

Finally, the two chatter bugs stopped. Silas' mouth dropped and Bror smirked, lifting an eyebrow in my direction. "I can take you to the room behind the curtain," Bror said. He laughed under his breath as I followed behind him. Silas looked at the heavens, muttering under his breath.

THE GOOD NEWS WAS I WOULDN'T GET FROSTBITE WALKING around Tidings in my new boots and jacket. The bad news was that I spent too much money on clothes I'd never wear again after the next three months. Bror said he would send "the dogs" with my bags to be delivered this afternoon, which I thought was a rude way to refer to his employees.

Silas walked me to Fika & Friends, a packed café with customers eating muffins and drinking hot beverages outside on the sidewalk. Dagny sat at an iron bistro table on the sidewalk, nonchalantly petting a beautiful, silky brown-and-black dog. I reached my hand out and he nuzzled his nose under my palm, begging for ear scratches.

"What a good boy you are," I said in a baby voice, because that adorable dog deserved all the spoils. I'd always wanted a dog—maybe someday, when I was settled down.

"Yes, Snøfnugg, what a good *boy* you are," Dagny said in a sarcastic tone. "Snøfnugg is a very naughty girl, actually. Her middle name is Chaos."

"My apologies, Snøfnugg," I whispered in her black floppy ear and kissed the side of her snout. Snøfnugg jumped on me, knocking me on my butt and covering my face with kisses. I giggled like I was being tickled to death. I tried to pull her off me, but she was easily a hundred pounds of muscle and fur.

"Snøfnugg, off!" Dagny commanded. "Silas, control your nutty dog."

"She's yours?" I turned to Silas.

"Yeah." He crouched down and scratched her ears. I could tell he'd let her get away with anything. They had strong mutual love. "Dagny watches her for me when she can." He turned to Dagny, "We'll be out after we order."

Inside, a fresh spruce tree in the corner was ordained with pink lights and red-and-white sparkling peppermint candy ornaments.

"What's with this place and peppermint?"

"Peppermint is our number one exported item." Silas guided me in front of him in line with a gentle hand on my waist, pointing at the chalkboard menu on the wall. I held my breath as I positioned myself in front of him, the tight line of people forcing us to squeeze closer. Nerves fired up and down my spine and it ached for a touch on my lower back that never came. "The peppermint factory employs most of the residents." He was still speaking, but I tuned out whatever else he said. I was too busy focusing on my nipples not hardening despite the velvet bra I found at the boutique. I took a deep breath, heard him say something about the railroad, and tried like hell to gather my wits about me.

I scanned the room, taking in the charming space that resembled a real log cabin. A piercing scream cut through the air, and I followed the panicked gazes of the guests toward the front door. Silas barreled through the crowd, charging for the exit.

I gathered with the crowd at the window. "What's going on?"

"I told you that dog was a menace!" Dagny shouted over the heads of lookie-loos.

I held a hand over my gaped mouth as I watched Silas run out into the street. Snøfnugg circled a stopped car with a broken headlight, dragging the table behind her around and around.

"Snøfnugg!" Silas bellowed. "*Heel!*"

The driver shouted, cursing at Silas. I don't think Silas wanted Snøfnugg to heel in the middle of the street, but that's what she did with her big, furry body. Flat on the snow-covered road, tongue lolling out. Silas untethered the leash from the table and picked her up, while she latched on to him. Her front legs and paws wrapped around his neck, and he held her like a toddler. He handed the driver something from his wallet, and then put the phone to his ear.

"Oh God, he's going to bring that mutt in here," said a blond woman wearing oversized —and ugly—sunglasses indoors. I'd been here for only one week, but I could even spot a tourist now. They dressed like they were on a modeling shoot for high fashion in the snow.

Silas sat in a chair with the shaken pup still gripping him like a giant sloth. He apologized to the patrons, but none of them, except for the fake snow bunny in the corner, seemed to care that the dog was a little nuts. Once she planted four paws on the floor, she became the people's dog, making her way table by table to receive reassuring head pats and scratches.

I ordered two peppermint-infused coffees and watched Silas instruct Snøfnugg to lay down by the front door. She did as he commanded, but when she looked up at me, she bolted across the room, fluffy tail wagging everywhere, slapping human legs along the way. Silas jogged toward us. She sat perfectly still at my feet, locking eyes with me. The closest thing I had to a pet was a desert tortoise my high school kept as a mascot. I'd show up before school to try to be the first to feed Tortellini, and watch as he chomped on his lettuce and other discarded vegetables the grocery stores donated.

"I'm sorry about that." Silas reached for the pretty dog's collar, and I shooed his hand away, wanting to indulge my hands in her soft fur.

"No problem." I kept the baby voice to a minimum as I rubbed her ears and scratched her chin. She responded with licks on my hands and face.

"Whenever she comes in here, she goes around on a begging tour like she's so starved for attention and food." He shook his head in disbelief. "I thought she could do her panhandling outside, but lesson learned."

"See?" I told the dog directly. "You're a good girl."

"Yeah, poor Snøfnugg is misunderstood," he said, tone laced with sarcasm.

"Silas, you're scaring the people with that mutt!" Ginger stood behind him, looking like a looming storm cloud in her all-black ensemble.

"She's not a mutt, she's a—"

"I know, I know, she's a 'very expensive breed.'" She rolled her eyes in dismissal and leaned into me, whispering loud enough for him to hear. "Only Silas is allowed to tease his baby. He's very protective of her."

"Does everybody always show up here at the same time?" I asked.

"I spend my days walking up and down this street checking in on the staff. I heard the commotion and came over to check things out." Ginger looked between me and Silas, a quizzical expression on her face, then settled her gaze back on me. "*You* were my next stop, actually. Things are going well at the lodge? And how amazing is that large bathtub in your suite?"

My memory flashed to last night's steaming bath, where I indulged in luxury and self-care unsuitable for public conversation. I searched my brain for a response that didn't center around my hands being between my thighs. I couldn't help it—for fuck's sake, there were hot Viking men everywhere. And Silas with his dimple and large, capable hands. "Uh, yeah. It's hot," I stammered out awkwardly.

"Well, I'm glad I caught you here. I wanted to see if you'd like to come out on Friday with me and my friends. A fresh batch of climate researchers are coming in." She arched an eyebrow conspiratorially and lowered her voice. "Trust me, it's the best part about living here." That explained the massive list of reservations I filled this week. Some names requested specific rooms as if they were regulars.

"Can't seem to get enough of those, Ging?" Silas said.

She swatted his arm. "It's cold and lonely up here," she explained in her defense.

I tried to meet their banter. "I mean, there's always Allan." Ginger and Silas stared at me with a cold expression. Silas broke the tension and exhaled a wheezing laugh, nearly falling over his knees. I pinched my lips together, desperate to keep my smile tight.

Ginger blushed, embarrassed by a normally demure Silas breaking character with attention-grabbing chuckles. "Like I said, Friday night. Dress sexy, but ya know, *cool.*"

"How do I dress sexy here when all I want is to wrap myself in a fur blanket? I'm actually jealous of Snøfnugg's coat."

"You can't have it," Silas said, his serious tone an abrupt end to his uncharacteristic guffaws.

"Yeah, no shit. She was making a joke." Ginger poked him in the ribs.

He distracted himself by petting his dog's jaw, speaking directly to her. "I guess mine fell flat." Dagny and Ginger liked to tease Silas, and there was loving banter between all of them. But his laughter ebbing had left something sad behind in Silas' expression.

Ginger leaned into me. "It's plenty warm inside with so much body heat. Make sure you bring out the titties and ass, my friend." I'd never met anyone in HR so open about dating and sex. Many lines seemed blurred in Tidings.

"You going out with her?" Silas asked as Ginger scurried off to tackle the next item on her long to-do list.

I shrugged. "I didn't realize I was working in some sort of hostel for horny nerds." *Is he scowling?* "What's that look for?" I couldn't get a read on this guy; sometimes he was passively neutral, other times his face expressed sadness or frustration. "Is 'horny nerd' an insult?"

"Actually, I—" Before he could get a word out, he reached for his ringing phone in his back pocket. He held the phone to his ear and huffed out *yes* and *yeah* and *okay* and *be right there*. He looked at me with a flash of regret. Dagny rolled her eyes at him.

"Snøfnugg, up," he commanded. "Go to Dags."

The fluffiest, cutest dog in the world bounced over to Dagny, who slipped her a piece of croissant from her plate. "Yeah, yeah I got her," she said to Silas. She waved off my look of confusion. "Happens all the time."

"I have to go to work," he explained, buttoning up his jacket and pulling out a pair of wool gloves from his pocket.

I nodded in understanding, like I too was a very important person on call. "Thank you for your help today."

"See you later," he muttered. Dagny tossed him a sly smile and a wink. He shook his head toward her, engaging in silent conversation.

I MADE IT BACK HOME AS THE SUN SET AND THE FIRST TWINKLES OF the night sky appeared. My new wool layers and parka kept me from going into hypothermia, and for the first time since arriving in Tidings, I could feel all my toes and fingers.

Parked like a semi-truck, four Huskies waited alongside the curb in front of the lodge with a small red sled behind them. A note strapped to the collar of the dog in the front, who nuzzled his nose in my hand as I gently approached him, said:

Deliver to Alice Woods at Evermore Winter Lodge

When Bror had said he would send the dogs with my new clothes, he literally meant that. No one could pay me enough money to wipe the smile off my face.

"Thank you, pups." I stacked the packages under my arms and watched as the alpha dog rose, the others behind her following quickly. They shook a layer of fresh snow off their fur and trotted down the street, empty sled pulled behind them.

I retrieved the key from my jacket pocket and went inside my toasty room where the fireplace was already warmed up. I unpeeled the layers and hung my outerwear on the nearby iron coat rack.

I reached for an orange from the fruit basket, shedding my clothes along the way to a steaming, hot bath. Fully submerged, I peeled the orange in the tub, tossing the peel onto the floor—until a noise outside the bathroom froze me in place.

"Alice?" called a man.

I fumbled out of the tub, spilling water across the tile floor. My feet slipped on the orange peel, and I collided with the wall. In a rush to grab a robe off the hook, I stubbed my toe against the door.

"Just a minute!" I yelled, grabbing my foot and cussing in my head.

"Sorry," he said. "It's Silas. You left your purse at the café. I brought it for you." I heard cursing and loud footsteps.

I brushed out my wet ratty hair and twisted it tightly along the nape of my neck. "You left *before* me," I replied, as if the fucking logistics were more important when I was naked and wet on the other side of the door. The front door slammed, and I was met with momentary silence.

"Hello?" Then a knock. "What the hell is going on?"

I adjusted the belt on my robe and stomped out of the bathroom. I opened my front door to find Silas with his fist lifted about to knock again. "Shit. Sorry," he mumbled and turned around, flustered as all hell.

"*Why* did you break into my suite?"

His face was red, wrinkles creasing in the pinch of his brows. "I am so sorry, Alice. Ginger told me you were expecting me, and you'd left the door unlocked. I came this direction on my way home from the hospital, so it was a quick stop," his voice was muffled. He was mortified and nervous. I could blow out a single hot breath and knock him over.

I crossed my arms and glared. "Do you make a habit of entering people's houses without an invitation?"

"*No*, god," he replied, indignant. "Your door was open, I just walked in."

"It was open?" I shrieked, quickly examining the door handle for a malfunction. "You're lucky I didn't chuck a glass vase at your big head."

"I'm sorry, I won't do that again. And I'll have a strongly worded conversation with Ginger."

"Good luck," I said to his back as he walked down the hallway. I bit my lip, hesitated, then launched without thinking. "You were at work?"

He paused, looking over his shoulder. Our eye contact heated me, beads of water dripping down my back like cascading lava. "Uh, yeah, sometimes it gets too busy for one guy. I help when I can."

"Does anybody help *you*?"

His gaze lifted from the ground, painstakingly slowly. I held my breath until his eyes met mine again. "No, I'm alright."

"You're on your way home then?"

He nodded.

"A glass of wine to clear the air?"

I didn't wait for his reply and walked into the kitchen, intentionally leaving the door open this time. I perched onto my toes and grabbed two wine glasses from a top cabinet, and a bottle from the curated selection, hoping a deep Cabernet would lighten the tension.

Silas leaned against the open door and tucked his hands in his front pockets. I was still learning him, but I'd seen him do this mannerism a few times before, including when he had sheepishly apologized to the patrons in the café for his dog's rambunctious behavior. His gaze looked everywhere but at me, and I knew something was holding him back from saying yes. The least I could do was bail him out.

"Oh shoot, I promised Ginger I'd go to Pilates in the morning. A glass of wine this late probably isn't a smart choice." I only noticed the droop in his shoulders because I was looking for a response from his closely guarded body language. Not even an eye roll from the man.

"Some other time then," he murmured, a faint tremor in his exhale. Though I knew he didn't mean it, it was the courteous remark to say when someone canceled plans you didn't want anyway. He turned on his heels, leaving the room before I could piece together the words that danced on the edge of my mind.

CHAPTER 9

ALICE

I didn't give a second thought to Ginger's suggestion for my outfit tonight; the whole tits-and-ass thing was overdone in 2006. I wasn't sure if she was trying to use me as bait or some flex on her dominance. I threw on a gray sweater I pulled from under the pile of clothes tossed without regard on the floor next to my bed. I hadn't unpacked yet. Empty hangers and bare drawers sat as a reminder that this was temporary.

I unhooked my tight bun, tossing pins, and a hair tie on the countertop. I curled gentle waves around the ends. Touched up the charcoal liner on my eyelids and added a pop of pink lipstick. I didn't need the extra layers of a coat, scarf, or gloves. I only had a brief walk down the hall, past the front desk where I gave Elvin a smile and wave, then through the side door into the restaurant.

In a corner booth, Dagny and Ginger introduced me to their eclectic group of friends: a bartender and DJ named Anton, a purple-haired hair stylist with a tattoo on her neck named Annie, and Bror, the boutique owner.

And of course, Silas was there. I waved politely, stealing a moment to take him in. He looked tired, but I doubted there ever was a time he didn't. Flashes of last night cradled my thoughts. How a simple, accidental tug of the belt on my robe could have had me standing naked and wanting in front of him. He wore a tight, green crewneck sweater that wasn't modest about his covered shoulder muscles. Green, I was beginning to understand, was his favorite color. And it became my favorite on him too, enhancing the brightness of his eyes, and pulling flecks of gray tucked in his brown hair to shimmer under the lights.

"Hi," I said.

He flexed his hand around the beer mug.

"Ignore the sourpuss," Ginger said, flicking a hand in Silas' direction. "He's mad because I forced him to come out here instead of staying at home playing with his toys." She leaned across the table, placing a drink I didn't order in front of me.

He put his beer glass to his mouth and muttered, "See if I'll save your finger from frostbite."

"Sure, you would," she said, patting him on the head.

Silas pushed back from his seat and stood. "I'm leaving."

"Shut up and sit down."

My facial expressions were as transparent as cellophane, so I covered my face with my drink, taking sips of the gross concoction Ginger ordered for me.

"What is this?" I grimaced.

"Peppermint mojito," Silas and Ginger said simultaneously, then went back to their bickering. I pushed the drink aside.

I quietly observed as the group tossed familiar barbs

and inside jokes at each other, looking more like a sitcom family around a dinner table than merely friends. Silas remained pensive. A faraway look in his eyes I recognized in myself before.

Should I reach out a hand and rescue him from here?

Dagny jabbed my shin under the table with her pointed heel.

I reached for my leg. "*What* the—"

"—that guy over there is staring you down." She pointed to a man in an orange beanie sitting at the bar. I glanced up and connected with his smirk.

"Why?"

"Because you have something gross stuck in your teeth," Dagny jeered.

I flinched and covered my mouth.

"I'm kidding. He's obviously attracted to you."

"Do you know him?"

"Brett? Yeah. He's a regular researcher. Comes up here a couple times a year."

Anton finished his drink and pushed it to the edge of the table. "Ew. He eye-fucks anyone with a pulse—no offense, girl," he said, a decimal too loud. The family at the table next to us looked horrified.

Ginger grumbled. "Not just anyone. Brett has standards."

The table broke out in laughter, except for Silas, who looked even worse for wear than when I'd arrived. He tensed, angling his body away from the group. I was still the new girl here—despite being embraced by this quirky group—and I hesitated on the proper way to insert myself into their dynamic.

I kept myself on edge, waiting for someone to confront me about the viral video. It was only a matter of time before someone got curious and Googled me. But for now, I had a quiet advantage. The lousy internet worked in my favor. Texts took forever to send, pictures got stuck in limbo, and search engines might as well run on wishes and prayers.

"Maybe she doesn't want you to set her up," Ginger said. "What do you think, Silas? Should our new girl go talk to our old pal?"

If eyeballs were weapons, Ginger would have disintegrated into a ball of dust from the way Silas looked at her. I cleared my throat and pushed my chair away from the table.

"I should leave," I said.

"Oh no, you don't," Dagny said. She gave my shoulders a push, nudging me out of my seat. "You just got here. Go talk to him."

"This whole interaction is making me sweaty," Anton said.

The group prodded me forward, save for Silas, who sat with a wrinkle pinched between his brows. I held my drink in one hand as I maneuvered around the table, squeezing behind Silas', my ass brushed against the back of his chair, and my stomach twisted. "Sorry," I murmured.

At the bar, I ordered a new drink without peppermint syrup and drummed my fingers on the counter. I glanced at my group of friends, catching Ginger clenching her teeth at Silas. I whipped my hair back, tendrils grazing over the rim of my drink.

I raised my eyebrow at the handsome researcher, giving him an expression that I hoped was more of a flirtatious smirk and less symptomatic of a stroke. I was nervous and felt like an awkward baby deer wobbling on unsteady legs.

He flagged the bartender down, ordering an Old Fashioned with top-shelf whiskey. "I don't drink often, but when I do, it has to be the good stuff," he explained when my eyes widened at the expensive bottle.

"Once I felt really fancy with Trader Joe's brand of champagne."

He indulged me with a pity chuckle. My cheeks heated at his flat response.

"I'm Brett." He reached his hand across the sticky bar top. "I'm with the Anchorage crew for a few weeks."

"Alice," I replied. Our hands clasped, and I wanted to pull back and wipe off the sticky sheen he transferred to my palm. "I'm from Arizona, and not a researcher."

He looked down at our grasp, his thumb toying with the back of my hand. "What's back in Arizona for ya?"

The greatest humiliation you'd ever heard.

"Not much. You know how it goes—Tidings found me and now I work at the Evermore Lodge."

He eyed me over the rim of his drink. "You're the new Carly."

I quirked a brow, confused. "If Carly worked for Elvin managing guests, then yes."

Brett's eyes never left my cleavage as I watched a red flag sprout out of his head like a damn weed. Brett was attractive in a conventional way. Hazy blue eyes, dirty-blond hair and broad shoulders. But something wasn't quite right. The alcohol pickled my brain, and my judgment felt wonky.

He licked his lower lip, which gave me the sudden need to throw my drink in his face. "I think we're on the same page here," he said, reaching around to squeeze my ass.

Yeah, I'd like to throw my drink in his face. Violently.

I turned from him, squeezing my knees tight, which was not an effective form of communicating my aversion as his thumb stroked my hip. My jaw tensed and I put a hand up between us.

He leaned forward, tugging on the jean material encasing his thighs. "You are fucking hot. I'd like to get to know you better somewhere quieter."

"I'm not really looking for a hookup." I glanced back at the table; everyone but Silas had lost interest in me.

I stood, scooting my barstool under the counter and backed up. Brett's icy blue eyes looked over my head as someone stepped into our space, and he nodded in their direction. "'Sup, man."

I turned over my shoulder, looking Silas in the eyes as he gave me a well-worn look—a direct gaze, steady and engaging. It made me feel like everything might be okay, after all.

"You good?" Silas looked at me with authoritative concern, like he'd be willing to grab this asshole by the collar and chuck him out the door.

I hummed a response, slurping the last of my drink through the straw. I could take care of Brett myself. I was about to leave before Silas and his male version of resting bitch face waltzed in.

Brett smiled wide, tilting his mouth to the side. "Delilah and I were discussing our thoughts on settling down, starting a family." He waved down the bartender, but I kept my focus on Silas, whose eyes raked over me as if he were scanning for signs of trauma. I rolled my eyes at Brett; he was so unserious. Good riddance.

"That's not her name," Silas said. He leaned in closer; his warm breath grazed my neck. "Are you okay?"

I responded with a supercilious nudge of my chin, as if to say, "Back off." His eyes ping-ponged between Brett and me, settling on a glare at Brett like a stare down in the Wild

West. He nodded at me and walked back to the table, speaking to Dagny, who responded with her own nod. Brett was yapping about something, and I watched Silas grab his jacket off the back of the chair before leaving out the front door. Ginger looked pissed, pointing her finger at Silas as he snubbed her.

I wasn't sure what to make out of what happened between Silas and Brett. It was hot, if not mildly patronizing, when Silas had jumped in when another man grabbed my ass without my consent.

"What's that guy's deal? Kind of a dick."

Turning back to my present company, I sneered at Brett. Perhaps Silas was incensed, but his attitude wasn't without merit. My throat bubbled with rising guilt. He was looking after me when he saw me flinch at the unwanted touch. I hadn't known him long, but I knew enough; Silas was a helper. He found pockets of need where he could be of service and inserted himself.

I pushed my drink away and looked at Brett, mulling over how to deliver some lame excuse about needing to leave immediately and why he definitely wasn't coming with me. But I owed this man nothing—and he didn't get a word from me. I walked with purpose, following the route Silas had carved through the tables and chairs. Brett scoffed, but I didn't turn back. I'd never talk to him again. I didn't give an explanation to my friends at the table either. I ran out the front door and whipped my neck around, searching for the man who always seemed to suddenly appear whenever a social contract was tested.

I opened the door to the harsh sting of air I was still acclimating to. I wrapped my arms around myself in a tight hug, suddenly all too aware that I didn't have a fucking coat. I'd left it in my suite thinking I wouldn't leave the building tonight.

Perhaps my greatest flaw was impulsivity. My rash decisions didn't often make sense in retrospect, but I operated on vibes, what felt right in that moment.

I tip-toed across the icy sidewalk and rounded the corner. My lungs pierced on the inhale. Thick, heavy plumes of breath surrounded my face with each exhale. Against my better judgment, common sense, and fully developed frontal lobe— I continued chasing after Silas in the cold, dark night, acting on a swirling feeling in my gut that I needed to apologize for dismissing him when he was being a perfect gentleman.

One thing I knew with absolute certainty, an invisible force, potent and unyielding, coiled around my body and pulled me toward him. Since arriving in Tidings, I got the sense that there was something different about this place. Whether it left me powerful or powerless, was still to be determined. It was obnoxious—I was trying to stay low-key, not add more drama to my life.

I spotted a figure one block down and took a risk to follow him. It had to be Silas. Breathless and sputtering to myself in the frigid fucking cold, I was extra cautious of my steps, relying aggressively on my stealthy tip-toeing skills, to avoid falling on my ass and breaking a bone. I imagined my cracked tailbone, fused to the frozen ground, dead before someone found me.

The moving shadow crossed the sidewalk, illuminated by the glowing lights strung across the street. I made it to the crosswalk sign right as it displayed a ten-second count-down. I gunned for it, tiptoeing for purchase across the icy street.

Hang on. Hang on.

I couldn't lose him, or my impetus.

A car turning left honked its horn. "I'm so sorry, so sorry," I shouted back, not losing any momentum in my hobble. I crossed the street in one piece and made it back to the sidewalk, panting and straining my neck for which direction to go.

I turned left and galloped a few steps before I smacked right into a body. His abrupt stop accidentally clotheslined me, an arm to the throat, and I wobbled my arms like a cartoon rabbit who slipped on a banana peel. As I fell, my hands failed to break my fall as they scraped against the ice. The skin on my palms cracked, going from a shade of red to outright crimson blood.

Silas leaned down, his eyes an inch from mine as he scanned my face. He offered a hand and gently lifted me, one arm supporting my lower back and the other under the crook of my elbow. "You're lucky you didn't hit your head." He looked so handsome standing under the light, a black beanie covering his head and stubble warming his rosy cheeks. "Are you injured?"

"Just my pride. And maybe my ass." I tried to catch my breath, but my lungs were on fire. "Do you think I broke my tailbone?" A wheezing sound came out of my mouth and Silas stepped closer, placing a hand on my back, right where my lungs rose and fell in rapid measure.

"Where's your new coat? And you should never run in this temperature; it can cause bronchoconstriction, and—" he put his hands on my shoulders and braced me, "as you can tell, wheezing."

"*Bronco* what?" I gasped, rubbing my chest. The burn intensified.

His fingers splayed where my ribcage met my waist. The comfort and heat from his hand distracted me from my health crisis. He softly whispered instructions to take measured, controlled breaths, slowing down my heart rate. But when he smiled at me and told me I was going to be okay, every nerve in my body lit up like the one-hundred-foot tree decorated at the end of the block.

"Come with me inside; you need to warm up." Silas extended his arm for me to link onto, but I held back the pain radiating from my tailbone. "Your hands are bleeding." He lifted them closer to his face to inspect.

"I don't need stitches, relax."

"No, you don't." He gently held my ice-cold hands between his, before he pulled back and took his gloves off. "Here, wear mine."

"But I'm bleeding."

"I have a thousand pairs. Keep them."

My hands warmed from his wool gloves, and I muttered a thank-you. We walked gingerly to the nearest building, a bistro and bar with an overpowering scent of espresso and peppermint. We sat at a small wooden table for two, and he ordered a kettle of hot tea to share.

"Do you feel better?"

I cleared my throat, preparing to sound convincing. My lungs burned, my lower back ached, and the cuts on my palms and knuckles irritated me. "Totally."

"Do you have asthma? This is the second time you've had a wheezing attack."

"No. It seems to only happen in front of you."

"You were breathless."

"I was not! Maybe *breathy*. Breath-ish."

The warm water soothed my itchy throat, and I took that moment to ponder why I chased him like an absolute loon in the cold, dangerous night. "I—uh—came to say thanks for checking on me at the bar."

"I'm sorry for inserting myself. I overstepped." He cleared his throat on a sip of tea. His cheek twitched and I couldn't take my eyes from that spot. "But I sensed you were uncomfortable."

"Well, he was outrageously assuming... and slimy." The muscle near his jaw twitched again. The waitress approached to order our food, and remembering I didn't have my wallet, I passed.

"Let's get the board of their famous petite fruit tartlets to share," he said. "My treat." His jaw had a mind of its own; it flirted with me in an obscene way. It twitched and hallowed, sparking a new wave of heat inside me. "I don't mean to be presumptuous," he added.

You can presume all the things with me, I thought but didn't verbalize. "But did you chase after me because Ginger told you to play nice with me?"

Yes. No. I think you're gorgeous. "What?"

The server delivered our beautiful display of desserts. "May I offer you both a complimentary peppermint hot chocolate? Our house specialty."

I held back a gag and feigned a smile. "No, thank you. This is enough sugar for me."

"Same here. Thank you, Natalie," Silas said. He couldn't hide his smile and chuckled as he split a lemon tart down the middle with a miniature knife, then handed me half. "Overdone it on the peppermint already?"

"I *hate* it—"

"Shh," he cut me off. "Don't let anyone hear you say that."

I whispered, "I never knew people could be so protective over fucking peppermint." I took a sip of water, angrier than I should have been. Peppermint had been forced upon me against my will, and it would be one thing I'd never miss about this place.

"You're settling right in. Before you know it, you'll be a regular."

I coughed lightly to clear my composure. "But I haven't met Lucia yet." I wasn't clear who she was or what her relationship was to him.

Silas chuckled. "I hope you don't meet her, though at your rate you're probably not far off unfortunately." He laughed a low rumble. It made me want to lay my head against his chest.

"Does she live in Tidings, or do you visit her somewhere else often?"

"Good God," he said, scrubbing at his stubble with his palms. "Who told you about Lucia?"

I rolled my lips, contemplating before I inserted myself further into somewhere I didn't belong. As if a switch flipped on, we both said: "Dagny." I said it as a confession; he said it confidently, as though her schemes had affronted him before.

"Lucia, is *Saint Lucia*." He removed his black beanie and combed his fingers through his hair. Distractingly tousled and sexy. "Saint Lucia Medical Center. Folks call it Lucia for short, and Dagny jokes that I'm dating the hospital since I spend most of my time there. Dagny tagged along with me to Tidings when I got the job. I'm not sure why I thought it would be a good idea to have my little sister in such a small town where the only way out is a train or a helicopter."

"I never thought to ask the name of the hospital." Dagny said she was studying for the medical school entrance exam—a family thing she explained. It made sense now. "How did I not know Dagny was your sister?"

Silas leaned in, lowering his voice again, which set my

nerves on edge. Out of frustration, I wanted to scratch my nails down his arms each time I felt his voice boom in my chest.

"Does that mean you're not asking about me?"

I rubbed at the heat blooming across my neck and teased. "Why would I when you already seem to appear everywhere I am?"

"Or are you the one appearing wherever *I* am?"

"You were in my house while I was in the bathtub, remember? I've yet to be in *your* hospital."

He clasped his hands around the mug, and a proud smile spread across his face. "That's because I saved you from hypothermia. But go ahead. What would you like to know, Alice?"

I had a thousand questions; I didn't even know where to start. "Is Allan the coroner? When he hurled himself across the lobby at me on my first day, he acted like he hadn't talked to a breathing female his whole life."

Silas sputtered his drink on a sip, laughing. "Allan is our surgeon. He's a little choppy around the edges, but he's loyal and good at his job."

"Is that a surgeon joke?"

Silas eyed me with amusement. "The lanky guy is Erik —he takes care of the admitted patients. Henry looks like a blond linebacker and is double-board certified in derma-tology and radiology. He's incredibly annoying."

"Are there any women at that hospital?"

"Of course, those are just the guys you saw that night. Can't blame them for not wanting to spend their night off with us assholes," he said, his smile fading slightly.

He offered me the last bite of a mint chocolate tart. My eyes rolled back at the decadent flavor. Silas flagged down the bartender and ordered the house special for both of us. "A rite of passage for all first timers in Tidings," he said.

I watched the bartender rim two shot glasses with frosting, dip them in crushed candy cane, and pour in RumChata with a splash of house-made eggnog.

Our knees brushed underneath the table, and when Silas leaned in to toast our shot glasses, his breath carried across the space between us, landing on the delicate spot on my neck.

I tossed the drink back and audibly groaned, soaking up the taste. "Finally, something with peppermint that's decent." I licked the remnants of the frosting off my lips and his gaze fixed on my mouth.

"Why did you come here in the first place?" I asked.

"An opportunity I couldn't pass up."

"Well, I yelled at Siri to find me a job far, far away. I had a lot of tequila that night. Next thing I know, Ginger was calling me."

"Nobody comes to Tidings by accident." A flicker of light caught his eye. Silas was cerebral, his decisions rooted in fact. This science-backed professional couldn't entertain silly ideas about destiny, yet something still glimmered when he talked about it.

Blame it on my near-death experience tonight, but I was feeling renewed and confident. I had Silas right in front of me and I had so many questions about Tidings. About him. "Why did you name your dog Snøfnugg?"

"It means 'snowflake' in Norwegian. She's big and goofy, maybe a little flaky. But she's the best dog in the world." He kicked up a smile, in the same way he talked about Dagny. Like only he was allowed to say some disparaging things about his sister and dog. Everyone else better watch their mouths. "Do you plan on going back to Arizona?"

I laughed. *Yeah, sure, hot doctor, let me tell you all about being the laughingstock of The Grand Canyon State.* "I'm embracing my nomad era. Kind of in between jobs right now and taking a sabbatical here in Tidings. Maybe teach English abroad next. I studied anthropology in college. I thought I could become a museum curator, but that was dumb and naive."

"Why naive?" he asked politely.

"My sister calls it a degree in puppetry. Mostly worthless." I waved it off. "She's probably right. It's not like it set me up for success like becoming a lawyer or doctor or something. I've got a lot of interests, but nothing I was ever sure about career-wise. You're lucky that you figured it out so young."

He scrubbed an eyebrow with two fingers. "No, I wouldn't say that." He pulled his phone out of his pocket and scrolled. I anticipated him having to leave quickly, like he had every time we were in the same room together. Understandingly, with hospital emergencies he didn't have time to spare. "I have next Saturday free. I could show you the cheesy touristy things."

I looked up from my drink, biting on the straw. "Are you sure? I only have Mondays and Tuesdays off."

"Working nights is a real asshole move," he said, solemnly. He brushed aside his emotion and suggested I ask Ginger or his sister to take me out on my off days, show me around town. I was still reeling from what he said, almost like a self-deprecating joke, but his eyes had real emotion in them. I felt lucky to be the one on the receiving end of it.

Silas stood, offering me his jacket. I refused but he gave

me an impatient look. "I could wait all day. But Snøfnugg's at that snow park and her time is almost up. You don't want to make her wait for her daddy, do you?"

My dizzy brain swirled in RumChata couldn't ignore the dirty euphemisms that my brain latched on to. He gripped my elbow when we made it to the sidewalk, completely aware I was buzzed and now trying to navigate the icy, hard sidewalks was a death wish.

"I should have had you wait while I got my car to come get you," he said through clenched teeth, muttering quietly. Berating himself.

"I'm okay."

"Really? Because you look like you're about to break a leg any second in those damn shoes."

"Well, good thing I know a fantastic surgeon."

"He's mediocre," Silas corrected.

"Are you jealous?" I teased.

His nose scrunched up. "Of Allan? Ha."

"He's nice," I countered. "A little nerdy, but the right girl could work that out of him."

Silas' arm dropped, wrapping his hand around my waist as I wobbled over a chunk of ice in front of the restaurant. "I've got you." His words tickled the delicate skin behind my earlobe.

He opened the door and released his grip from around my waist, placing his hand on the small of my back to guide me forward. Ginger gave me *that* look with her eyebrows, and Anton lifted his chin in a slight nod of approval.

"Well, I'm headed home," I said to the group, evaporating on the inside from the heat from Silas' hand. I waved to the table and turned toward the interior door connecting the restaurant and lodge. I felt a rush of air behind, knowing Silas was quick to follow.

"Well, at least you don't have to call for a sober driver," he said. We paused at the front desk, and before I could wish him a good night, he leaned in, placing one hand against the counter, caging me in. "Drink some water before bed."

"I'm not drunk. That drink had a lot of sugar in it."

Silas' eyes danced around my face. I wanted the warmth of his mouth more than a good night's sleep. I'd be hungover all day tomorrow if it meant tasting him. He shifted away, dousing my flame in a bucket of water. "Get some good rest."

"Good night," I replied and walked to my front door. He turned back and grabbed my hand before locking his fingers around my wrists. My breath hitched, caught off guard by his spontaneous touch. The rugged lines by his eyes drew me in.

He sure was pretty to look at but getting involved with *anyone,* even a handsome, kind man like Silas—especially Silas—in Tidings was a disaster waiting to happen. He was settled here with work. He had his sister and friends who were like family. He would never leave, and I'd need a lobotomy before I lived here for more than three months. Not a chance in hell. And I seriously meant hell would literally have to be frozen over before I became a resident of Tidings. My bones hadn't felt warm since the day I left Arizona.

Without a word, he hesitated then released my hand and nodded as he walked away.

In the short time I'd been here, I already let the curtain down, exposing vulnerabilities far too easily. I didn't get sloppy drunk or let my insecurities fly around my ex-boyfriend Mark. But for someone who took a plane and train to get as far away from my shame as possible, I continued to drop the ball around Silas. I had to shut it down before I created another wave of disappointment in my wake.

"Thank you." I hesitated, not sure what exactly I was thanking him for. But I wanted to steal another moment to look at him before I closed a door that couldn't open again. For a millisecond, I pretended I knew what it felt like to be his. "For tonight. For your friendship."

He dipped his head and offered me a soft smile, then he walked out into the frigid cold night.

CHAPTER 10
SILAS

"*Thanks for your friendship,*" I repeated Alice's words in a sing-songy, sarcastic tone as I forcefully tied my laces. I grabbed my foot, holding it close to my hip to stretch my calf, then switched to do the other side before going into dynamic lunges. Since Alice had friend zoned me, I'd gone insane; that was the clinical term of rehashing the same line repeatedly, expecting a different conclusion, but left with the same defeating feeling.

A friend was not this disruptive in my life. It wasn't just the blood pulsing chaotically through my veins, or the tightness in my breath. If we were just friends, I'd have to rethink every other friendship I had, because this—what I felt for her—was unlike anything else.

I was helpless, unable to stop replaying that scene— flashes of her smile, then her downtrodden face, cycling in my mind. And just when I wanted to tuck a loose strand of hair behind her ear, she thanked me for my damn *friendship*.

I needed to run her out of my head before I did something I'd regret, like call Elvin to tell him to give her the night off so I could show her *exactly* how I felt about being *only* friends. When her lips curled into a satisfied little smile as she set the empty glass down, finally appreciating something peppermint flavored—I was *appreciating* her. My gaze couldn't help but follow every movement—the flick of her wrist, the way she wiped a tiny bit of frosting off her mouth with her finger, then licked it off with a casual grace that made my stomach tighten.

Stopping warmup stretches earlier than normal, I was in a rush to run my feet like a rocket, blasting on the tread. Sore quads were a problem for future me. My mind was wound too tightly to wait.

"That's it, Hill, run it out, bro," Henry said, running at max incline and a speed a former Division 1 athlete could handle easily.

"You're still fucking here," I stated. I turned the speed up and immediately regretted it. I couldn't back out now, or he'd never shut up.

"Got to make sure you don't quit," he said casually, not even breaking a sweat.

"Shut up and let me run."

"You are one grumpy asshole, man. I thought you fucked that Arizona chick."

I glowered at him as he chomped on his gum, tossing a nonchalant smile at me. "I will kill you."

Henry was the absolute worst. We didn't need a fucking dermatologist anyways. Between the family doc and surgeon, we were perfectly capable of diagnosing a suspicious mole. Then outsource radiology readings to a virtual doctor in Washington, and we could dump Henry's body at the base of the mountain for the moose to eat.

All my life, I'd surrounded myself with Type-A people,

hypercompetitive people. Alice was a flighty, disorganized, messy thing. But refreshingly flexible and free-spirited.

Before we had our alone time, I was cranky and bent out of shape. I desperately wanted to be home, but I came out at Ginger's insistence. I knew Alice was the hottest new thing in Tidings, so fucking sue me for wanting to make her mine. I saw her eyes glaze over when she watched friends laugh together, or spotted grabby, happy couples. I felt her sadness, too, and forced myself from climbing over tables and chairs to get to her and hold her.

"You moron," I said out loud to myself. I didn't need Henry next to me; I was good at berating myself. Shit, I was sappy as hell over this desert wildflower who stumbled in here, looking like she belonged in Tidings as much as Snøf did in Palm Springs.

I wanted Ginger to give me more insight into Alice. She was a fascinating new discovery, and I was compelled to gather research on her. Did she leave Arizona because of a broken relationship? Was she seeing anyone? Of course, Ginger wouldn't give me shit other than Alice was here on a temporary contract. She said, "If you want to get to know her, go ask *her*, you wimp."

I picked up speed on the treadmill, easily done when I pictured Brett, the researcher, touching Alice. I wanted to pound in his nose, blur out that smug look he carried. We were friends in undergrad until he turned everything into a competition: lab work, professor's approval, girls.

Mostly, I hated that he never let me forget the Carly shit. He gave me shit and played up his fantasy that he was the alpha male when he was nothing more than a bombastic prick. And when he touched Alice, I lost any remaining sense of control.

I waited for Alice to arrive while listening to Ginger and

Dagny play up how excited they were to set her up with Brett. I knew both those women well, and even knowing they were setting Alice up with Brett to aggravate me didn't stop my blood from boiling over.

My intrigue—putting it lightly—with Alice had arrived at the worst time, which only made matters more complicated. I had career opportunities to consider and needed to decide soon.

Sweat poured down my head. I took my shirt off and tossed it on the gym floor. I was lost in the rhythmic hum of the machine and the pounding of my feet, but not enough to break the hold of my thoughts about Alice. I wondered why she ended up in Tidings. Not her bullshit "sabbatical" story, but her real *why*.

It was my fourth year in Tidings, and I still remembered my first day as if it was yesterday. Back then, I wasn't nonplussed like Alice who was adorably wide-eyed and terrified. It was a magical experience for all first timers, except for this beautiful girl from Arizona who looked as out of place as snow in Death Valley. If she could be convinced to stay through the winter, it'd be a cinch for her to fall in love with the place during sommar. But what did it matter if I wasn't here anyway? I was leaving. We would go our separate ways.

I upped the speed dial to a grueling pace, no longer concerned with Henry's speed, though I saw him in the corner of my eye, a pace behind me. I ran my fingers through my sticky hair, giving the wet strands a shake. My breath was choppy and even with all my focus on the steady beat of my exertion, I couldn't get the image from last night of her shivering and flustered out of my mind.

"That's it, Hill." Henry's voice carried from my periphery. "Run it out. Get that bad energy out of here." He egged me on. I was running for my own lucidity.

I'd crafted my path in life in a completely technical way. Strait-laced with clear direction. Relocating to Tidings was the most spontaneous decision I'd ever made. And the riskiest if the statistics for moose-versus-people injuries were accurate. The regular town moose, ironically named "Marshmallow" by the hospital staff, had snuck into the emergency room enough times that there was a tranquilizer dart with his name on it secured next to a fire hydrant by the entrance.

For years, Ginger had incessantly nudged me to find some wild girl to stir up my "humdrum, vanilla life," as she referred to it. She didn't know what went on in my bedroom and I wasn't going to correct her on her assumptions; some of the thrill was being unassuming. Alice fit the bill—she was hyperkinetic and reckless enough to satisfy Ginger's annoying insistence on shaking things up for me.

Alice's eyes held pain, maybe a broken heart that left her no choice but to run as far away from Arizona as she could to escape the pain. Those stories were a dime a dozen in Tidings. City girl flees to a small town to heal from a bad breakup or existential crisis. At least they pretended to be happy to be thrown into the chaos, but Alice wasn't attempting to fool anyone. I envied her freedom, to be honest.

I increased the speed to max, chasing wild, tangled thoughts, like maybe if I stayed close enough to her, I'd finally get the courage to speak the words I'd kept quiet for far too long.

At least now she had appropriate clothes and wasn't wearing those flimsy excuses for shoes. I wanted to see more of her, but not as a patient with a black toe.

I slowed my pace on the treadmill, taking large breaths to bring my heart rate down. Once I got to a comfortable walking pace, I pulled my phone out and shot Ginger a text asking for Alice's number. She replied with the phone number and an emoji sticking out a tongue, asking why I wanted it.

Just the number would have been fine, Ginger.

She hurried her way into my personal business like a water bug scurrying across the floor, annoying me like the pesky older sister I never wanted.

> Ginger: Want some advice?

She responded before I did.

> Ginger: Alice is blunt and likes it reciprocated.

> Silas: I've got it.

> Ginger: Don't half-ass it. Give it to her.

I threw my head back. *That's the whole point, Ging.*

I'd be a gentleman, of course. But Alice had me feeling like a grizzly bear waking up from hibernation. Fucking starving.

> Silas: Will do.

Four long years later, and the best part about my life was a strange new girl who made me hold my breath.

A sweaty towel hit my face and Henry laughed in my direction. "Your favorite radiologist is on call tonight. See you later, jerk. Hope you feel better now."

❄

WORKING NIGHTS AT A HOSPITAL WAS ALWAYS A NIGHTMARE. AND when it was a full moon? Absolute chaos. I didn't have one sip of water all night, but I had three drinks with ingredients of caffeine, sugar, and arrhythmia. My energy level rode the adrenaline wave, and now I'd peaked. I felt the impending crash.

I treated a nasty flesh wound in a man's arm from a kitchen knife accident, or so the wife said. I left that story to be determined by the police. A woman almost died from alcohol poisoning. A smoker with a COPD exacerbation couldn't find his lungs to breathe on his own. To top it off, I pushed a dislocated shoulder back in its socket for a stupid teenager who'd had a physical altercation over a damn video game.

Nearing the top of the hour before the end of my shift, I took a moment to bask in the glimmer of the early dawn streaming through the windows in the main hallway. The sun peeked above the mountains, casting a pink and purple glow over the snow. As much as Tidings drained me, the view never got old.

"Dr. Hill," a familiar voice said as he approached me.

"Page," I replied.

"Shift is almost done. Nightcap?" Justin Page, the daytime emergency medicine physician, clocked in to relieve me. As our routine went, he offered me a fresh cup of scalding hot coffee. Justin was a veteran physician with ten years under his belt who'd paid his dues with the shitty shift when I arrived in town.

I glanced at my watch, grateful for the six o'clock hour approaching. I loved my profession, but working night shift was a special kind of exhausting. My nocturnal sleep schedule was well settled but it still felt like my body would never fully adjust. Modern-day humans weren't suited to this lifestyle. Every sunrise, I inched closer to full burnout.

But if I wanted to return to a normal life, not one of a vampire, I'd need to make changes. And that required relocation, since the opportunity for day shifts wouldn't open for the foreseeable future.

Nobody knew my plans. But once word got out, admin would do whatever it took to keep me, including a raise I'd be foolish to say no to. I couldn't stop fantasizing about being done here. Being somewhere warmer and calmer. My recent week in sunny California had thawed my bones and given me a serotonin boost so strong I felt briefly manic. For a moment, I was back on the beach listening to the waves crashing on shore as my skin heated.

But this was my reality: a mountain of snow and a colleague to my left.

"Thanks." I inhaled the decaf coffee before I took a scalding sip. As we did every day at that time, we stood shoulder-to-shoulder looking out the window. The still part of the morning was the best part of any shift. It's that break between night and day, a lull of serenity where things were quiet enough to hear your own thoughts for a moment. "Ready for handoff? It was a doozy."

Justin chuckled good-naturedly. "Always is on a full moon."

"No suspicious foreign objects in anuses, though."

"Ah man," he joked. "It's been a while since we've seen weird butt stuff."

I shrugged casually. "What can I say? People must be taking a break from experimentation."

Justin snorted. "I'm trying to get some vacation time

with the wife in a couple weeks. Think you'd want to switch things up and we could have the per diem cover nights?"

"If admin approves."

He nodded in agreement. "Figured it'd be a nice break for you. I know dating life is impossible with the night shift."

"Suddenly concerned about my dating life, Page?" I gave him a side-eye, his brows lifted in curiosity. I took another sip of coffee. "You must have had a recent run-in with a gossipy redhead."

"My *wife* talked to Ginger."

"Dear God." I ran a hand through my hair, the product I styled it with thirteen hours ago long gone. My reflection drew my attention to the cowlick that never stayed down without industrial-strength gel.

"So?" Justin pressed. "The new Carly?"

I scowled. "She is not the 'new Carly.'"

Another fantastic reason to leave Tidings was that wherever I went, people hounded me about her—I mean, *it*.

Carly was a failed science experiment gone awry. A botched attempt to solve Elvin's staffing issues. Last year, Elvin wouldn't budge on hiring help, even though the whole damn town knew he needed it behind the desk. So, Ginger hired "Carly,"—an A.I. assistant who answered phones. It wasn't common knowledge, except to Elvin and Dagny, that Carly was not a human.

One day, I called to ask Elvin if he had any extra rooms for an out-of-town patient's family, and Carly answered the phone. Her voice was light and friendly, catching me off guard on a difficult day at work.

I spent a few days giving the front desk a call to chat with her. When I finally got the courage to ask her if I could stop by to meet her, Dagny—who was listening in on the conversation on speaker phone during a lull in restaurant traffic—yelled at me with a barrage of insults: *You dumb ass! Where did you get your medical degree? Online?* Within an hour, the whole damn town knew I hit on a robot. I threatened Ginger to immediately get rid of Carly, or Tidings would be a doctor short by the next day.

Justin instantly looked gleeful, and I realized my slip up. "Ah. You admit, there is a *she*. A real one, though, right?"

I gave him a subtle middle finger, tucking it in the pocket of my fleece vest. "She's just different. Funny. We had some run-ins before I officially met her in Tidings, and it felt—"

"—Serendipitous?"

"*Interesting*," I corrected, giving him a side-eye.

We walked to the doctors' office, a small former closet behind the nurses' station in the emergency department, as I went over the night's patients and who was still on deck. No one was sick enough to spend their weekend in the emergency department. They could have saved our shared time by scheduling an appointment with their family doctor or had their prescriptions filled before they ran out. But I'm not to judge, only to heal.

At the end of every shift, I was utterly exhausted, teetering on the edge of hallucinations.

Still, I desperately wanted to see Alice. I needed to lay eyes on her.

My skin itched as I meandered through the lodge lobby, not from the well-worn hospital scrubs I'd worn all night because I'd already showered and changed into my regular clothes, but from the same indescribable feeling that had me pushing through the brink of exhaustion to bring a breakfast pastry and coffee to impress a woman.

Only she wasn't there when I stopped by the front desk

of the lodge. I awkwardly left the delivery with Elvin, dodging an explanation as to why I wanted to visit with his beautiful new employee, and instead, pretended it was for my sister when she came on shift at the restaurant next door.

As I stepped out the door into the frozen air, a gentle breeze caressed my neck, carrying with it the warmth of the desert air. I paused, entranced by the lingering fragrance of dry earth and delicate florals, like Alice had walked through here only minutes ago. She wasn't there, but her essence lingered in the air.

I smiled and continued into the cold.

When I returned home, I didn't even make it out of my shoes before I fell face-first onto my couch where I slept until noon. My dog woke me up with wet licks on the bit of skin showing between my socks and pants.

I opened the back door for Snøf, and that burst of familiar yet never tolerable cold punched me in the face. "Go on," I commanded. She rose and wagged her tail before she gleefully swan-dived off the balcony into a pile of snow.

I shut the door and grabbed my phone, knowing my dog would be out there for a while digging and burrowing in the snow.

Silas: Hi Alice, this is Silas. When you're free, I'd like to show you the best part of Tidings.

Alice: Sign me up.

CHAPTER 11
ALICE

"Stupid nice, hot guy has me all distracted," I said over the lip of my steaming coffee mug. I blew on the scalding liquid to cool it down, before taking a life-preserving sip. I found the best seat in the cafe, a velvet chair at a small table tucked in the back.

Overlooking the mountains to the west, today the sun glowed to make the mountain peaks a shade of mulberry pink, almost too mesmerizing to be real. Reminiscent of a snow globe, with a gentle shake, snowfall would bury me under its powder. Tidings was a serene tableau frozen in time. I couldn't see it or touch it, but the air shimmered with a quiet energy of something *different*.

I curled my legs underneath my seat and stared at the blinking cursor on my blank email. The cursor might as well have stuck a tongue out taunting me. When I rubbed the soft part of my wrist, I could feel the heat where Silas' finger pads had burned into my skin days ago. I jumped when a text from him appeared after I'd been thinking about him all morning, as if he had read my thoughts.

But I had work to do. I tucked my phone under a stack

of books on a chair next to the table. I had left Arizona to catch my breath, buy time, and figure out next steps after becoming another statistic in the public humiliation era. But I had also left behind an investment in my shitty ex-boyfriend's finance app.

I changed my password and took full control of my money.

My payday would come; I'd be sure of that.

Opening my account, I took a deep breath, bracing myself for the mess ahead. I scrolled through my portfolio, carefully examining each company Mark invested in. I dug into the financials, analyzed market predictions, and searched for any sign of where things had gone wrong. Was it time to cut my losses and sell everything off? Or should I just bite the bullet and work with a real financial planner—someone who actually knew what they were doing?

My cryptocurrency investment was a wash. If it wasn't real money, how was I ever going to find it? I had no idea where to even begin. I avoided texting Mark, though—asking him felt like I might contract leprosy just through the phone. He was a high-risk contact.

Mark and his circle of arrogant finance bros had screwed me over, but the truth was, I only had myself to blame. I had trusted him. I had believed in his promises, in his confidence, in his ability to "make it all work." And now, I was left cleaning up the mess they'd made, regretting every decision that had brought me here.

At the end of the day, it was my fault.

I was determined to learn from my mistakes. Right my own path.

Which was why flirtations with Silas were a bad decision, unless we could keep it completely emotionally void. I would never adjust my life for a boyfriend again. Sure as hell, I would never find a happily ever after in this snow-covered hellscape, no matter how handsome and nice the man.

But Silas sure was pretty to look at. His offer to show me around made me wonder if the "best part of Tidings" was a euphemism for his dick. I mean, he looked like he knew what he was doing with it.

I want to scrape my fingers through his hair.

He looks like he'd talk me through an orgasm.

I lowered my head and blushed. Looking at my phone on the chair next to me; it lit up with a text from my mom. I wanted to chuck it in the snow. My parents deserved an update and to hear I wouldn't be home for the holidays. There was only so long I could ignore them before my face ended up on a missing person's website.

The sound of metal scraping across the floor pulled my gaze up to Ginger, claiming the chair across from me. She launched immediately into an unsolicited summary about her wild night with a new tourist in town.

"He had the worst voice; it was really gravely, but not at all sexy. It was like he smoked a pack a day for forty years. I told him to keep his mouth shut unless it was licking or sucking on something. Then he told me I sounded like a shrill wombat before he flipped me upside down as he was standing."

I chewed on the straw from my water glass, performing mental gymnastics to keep up with the sordid details that would have her arrested in another state. "I'm surprised you're walking today."

Ginger waved me off. "I do a lot of exercises. I have a strong pelvic floor."

I fumbled my drink down my shirt. Ginger eyed me wiping the back of my hand over my sweater and tossed napkins at me. "You're wearing more coffee than drinking it."

"I'm a bit out of focus."

Ginger rested her chin on her hand. "What has you so distracted?"

"Trying to do some budgeting. My mom called."

"And Silas finally got the balls to ask you out."

I tossed a wet napkin on the table, accepting the stains for what they were. Any more spills and I'd look like a spotted leopard. "Do you have my phone bugged for surveillance?"

"I find things out the old-fashioned way. I get people to talk through any means necessary."

"You did convince me to come to Tidings, so you must have seriously good skills."

Ginger pursed her lips, face stone-cold sober. "It wasn't me. Only the people who need to be in Tidings do."

I turned my hand outward, gesturing for her to go on.

"Certain people can't be here. It messes with fate, and she gets prissy about that." She spoke of fate like a stern grandmother with control over an inheritance; *behave and you'll be rewarded.* "Alice, do what you were called here to do. The rest will fall into place." Her hair looked a red shade darker under the lamplight. I cocked my head at her expression, a smile creeping across her face. "Oh, and you can't avoid talking about Silas forever."

"Yeah?" I asked. "And why is that, Pumpkin Spice?"

"Because he's behind you. And he's coming this way."

My stomach dropped as I turned my head over my shoulder to see Silas approach our table. He was carrying a carrier with four coffees and tossed a familial smile at Ginger, reserving a sly smirk for me. Heat prickled beneath my sweater's collar.

Silas commanded space in the room like air belonged to him, yet in a subtle way that made him approachable.

From the smoldering way I caught him eyeing me, I allowed myself to indulge in thoughts that there was something brewing between us. Perhaps a few weeks of playing around would feel good. A boost of confidence when I needed it most.

Tidings was a once-in-a-lifetime experience. And Silas, he was a once-in-a-lifetime man. A ruin your life kind of guy—not financial ruin or with a sexually transmitted disease—but in a way that was impeccably crafted. He'd elevate my standards for the next guy to be a philanthropic astronaut who looked hot in flannel.

Ginger kicked my boot under the table.

"Right, yes I agree." I missed what he said in my lusting stupor.

Silas and Ginger stared curiously at me; my response must have made no sense. I was flustered and covered in coffee stains, looking like I needed to be shrouded in a smock.

Would that emergency helicopter evacuate me out of here, right now please?

Silas cleared his throat. "I've got to get to work. Just wanted to say a quick hello."

"Double shift?" Ginger asked him.

"Came home and slept for a couple hours. Took Snøf on a walk, now loading up on caffeine for me and the team."

"Is that safe?" I asked, "Working back-to-back?"

"That's what he's trained to do," Ginger said. "Right, Silas?"

Why wasn't Ginger more concerned with his well-being? The dark circles under his eyes were a cry for help. I interjected before Silas could respond. "Should he have to?"

Ginger all but lit me on fire with the expression on her face. I expected to get a tongue lashing to the tune of, *Can you shut your big fat mouth for once?'*

"It's the life I signed up for," he shrugged. "No problem here."

"Other than caffeine-induced arrhythmia?" Silas lifted a brow, likely at my unexpected use of medical terms. To this, I responded, "Late nights anxiously deep diving WebMD's website."

He laughed and the skin around his eyes softened. I wanted him to linger and keep that expression on me. I liked making him smile.

"Coffee delivery is your love language," I said. "Your co-workers appreciate it, I'm sure."

"As much as Alice loves to wear it," Ginger added, pointing to my stained sweater.

I blushed, and Silas offered a sympathetic chuckle. "Well, have a good day, ladies."

Ginger and Silas had a similar dynamic to his and Dagny's. Like siblings, they bickered over who was smarter and stronger, but ultimately teased one another in love. The kind of taunting that only helped them become better.

"I've got some meetings, too. See ya later," Ginger stomped out the door after Silas, reaching for a cup of coffee in his beverage holder. He tried to slap her hand away, but she stuck her tongue out. I watched as they walked away, disappearing around the corner.

Silas seemed to have a secure, happy life here—at least, that's the version he wanted everyone to see. But underneath, I could sense something quieter, something sadder, simmering just below the surface.

❄

I stayed hidden in my suite instead of accepting Dagny's invitation to Fire & Ice that night. I numbed my loneliness in a leather chair by the fire, tapping absentmindedly on the lock screen of my phone. After gathering the nerve to call my mother, I almost hung up after four rings. Then, just as I was about to, her soft voice surprised me with a warm hello.

"Alice, what a lovely surprise."

"Hi, Mom. How are you?"

"I want to hear all about Canada," she said with a burst of her familiar enthusiastic, bubbly voice. "Are you draped in furs?"

As a child, I always complained about being too cold, often curling up next to the floor heater, stretching out my pajama gown over my knees. "Not in Canada. But it is cold. I'm sitting in front of a fire right now looking out my window. Every inch is covered in snow, and more is expected tonight."

"I still can't believe you, of all people, ended up *there*."

That was the first thing we both agreed on in a while. "Do you think it's karma?"

"For what, hon?"

Already feeling cut open, I went for the dagger. "It's not a mystery that Dad thinks I'm a loser."

In college, I didn't care what he thought about my choices. I knew I'd figure it out eventually. But now, in my early thirties, I began to regret adopting petty disagreements and holding silly grudges. "The last email he sent was one line. '*A person without a plan is as reliable as a bicycle without tires.*'"

"'Loser' is not a word I've ever heard your father use about you." *He doesn't know about the cryptocurrency scam yet. Or the NSFW image that made me viral for a week.* "He doesn't want you to waste any of your unique potential."

"Well," I said, holding my voice steady. "I am enjoying it more than you'd think. And it's giving me time to think about my next plans."

I waited for a response.

A hiccup would suffice.

No one from my family knew about what happened in Arizona—I hoped, anyway. My sister would have given me an earful already. So far, most articles were only on trashy, click-bait websites. As far as I was concerned, I was old news, and some sad person was the latest victim in the ever-spinning wheel of public shaming.

"Hello?"

"You're on speaker." My mom's voice carried over the sound of water, like she was filling a pot of water to boil.

"Alice," my father's voice was low and authoritative. "Did you move there for a boy?"

I rolled my eyes. "No, Dad."

"Is Mark with you?" Mom asked.

"We broke up. I'm fine though—it was my call," I lied. "We weren't a good match after all."

"I never liked that punk," Dad said. "He looked like a sleazy car salesman."

"What are the men like there?" Mom asked.

Images of Silas' hand on my elbow flickered through my mind, and the frown on his face when he turned down my offer of wine the other night. I overanalyzed him, trying to find meaning in whatever I imagined "us" to be. I was a grown woman—I could ask him outright. But with my expiration date on my time in Tidings, I wasn't confident either of us would want to get involved.

"Not sure, Mom. I'm focused on work."

"Good idea, kiddo," Dad hollered. An unexpected wave of emotion rolled through me. It felt good to hear my dad compliment me, even if they would soon be angry and disappointed at me for getting fired in a public setting.

Did I have arrested development? Maybe it was all those damn participation trophies that helped me scrape by in life, assuming it would all get figured out soon enough on its own. Was anyone else in their thirties still trying to figure it out, too? Ginger and Silas were clean-cut professionals. I was one job away from becoming a performing troll in the circus.

My phone buzzed with a text, and I pulled it away from my ear.

Silas: I hope you're relaxing by your fire, enjoying the snow falling tonight.

Heat bloomed in my cheeks, a welcome sensation against the frigid air permanently nestled under my skin. I sent him a picture of my view, a roaring fire and outside the window, snow was coming down hard. A glimpse of the skin on my leg appeared in the corner of the picture frame.

Alice: Didn't take you for a voyeur, Hill.

I chewed a thumbnail between my teeth.

Silas: Would you let me in if I was?

My name came through the speaker, and I fumbled the phone. "Mom, Dad, love you. Got a work thing to deal with. Call you later."

"Alice, one second."

"Yes, Mom?" I replied, trying to mask the impatience in

my voice. I wanted to hang up and turn my attention back to Silas, but something in her tone made me hesitate.

"It feels good to hear your voice." Her words hung in the air for a long moment. It wasn't the kind of thing my mom usually said, and it caught me off guard. I hadn't realized how much I needed to hear the softness in her voice.

I felt guilty keeping the truth about what happened in Arizona from her. But I wasn't ready to talk about it with anyone. A gnawing anxiety festered inside me; the longer it stayed buried, the bigger the fallout would be.

"You too, Mom," I said, the words feeling heavier than I'd intended. A wave of nostalgia washed over me, the distance between us suddenly feeling less like an impenetrable barrier and more like a miscommunication. I wasn't ready to bridge that gap, but at that moment, it didn't feel as impossible. "Love you."

"Love you, too," she said softly, then the line went silent.

I moved to my bedroom, making a mug of hot tea along the way. I was feeling... emboldened. Like in the way I hid from the truth was maybe my new superpower. I felt audacious. And Silas' attention made me feel desired. For the first time since I arrived in Tidings, I felt *hot*. The desert summer sun seemed to suddenly be in the room with me. I tugged the cardigan off my shoulders and took a deep breath. My nipples tightened, not from a cold breeze, but from an internal heat.

Alice: You still have to pass my ten-point inspection list.

Silas: Easy. Hit me with the first one.

Well fuck, I had completely made that up and now had to come up with something.

> Alice: If you could have one wish, what would it be?

> Silas: That's serious.

> Silas: Uh—world peace?

> Alice: Okay, Miss America.

> Silas: To be happy.

Even through text, I felt sadness in his words. Each day, he wore a mask of indifference. I knew what it was like to live a second life. Everyone had something to hide.

> Silas: So… Are you going to let me in?

I glanced down at my appearance, considering.

> Silas: I'm kidding. I'm at work.

I sunk back into the chair, feeling a wave of disappointment crash over me.

> Alice: Slow night?

> Silas: You can't say that!! You'll jinx it.

> Alice: Sorry! I knocked on wood three times.

I watched the screen as three dots appeared in a text bubble.

But a message never came.

CHAPTER 12

ALICE

Silas: Did I bore you to sleep?

I'd fallen asleep in the chair with my phone in my lap. The vibration jolted me awake, and I wiped drool off the side of my mouth.

Alice: Not because of you. I just crashed.

Silas: Must be nice. I'm just getting to bed.

I squinted at the time on my phone—it was nearly eight in the morning. He must have been run ragged.

Alice: You good?

Silas. Yeah. Thanks for asking.

Alice: Good night then.

My day, however, was only beginning. After the busy morning checking in a new group of guests who arrived on the red-eye train, I stepped into the back office and

140

returned my mom's incessant voicemails from the morning. She answered winded, speaking before she caught her breath.

"You might not call me much anymore," she said, "but I know my daughter well enough to know when she's covering up something. There is no way you moved somewhere with snow if it weren't for a boy. Sorry, it doesn't check out."

Mom always knew when Andrea and I had something to hide. A mother's intuition was not to be overlooked.

I attempted to dismiss her with humor. "Our ancestors are Scandinavian," I said. "I was built for this."

"You wear a cardigan in the summer... *in Arizona.*"

"The men in my office always turned on the a/c like they were freezing meat."

"And last I heard," she argued, running over my words without hearing them, "it was twenty degrees where you are, and that's before the windchill."

"When did you become a meteorologist?"

"It's suspicious, is all."

I let her have that one. Nothing about Tidings was credulous. I still felt like this was a plot of a *Saw* movie; if I didn't find the escape key, I'd be forever trapped in a peppermint torture chamber.

"I didn't move here for a boy. I can assure you."

Would I stay for a boy? Whoa, where did that intrusive thought come from?

She waited patiently without a word, priming me to start spilling.

"To *escape* a boy, maybe. I wanted a fresh start."

Mom hummed and I pictured her sitting cross-legged at the kitchen island, furiously tapping her almond-shaped nails across the granite countertop.

"So... what has the crazy neighbor been up to now?" To remove the focus from me, I gave my mom space to deep dive into the latest gossip session, to which she took full advantage. One thing I knew about Shelly Woods was that she couldn't help herself around a juicy story, especially involving someone she disliked.

"Oh!" she exclaimed at the end of the saga. "Andrea is in New Mexico, digging rocks and snorkeling, probably drinking margaritas and smiling in the sun." I made a mental note to cry about that one later. Surely my peppermint hot cocoa and thick layers of wool boot socks would not rile up any envy... "We're meeting her for the holidays." For the first time, my mom sounded wistful—but then she hesitated and spoke softly. "It would be so great to have my girls together."

Emotion swelled in my chest. It'd been years since we all gathered. It was easy to pin it on my sister's unpredictable travel for work, and it became the expectation that we were cordial but distant. My parents never pestered me, and I hated that. I *wished* they asked more to spend time with me, insisting on a cramped family vacation where we teased and laughed at each other.

"I can't this year, Mom. Maybe for your birthday next year?"

"Yes," she said quietly. "That would be lovely."

"I love you. I'll call you again soon."

"I love you, too, Alice."

"Room service," a voice from the other side of the door called, coupled with a knock. I pushed myself up from my chair behind the desk and opened the office door to a tall drink of water. Literally—Silas held his large water bottle in one hand and slung his black backpack over one shoulder. He ran his hands through his already messy hair in pensive thought.

"You resetting in there?" He gently tapped his fingers on the side of my head.

I was sure the expression on my face was a textbook example of dazed.

"I asked when you're off today," Silas said.

I shook my head, recalibrating. His persistence to see me was satisfying, like that feeling of coming home after a long day at work, changing into my favorite pair of comfy pants, sinking into relaxation. Silas felt *familiar*. I knew he always raised an eyebrow with every inflection of his voice when he asked a question. He drank decaf coffee after working the night shift, because he believed it was some sort of personal infraction not to have a dark roast in the morning, even if he had to sleep on an opposite schedule. Silas was consistent. Reliable.

"Two days in a row of seeing you when you get off shift," I said, instinctively reaching my hand toward his face —a bold move. But here he was, alone in my office, wearing an expression that ached for comfort. I grazed my thumb across his cheekbone. "Your under eyes are darker today."

"That rough, huh?" He turned his head, leaning it into my palm. For a second, his eyes closed, and he released a long breath.

My toes flexed in my shoes. I wanted to say more. *Be* more for him. But we stood silent, with our fingers lingering together. He lowered our hands, and his knuckles brushed my waist.

"But yes," he said, and I lifted my gaze from where our hands connected and watched a smile line pop next to his mouth. He rested a thigh on the edge of the desk, and I turned away, feeling flushed. "A bunch of dumb shit, really. Couple teens snuck out to the little cabin in the woods during the day, got lost on the way back, and needed treatment for hypothermia around midnight."

"I don't know anything about medicine, but getting cold injuries sounds like par for the course around here."

Silas' pants creased where his hip met the edge of the desk as he looked around, speaking softly so only I could hear. "Frostbite on genitalia." I scrunched my nose and frowned. *Ick.* "So, that was a very pleasant conversation with their parents, as you can imagine."

"I can assure you," I said, distracted by the wrinkles in his scrub pants, stretching across his thighs. "I was not that dumb of a teenager."

"Oh, I was."

I scoffed. "Silas? A bad boy? I don't believe it."

"Believe it. I threw toilet paper on a tree during a senior prank."

"Alert the FBI," I said sarcastically, twisting a pen between my fingers before pointing it at him. "And I thought you were perfect."

"It was the beginning of my wild streak. Still became a doctor though." Silas chuckled and straightened his posture. The room filled with silence, and he cleared his throat. "Anyways, I thought I'd come get your answer in person. Are you free next Monday?"

My pulse fluttered in my neck. "I am," I responded with a guttural voice, and cleared my throat. "What do you have in mind?"

I refilled my coffee from the carafe on my desk, lifting it up in offering. He politely shook his head. "Right, no caffeine," I said.

"Play in the snow. A little day trip on the snowmobiles and picnic at the small cabin we can rent for day use." He picked up a candy cane paperweight on the desk and fiddled with it between his fingers. "'Cabin' is a generous word—it's basically one room with a fireplace and a small cot. A safety shelter when people are out in the wilderness."

The idea that there was more wilderness than what Tidings already felt like to me was laughable. "You want to take me where people get frostbite on their genitals?"

"It was just the male, since it was... out. You needn't worry. Your breasts and genitalia will be warm enough."

I sputtered on my sip of coffee, cursing softly. He gazed at my chin, exploring.

"I'm clumsy," I said. Silas moved his hand with deliberate ease, tracing the warm drip running down my chin. The slow, measured action sent precarious shivers through my body. I leaned in to his finger, offering the expanse of my neck.

Then, with a slow, teasing flick of his finger, he brought it to his lips, savoring the moment with a glint in his eyes. I released a shaky exhale. "Best coffee I've ever tasted." He left me with my jaw on the floor as he stepped out of the office. From outside the door he said, "I'll let you get back to work, Alice. See you Monday."

I REPEATEDLY PRINTED AND STAPLED GUEST RECEIPTS. A MUNDANE, mindless task that had me second-guessing most of my life decisions. And for better or worse, left plenty of opportunity to think about the unexpected sex appeal Silas dropped at my feet earlier, leaving me in a cloudy haze of desire.

How dare he touch me like that and walk away, like it was nothing.

The lodge, and all of Tidings it seemed, liked to keep a paper copy of everything. The computer system was as useful as the 1993 MACDOS. Not wanting to be rude and judgmental of their methods, I bit my tongue and tore another perforated edge from the paper that chugged out from the clunky printer.

"I'd hate to be kicked out of Tidings because I offended Elvin over his preference of vintage office supplies," I muttered to myself.

"If I had it my way, we'd have ink and quill," Elvin said behind me. I jumped, slicing a finger across a corner of the paper and cutting open a piece of fine skin between my index finger and thumb. I put my hand in my mouth and sucked on my wound.

Elvin smiled fondly at me, the apples of his cheeks pink as a piglet. From a drawer, he removed a first-aid kit and handed me a small bandage.

"When you're done with that," he said, "there's some sorting in the back that needs to be done. A few boxes of *ancient* paperwork. Some can be burned, though."

I crinkled my nose and turned my back, hiding my embarrassed face. "They invented paper shredders so you don't have to do that anymore."

My phone pinged with a message from Silas.

> Silas: I can't stop by this morning because of some errands I need to run. But didn't want you to think I forgot about you. I'll pick you up tomorrow morning at eight.

Smiling became increasingly easier from the feeling of seeing his name flash across the screen. I hadn't heard from him since he left me in a haze of lusty smoke in my office yesterday. It started to feel like more than a simple crush.

Crushes felt pastel and featherlight; this felt heavy and thick, like warm molasses sliding down my throat. Intense and overwhelming—and yet, somehow, welcomed.

Alice: Looking forward to it.

"Elvin, what do you know about this cabin in the wilderness?" Saying it out loud sounded like somewhere a person dumped bodies. I opened the browser app on my phone, surprised the Wi-Fi was working smoothly, and searched for things I'd need to know to not look like an idiot.

Like how to ride a snowmobile and how to dress warm for our snowmobile date.

Oh god, who was I?

A date in the snow didn't sound like my cup of tea, but it beat the hell out of touring the peppermint factory.

"It feels like you're at the end of the snow-covered earth," Elvin's voice carried from the office. "Everyone has to see it once." I heard his jolly chuckle and footsteps as he crept out the back exit. "I'm out of your hair for today," he added.

After work, I met Ginger for drinks next door. Over a sip of wine, I said, "There's a niche webpage for everything."

Ginger sat next to me at the bar, inhaling a charcuterie board stacked with soft cheeses, cold meats, olives, and roasted nuts. "I know someone local who makes great leather collars with matching lace sets," she said around a mouthful.

I shook my head. "That is not what I meant." I plucked a green olive from the plate, making a sour face at the blue cheese I didn't realize was stuffed in it. "Silas is going to take me to the wilderness. Do you know about that little cabin?"

"It's his go-to spot."

A lead weight dropped from my throat to my feet. Of course he had a routine with the girls he dated. The man was built with the mechanical inner workings of a clock; he was never off and stayed on cue. And he was so damn good at getting us to swoon.

"Holy shit," Ginger said. She rested the back of her hand on my forehead. "I was kidding. But you look like you're about to throw up."

What or *whom* he chooses to do in Tidings was none of my business. It could never be my business. It was his home after all, and I was on loan. I'd be gone before we knew it, and then the next girl at the front desk, wide eyed and fucking clueless, would be enraptured by the magic of Tidings... and the hot doctor with an adorable dog.

"You're the first girl I've seen him pursue in years. And back then, it wasn't anything like this."

I cleared my throat and shook my head. "Pardon? I thought I heard you use the word *pursue*."

"You heard correctly."

My thoughts spiraled back to Mark. He was relentless in *pursuing* me... he knew I had expendable money at the time because I bragged about my savings account and my financial plan. Then he ruined my life with his bad ideas and stupid boat shoes. "A little risk now for a big payoff later," he delighted in, encouraging me each day as my investments soured. I was going to get back every dime I wasted on that asshole, and walk away richer and smarter. What a fucking sucker I was to fall for his... pursuit.

"Do I have 'gullible loser' tattooed on my forehead?" I asked Ginger, swallowing the last tannins of my red wine and signaling to the bartender for a refill.

Ginger raised her eyebrow at me, one I could picture her giving across a table in the boardroom signaling her impatience. "Get to the point."

I lowered my voice. "What does Silas want from me? If you say he hasn't pursued anyone in a while, then why me?"

Ginger leaned back on the bar stool and looked me up and down. She tilted her head in the direction of my lower half. "Have you seen that ass?"

"You're an anomaly, Ging. Half the time you scare the hell out of me with your serious face and then the other half you're no better than a man, objectifying everyone."

Ginger set her glass down on the bar top a little too hard than necessary. She turned to face me, crossing her knees. "You dummy."

"Your friendship skills could use some thawing out. A little too icy, no?"

"I respect you, but girl, if you don't figure this out soon, I'm going to lose any composure I have left."

"Why the hell would you respect me? I am nothing special."

"You took a blind leap of faith to come here," she said.

"A fool's errand, no?"

"Everything that happened brought you here. Fresh start, fresh air. It's good for you."

My grip tightened around the stem of my wine glass. "You know, where *I* come from, people don't speak in riddles," I said through gritted teeth. "Here, everywhere I go it's a mystery surprise box I have to unravel. Elvin acts like some sort of seer. You're a breadcrumb thrower. Can anyone just be upfront?"

Ginger tossed cash on the bar and pulled her jacket off the back of the chair.

My breaths became short. My vision tunneled. I had gone too far, and it was too late to take it all back and shove it back inside. I closed my eyes. "Look, I'm sorry…"

But then Ginger pulled me up by my arm and told me to grab my coat and purse. "Don't apologize; things are just starting to get good."

She grabbed my elbow and pulled me outside as I fumbled to tie the belt around my wool coat. She hailed a Tidings' taxi—a two-person carriage pulled by a snowmobile.

"What, no sled dogs?" I groaned. I would never get used to the modes of transportation in Tidings. "And another thing about this place, do you know sled dogs delivered my clothes from the boutique?"

"Pretty damn cool, don't you think?" She smiled and Ginger's surprisingly soft tone was comforting like a salve on a chapped, delicate part of me. There weren't many times Ginger softened around the edges, but when she did, a wistful air surrounded her like glittery snow blowing in a gentle breeze. She spoke about Tidings in reverence, and with mysterious magic lingering in her words.

We sat next to each other in the carriage, and I gripped the safety bar in front of us holding on for balance as Ginger relaxed against the headrest, nonchalantly giving the driver the name of our destination like she was in a yellow cab in New York City.

Minutes later, we arrived at a bar at the end of the main

drag, right before the hiking trails and unmarked roads that lead up the mountain.

It was packed, bodies in every chair, standing room only at the bar and in the back. Hot breath and loud music filling the air. I awkwardly squeezed through the tight space, bumping my ass on chairs, reciting, "Sorry, excuse me."

Behind me Ginger was graceful and tranquil. Everyone shimmied their chairs around her as if she was royalty. She acknowledged people who waved to her, most I didn't recognize. Employees from other businesses, staff at the hospital, and the bartender, and servers. She pointed out tourists, easily identifiable by their phones strategically aimed at a staged vignette of a peppermint drink and evergreen boughs manipulated into centerpieces.

She nudged me with her elbow, calling my attention to a table in the corner with the new group of researchers here on assignment.

A handsome man with bright eyes and gray strands peppering his facial hair, lifted his drink toward her.

She waved, offering a meek, "Hello, James." She turned to me and said, "Grab a seat and order some food to share. I'll be right back." Ginger stepped aside to make a phone call.

"You dragged me here to ditch me?"

"I need to talk to someone real quick. We're all friendly here."

I ordered a drink, a cocktail mixed with nutmeg and orange with a cinnamon stick for garnish, and a platter of the best greasy kind of happy hour delights.

James and another man stopped by our table. "Hi, I'm James, and this is Drew. May we join you?"

I gestured toward the empty chairs at the table, tossing them an indifferent glance. I'd never been nervous to get to know new people and usually adapted to new settings without a fuss. But I was confused and maybe a little slaphappy toward Ginger who had forced me out of the warm bar, into the cold air to ride in a carriage down an icy path only to ditch me with random guys.

"Have a seat. I'm Alice, a friend of Ginger's."

"Nice to meet you Alice," James said. "How long have you been in Tidings?"

"Not long." I kept an eye on Ginger, who paced in a continuous small circle fast enough to burn through the soles of her shoes.

Drew did the typical prodding, trying to figure out my life story, namely if I was single. He was good-looking in conventional terms, but nothing that stole my breath, or made me stumble over my words. No—only Silas could get me to hyperventilate and spill my coffee all over myself.

James kept looking over his shoulder at Ginger, letting me know that I wasn't the only one waiting anxiously for her to get off her phone and join us. He certainly looked like a smitten kitten hungry for a bowl of cream.

I pulled my phone from my purse, snapped a picture of my empty cocktail and sent it to Patrick.

> Alice: This is not tequila, but I miss you. Come visit.

I stood, wobblier on my feet than I anticipated. Drew stood quickly, holding me upright at my waist. "You good?"

"Fine, fine." I smiled. I felt the heat of his hands on my waist. I shrugged and put space between us.

He lifted his hands in an apologetic manner. "Sorry, was trying to keep you from falling." His face was close to mine, sour whisky breath fanning across my skin. "Let's get you some water."

The effects of the wine and cocktail combo swirled in my head. I'd make a mistake drinking tonight when I had to ride on a snowmobile tomorrow. I envisioned myself puking off the side into a snowbank, holding on for dear life. Silas would be so disgusted he'd kick me off and tell me to walk home. Rightfully so.

No, Silas wouldn't do that. He's responsible. And polite.

My thoughts were all over the place. "Have you ever been to the yurt here, Drew?" I wiped spittle from the corner of my mouth. I struggled to get the correct pronunciation of yurt out of my sloppy mouth.

"The what?" he asked.

I looked at his eyes, bright blue like glacier water and strands of blond hair poking out from under his beanie.

"I think she means the cabin the locals talk about thirty kilometers west," said the other guy whose name I forgot.

"I don't know what to wear. Any ideas?"

He laughed and placed his hand on my lower back, drawing small circles as we waited at the bar for my water. I lifted a shoulder, putting more space between us. I knew these guys had a slutty reputation, but this was becoming the horniest town off the map.

"Do you not have women on your home planet?" I asked. I knew I wasn't making any sense but how do you stop a train with rusted brakes?

"What?" He leaned in, and his breath tickled my ear like an annoying fly buzzing by.

"You people... I mean, scientists. Researchers. You come here to test the temperature of the snow and hook up. Like you've never seen women before."

"Test the temperature of the snow?" He spoke slowly, annunciating each word like I was speaking gibberish.

In the mirror on the wall behind the bar, suddenly I saw one and a half reflections of me and two of… Dustin? Derek?

He scratched the back of his neck and adjusted his beanie. "Y'know, James said Ginger was a firebrand, so it makes sense that the company she keeps would fall into place," he said, his Minnesotan or Canadian accent—who could tell the difference anyway—thicker than before.

I asked for another glass of water after I chugged mine in a most unladylike fashion. I didn't give a shit.

"What did you say your name was again?"

He started, but then a shadow loomed. Another reflection in the mirror. This time I was certain it was real.

Silas glared—*fucking glared*—at the horny scientist next to me.

I turned around and smiled until my cheeks ached. "Silas, this is Doug."

Silas stared at Doug. Doug looked utterly confused.

"That's not my name," said *not Doug*.

I hiccupped. "Ginger introduced us."

Silas clenched his teeth. "Did she now?"

Doug, or whatever, rolled his eyes. "This chick's weird."

I stuck my tongue out as he walked away.

"You're wasted," Silas said from somewhere in my periphery.

"You're hot," I said as I watched my filter fly out the window.

"Let's see if you say that without your beer goggles."

"I wouldn't have agreed to go with a strange man to your yurt date sober if I didn't think so." I brushed my hand across his waist, shocking both of us if his twitch was any indication. For me, it was the muscle that came out to say hello. "You're also kind and trustworthy."

"Just Google me and let me know if you find anything

troubling." My stomach swirled. His lips grazed my ear when he spoke, while his hands tucked my arms through the sleeves of my heavy coat. "And it's not a 'yurt,' it's a small permanent structure. Some people generously call it the 'little cabin.'"

He didn't take his eyes off me, not even when Ginger not-so-subtly kicked his shin with the pointed toe of her boot.

"Psychotic," Silas said, looking directly at Ginger's face.

She scoffed and pointed at her chest. "I'm a mastermind."

I had no idea what was going on between them.

"Did Ginger call you to rescue me?" I asked Silas. "Because I didn't need rescuing. I'm not a victim or a damsel in distress." I was getting fired up, and just to prove a point I tucked my arms in at my side.

Silas draped an arm over me, and I felt like I could purr at the feel of his arm around my shoulder. He scanned my face and hesitated. "Ginger's got a bad habit of sticking her nose in other people's business."

"So what's your business then?"

He untucked parts of my hair that were trapped underneath my jacket collar. "You," he said.

Ginger smiled like a sly fox and gave me a delicate finger wave. "See ya."

"I'm not leaving," I slurred. I had a lot of questions about what the hell was going on and what Silas meant when he said I was his business.

"Yes, we are," Silas said, ushering us to the door.

Ginger's chuckle rumbled through the bar, and I saw a swarm of men in the front of the bar eye her like she was a lonely queen bee. "Hello boys," her husky voice called out.

I tripped over my own feet, and Silas caught me before I

could fall like a newborn fawn still wet behind the ears. "Where are we going now?"

"Your place," he said, grabbing my hand and holding the door open with his other shoulder.

A sliver of sobriety entered my bloodstream when the piercing cold air slapped me across the face. "That's awfully forward."

We walked arm-in-arm, and I nuzzled in closer, like he was my own personal heater. "I'm getting you there safely, putting water, and ibuprofen nearby. Then I'm going home."

"The hero complex must be exhausting."

He flexed his jaw and made a movement like he was passing a marble from cheek to cheek. "I'm just doing the right thing."

"I meant what I said earlier. You're hot. Like stupid hot. With your... face." That earned me a laugh. Good, that saved a little bit of my dignity. "Please don't judge me. Ginger left me all alone and I got accosted by whatever his fucking name was."

"He accosted you?" Silas stopped, and the lights strung across the nearby building's facade cast him in sharp contrast. I looked at him—*really* looked—at his handsome yet drawn face. Overworked and over worried. A week's worth of sleep waited for him.

"His offensive breath did," I said.

We rounded the corner past a group of senior citizens gathered around a fire pit, sipping on peppermint-flavored something. I was like a peppermint hound dog by now. I was freezing and my feet ached.

Silas sensed my discomfort, encouraging me with a quickening pace and a gentle tug of my elbow. "Up here a few more cars. Not a lot of open space tonight."

"Ginger made us ride on a snowmobile carriage," I said. Silas opened the passenger door of his truck and secured me in the front seat. I'd be embarrassed tomorrow when inevitable flashbacks of him clicking the seatbelt over me appeared. A slice of exposed skin between his jaw and scarf wafted that familiar warm scent. I couldn't help myself. I had to sniff him—very obviously sniff him desperate for one more hit. "What did you mean that *I'm* your business?"

"Alice," he said my name with a *tone*, like he had to repeat himself. "What did you tell the asshole at the bar?"

CHAPTER 13

SILAS

I woke up later in the afternoon than normal after a shift, but my body pleaded for more sleep, even as it fought with other things it seemed to crave more recently. In a daze, I reached for my phone to see texts and missed calls from Ginger, who gave me the play-by-play of her evening plans with Alice. I hadn't grasped what she was alluding to when she called me again.

"What do you want, Ginger?" I asked her; my voice was heavy with sleep.

"I'm trying to help Alice get to know Tidings better."

"By bar hopping?" I sat out of bed and ran my fingers through my hair, still full of gel from last night. I'd come home so exhausted I didn't even make it to the shower. I was lucky I made it to my bed.

Dagny helped me with Snøf on days or nights when I couldn't get her into doggy daycare, but right now, my dog looked pissed. She stood at the backdoor with her brows furrowed; my dog was glaring at me. "I'm coming, I'm coming," I said walking to the door to let her outside.

"Ew! What are you doing exactly?"

"I was talking to the dog. She needs to go outside."

The background noise of cheers and loud music came through the phone. "So do you. Come meet us at Frozen Hearth," she said, then lowered her voice to a whisper. "Some dudes are hitting on Alice."

She knew exactly what to say to get me acting like a possessive lunatic. I asked Alice out on a date to the little cabin, though maybe she didn't fully know it was going to be a date-date. The local folklore always built up the location like it was a mystical realm, somewhere that gave you a transformative experience, if you were there at the right time.

For me, the highlight was the 360-degree windows wrapped around the structure. The views were unmatched; although I hadn't experienced the Northern Lights there yet, it was like no other place on earth. I knew Alice was skittish about Tidings, but the feeling of being alone under the Northern Lights and the vast plains of snow was my plan to win her over.

Or at least see if everything they said about fate around here was right.

I didn't want to overwhelm her, but I also didn't want anyone else to be *over*, or under her, either.

"Damn it, Ginger."

"You've got no one to blame but yourself, lover boy."

Someone who sounded like Alice called Ginger's name. "Is that her?"

"Yup, and we are about to go on a double date with some hotties so get here now. Bye." She hurriedly said and rushed to hang up the phone.

I dressed at lightning speed and drove down to the bar before my truck was fully warmed up. My hands were freezing on the steering wheel, waiting for it to heat up. By the time I got to the bar, Alice was loose and flirty with a couple guys I recognized. The caveman attitude wasn't familiar to me, and I fought with myself to act more chill than I felt on the inside. Because something about her smiling at them made me want to punch their lights out.

I got her away from them and in my truck faster than I'd check a patient's pulse in ten seconds. She was sloppy. Tidings' cocktails were sneaky, deceivingly delicious and strong. I'd formulated a plan to take her back to her suite and make sure she was good to go for the night before heading home.

"Alice." I'd repeated her name four times before she looked up at me. "What did you tell the asshole at the bar?"

She waved me off. "I don't know what to wear," her voice was breathy. "You don't know how many bloggers linked outfits. Imagine getting a commission from your snow-style blog."

"I don't speak this language," I said, shutting the car door before I jogged across the front of my truck to the driver's side. We waited in silence for the heater to warm up as she blew warm air into her closed fists. I forced myself not to reach across the center console and pull her into my lap. "The seats will take a moment to warm up."

It was tensely quiet; the only sound was the rev of the engine as it worked overtime to get the heater on. My other senses were whipped with rapid-fire precision. If warmth had a smell, it would be her. She was wool, delicate vanilla, and comfort.

"Can I ask you a question?" she asked. I turned my head toward her, lifting my brows. "Is the cabin in the woods a secret cult thing where I have to take a blood oath?"

I shifted into reverse and our eyes met over my shoulder

as I maneuvered out of the tight parking spot along the curb. I put my arm behind her seat and winked at her. "Don't be ridiculous, Alice." I tilted up my lips in a sinister smile. "We don't just want your blood. Your organs are the high value."

We were silent as we drove through snow-covered streets. The windshield wipers on a low speed knocking off large flakes as they trickled down. She cleared her throat. "Oh, good. I was worried you were taking me there to have sex."

Fuck.

I found an open spot alongside the curb in front of the lodge and held onto the gear shift with a white-knuckle grip before thrusting it into park. I slammed my door shut, letting out an indecipherable grunt I didn't recognize as my own voice. Her off-the-cuff comment sent a jolt of energy straight through me. I opened her door and leaned in, reaching over her body to unbuckle the seatbelt. I lingered, taking in the matching competitive grin she gave me until her smile dropped to that of a cornered mouse, a hungry cat peering in.

"Are you mad at me or something?" she asked. "Is this about the cabin?"

Again, I grunted like an idiot and reached for her hand to guide her down the sidewalk to the front door of the lodge. "I don't want to talk about the fucking cabin."

"You know I was fine back there." She tried to pull her hand back, but I wasn't fucking letting go. "I wasn't getting drugged and dragged off to his secret research lair." She giggled and hiccupped. Adorable, but she was wasted. She swatted my hand away again and fumbled. She would have fallen on her ass if I didn't have my arm around her. Every night at work I waited for her to come in with a swollen ankle. The girl with sunshine streaked in her hair was a mess on these icy sidewalks.

"Let go," she protested. "I can walk."

"Once we get to the door. You should always be escorted on these icy sidewalks."

"Like a prisoner?"

"Sure." And a part of me liked the idea of her being my prisoner, locked in a room together all night. All week.

"You're being moody tonight."

We made it to the front of the lodge, and she let out a sigh of relief.

"And you are inebriated."

"What's the big deal? I'm a grown woman."

"Key?" I ordered with my palm out. We stood outside the door to her suite as she fumbled through her purse. She swatted and huffed through whatever women kept in their bags. Ultimately, she became too frustrated to keep her fishing expedition going and tipped her bag upside down, dumping all the contents on the floor.

I gave her a stern look. "Really?"

She squatted, filtering through lipsticks, tampons, and—

"Alice, is that a cactus?"

She bit her lip.

I reached down and grabbed the three-inch-long live cactus in a mini terracotta plant. I examined it, touching the spikes to confirm it was real.

She smiled and forced a hiccup down. "Desert girl," she pointed to her chest, her words heavy and tipsy. "To always have a piece of it with me." She quirked a smile like she was reminiscing over a fond memory, but her tone sounded sad. I didn't know why she left Arizona. We hadn't talked much about her life before Tidings. But for the first time, she didn't speak about Arizona in reverence for its weather opposite to Tidings, but like she painfully missed *home*.

"Ah! Got it." She held up a key and secured all the loose items back in her bag. "Isn't it cute?"

"I've never referred to a key as 'cute'."

"The antique element," she flashed it in front of me. "It's a dainty, old fashion charm."

I assessed it like it held the answer to a secret riddle. That brass key brought her joy like that cactus. Her bag was full of mysteries and happiness. I got so distracted by the cactus I missed my chance to learn more about her, hoping she had more clues to give away. I shrugged. "I guess I've been in Tidings too long."

She gave me a sympathetic frown then struggled to get the key in the lock. She was drunker than she'd admit. She stopped trying to put the key in the lock and tried to wave me off with a tension-stuffed standoff. "Well, I'm home. Thank you."

"Anytime." I pulled the key from her hand and inserted it in the lock, easily turning it, and opening the door for her with one hand.

"Would you like to come in? I have a nice view of the snow. The snow has really grown on me."

I bopped my finger on her nose. "I can tell when you're lying." She about turned a shade of green as she forced the statement out of her mouth.

She nodded. "Then a nightcap it is. And you can tell me everything I need to know to prepare for my first cult meeting tomorrow."

"Do you have tea?"

She glared at me like I said I hated her favorite book. "Yes, but I don't make peppermint tea in this house."

"Something besides alcohol then." I took a seat on the sofa across from the fireplace as she heated up the kettle.

I watched her work around the kitchen, acknowledging how random it felt to finally be in the suite at the lodge I walked past almost every day for four years. How many nights I grabbed a drink with the guys at the restaurant, or popped in to check on Elvin, never imagining one day a woman from The Grand Canyon State would have me chomping at the bit to see her.

And do other things to her. *For* her. *To her.*

"What's your favorite book?" I asked. I needed to know more about her, even if it was a book or movie or drink preference. She was self-deprecating almost to a fault, like that was a protective measure to hide a flaw she was insecure about. Something I'd learn about her sooner than later.

"Hmm." She hummed from the kitchen, pouring hot water over tea leaves steeped in a strainer. "*War and Peace.*"

"Really?"

"God, no." She carried two cups on a tray and bent to set them down. Her sweater drifted and I flicked my eyes away before I took too much liberty appreciating her cleavage. "Okay, but you can't laugh."

"Please tell me it's Sasquatch porn."

"What? No," she said. "Do *you* like Sasquatch porn?" She stood in front of me seated with her hands on her hips. She looked hot in her scolding pose.

I leaned back on the couch, cupping the back of my head with my palms. If she was acting like she didn't notice my biceps flex, she was a terrible liar. "It was a thing Ginger mentioned once. Go on, I want to know."

She fiddled with the tight hairstyle that always made her look like a librarian or flight attendant—both super-hot fantasies—and I watched as she laid a few metal pieces on the coffee table before unwinding her long hair from its secure hold. Alice was consistent with that hairstyle, and it always surprised me when I realized how long her hair was. She had it so tightly wound I was impressed at the skill it took to minimize her length. She was always beautiful to me, but I really liked her hair down like this. Like she was relaxed. Relaxed around me.

She tucked a stray hair behind her ear and the line of little earrings she wore glimmered along her earlobe. "Have you seen those books that always have a picture of a bakery or some small shop, and an animal? Usually a cat?"

"No, but I'm intrigued." I waved my hand as if to say, *keep going*.

"They're kind of murder mysteries, but not gory or anything."

"The cat gets murdered?"

"No, the cat is like a... sidekick."

She found a seat next to me, and I was pleasantly surprised she didn't hug the other end of the couch, but put herself within my arm's reach. From a closer vantage, I grew more fascinated by her hair. The color wasn't brown, but it wasn't blond either, somewhere between like it had been tanned by the sun. Bronzed.

"Anyways, I like those books. There's always hijinks and, yeah, it's about a murder but it's cozy." She rambled and I'd never been more entertained in a conversation about books.

"A cozy cat murder?"

She nudged my side with her elbow, and I feigned a cry of pain.

Alice grabbed a cup and handed it to me, watching me as I took a sip. It was a mix of cinnamon and apples, maybe. Definitely not peppermint.

"It's good," I said.

Her lips hovered over the lip of her mug as she gently sipped, careful not to burn her tongue. She wiped the side of her lips with her fingertip. "I didn't like any of the guys trying to... talk to me."

"No?" I was close enough to rub her thigh with my thumb. It took supreme concentration not to touch her more.

"I thought perhaps you didn't either." She set her teacup on the table and repositioned herself to face me, her knee rubbed on my thigh. Warm and floral perfume or hand lotion or whatever the fuck she put on to smell like that drifted. It drove me fucking mad. At first, I was obsessed with the fresh scent because it was something new besides the sterile hospital or peppermint, but it was an undeniable craving—a necessity.

"Are you praying?" her voice refocused me, and I pulled my hand back, not realizing I was running my fingers through each soft strand. "You closed your eyes and muttered something about the holy spirit."

"You're drunk."

"No, I'm not," she couldn't even say it with a straight face. "Okay, yes, I'm drunk. But I ate a lot of corn nuts."

I pinched her cheek, and she didn't flinch. "I really want to kiss you," I whispered. "But not when you're inebriated."

"I'm undrunk now," she laughed, the kind of goofy sound where a snort went through her throat. Yeah, she was toasted.

"I've kissed a lot of guys while drunk, y'know."

"I'm not a lot of guys."

"No, you're not." She leaned forward and stroked her nose along my jaw. "I like you," she murmured on a drunken breath. "But a guy like Silas shouldn't like a girl like me."

I wrapped an arm around her waist and scooted her closer, a breath away from sitting on my lap, as my pinky skimmed along her hip bone. "A guy like *Silas*?"

"You're thirty-something years old, and your life is all figured out," she rambled. "I bet you can make a really good poached egg and have a healthy 401k. I'm, uh—well, admittedly, in a temporary place right now. I enjoy hanging out with you, but—"

"Do you like poached eggs?"

She kept talking over me, hell, talking over herself. "It's not that I don't have a 401k, I do, somewhere. I think I have to update my mailing address."

"Alice."

"I should probably figure out my username."

"Alice," I whispered her name, just enough so she could feel the heat of my breath against her ear. I saw her breath catch at the base of her neck, the tiny shift in her body telling me everything I needed to know. "We're all just figuring this whole life thing out as we go. Might as well enjoy the company while we can."

I pressed my lips to the divot in her neck, the small part above her collarbone. She sucked in a breath, and that sound... fuck, that sound did something to me.

"I should go." I abruptly stood before there was any chance of changing my mind. Alice had had too much to drink, and I wasn't an asshole, no matter how *undrunk* she claimed she was.

I placed a glass of water next to her cup of scarcely touched tea. Her eyelids were heavy, and she was fading quickly. "I don't know your bounce-back rate after drinking, but let's take a rain check tomorrow."

"You mean a snow check?"

I glanced up at the ceiling, pinching the bridge of my nose to hold back a laugh at the awful joke. But despite myself, a smile tugged at my lips. I leaned in and pressed a soft kiss to her cheek, my lips lingering against her cool skin for just a moment longer than necessary. "Your cheeks are cold."

"This may come as a surprise to you, but I am always cold here."

"No snowmobiling tomorrow, especially if you're hungover. But let me make you dinner?"

"S'kay." She swatted my chest, dragging a finger down. Puckish as hell.

I closed the space between us and our chests brushed. She didn't back down, but leaned in, giving the faintest roll of her hips.

"Silas," she said in a shred of a whisper.

"Alice," I murmured in return, my voice low, the words almost lost between us. I was fading fast—fighting the urge to close the distance between us, desperate to finally kiss her, to taste the sweet promise of her lips, and to see if the rest of her body carried the same intoxicating honeysuckle scent as her neck.

"You're so..." She trailed off, her words hanging in the air like an unfinished thought.

"Thirty-four," I answered, my voice a quiet, steady pulse.

She cocked her head in confusion, and I used that opportunity to deliberately draw my nose down the curve of her neck.

"I'm thirty-four," I repeated, my lips brushing the edge of her ear.

"I'm thirty-three," she whispered, her voice a little unsteady now.

Her breath brushed my ear with the faintest exhale, like the softest, sweetest moan, and it set something deep inside me alight.

"I'm from California," I added, my words barely more than a hum, my lips still dangerously close to her skin.

"I'm from Arizona," she murmured.

I cleared my throat and stepped back.

Her head tilted slightly, and she blinked a few times, as if the distance between us didn't quite register. "Why...?" she murmured, her voice a little slurred, the question hanging in the air.

"You can't string together a sentence without sounding like a keyboard with a broken space bar." I rested my hands on her shoulders with enough space that we looked like two middle schoolers at a chaperoned dance. "Drink water and take an ibuprofen."

"Yes, sir." She did a dramatic, awful impression of a salute.

"I'll call you in the morning. Maybe ten or so, assuming you'll sleep in."

"I'd sleep better if I wasn't alone."

"Some other time, we'll do this the right way."

And then I fucking ran out of that suite like that damn roof was about to collapse. Because my self-control was crumbling under all her pressure.

CHAPTER 14

ALICE

I opened one eye to a punchy redheaded woman peering over me, and a pristine, fresh blanket of snow out the window. It was awful.

I forcefully grabbed the blankets and pulled them up over my face, rolling over to hide my body from her. Memories of last night streamed through my mind like shadows in a dark room.

Silas walked me home.

Silas saw me drunk.

He told me he didn't like other guys talking to me or asking me to go to the cabin—oh god. I fumbled for my phone to double check I didn't send any embarrassing texts last night. The light burned my eyes and I tossed my phone.

"Get dressed; we've got a hot barre class," Ginger called from somewhere in my room. "Not a *bar*, which, by the way, is exactly what you smell like." I had a pillow pressed over my face, trying to block her out, until she yanked it away and tossed it across the room, out of my reach.

"Is this in my employment contract?"

"I'm here to level you up. Chop chop."

"I see we've reached the part of our friendship where you let yourself into my room," I grumbled. Truthfully, I loved that we had become close friends so quickly. I didn't have a group of close friends back home, since most of them now were married with kids doing their own domesticated shit. Ginger quickly became a friend I'd dearly miss when I left Tidings. I had a feeling she had that impact on everyone who came into her consuming orbit.

Silas was a gentleman last night, but I was secretly pleased he wasn't around to smell me like this. No one had ever been so gentle with me before. Gentle like a quiet, predatory bear, looking for both a fight and a fulfilling meal. That's twice now that Silas inserted himself between me and another man. Jealousy perhaps?

God, I wanted to be on the other side of that feasting mouth.

"Have you ever fucked someone out of your system?" I asked with an arm draped over my eyes.

It seemed like a smart plan. I'd be gone before things got too awkward or emotional or we had to do the "let's be friends" talk. We wouldn't have to duck around public places to avoid each other, instead, peacefully going our separate ways, grateful for the memories and wishing the best for each other. Saying it out loud felt like it came out of left field, but I'd been thinking about him like this for weeks. And the dream I had last night blurred into the drunken memories of his hands on my hip, his breath on my skin.

"Duh," she replied. I felt the mattress dip when she sat near my feet.

"But does it work? Someone you are super attracted to. You do it once and then common sense settles in about why it'd be a bad idea to do it again."

I'd drive myself crazy thinking about his smart mouth

and hands for the rest of my life if I never had the chance to taste him myself.

"For me, yes. For them, no. Men are clingy as fuck."

A temporary fling could be what I needed before the next phase of my life. After Tidings I'd move somewhere new, become serious about my career, then settle down.

The idea of making my family proud fueled my dreams of a stable future—to feel like I belonged. I envisioned budgeting my paychecks for a cozy cottage and sharing my life with someone dependable. The little details—like putting a chicken in the crockpot and enjoying playful teasing at family dinners—tugged at my heartstrings.

Preferably somewhere without caribou walking through downtown or peppermint hot cocoa year-round. Somewhere warm and glowing.

Which would be somewhere without Silas. Damnit.

"Up you go," Ginger forced me out of bed by pulling on my fucking toes. From my new position on the ground, I reached up, pawing around the nightstand for my phone. I smiled big at a message from Silas.

"Let's go, we're going to be late," Ginger yelled as she tossed workout clothes at my head. I had enough time to read the messages from him.

> Silas: How are you feeling?

> Silas: Let me know when you're awake.

> Silas: I thought about you all night.

> Silas: Tell me you'll come over for dinner tonight.

> Silas: Also, I'm sorry to be so forward.

Silas: Text me when you wake up.

Adorable.

I dressed like a blind mouse, pulling on whatever Ginger threw at my feet, and no one could pay me to wipe the smile off my face.

"I hate you," I muttered every ten feet as we walked down the sidewalk to the community recreation center. I could still be cocooned in my snug nest of fluffy blankets and cushy pillows instead of marching through god's least favorite biome to go fucking exercise.

"Doing squats in the heated room will make you feel like you're back in Arizona, so quit bitching," she demanded.

"Doubtful," I said.

We grabbed our mats and a clean pair of barre socks from the basket at the entrance. The room was full, but we found a spot in the dead center, like the free space on a bingo board. We started our warmups, and I immediately regretted showing up. The remnants of last night's cocktail sloshed in my gut, and I promised myself that if I didn't throw up, I'd never drink again.

By the time we made it through warm-ups, every muscle and tendon moved freely, without any stiffness, relieved to move again without creaks and tightness. Either my body was crying happy tears or bad decisions oozed from my pores. Halfway through six minutes of laborious plié squats, I whispered in her direction. "I think I have a date tonight. Silas wants to date *me*." She eyed me with a knowing expression. "You knew that, didn't you?

"Yes," she replied.

We followed the instructor into a wide-leg bend, and I frowned as my inner thighs screamed from holding the stretch too long. "How'd you know?"

"Not about tonight," she replied, "but *you* and him, yes." She winked and gave me an approving smile. "So, what's the plan?"

"Dinner at his place."

Her brow arched. "Bold. Nice work."

My stomach tightened, but it wasn't from the ballet-inspired movement. It was something I hadn't felt in a while. "I'm nervous."

"Ah. Virgin?"

My cheeks heated when a girl next to us tilted her head clearly listening in on our conversation.

"I've never been nervous for a date," Ginger added. "Not once."

The bleach-blond girl in front of us turned over her shoulder to toss a dirty look, clearly annoyed at our in-class conversation.

Following the instructor's motion, I pulsed in a deep, wide-leg squat and arched my left arm over my head. "A lot of dating in Tidings for you?"

"You know the drill by now," Ginger said, leaning to her left. "A dozen researchers come through every few weeks, then the rotation starts again."

I raised my brows and pursed my lips. *Good for her.* With a name like Ginger, hair to match, and a body sculpted by a goddess, there was no doubt she had men lining up to worship at her feet.

At the end of class, we stood side-by-side in front of the locker room mirror. The space was outfitted like a high-end spa, with every amenity we needed to freshen up. I watched in awe as the living bombshell brushed her long hair, propping it into a bouncy ponytail fifty layers thick.

Ginger grabbed a brush before I could hoist my hair into

its standard tight bun. She went to work, giving me a similar perky style. "For what it's worth, Silas is a good man. He doesn't rotate through tourists or one-time visitors."

I didn't *want* to care about what he did or who he was with, but the truth was, I did. I couldn't pretend otherwise anymore. Silas' consistency was nice, but it was also terrifying. It was easier when the guy you had a crush on was a walking red flag and flakier than a pastry.

He moved through life like a perfect clock, never missing a beat. I felt like a tumbleweed, going wherever the wind took me.

Ginger tugged on my ponytail. "I know everything, remember?"

She walked briskly, no time for meandering. My body temperature was at a fever level, and I was grateful to feel warm enough that an extra layer over my cropped sleeveless top would be too much. We left the locker room and walked to the foyer.

"What else do you know about him?" I asked.

"He's overbearing. Drives Dagny crazy with the macho brother shtick."

I sipped lemon-lavender ice water, listening to Ginger's thoughts drift toward dirty gossip about researchers and tourists. There was even a list of bad-acting permanently banned people from Tidings.

"What do you have to do to get banned from Tidings? Insult Elvin by telling him he needs to get with modern times?"

She paused, placing her hand delicately on my elbow, and looked up at me. "The old-timers like Elvin are good people. They're not judgmental or think their way is better than others. They're protecting Tidings and its *magic*." She whispered magic like a starry-eyed kid on Christmas Eve, or someone with reverence for a closely guarded family recipe.

"Maybe they could use some of that 'magic' to make it just ten degrees warmer." My feet came to a screeching halt, the heel of my shoes leaving a black scruff on the white floor, and flung my arm in front of Ginger like I was holding her back in the passenger seat at a poorly timed yellow stoplight.

Through the door to the basketball court, a silhouette caught my eye. I stood to the side of the window peering in, Ginger pressing up on her tippy toes to see over me.

"Massive shiny objects." Ginger's tone was raspy.

Eight men, half of them shirtless, ran up and down the basketball court, their bodies gleaming with sweat, each step pounding like a wrecking ball against my chest. Sharp squeaks on sneakers met the sounds of heavy breathing.

And today was my lucky day because Silas was on skins.

I couldn't take my eyes off him. As he crouched low into a defensive position, knees bent, muscles rippling beneath his skin. His arms were raised, taut and ready, blocking his opponent with a kind of fluid strength that made my pulse race. As he shifted, I caught the motion of him tugging the bottom hem of his shorts higher up his thigh, revealing a glimpse of hardened muscle—smooth, defined, and dangerously tempting.

I felt a wave of heat rise in my chest, my breath catching in my throat. I couldn't look away. My heart hammered in my chest, and for a moment, I thought I might actually stroke out.

I should not go to the gym when I'm ovulating.

Ginger gripped my arm as we stood like slack-jawed voyeurs. Sweat poured off their toned bodies. Someone dunked the basketball, and another guy slapped his ass—a common gesture among athletes—but the way Ginger salivated it looked like she had new weekend plans.

"Two at once?" I tossed around the idea to her.

"Don't be so nonchalant about that." She tightened her smile and shrugged her shoulders, a blush creeping up her cheeks. "It's serious business."

Silas made his way over to the bleachers, grabbed a small black towel to dab at the sweat pooling on his forehead. Wet strands of hair clung to his skin, damp and tousled, framing his face with a raw, untamed look. The sight of him, all sweaty and rugged, sent a rush of heat to every nerve ending between my thighs. The soft wisps of hair, so close to my reach....*fuck.*

I ducked below the window, maneuvering into an awkward crab walk. "They saw us gawking," I whispered in a panic to Ginger.

"Why do you think they play without their shirts anyway?" Ginger asked, her tone laced in sarcasm. She leaned against the wall.

Still hiding, I crossed my arms as a chill transferred from my stomach to my arms. I was wearing only a blue sports bra and itty-bitty black spandex shorts. I reached for my bag to grab more clothes, but Ginger snatched my duffle out of my hands.

"What are you doing?" I hissed.

"He's not wearing a shirt, either. I want to see how this plays out."

"You're an enabler." My heartbeat quickened. Silas was four breaths away. "I look okay?"

"Glowing."

"You mean sweaty."

"I mean, it's going to send him into orbit."

I stood back from the door when it swung open. "What

are you doing here?" Silas grinned, playful in his tone. He knew damn well what we were doing—nothing but Peeping Janes.

My brain worked overtime to find words and form a sentence. I had to force them out of my mouth. "I took a barre class with Ginger."

"Did you like it?"

A prickle raced around my spine. "So much."

When he spoke, his voice seemed to be directed to the dips and curves at my waist, each word brushing against my skin. "I've heard it's hard," he said. "Was it hard?"

A bead of sweat released from my neck, flowing down my chest, getting trapped in between the canyon of my breasts. My mouth dried. I looked toward Ginger, who suppressed a smile so hard her cheeks swelled to a pinched peachy color, and offered no saving.

Silas casually leaned against the wall, his bicep flexing with ease. He knew exactly what the hell he was doing. He grinned, fake subtlety not fooling me.

I pleaded with my dumb brain to make smart words. I entered the bargaining stage—I offered an organ on the black market in exchange for a coherent response. "Very."

Ginger rolled her eyes and tightened her cardigan belt over her attire. She threw my jacket and pants at me. "You have that appointment, Alice, remember. We got to go."

Silas' wide, beaming smile tore something open inside me. As he stepped closer to me, I counted the number of droplets draining down his chest. His voice was low when he said, "I'll text you my address."

"K." I waved with my fingers, and Ginger jerked me by my arm down the hallway.

"Oh my God, he has you dick stupid."

"It's nothing."

"Nothing?" she questioned with a heavy dose of skepticism. "If I didn't know you were in *heat*, I would've thought you were having a catastrophic medical event."

Of course, I was heavily attracted to Silas. He was timeless, like war-torn lovers reuniting. Nonsense like acts of war and desperate, foolish games made sense if the man was someone as charming as Silas.

I thought I could keep a boundary between us, but each day that weakened like a flimsy wall made of straw. The closer I became to my new friends, the harder it was to stay neutral about my time in Tidings. When I thought about leaving, a twinge of uncertainty sluiced through me.

We stopped in the foyer to dress before we went outside. "Am I *conquestable*?" I asked Ginger, pulling on my sweatpants and zipping up my parka. She gave me a look, and I tried to explain. "Like would I be someone that a man would endure a conquest for?"

"Are you asking me if you're Helen of Troy? Cleopatra?"

"No." I took a deep breath before opening the doors. "You said Silas was pursuing me, and I haven't stopped thinking about why he would do that."

"We've been over this." She held her hands out like a female presenter on The Price is Right, closely examining above my waist—the prize, she seemed to suggest. "And now he's seen that perky chest out of a sweater and oversized feather-stuffed jacket."

I rolled my eyes. If Ginger thought that's all I had to offer men, I was never going to date again. "I'm more than just a body, Ginger. No offense, but I don't need to sling my vagina around."

"Is that what you think of me? Didn't take you to slut shame, Alice," she said, anguish undoubtedly behind each word. "Intelligence and sexuality are not mutually exclusive traits, and my sexuality is a natural and empowered expression of self-confidence and desire."

"No," I shook my head, my face flushing with embarrassment at my outburst. "I didn't mean it like that." I wanted to apologize, to explain myself, but doing so would mean admitting what lay beneath my fragile self-esteem. I was a stale, unemployed woman with nothing to bring to the table. Self-deprecating humor and bouncy tits were not going to win out in the end. That wasn't how the real world worked.

We didn't speak for the remainder of the walk. I went to my room, and she went to her lab or wherever she went to concoct her evil plans. Ginger had a mysterious layer draped over her. She always appeared to be three steps ahead of whatever I was thinking, with an intelligent reply for everything.

She alluded to magic in Tidings, as if it was something omnipresent or sentient. She was the scariest woman I'd ever met, but she seemed to tuck herself in when she'd mention the magic of Tidings. Ginger, the girl with her boot on everyone's neck, was also extremely superstitious.

I cried in the shower then plopped myself on the sofa with my phone, texting Patrick before typing my name into Google. My stupid viral story had been pushed to the second page of searches, and instead, thankfully, the first page was linked to my private social media accounts and Pinterest board I hadn't used in months. No better time to try a new recipe or craft project than when you're locked inside a snow globe.

Patrick texted back his disappointment that there wasn't a dating app in Tidings named "Ho Ho Hoes."

Patrick: This could be a grand business venture.

Alice: I'm not inventing a slutty dating app for the North Pole.

Patrick: Are elves there?

Alice: Elves aren't real.

Patrick: That you know of…

I paused my back and forth with Patrick when Silas' name flashed across my screen.

Silas: I'm held up a bit, would a ride share be okay? I'll get a safe car to pick you up tonight.

Alice: Thanks. See you at 6.

CHAPTER 15

ALICE

From the back of a decked-out Subaru that could easily maneuver up a snow-covered ski hill, I gave myself a pep talk. I wasn't in the mood for small talk with the driver and was left alone with my own thoughts, terrifying as they may be. I needed to be crystal clear with Silas that I was here for a good time, not a long time. I wanted to get to know him without getting my heart broken, and if we were on the same page going into it, that wouldn't be a problem. It could be fun, and hot, then we would part as pleasant footnotes in each other's history of our time in Tidings.

Be that as it may, tonight was clearly a date. Silas greeted me at the door with a gentle kiss on my cheek, offering me a glass of wine.

I unfastened my heavy winter coat, giving me time to flutter my eyes around his house. Built like an expansive log cabin, the vaulted ceilings gave it an airy, open feel, yet cozy with a bright crackling fire, plush leather furniture, and thick rugs over the hardwood floors.

It was more than simply inviting; it was somewhere that felt... like home. My suite was luxurious and comfortable, but it never let me forget it was temporary with a foreign smell that never settled.

As Silas moved about his home confidently and relaxed, I scanned the books on his shelf, running my hands across the spines. Bible-thick, intimidating medical texts on the top shelf, and below was a collection of biographies and sci-fi. "Typical nerd."

"I heard that!" He shouted from the kitchen, his voice carrying over a loud sizzle. I could smell the delicious aroma of butter and garlic sautéing. I picked up a picture frame of a group of young kids I presumed were Silas, Dagny, and their siblings. I hoped to find evidence that Silas had not always been *this* way. That before he blossomed later in life as a perfectly handsome and confident man, he was just another awkward, lanky teenager like a wobbly foal searching for its legs.

"Son of a bitch," I muttered under my breath. "Of course, he's always been hot." I pulled a book out with the letters USMLE. "What's 'you smile?'"

"Show me?" He carried two glasses of red wine from the kitchen, clinking his glass against mine and holding eye contact as we sipped. I forgot what we were talking about, and a heaviness settled between my ears. He tucked my hair behind my shoulder, grazing his fingertips across the back of my neck. "What did you ask, Alice?"

I cocked my head toward the bookshelf, pointing at the letters. "U-S-M-L-E. You smile."

His eyes widened and he shook his head. "No. No. Not 'you smile,' *definitely* not 'you smile.'" He wiped his hands on the towel tucked in his back pocket and reached for the book. "This was the most important, most dangerous, most terrifying book of my life. It was the first board exam you take during med school. If you fail it, you can kiss being a doctor goodbye."

"Need therapy for that trauma?"

"I still have nightmares."

"Maybe you guys should be compensated for pain and suffering. And get rid of the book if it's such a trigger."

He pinched my chin gently between two fingers, biting down on his lips as he scanned my face, then tucked the massive book back on the shelf.

"Did you ever get an *F* in your life?"

"Be real, Alice."

Snarky Silas was so hot.

I followed him to the kitchen, prodding for more. "What about a *B*?"

A cocky smile answered in reply. No words necessary.

"What aren't you good at?"

"Wouldn't you rather be surprised?"

"Not particularly. I don't like surprises."

He sharpened a knife with a tool he removed from the drawer. I watched in total horror as he finely chopped mushrooms and onions. With precision like a world-class chef, he sliced the knife through the vegetables at lightning speed. I covered my eyes with my hands in case he cut off a fingertip. The sound of the knife reverberating off the cutting board came to a still, and footsteps filled its space.

"Hey," he said, pulling my hands down, "Trust me. Relax. Drink some wine."

"You're dangerously close to the sharp edge of the very pointy, very stabby knife and I'm not really good with blood."

He moved back to his position as skilled chef in front of the cutting board. "Well, I am, so it's fine."

I scoffed. "But if you start to lose a lot of blood and go into shock, who's going to have to save you? Me."

He picked his gaze up from the cutting board, narrowing his eyes at me as he flawlessly tossed a mushroom from one hand to the other, dropping it on the board, then mincing it into tiny pieces.

I was more desperate than ever to find a flaw in him—that was my new goal. And if I failed, I'd turn him over to the government for scientific experimentation.

"You're sick."

He grinned with a mischievous glint in his eye. "Can you trust me?"

I huffed out a laugh. "That's asking a lot. A strange man with a knife wants me to trust him."

"Come here," he said, and nudged his chin toward his left shoulder, showing me where to stand. I watched as he tossed the mushrooms and onions in a small saucepan with butter, garlic, and sprinkled in salt and pepper. As the ingredients sizzled, he put his hands on my shoulders and the intensity of his eyes burned into me. "You have to relax. I'm safe. You're safe. Your biggest concern should be that Snøfnugg's going to jump on the table and steal your steak."

My gaze mirrored his to the oval dining room table, two place settings arranged across from each other, intensifying the sense of intimacy—the building of trust. I hated having secrets, but no one gave me the guidebook on how or when, or even if it was necessary, to confess an embarrassing incident.

Silas moved around the kitchen in a well-accustomed measure, at ease with utensils and the precise temperature at the gas stove for cooking meat on a stainless-steel pan. "Have a seat," he said. I made my way to the table where I was served like a fine dining restaurant, topping off my wine glass before presenting the carefully constructed plate before me.

I'd never been more romanced in my life. He'd pulled out all the stops for this brief and wild love affair.

And if he didn't know what he was doing, he was lying. But why the hell *me*?

"Did you invite me over for a fancy steak because I have nice tits?"

He reared back, reaching for a napkin that he balled into his fist and held at his mouth.

"I thought nothing shocked you," I teased.

"You do," he said, fighting for air.

A teasing smile played on my lips. I wiped the corner of my mouth with the silver linen tablecloth I had draped in my lap. I turned up the dial, moaning over a perfect piece of steak and complimented his skills. Cooked to a perfect medium, coated with mushrooms and onions, served with baguette slices topped with black truffle butter, and mashed sweet potatoes.

"You know, if being a doctor doesn't work out for you, you could always be a private chef. I bet you'd make a lot of money cooking for thirsty women."

He hummed a response, and a pink tint spread across his cheeks. "So, am I here because of my tits? They're that steak-worthy?"

"No," he said all too quickly, and then shook his head like he was reversing his explanation. "Yes, I mean, they're all kinds of worthy but—" he blushed. "You caught me off guard and I am still trying to find the right way to say this."

"You're not being graded. Tell me what you're thinking. No filter."

His eyes flicked down to my chest and if his white-knuckled grip on the stem of his wine glass was any indication, he was hanging on by a thread. I found it utterly delightful.

"I like being around you," he said. "You're funny... and yes, very beautiful."

As a woman who frequented college bars for years, I was no stranger to flattery. I wasn't as familiar with sincerity, and his emotions lit up across his face like Christmas lights—vibrant and impossible to ignore. I wanted him to stop talking about me, and instead pull me onto his lap and show me what he *thought* of my glorious tits and long hair.

"You have caramel cake for dessert."

"It's from the bakery," he replied, settling his face in one hand. "I thought you'd want a change from all the peppermint."

"Well, that was very considerate. By the way, about peppermint... doesn't anyone get tired of it?"

"Maybe the transplants." He poured the last of the Pinot Noir in each of our empty glasses. "But to the locals, it's their bread and butter."

"Have you always liked to cook?"

"Not until I bought a cast iron skillet with my first big-boy paycheck. Probably one of the best purchases I've ever made, and it's earned its cost per use."

"I get that." I twirled my finger around the rim of my wine glass. "The best purchase of my life was wool socks at Needle & Wool last week. Now I don't have to worry about losing a toe."

Silas grinned and adjusted himself in his chair, crossing one leg over his knee. His foot bumped mine and we stilled inconspicuously. He stood and reached his hand out for mine, walking me to the living room, before standing chest-to-chest, boring his eyes into mine.

"Look, I think what you were alluding to is... am I trying to wine and dine you, then fuck you?"

Another observation—Silas Hill had a dirty mouth. And it ignited a deep, primal warmth through my veins, the kind of heat that sparked a thousand other ideas of things I wanted to know about him. Mostly involving the removal of clothes, and what his body would unleash when it was set on fire.

Boom.

CHAPTER 16

SILAS

The dim lighting reflected off Alice's hair, shimmering like a golden halo, effortlessly catching my eye. But her expressive eyes were wide and unguarded, as if my directness had shifted something in the air between us. I moved to the sofa, relaxing against the softness, and crossing one leg over. A perfect opportunity to drink her in — every curve, every subtle shift, every silent reaction.

I hadn't come this far to stop now.

"And the answer is yes. I absolutely want you, Alice." Now that I'd said how I felt, I made it obvious... my gaze ran up and down her body, taking in the rapid rise of her chest, to the nervous tight fists she held under her chin. She unclenched one hand, and bit down on her thumbnail. I groaned and cleared my throat.

I was about to pull her down to me when she crossed her arms and said, "You say that to all the women you bring here?"

"I've never brought a woman here for that... I can see how you might think that, but I haven't had a lot of free time for that kind of thing." She stood as I sat on the couch, towering over me. I'd let her be imposing for as long as it took for her to get comfortable. I bit my lip to hide my smile.

"Everyone has time for hookups."

"Sure." I leaned back against the couch, resting my head on my hands. "But I'm not lying. This house is a virgin, if you will."

She rolled her eyes and scoffed. "I wasn't born yesterday."

"Take a seat, Alice." Her expression flinched, and I chuckled.

She exhaled a deep breath and sat on the other side of the couch. Fair enough.

"I'm not trying to be jealous or anything; I just don't care for bullshit."

"I don't either," I said, agreeing with her. I patted the open cushion next to me, and she maneuvered her body a bit closer with a wiggle of her hips. That would do for now, but I desperately wanted to eliminate anything that could be viewed as space between us. Alice's long hair was pinched behind the couch, and I picked it up, rolled it around my fist and tossed it on the other side of her shoulder. With casual indifference, I reached my arm across her back and rubbed the strands between my fingers.

"I like your hair like this," I said softly. "Your bun is hot in a serious type of way, but this looks more like you."

She smiled and leaned into me. I kissed behind her ear, teeth delicately skimming across her skin. Her neck rolled like a cat, exposing the best spot to make her purr. I whispered, "No man is waiting for you back in Arizona, right?"

She blew out an exasperated sigh. "No, not anymore. We moved in together too fast. It wasn't right... and here I am."

I didn't know how to feel about that answer. She was running from something. Searching for new beginnings.

She flinched as I drew my hand back from touching her, even though every other part of my body ached for her. "Are you okay?"

"Yeah, I'm not hung up on him after all. Rebuilding my life is more complicated than getting over a shitty guy."

"How so?"

She reached out, stroking a thumb along my neck, and I clenched my fists by my side. She watched the circle she drew just below the angle of my jaw. I needed a distraction while she talked it through. I turned my gaze to a set of beady eyes staring back. I slapped the empty cushion to my left, inviting my dog up.

Alice reached across my lap to scratch Snøf's ears—so much for slowing things down. I flinched and grabbed her hand, holding it across my waistband.

"What about you?" she asked, watching as her hand rested close to where a bulge was forming. I let go, instantly missing the warmth of where her hand had been for a microsecond.

"I was so focused on getting into med school, and then once I did, there was zero time for dating, since every test can make or break you."

"So, you never had relationships?"

Snøfnugg's head curled and relaxed in my lap as she looked up at me with droopy brown eyes. Alice sipped her wine before scooting into me. I hadn't talked about Lia in years. It wasn't that I was still hung up on her—she was just a chapter that no longer mattered. She wasn't the right one for me, not in the end. I see that now. But back then, I think I just wanted to check "long-term relationship" off my to-do list, like it was some kind of accomplishment rather than something real.

"Mostly stress-relieving hookups lately."

"Couldn't picture you as a one-night stand kind of guy."

"It wasn't to be a jerk. I was pretty clear up front what my priorities were."

"You got through schooling, and now your reward is the snow bunnies or whatever Ginger referred to them as." Pressed together, our palms reached nuclear levels of heat. Only one dog ear and a zipper separated us from a hand job.

"I don't date tourists," I said emphatically.

But I wanted to get to know *her*. Unfurling her tight, slicked-back bun was a good first step, like she'd let me see her natural hair as it lay. But the conversation felt like we were dancing around, avoiding the real situation and searching through deep, murky water for something we could simply find with a spotlight—the truth.

"Is this a date or just steak and snuggles with your dog?"

"I didn't have the dog in mind when I thought about you on the couch with me," I replied, scratching Snøfnugg's ears. She was full-on snoring.

Alice pulled her hand from the dog's head, and my eyes focused on my knee where she stroked her thumb. She lifted it up like she was unsure of herself. We stared awkwardly at my now bare knee, and she tapped her fingers along the couch, as if examining the craftsmanship.

"I don't always think through my decisions," she confessed.

"With me or in general?"

"Don't you think you're special," she teased.

I bit down on my cheek then grinned. "And you don't?"

"It's beneath you to fish for compliments."

I clicked my tongue. "If I was, I'd probably take my shirt off and ask if my six-pack was symmetrical."

"Well, I've already seen it and I hate to break it to you but it's disgusting," she laughed, leveraging the movement of her bouncing shoulders closer toward me.

I ran my thumb across her bottom lip and her breath hitched.

"I wouldn't—" she stopped herself before she finished her thought.

"What?" I was shocked at my own breathy tone sounding like a plea.

She shook her head and smiled. "Nothing."

I was exhausted. Tired of trying to unravel what Alice kept to herself. Tired of Tidings and the thinly veiled threat that fate was somehow to blame—or thank, depending on how one felt toward it—for the "gifts" it bestowed upon those it called here.

Ginger and others had said since day one that *Tidings only allowed in those who it wanted to be here*, like it was a breathing body with a brain capable of making decisions.

But all I'd ever felt was pressure. Fucking pressure to save lives, to smile, to not offend anyone, to be grateful to even be here.

Allegedly, magic was all around me. All I had to do was pull my head out of my ass and embrace it. But if it was magic, why was I hanging on by a goddamn thread, so bare it would snap with the next lightest pull?

Alice was the most out-of-place tourist or temp I'd ever seen in four years. For fuck's sake, she didn't even have a winter jacket. Yet I'd been tethered to her like that invisible gossamer thread Ginger warned me about.

I was a scientist. Cerebral. Critical thinker. We were responsible for our own decisions—and our own destiny.

Nothing would pull us here or keep us here against our will. Alice wasn't here to stay, to build a life in Tidings. She was essentially a tourist with a paycheck. Soon she'd be gone, and I'd be someplace else, too, with a broken heart.

I began to push myself out of the couch, to stand up like a man and tell her whatever this was—if we were anything at all—had to end before it confused the both of us more. Or made things more painful.

She blurted out, snapping my thoughts apart. "Do you like hockey?"

"Hockey?" I asked perplexed, like she suggested we rob a bank. The flippant turn in conversation was enough to make the wine swirl in my brain, too. "Sure, I guess. I don't have time to watch a lot of sports. But I don't hate it. Do you like hockey, Alice?"

She shrugged non-committal. "Can't say I've ever watched a game.

"Huh," I muttered. Was this twenty questions time? "Are you happy in Tidings?"

"I miss skirts."

"You can wear skirts here." I used every psychological trick in the book to keep my eyes from looking down at her hips, imagining her bare legs in a skirt, wrapped around me. God, I could slip in so easily—

"—not if I want to keep my lower appendages, which I happen to be a fan of."

"I am too." I nudged the dog off the couch, my composure all but fucking gone.

She cleared her throat. "But overall, Tidings has been good to me, though I don't know why I deserve that."

"You don't need to be so self-deprecating." Anger seeped into the words, layered with frustration, confusion, and a rush of rising blood pressure. "You're beautiful and intelligent, and witty enough without sacrificing yourself."

"It's not for the expense of a laugh." Her outer shell hardened. I could see walls rising like a surge barrier, holding back encroaching flood waters. "I'm—"

"Defensive? Guarded?" I answered for her.

Her eyes flared. A bear poked. I clenched my jaw so tightly I thought I heard a tooth crack.

"Protective." She stood, releasing herself from our embrace. A cold gust of air blew across my arm where her head had rested.

"Protective of what?"

"That's enough vulnerability for one night."

I reached for her, wrapping an arm around her lower back and holding her steady like a kickstand.

"Hey," I said, my voice like a plea. "What happened?"

"I should go. I'm sorry I ruined this evening." Alice's palms rubbed against the wrinkles in her shirt when she stood, then she walked toward the door.

"You didn't ruin anything," I called after her. "I wanted to spend my free night with you."

She hurriedly zipped up her heavy jacket and tightened the belt so hard around her waist that I thought it'd knock the air out of her lungs.

"Silas, I am not someone really worth getting to know."

"Why don't you let me be the judge of that?"

"You're too goddamn nice. It's a little unnerving if I'm being honest. Look, Tidings is a placeholder. This was an unusual opportunity. One that fell into my lap. Literally a call out of the blue. You've got a mortgage and a dog, and dinners planned for next week. I don't even have an electric bill in my name."

"Too nice?" I rubbed the back of my neck and crossed

my arms, fixing my gaze at my feet. If I wasn't too nice, then I was a grumpy asshole, according to Ginger. Right now, I was teetering on combustion, and not just from my dick. "Wrong place, wrong time, right?"

I exaggerated a smile and felt a tightness pull across my chest. A crushing blow, just like it was the last time I had my heart broken.

"Right. Thank you for understanding." She tightened the bag straps over her shoulder; the hesitation on her face made me think she was pleading somewhere between *"Let me go now"* and *"Say something to save me from myself."*

"Can I drop you off at home, please? I'd feel better taking you than an Uber with the way this snow is coming down now."

We drove in silence. I parked in front of the lodge, keeping a firm grip on the gear. My eyes didn't meet hers as I unlocked the door. My thoughts were coiled and kinked along the path, like we were losing air in the cab of my truck. The lack of oxygen made me dumb.

"Look, Alice—"

"—Thanks for the ride." She slammed her lips shut, holding back anything else burning on the edge of her tongue. "Self-preservation is all I know right now."

I swallowed hard as I scanned her face. At first, I was interested in the asymmetry of her face. One eyebrow had a stronger arch than the other, her cupid's bow pointed slightly dramatically, and her brown eyes reflected hazel tones in different lighting.

The wheels were spinning behind her eyes, like she was contemplating the right words to say next.

"I don't expect you to understand," she continued, "and I wouldn't want you to ever know what my life has been like. You are unscathed, and I mean that as the nicest compliment I can give."

"On a scale of one to jilted bride left at the altar, how bad?" I shifted my weight across the seat and rolled my head along the back of the leather headrest toward her. I held her eyes and she stared back. She didn't bat an eyelash. My vision traced the heart shape of her face, fixating on the wrinkle that popped out next to her mouth when her lips twitched.

Silence became the third person in the car with us. She blew out a breath that fogged the window.

"I know what it feels like to have something clawing at you from the inside," I said, gripping the steering wheel and overthinking how much to reveal. Something tightened in my throat, and I briefly considered shutting my mouth entirely. But I turned to her again; she looked like a spool of thread about to unravel down a long hallway. I swallowed hard and spoke so quietly it could have been only for me. Perhaps it was. "Crying out to escape. And no one to hear."

Her eyes welled with moisture and without a word, she jumped out of my truck like her hair was on fire, landing ankle-deep in fresh snow. I wanted to steal a glance over her shoulder, but it never came. I wasn't sure if I was disappointed or impressed at her restraint.

CHAPTER 17

SILAS

I'd blown Ginger off too many times to play the exhaustion card again, so I had to show up when she asked for help to make snack bags for senior bingo night. Because I wanted to keep both of my testicles, I avoided arguing with her that the sugar overload would send elderly heart failure patients to my emergency department tomorrow night. Ginger would make an excellent drill sergeant. Or an embalmer.

I was on the dumb end of the candy-making assembly line tying a twisty knot on a plastic bag full of white chocolate-peppermint-coated pretzels and raisins. Alice would hate this. I could hear her complaining about the peppermint, maybe offering an alternative flavor like marzipan.

"Something funny, Hill?" Ginger using my surname had always grated on me, like a coach tearing down a player for a bonehead move.

"Alice hates peppermint," I said as I twirled a plastic bag tie closed. "If she were here, you'd never hear the end of it."

"Maybe you should have invited her like I suggested. Team building and all that."

"Isn't that your job?" I scoffed. "I'm not on her team, anyways." In any sense of the word, it seemed. I wondered why I even put forth effort if I were to only be banished to the friend zone with Alice. Time wasn't exactly on our side, either. The clock in Tidings was ticking like a time bomb.

"Ah," she nodded. "Landing in the platonic bubble by a love interest is something you do to yourself, Silas."

I snapped my fingers, indicating for her to hurry up. "I'm out of bags. Less talk, more work." I sidestepped deep diving into my relationship failures with the Ice Queen like I avoided multidrug-resistant gonorrhea.

"Must suck to get friend zoned. How does it feel?"

"If I'm not mistaken, *I* drew the line on you years ago."

"Ew, don't remind me. That's when I was lonely and desperate." She gave me a steely eye. "Don't say it. I'm still desperate... but controlled."

Ginger and I had a blurry relationship. Somewhere between a brother and sister pestering each other, and an ex-girlfriend (which she was not) who stalked my social media (which I hadn't used in years). She was part of my onboarding process to Tidings, but she didn't officially work at the hospital, so we became friends instead of colleagues. She turned that into a license to share too much personal information. She was helpful, reliable, and a party owl. A good friend, despite her tendencies to annoy the hell out of me, she was unabashedly honest, loyal as a Marine and protective of the people in her life. But nosy as hell.

Ginger paused at her station to furiously type out on her phone, simultaneously speaking to me. "I do like Alice, you know. She is less...*froufrou* than other prissy bitches who have circled your block."

"Prissy bitches?" I held my empty hands out and snapped my fingers, signaling my boredom in the lame section. Ginger's hands moved quicker, stuffing the bag with pretzels and tossing a few new ones my way before I growled again.

"Remember Jenna? She threw your phone in the snow."

"She was insane," I said with a pointed glare. "She was jealous I was on the phone with my mom."

"Yeah, she really put your relationship on ice."

"Wasn't a relationship," I muttered.

"That's probably why she was so pissed then."

It was past due time to admit that the regular rotation of temporary visitors had gone stale. I was tired, completely exhausted if I were honest, of the same in, same out. With the women I'd see, it always began with small talk over drinks, or dinner if my time was generous, then back to her hotel. We'd fall asleep with her moving over to snuggle, and I'd placate her until she fell asleep. I always left a note on the table and went home quietly in the night.

I didn't lie to Alice. I didn't seriously date and I never brought a woman back to my house. I wasn't an asshole to women. I respected them, which was why I told them exactly what to expect from me —I never wanted to go through what I did with Lia again. On either side.

When I spotted Alice on the train, I instantly knew she was a first timer. That petrified look on her face told me she thought she was entering a cult and regretted not asking more questions before agreeing to come here.

Despite drowning in a sea of work emails that begged for a scowl, I couldn't help but smile at her across from me. I caught her reflection on my computer screen, and I couldn't resist tilting it, ensuring it framed her face perfectly. She was gorgeous, and her expressive moods amused me. The woman would be terrible at poker. Or delivering STD news to a patient.

Ginger clapped her hands in front of my face, earning a displeased look from me. "I was saying…" Ginger waved her hands in an arc like a name broadcast in Hollywood lights. "*The Reformed Playboy, M.D.*"

"I was not a playboy. I don't have the sociopathic tendencies to qualify."

Ginger harrumphed and muttered something under her breath about mansplaining. She walked back to her station at the front of the table, giving me space to breathe and a much-appreciated reprieve from her hovering.

I couldn't shake the returning thoughts that my time in Tidings was up. It felt like that sensation when you realized it was time for a haircut. Strands fell a bit too long, and your ears started to itch, signaling change was due.

Years ago, I thought Tidings could be my forever home. I couldn't imagine walking away from its magic and adventure. It was like no other place on earth. Each year, I continued to push aside small, pestering grass-is-greener contemplations, knowing once I had a glimpse of those purple and green Northern Lights, I'd fall for Tidings all over again.

I'd been under Tidings' spell long enough. I was an asshole who couldn't decide if it was my forever home or a place I couldn't stand a second longer.

I decided months ago that I needed a change for my mental health and to rescue my precarious Vitamin D levels. I knew it was time to put Tidings and its promises behind me—and then that woman from Arizona arrived and I was so far gone for her I wanted to convince her to stay with me.

Something stronger than Tidings' enchantment overpowered me. And suddenly, I wanted a white cottage with green grass, swinging on a hammock under a willow tree... with Alice.

"How's Dagny's studying coming?" Ginger asked.

I grunted. "She's not taking the MCAT seriously."

"Maybe it's the right amount of serious for her."

I pointed my finger at her. "Don't you start."

"Don't you point your finger at me. I'll saw it off."

Damn, she would, too.

Dagny had followed me to Tidings, committing to studying a year for the MCAT and then she'd leave to go to medical school. But one year turned into two and now she was trapped in Tidings' black hole of despair.

I didn't care if I was a brute for assuming responsibility to keep an eye on my little sister. Med school wasn't for the weak, and it was important to have support nearby. I wanted to give that to her. If Ginger was a nosy, bossy "big sister" to me, then I was the grunting caveman to Dagny. But Dagny and I shared a last name and I'd been raised to safeguard what was mine.

"You know I have to keep my head on a swivel for Dagny," I said.

When Dagny went through a difficult time in high school with some asshole boys, I was a first-year medical school student. I was forced to watch from hundreds of miles away as she was on the receiving end of social media bullying. She lied to my parents, skipped school to go be a cliché and skip rocks at the river under a bridge. A passerby called the police about a homeless kid needing a welfare check and when he showed up at my mom's office with Dagny in tow, it was enough to kick-start my scary big brother persona.

One night, after a group study session, where I spent

more time tracking cruel comments on her page than paying attention to the guide for my first anatomy test, I couldn't take it anymore. Instead of going back to my shitty studio apartment, I turned onto the interstate and drove five hours to my childhood home.

By morning, I was following one of the assholes along his walking route to school. I towered over his punk ass with my six-foot-one frame and muscles of a grown man. I don't remember all I said, but it was enough motivation for him to lay off my sister. I may have tossed around arrogant med student bullshit like, "I know how to put you to sleep and remove all your toenails." I grossly exaggerated my medical skills (of which, I had precisely none), but a stupid teen boy wouldn't know that. The next day, I was back in class, having excused myself with a bullshit story about a stomach bug.

After that incident, Dagny was understandably mortified and hated me. She put me on ice for a few weeks until she came around, realizing how peaceful her life had become once the bullying stopped. I would always protect her from the bad guys and help her in whatever way she needed. And I hadn't stopped looking out for her since.

My phone buzzed in my back pocket, pulling me out of my deep thoughts. Hoping it was an emergency to call me into work and get me out of the hell hole candy stuffing work with Ginger, I was surprised to see a text from Alice. I hated how things ended last night, and I'd thought about reaching out to her a hundred times, but I figured giving her a little space was the best move. I was going to give her that space for twenty-four hours and if she hadn't reached out, I was going to grovel on my hands and knees.

Alice: Did you find a wool mitten in your truck? Sorry to bother you. If you find it, let me know where you are, and I'll come get it after my shift! Thank you.

I thought back to last night when I opened the door to see her on my porch. She was bundled up holding her wool-covered hands under her chin. I took each glove off, stroking my finger down her hand in a way that was unnecessary in a practical sense, but proved me right—we'd be explosive together.

We bobbed and weaved around whatever this was between us since the first day we met fighting over suitcases. The tension in the air between us was thick, but we never said it out loud.

The low-cut sweater she wore last night made sitting across from her at dinner an act of courage under fire. She threw out a question about her tits like we were having a neutral conversation about the damn weather, and the rest of the evening was a fight for my life under a lust-filled haze. I strained my eyes so hard the rest of the meal trying to keep them above her chin I thought I'd gone cross-eyed.

Alice's tits were spectacular; I wasn't fucking blind. A size slightly bigger than each palm, perfect for squeezing together and—

"Hey dummy." An honest-to-god spit wad landed on my cheek. I flicked it off and tossed an infuriating glare at the disgusting redhead in front of me. "Don't overthink it. It's going to work out in the end. Trust the Tidings' process."

I hesitated, scrubbing a hand under my beanie. "You mean Alice?"

She nodded, agreeing with what we both understood. I'd seen this work in Tidings before, the so-called magic, bringing couples and serendipitous events to the front, but I had never been in the center of it. I'd only recognized it when a little fireball from Arizona coincidentally began appearing everywhere the day I returned to Tidings *after* setting plans in place to leave.

Ginger tossed the last bag of snacks my way, hitting the edge of the table and spilling all over the floor. "Oops, can you get that? Gotta run!"

"I'm going to start calling you Coriander like Alice," I shouted to her back before she tossed me a middle finger over her shoulder.

Smiling at Alice's name on my phone still wedged in my palm, I lingered on the moment, contemplating my next move.

Silas: I can bring it to you.

I SEARCHED MY TRUCK AND FOUND ONE LONE WOOL GLOVE TUCKED between the seatback cushions. Even if I didn't find it, I would have bought every pair in this damn town if it gave me an excuse to see Alice today. I inhaled it, the aroma of warm vanilla and honeysuckle permeating my senses. I was drunk on her fragrance.

We needed to work through whatever the hell happened last night because I couldn't get her off my mind. The argument clawed at my brain like a hungry eagle scouring a lake for dinner. I knew I could be a patient, listening ear ready to give her whatever she needed.

I was on my way to the lodge when I received a call from my colleague that he desperately needed help. I grunted, but turned my truck around, driving through a fresh layer of unplowed snow. It was heavy and sticky on the back tires that fish-tailed on a hidden sheet of black ice beneath the powder.

I had a bad feeling it was going to be a difficult night.

My phone buzzed in the front pocket of my fleece vest. I held it between my ear and shoulder as I continued typing the patient's treatment plan for discharge.

"What is it, Dagny?" I said impatiently.

"Did you register me for the spring exam?"

"Yes."

"I didn't ask you to."

"I'm really busy. I'm exhausted. I don't have time to talk to you right now, especially if you're going to act like a petulant teen."

Pete jerked his spinning chair to a stop.

Dagny persisted. "We've got to talk about this, Si."

In my gut I knew what she wanted to say. I think I'd known it for a long time, but I never wanted to admit I had been wrong about her. I thought she could handle medical school. She was bright and smart, and I never wanted her to waste her potential.

"I've got one more note to finish and I'd like to go home," I said curtly. "It was a hell of a night."

"Make time to talk to me this week."

"Sure, okay." I hit the end button and tossed my phone on the desk. My fingers raced across the keys finalizing my notes. I logged out of the electronic medical records and removed my ID badge from the card reader. I stood and was met by a brick wall of a former soldier.

"I know you're stressed out," Pete said, arms crossed

and unmovable. "But get it under control. Talk shit at *me*. But not Dagny."

Red hot fury whipped inside me like a hungry, demolishing tornado ready to destroy everything in its path. I wasn't always like this. I prided myself on being sympathetic and found strength in my compassion, which made me effective and good at my job. The fuel was lighting a fire inside me, taunting me to let myself go.

A shit-ton of personal disillusionment didn't put me in the position to help anyone else.

"Mind your own fucking business, Nurse Pete."

I stormed out of the hospital without looking over my shoulder. When I got home, I laid in bed and stared at Alice's name on my phone, thumbing the blue button over a text message I so badly wanted to send.

CHAPTER 18

ALICE

A common misnomer when a woman comes to a small town is that she's looking for a hunky tree farmer to give her a modest ring and change her pathetic life around. Embarrassingly, I had romanticized that notion when the opportunity to flee my messy life in Arizona and come to Tidings came calling.

Tidings was like any other town—a place where I didn't belong.

Bumper Austin from that corny tabloid website emailed me again, pleading for an interview. No way in hell was I going to talk to him. I wanted this incident dead, and telling my side of the story wouldn't help the situation; it would only bring it back to life. I made a mistake I was fired for. There was nothing more to explain. I blocked his email, tossed my phone on the desk, and laid my head down.

"Are you done with the melancholy, pensive bullshit?" Ginger leaned over the front desk, her black glasses drawn underneath her chin. Her fiery hair was curled like an old Hollywood starlet with voluptuous, shiny curls.

"I'm fine," I said. I stapled paper receipts, succumbing

to Elvin's antiquated system. The overstuffed filing cabinet was working harder than a pencil skirt at Thanksgiving dinner. Earlier, I filled a box with decade-old customer receipts and stacked it against the wall in the back office. One of these days, Elvin would have to let these old receipts go. Today's box was dated from the eighties, for crying out loud.

"Lest I remind you, *Gingersnap*, you hardly know me."

"Haven't heard that one before," she muttered, tacking on a curse word under her breath. However possible, Ginger sounded more exasperated than normal. "I'm surprised no one has asked you if you'd ever been down the rabbit hole, *Alice*. And I know you well enough."

"I did and it brought me to a strange land called Tidings." The stapler jammed and I pulled a paper clip out to fix it, failing to finagle it loose. "Damn thing," I said to no one, smacking the stapler against the desk. "If we used modern technology I wouldn't be fighting with a stapler."

Ginger pulled the stapler from my hand, eyeing me like I was an unhinged woman with a weapon. She opened the top and stuck a long-manicured pinky nail in the slot, removing the jammed staple. "Do you know why I offered you the job?" she asked. "Maybe why I hired you out of the thousands of applicants?"

"You won't convince me that there were a thousand people who wanted to come to this tundra and work at a glorified hostel."

Ginger walked around the side of the desk and hunched over the back of my chair, holding me in place. She opened her laptop and furiously scrolled through an endless list of names and contact information on a gorgeous, color-coordinated Excel sheet.

I hadn't looked at a spreadsheet since I left Arizona. I missed that.

"If Elvin would approve the hours, I'd work extra to transfer records digitally. I could research and find the right software that even *he* could use once I left. This is a whole mess," I waved my hand in front of endless stacks of customer receipts. "Why is he so stubborn? This isn't effective and a waste of paper. Climate change and all."

"This is a list of everyone who applied for the job," Ginger said shoving her computer screen in my face, forcing me to look at the dozens of names who could take my position in a heartbeat.

Dispensable, replaceable, unremarkable. It was the same as always for me.

Freshman year in college, I had made quick friends with my dorm mates. We were flying high on fearless autonomy and the riskiness that came with newfound independence. No parents to hover or micromanage. But it was only shallow relationships built around parties, boys, drinking —experimenting. After the initial amazement simmered down, we drifted apart. They each found friends better suited to their interests and studies, and I was left standing alone in a large room. Literally. I organized a cookie decorating party for Valentine's Day in the dorm's recreation room and no one came. I spent the rest of the day hand delivering cookies across campus and became known as the "Cookie Girl" for the rest of the academic year. And not in a way that benefited me.

That hardly scratched the surface of feeling discounted and unnoticed. With Mark, his friends became my friends only superficially in group settings. And when I lost him, my money, and our apartment, so too gone was any semblance of a social life.

I wanted to understand why no one ever stuck around with me, not even my sister. If we weren't related by blood and parental guilt, I doubt we would even talk.

Here I was again, replaceable and forgettable, this time trapped in a snow globe like a frozen horror movie.

What was wrong with me? It wasn't anything superficial like halitosis. Was I... boring? Too accommodating? Lacking a backbone? My ex-boyfriend drained my bank account because I wanted to believe his promise to make me a millionaire in two years. I got swept up in the dream that we would travel the world, stay in five-star hotels, and enjoy fresh oysters and caviar, even though I hated seafood. Rich people loved it, and I thought I was going to be rich, too.

Tidings was my ultimatum—if I couldn't fix myself after this, I didn't know what the hell I would do with my life. I hated the snow and the peppermint everything, but maybe it could somehow be a saving grace. And that was the most asinine thing I'd ever thought.

Ginger perched herself on the edge of the desk facing me and closed her eyes. She looked like an exhausted single mom who worked two jobs. "I can't believe I have to do this with such smart, capable humans," she said.

I let out a dramatic sigh. "What are you talking about?"

She rubbed her temples. "You and Silas are intelligent on paper but quite dumb otherwise."

I stared at her.

She glared back.

Our staring contest continued until I widened my eyes and shook my head, giving her a nudge to finish her thought instead of leaving me playing a stupid game. "How are you the HR manager? Who can I report you to?"

She tapped her chest three times. "Me. Me. Or me." And

then she did something I never thought I'd see. She crouched down and held her head in her hands. Little noises came out of her and tears welled in her eyes.

I swallowed hard and tapped her shoe with the tip of my boot, like she was a badger that would snap at me if I got too close. I could handle snarky Ginger but this sensitive side of her scared the hell out of me. Emotional, crying Ginger was above my pay grade.

"Ging?" I said softly.

Her whimpers turned into full-on sobbing. I looked around the room hoping someone with experience to handle her would appear. I took a deep breath and crouched down next to her. "Are you okay? I was joking about reporting you. I'm sorry for teasing you so much. I thought that was our friendship —"

She pulled her hands off her face, scowled at me with red-rimmed eyes. "Tidings needed *you*, Alice. Probably more than you needed it."

I reared back. "To what? Swipe a credit card and hand over a room key?"

Ginger had real tears streaming down her face. I thought she was acting. Holy shit, she was genuinely upset.

"Nobody needs me, Ginger," I said quietly.

"Silas is leaving."

I flexed my eyebrows "Leaving what?"

"Here," she said, flinging her arms back with such force her knuckles hit the desk. "Tidings."

"What's your point?"

Her expression was so tightly restrained I wished we could capture her resolve and package it into an anti-aging serum. I gazed at her in awe. "How do you manage to keep your emotions so concealed? Is it the atmosphere? Did Tidings freeze your facial expressions?" Then, she smiled. It was subtle, but enough for me to notice. "You think I'm funny. Admit it. I won't tell anyone."

Ginger mumbled something under her breath and covered her mouth. I'd take that as a win. She gathered her composure, a nice reprieve from the ice queen aesthetic she usually wore. But her face was serious, like she was on the cusp of revealing a terminal illness with six weeks to live. "He's been trying to leave for a while. It took so much work to find you."

"I—" My tongue dried up and rampant thoughts searched for words. "What?" I sat on my heels, aware that at any point a customer would walk in, hearing whispers from women crouched down on the other side of the desk. "Ginger, enough with the riddles and the whole secretive mob wife demeanor. Tell me what is going on."

"Tidings wanted you and Silas here at the same time." Her voice was scarcely a whisper, more a fragile breath, barely touching the edges of sound.

A chill brushed my skin. I scanned the room like Ginger was referring to Tidings as a living *thing*, not a town, looking for her to pop up out of a corner.

Ginger rose from the carpeted floor and brushed off the back of her pants. She whispered, "Not any more than that. Tidings only brings the people who are meant to be here. Ask yourself: why are you here, Alice?" She tossed her bag over her shoulder, pulling her dark glasses over her eyes.

The door slammed shut behind her, leaving my mouth gaping, utterly stunned.

CHAPTER 19
ALICE

I picked at the smudge of red polish that had smeared before my nails dried, cursing at the small stain on my new white sweater.

From the inside of my suite, I heard Silas' sturdy voice on the other side of the door, laughing with Elvin. I opened the door and the sight of him took my breath away. He leaned heavily against the door jamb silhouetting his body, deliciously dressed in a heavy black jacket and matching scarf and beanie, with a backpack hooked over a shoulder. He dressed for warmth, but all I saw was a man dressed like he was up to no good. With the way he looked at me like that, I'd let him rob me. *Take what you want, Silas.*

He gave me a smile that punctured through my skin, simmering in my blood.

"Good afternoon," his voice was a low timbre. If he had any bit of nerves, his cool demeanor didn't show it.

"Hi to you," I piped out. I sounded giddy because I *was* giddy. He did this to me. I failed to hold my emotion in as my smile widened and heat bloomed beneath my layers.

I hardly slept last night thinking about Ginger's mysterious confession. Did Silas know Ginger was somehow behind this scheme to bring us together? Could he identify the emotions swirling in my eyes—intrigue, curiosity, longing?

But worst of all, I was laboring on skepticism and Silas' intentions with me.

Oh god, is it a blood-drinking cult?

"Shall we go?" he asked, reaching his arm forward. I flinched and tucked away my intrusive thoughts, hoping he didn't read my face to know I was thinking of him puncturing my neck with his teeth.

Despite the not-so-great way our last date had ended, Ginger's talk had given me a lot to think about. So when he texted me asking if I still wanted the ultimate Silas Tour of Tidings, I responded *yes*. Silas planned a full day of mandatory tourist to-dos, including a ride outside the city limits of Tidings to explore the wilderness and ending at the little cabin insulating us from the elements. The rest of the day would be a surprise for me, according to him. But he gave me enough information to be prepared. Snow boots and appropriate outerwear required.

Silas extended an arm, guiding me out the door first. I held my breath as I skimmed past him, hoping to feel an incidental finger graze, or a heated palm on the small of my back.

"Did you get enough sleep?" I looked over my shoulder and his eyelashes fluttered as he lifted his gaze, incinerating my insides. The tension was palpable. I cleared my throat, attempting to shake myself from the drunken spell he had me under. "I can't imagine working double shifts."

His shoulder bumped mine as we walked side-by-side. "I'm used to it," he said as he loosened the scarf around his neck like it was a necktie strangling him. But I didn't miss the way he ignored answering my question directly. "I thought about you."

Looking down at my feet, I blushed. "What did you think about?"

"How I don't want to disappoint you."

I clicked my tongue. "That's a low bar, to be honest."

He gave me a sympathetic smirk and I cringed at my self-deprecating joke. I didn't have a history to be proud of, nor the confidence to stand tall next to high achievers. I'd taken the opportunity to come to Tidings on a whim. Spontaneity was my forte, for better or worse. But over these few weeks I'd taken this blind leap of faith as a chance for a reset. I didn't have to glide through life on a whim anymore. I could do something I'd never done before and visualize the big picture. Perhaps that began with learning to practice self-respect.

A black horse outfitted in sleighbells on its harness stood at the head of a carriage waiting for us alongside the curb.

"That horse is a better parallel parker than me," I said, a lighter joke at myself this time.

Silas laughed. "First item on the ultimate tourist day, a horse-and-carriage ride." He tipped his head to the coachman and helped me up the steps.

"I've never been in a carriage before. Or this close to a horse's ass, unless you'd count my old boss."

Silas spread a blanket out across our laps and rested his arm above my shoulders on the seat behind us. The horse hitched in his gallop, and I squeezed Silas' leg over the blanket.

"Sorry, that startled me." I released my hand and searched through my purse for my mittens.

He handed me my missing glove.

"You found it!" I exclaimed.

"I'm sorry I didn't bring it to you earlier; I got really caught up with work."

We made small talk as the horse trotted through the main street. Everyone was out enjoying the bluebird day, a clear sky with fresh snow along the path.

For lunch, we arrived at a restaurant overlooking the roaring river, floating ice chunks racing downstream. Our window seat on the second floor looked like we were floating on top of the water, giving me a bit of apprehension. My fingertips pruned from sweat, the anxiety manifested in my body.

"Daytime is the best for the view here." He laid a white napkin in his lap and ordered us coffees and ice water, oblivious to my internal panic attack and completely unaffected by the precarious nature of our table dangling over an icy cliff. "I'm sure you were thinking it was unusual to go on a lunch date."

"I think it's more unusual to be a sneeze away from landing in that ice water below."

"Would you like to leave?" he asked earnestly.

"No, I'm a big girl. Very brave."

He lifted an eyebrow with suspicion, understandably so. "You can tell me if you're uncomfortable so we can make this more enjoyable for you."

"I didn't know I had a fear of heights."

He laughed. "Most people don't until they're stuck somewhere overlooking the earth below."

I took a deep grounding breath and tried to refocus. I wanted this to work because—damn—this was a once-in-a-lifetime opportunity that I should enjoy. But imagining myself plummeting into iceberg waters once was enough for me. "What are *you* afraid of?"

He smirked over the lip of his mug and winked. "Nothing."

We fell into easy conversation, long enough that the remaining sips of our coffee had gone cold, though our waitress topped them off twice. He told me about his experience when he first moved here years ago, and how lonely it felt to come home to an empty house after a long shift. Before long, he made good friends with his colleagues. And he loved that Dagny came up while she studied for the MCAT, until she had been studying a year longer than anticipated—a situation that rattled him more than I understood why. It was her business after all, her choice.

"You two seem close. I wish my sister and I had anything that resembled a relationship beyond the standard obligation." I hid the true reason for the distance between my sister and me: I was less interesting than the other aspects of her life that she'd need to put aside to make room for me.

"Dagny might not agree with you since she thinks I'm the world's bossiest older brother," Silas said. "She needs to get the MCAT out of the way and start the next chapter of her life."

"Why is she putting it off?" I asked, genuinely curious.

He shrugged, a subtle shift in his posture. "Your guess is as good as mine. You said your sister was a geologist? Where is she these days?"

"Your guess is as good as mine," I said, mirroring his earlier words. "But Dagny's seemed preoccupied lately. She canceled plans with Ginger and me a few times."

"You've made plans with them?" His eyebrows shot up, surprise flickering in his eyes.

"We even have a group text," I said, almost proudly, though I wasn't entirely sure why.

Silas' eyes widened even more, as if that revelation alone was enough to make him rethink everything. "Does that bother you? My relationship with your sister?" I asked, my tone softer now, almost tentative.

"Not at all," he said quickly. "You probably hear more from her than I do. Let me know if anything interesting happens." There was a weariness in his voice, an undercurrent of something unsaid that I couldn't ignore. He looked like he was carrying the weight of something he hadn't shared yet, something about Dagny that he wasn't ready to confront.

Feeling the growing tension between us, I shifted in my seat. "Do you know how much I hate peppermint?" I asked, hoping to change the subject, to lighten the mood a little. "But the smell is everywhere. It's like secondhand smoke. It clings to me no matter what. I can't get away from it," I said, my voice quiet, almost contemplative.

I didn't want to scare him off with the past I'd deliberately kept hidden in the shadows. I hadn't Googled myself in weeks, hoping the articles would find some darker corner of the internet to hide. And if he did ever find out I was the joke of the Southwest, we'd slice this thing between us off like a moldy part of a cheese wheel. Our fling was perfect for both of us. I'd wanted to kiss him from the first day I met him, and I suspected that we'd be heading there tonight, and god help me, I wanted to go further than that. I wasn't a classic romantic. I could separate physical attachments from deeper feelings.

Yet, I was terrified by how not terrifying he was. I felt strangely at ease with Silas.

"Alice?" His voice cut through my spiraling thoughts. "There's something I wanted to tell you."

My heart sank. "Sure," I said, trying to keep my voice steady.

"It doesn't change anything about us," he added quickly, his expression serious. "I just felt like you should know."

His words left me uneasy, and I tried hard to keep my face neutral, avoiding any emotion that might suggest fear or disappointment.

"I told you I hadn't seriously dated anyone in Tidings, and that's true," he began, his voice softening as he glanced around the room. "But during residency, I had a girlfriend. I was naive and thought maybe we'd get engaged. She broke up with me before I could even ask her. Honestly, it was for the best. I'm not heartbroken or anything. It's all in the past. But I wanted to be completely honest with you."

He bit his lip, a nervous gesture, clearly trying to hold back more words after the longest, most rambling speech I'd ever heard from him. Usually, Silas was quite composed.

"Did you love her?" I asked before I could stop myself. There was vulnerability in his gaze now, the kind that showed he wasn't sure what to expect next, but was wiling to face it.

"I don't know," he admitted, his eyes flickering with discomfort. "I told her I did, but I don't think you can fall out of love, and I definitely don't feel that way now. It was... safe, you know? But there was no spark."

Offering a comforting glance, I forced a sincere smile.

"No razzle dazzle, huh?" I teased, adding a dramatic flourish of cheesy jazz hands to lighten the mood. I wasn't upset at the context of what Silas told me, but it pained me that he had been honest with me, about something that made him uncomfortable.

I owed him my secret—one I wasn't ready to share.

Silas was charming as hell, and I couldn't understand why any worthy woman wouldn't want to be adored and cared for by him for the rest of their life. But why was he telling me this? Did he see us having a serious future? That thought sent a ripple of panic through me.

"Thanks for telling me," I said. "You didn't have to, but if it makes you feel better, then all's well, right?"

Silas hesitated, his eyes flickering between me and the window. He took a deep breath, the kind of exhale that felt like he was letting go of something he'd been holding onto for too long.

"Are you ready to go? We have an appointment in thirty minutes."

I smiled at him, tucking away my anxiety, and walked outside for the next phase of our date. The horse-led carriage took us to the snow park about a mile away. Silas pointed out monuments along the way and I shuddered when he showed me the peppermint factory. At a small hut-like structure perched among snow-draped hills, a staffer checked us in for our reservation of a snowmobile.

Silas tightened the straps on his backpack before picking up two black helmets, each with a sturdy visor and full-face mask.

"Well at least we're prepared to drive a race car 120 miles per hour."

"I don't mean to offend, but I wasn't sure if a girl from the desert knew how to drive one of these yet," he said as he clipped my helmet under my chin. I didn't take my eyes off his mouth and the way his throat worked when he swallowed. "I hope you're okay with me driving."

So okay. This was so, so okay.

"A smart choice, if you want us to live."

He tapped the outside of my helmet next to where my

ears were secured. "You can still hear me through the air vents, but once the engine comes on, you'll have to tap my shoulder or leg to get my attention."

I sat behind him and indulged in the required closeness of our bodies. I wrapped my arms securely around his waist. His backpack was small and snug tight to his body, and I rested my head on it like a pillow.

"Hang on tight," he shouted, his voice a louder, more commanding tone than normal.

Silas turned the key in the ignition and squeezed the throttle. The snowmobile roared to life beneath us, sending pulses and vibrations from my toes to my head. And most specifically, from my front through Silas' back.

"If you get scared, tap my leg," he yelled over the noise and grabbed my hand to show me where on his thigh to touch him.

I must have lost all common sense the second I agreed to come to Tidings. Here I was, placing my life in the hands of a man I'd only recently met. A capable, life-saving kind of a man. He hollowed me out and built a warm place to stay inside me.

At the first sputter of acceleration, I startled and squeezed his waist, closing my eyes.

"Open your eyes, Alice," he yelled over the engine.

"How did you know I closed them?"

"I could feel you. I'll take it easy on you at first. We won't go too hard if it scares you."

The words coming out of his mouth triggered a tighter grip instinct out of necessity for my fucking sanity. With my face tucked behind him and the adrenaline bumping courage through my veins, I yelled, "How do you know I don't want it hard?"

Silas gently released the throttle slowing us down. He

reached behind him and rubbed my leg. Quicker than I desired, his hand went back to the accelerator to speed us up over a small hill. I hated that accelerator. I was so jealous of that fucking accelerator and his hands squeezing it tight.

My skin was covered from head to toe in underlayers of wool and outerwear proofed for snow. Without an inch of skin to be brandished by the cold wind whipping past us, I was surprisingly warm pressed against Silas' back, the vibration of the diesel-fueled machine heating my core. Surprised I didn't hate it; briefly I thought the snow was beautiful.

Silas decelerated. I resented the idea of my perfect cocoon being ripped away from me. He stopped in front of a tiny wooden structure and turned off the engine.

"Is this where you go to hide the bodies?" I asked. He gave me a stern look through the visor and I was a weak-belly bitch for this man. "'Little cabin' might even be an overstatement."

"Actually, this is the cult's headquarters. The blood sacrifice ritual is around back."

I read the repartee in his eyes. "Do you eat your victims?"

"Only if you beg."

He reached his gloved hand into mine and helped me off the snowmobile, unbuckling the chin fastener on my helmet and removing it from my head. Without the tinted visor, I squinted into the sun, snow blind from the never-ending vast plain of snow. We were at the last vestiges of earth.

A chill ran up my back and I shivered even underneath stocky layers of wool and my winter parka that was as thick as a down comforter. "It's so cold."

"Yes, well, it is snow," he snarked. "Snow is, by design, below freezing."

"Cut me some slack. Until a few weeks ago, I'd never met a snowflake in my life."

He chuckled and draped an arm around my shoulder. His fingers tapped against it like he was playing piano keys, carrying the fresh and spicy scent of the nearby pine trees with the breeze.

"I'm forever fucking cold here." I missed how hot the Arizona sun felt on my skin, how it smelled warm, herbal, and floral.

He tucked me into his warmth. "We can start a fire inside."

"This is beautiful." And I meant it, but I had to force my frozen skin into a convincing smile. "I never would have experienced this if it wasn't for you. I'm cold but having fun. Thank you."

I was wearing snow pants, something I'd never in my entire thirty-three years on earth even looked at before. I was left with the only remaining option at Bror's boutique, a pair of hideous bibs. Suspenders draped over my shoulders pulling the pants up to an obnoxious high rise that created a shelf for my breasts and a long line up my ass.

The surrounding trees and isolating snow muffled the world into a serene silence. My heart raced at the breathtaking beauty. The snow-capped trees glimmered in the late afternoon light, like an untouched dreamscape. It felt like we were the last two people on earth wrapped in our own little world, with only the heavy weight of anticipation clinging in the air.

"So, now what?" I asked. We were so far from civilization it felt like we'd never be able to go back. Once you were here, you were here forever. It was a new world. A new reality. In the vast plains of nothingness but snow, nothing else mattered besides the present. Even as I tried to think about what I left behind in Arizona, it was like a movie reel that was jammed in the machine, images distorted and scratched.

"I brought dinner. It's nothing exciting, warm sandwiches from downtown. The aurora borealis is otherworldly here, even better than what you can see from your room."

From this vantage, the porch gave a full-circle view of the earth. A gentle hill rolled in front of us where the trees blackened in shadow from the sun. At night, the green and pink sky would reflect off the snow into pure magic.

"There's a lore about watching the northern lights from here." He stalked toward me with easy confidence—a cocky smile I'd learned he favored when he was teasing me. Playful even. "The *fabric of fate*,'" he said with air quotes, "If fate is pleased, the lights shimmer, like it's winking back at them."

I didn't know what to do with my hands, so I kept them tucked into my pockets. "Have you ever seen it, the magic or whatever?"

"No." Silas brushed his nose behind my ear, inhaling, and releasing a heated breath, skating along an exposed piece of skin. "You always smell so warm, like vanilla and yellow flowers."

I leaned into his touch, absorbing and transferring his body heat into me. His nose met that delicate, hypersensitive spot on my neck where scratchy facial hair tickled me, lighting me up from the inside.

"Do you believe in fate?" I asked.

I gripped the rail behind me and closed my eyes as his fingers laced in between mine, and he planted his lips on my jaw. The snow drifting from the trees—and his hot mouth—kissed my face.

"I'd like to find out." And finally, he took what his eyes pleaded for, locking his mouth onto mine. We kissed slowly, dreamily yet almost methodically, like we'd planned this moment for years, knowing our mouths would fit perfectly together. Silas' tongue brushed against mine and I couldn't resist the little whimper that floated between our mouths. He smiled in approval. My body was so flush with heat I unzipped my snow jacket and to my complete surprise I didn't regret the immediate brush of crisp air across my heated skin.

"You taste so good," he said. I tore my eyes from his mouth to the freckles dusting his nose, leftover kisses from the sun.

Silas grabbed my neck then slid his hands under my suspenders, toying with the cool fabric that created a gentle rustling sound, like leaves blowing in the wind. He pulled his mouth away from our locked lips, smirking like an evil mastermind who crafted a plan with red string and thumb-tacks on the wall.

Embarrassed by my awkward outfit, my cheeks flushed, a stark contrast to the chilled air around us. "This was all the shop had left. All the cute ones were gone," I said, sheepishly, exposed and awkward in the wilderness.

His grin widened, crooked and frisky as his tongue swiped over his bottom lip. Silas hummed as he ran his hands down my back, tracing the crisscross pattern of my suspenders.

"I love these," he said as he lifted them up off my shoulders and abruptly dropped them, snapping them against my sweater.

"They're ridiculous."

"Not a chance. I need to see this." Silas turned me around, putting the back of my outfit on full display to him. His hands took full, absolute liberty groping my ass. "Fucking hell," he groaned.

"What a dirty mouth you have."

"You have no idea," he said, breathless. He turned me around to face him. Pupils wide, glazed over and raring.

In a shocking revelation, I differentiated my hardened peaks from arousal and not sub-freezing temperatures. We stayed in that spot exploring each other, warming our shared cheeks through borrowed body heat until large snowflakes landed on our faces, startling us.

"Let's go inside." He led me by the hand to the entrance, a heavy steel door built to withstand bear claws and forceful moose antlers, he explained. He tapped his knuckles against a window adding, "Double-paned for our safety."

"Wonderful," I murmured. A delicious mix of fear and arousal swirling together in a heady cocktail. Heat built, contrasting sharply with the chill in the air. I couldn't find my lungs to take a full inhale.

"How many patients have you seen from bear attacks, by the way?"

He raised an eyebrow and removed his hat and gloves, tucking them into his backpack before dropping it on the floor inside the door as I followed him in. "You don't want me to answer that."

"That many?"

"No." He closed the door behind me, securing the deadbolt. His fingers glided across the nape of my neck, and he slid his hands under my beanie lifting it off my head. He reached for my gloves next, and even as he spoke in gruesome terms, his touch ignited every particle of my skin.

"Most of the people who get attacked by bears end up in the morgue. That's why the yurt is indefinitely limited to tourists. It's a huge liability. They'd go home in a body bag —or ashes. Family's choice."

Dark humor was a part of his coping mechanisms. His mental fortitude was built brick by brick from layers of compartmentalization, the joy of cooking, and the unwavering companionship of his dog. I was on the precipice of discovering his methods of pleasure. "Seen some shit, huh?"

Silas tilted my jaw, rubbing his thumb at my neck's pulse point. "I'd never put you at risk; I know how to keep you safe. You know that, right?"

"It's not *my* safety I'm worried about."

With a sly half-smirk, he asked, "Planning on eating me alive?"

"You're more likely collateral damage." With my track record, I wouldn't trust myself if my life depended on it.

"I'll take my chances," Silas said as he brought his lips to mine. His mouth was warm; his kisses saturated me.

It could have been minutes or hours for all I knew until at some point our bodies became so flushed with heat, we hurriedly stripped each other of the remaining outer layers and thermals. A heap of jackets, hats, gloves mounded at our feet on the wood floor.

"I promise I didn't have it planned like this in my head," he said between panting breaths.

"Undressing me out of my sexy suspenders?"

Silas chuckled, like he was hiding a bout of awkwardness. "We can stop, obviously. I wasn't thinking of taking you to the cult headquarters for a quickie. We really are here for the light show."

"Stop talking."

His hands flexed as he hooked his finger underneath my suspender straps. Slowly, excruciatingly slow, draping it down my shoulder. "Is this okay?"

I forcefully pulled the other strap down. "Yes."

Then he didn't hesitate to nearly rip my shirt off over my head leaving me standing in my pants and a red bra. Between strained breaths, Silas muttered curses and one-off words of appreciation: *adorable, sexy, and insane.*

I didn't see much of the cabin. A house tour was not a priority once we stepped over the threshold because his main objective seemed to be getting me nearly naked and laid out on a fur rug in front of the fireplace posthaste.

"I want to see you wear this forever," he said. Then thankfully saved me from overheating and removed my pants one leg at a time.

He left a trail of wet kisses down my heated skin as he lowered my pants—and himself—down my body, lifting my leg over his shoulder. I felt the hardness behind his pants skim across my shin, then my foot before he stopped himself at my center.

Silas was a curious kitten with a ball of yarn, toying with the bits of red lace and string—the remaining bits of fabric left on my skin. I leaned back on my elbows to watch his face light up from licks of flame from the fireplace. His eyes dazzled with mischievous wonder.

Here kitty, kitty.

"Pretty," he said, simply.

And I believed him.

I'd run out of excuses to describe Silas' sincerity. He'd never once led me to believe he was untrustworthy, and that was scarier than making a risky investment with every dollar in my savings. I wasn't losing money in this transaction.

Giving away my heart was much more ill-fated.

Either I'd leave in a few short weeks, or my sham life would catch up to me, and whichever one happened first would put an end to this... relationship. He was the most unexpected, and joyous, part of my time here. But I knew I couldn't have him beyond that; it was safer here where he was immune to my pathetic real-world life.

I'd be fucked up going forward without him, unable to ever find anyone so gentle yet endearingly commanding as Silas.

Any pretenses I'd held onto disappeared, and I lied back and let the hot doctor do whatever he felt like doing to me. I slowly rolled my neck like I was bathing in a vat of sticky honey, a similar sensation between my legs as he licked and sucked lazily from me. My back arched off the floor and he gently pressed a hand down on my lower belly, holding me in place as he continued his ministrations. A combination of tongue and fingers, sucking and nibbles. My orgasm swelled like a wave breaching the shore. Overwhelming. Crashing. And wet.

Reaching for his pants, I cupped his erection caged beneath his boxers. His hand landed on top of mine, linking our fingers together and pressing my hand right where he wanted it.

"Can I make a confession?" he asked.

"This feels like the right time for that?"

"Yes," he choked out, as my hand squeezed him, feeling the blood pulsing quicker. I reached beneath his boxers, stroking my fingers up and down his length, and rubbed my thumb on his crown where I felt a drop of moisture. He looked delirious.

"Well, go on. Speak."

"Woman." His breath was restricted. "I've been thinking about this since our hands touched at the airport."

"You thought of me giving you a hand job when we met?" I worked my hand the way his vibrations showed he liked it. Biting his lip and sucking in air each time I squeezed the slightest bit more. "A woman you had just met, whose name you didn't even know?"

He was so exasperated he sounded like he was running from a bear. "When I saw you, I knew I had to have you."

I climbed on top of him, seated on his legs, and he folded his hands behind his head. He grinned so bright it was like the Northern Lights personified. I wiggled his underwear down, fully exposing his body. He ached and warmed under my touch. I lowered my head, more than fucking ready to return the favor. "Next time I vote for simultaneous oral."

"Well, get your pretty ass up on my face then," he said, lifting his shoulders off the ground as his stomach flexed as he attempted to haul me up.

I hunkered down, digging in with my toes into the floor as I licked a full circle around his crown and sucked the tip. "Right now, I want to return the favor and give you my undivided attention." I lowered my head, never breaking eye contact.

"Jesus, Alice." I could have sworn that beautiful man might have cried as I took him to the back of my throat. He bit down on one hand and flexed a white-knuckle fist with the other.

"Relax, babe," I cooed.

"I c—can't. I want to touch, but—"

I sucked him harder and faster, giving one hell of an athletic performance all for the depraved goal of watching him fall apart. I linked my fingers with his. He gripped my hands tight, and I felt his entire body shake.

"F-finish, I'm going to finish," he sputtered. He let go of my hands and reached for my hair, tugging my face off him. He squeezed the base of his shaft and, with a moan, he came all over his stomach.

I walked on lanky, newborn deer-like legs to the kitchenette, grabbing cheap paper towels. "Sorry, this is all I could find." I squatted next to him, and he reached for my hands, but I held them out of his reach. "I don't mind. Let me help."

He stayed propped on his elbows, watching me wipe his stomach. His core shook and his breaths were still short, but he managed to say faintly above the sounds of the crackling fire,

"You felt so good," he croaked out. "*So* good." I smiled at him, his face pained as he came down from his orgasm. Or like he was holding something back. I nodded, encouraging him to keep talking. "I'm sorry I grabbed you like that. I couldn't speak and I didn't want you to swallow."

"Why?"

"I didn't want you to feel disrespected."

"Only you would be thinking of someone else's feelings on the brink of a toe-curling orgasm."

He gave me that cute smile, the one that reminded me he still had a playful side, despite the aging lines at the corners of his eyes and the flecks of gray in his hair. I finished cleaning him up and turned my head around looking for a trash can. "It's a pack-it-in, pack-it-out kind of place," he said. "Give it to me and I'll drop it in the outhouse in the back."

Laid out on my back, I admired the wood paneling from the floor to the sloped ceiling to prevent snow from melting and leaking through the roof. The beams were worn and faded gray, likely made from tight-grained and old-growth trees.

"When was this built?"

Silas' head rotated, his hair brushing against mine creating a soft friction. "It's probably a hundred years old."

I hummed a response. "It must have really good insulation."

Silas chucked and rolled over onto his elbow, boxers pulled back onto his hips. I snuck a greedy glimpse at what had been blessedly lodged in my face moments ago. I wasn't in love with his dick, but when I made him look like he'd crawl to the ends of the earth for an orgasm, I appreciated that control more than anything else.

"You watch a lot of house shows or something?"

"I majored in anthropology. My favorite class was historic preservation."

"Is that what you did in Arizona?"

I rolled my head to the side, finding Silas' eyes hazy and glazed. He licked his lips, and I squeezed my thighs at the thought of him tasting the remnants of me. His hand reached over, rubbing one nipple between his thumb and forefinger before going to the next one. I lost my concentration on how to sidestep talking about what happened in my past, but a sheen of mortification coated my clammy skin at the thought of telling him I had been fired.

"No, it was more of a hobby than a career."

"You like old houses?" Somehow the level of our voices dropped, and he was speaking in a near whisper now; his voice clicked and echoed around the crackling fire.

"Suppose so," I said, and couldn't help but smile. "They're intriguing. Withstanding years of battered storms, human behavior, cultural changes. It's nice that there are societies that protect them."

"I like talking to you, but maybe you should put a shirt on."

"Are my tits distracting you?"

"Absolutely."

I blindly swatted around the floor for the flimsy thing that had no business holding up my overstuffed breasts. Today I favored style over practicality.

Our eyes flicked away when they caught as we dressed in silence. Even though I'd had him in my mouth minutes ago, watching him put his clothes back on made me bashful. I watched from the side of my eye as he thumbed the button closed, swallowing the buildup of saliva pooling in my mouth.

"Come here," he said, opening his arms for me to walk into them. Stroking my back, he told me how much he appreciated me. He was so gracious and almost indebted, like he couldn't believe something so nice was done to him. *For* him.

"For the record," my voice was so quiet he had to lean in with his lips on my ear, "you could disrespect me any which way you want." I rolled my head into his hand, a soft place it liked to find itself, and kissed his palm.

A loud beep sounded from his backpack, and he quickly released me to retrieve it. Silas swore under his breath and said, "Damn. We have to leave right now. The snow is getting heavier."

I pouted with a full bottom lip.

He reached his hand out for me to stand with him. "I don't want to leave either, but it's for our safety."

"Isn't getting snowed in part of the experience of

coming to a small, snowy town? I think that's what the people expect."

"Unless you want to thumb a ride home on a moose. The weather isn't always predictable here. There was a slight chance of snow when I checked the forecast, but it changes in the plains quickly and aggressively."

He stroked my head, petting my hair down as he tucked my beanie over my ears. "I'm sorry we had to cut this short. I hope this doesn't feel... cheap."

"Cheap?"

"I honestly didn't think it would go that far. I wanted to get out of town; I wasn't expecting —"

"To go *downtown*?"

He rolled his eyes at my cringy joke, then rubbed my jaw with his knuckles. "We'll have to see the lights here another time, okay? I like you. And I want you to feel safe with me."

Damn it, he was going to make this so hard to leave in two months. Maybe leaving on polite, mutual terms would be the wrong approach. I could sabotage this, so that I'd leave a trail of fire in my wake; he'd give me a wide berth and say good-fucking-riddens. When this was over, it needed to be on his terms because I didn't have enough self-control to do the smart thing—not fall for Silas Hill.

I held my breath and bent down to tie the laces up my snow boots. On the ride back, a tear escaped and froze on my cheek.

CHAPTER 20

SILAS

We gathered in the vibrant town square, where cozy shops and restaurants glowed warmly from within and string lights twinkled overhead. As the clock neared eight, the businesses would close, inviting everyone to step outside with candles to sing winter folk songs. Alice and I explored a used bookstore, an antique shop, and a store filled with hide and leather goods.

At the heart of downtown Tidings stood the Orlog Sword, a magnificent white stone sculpture designed with a scaled hilt and pointed end, carved by the founders of Tidings a century ago. Legend—and to many, superstition—said it was infused with powerful spells to ensure that the city remained untouched by the passage of time.

The streets were closed to traffic, and in place of snow tires and all-terrain vehicles, was a large pen holding in more than a dozen reindeer, many with elaborate antlers and others displaying young velvet buds. Their fur was painted with freckled brown spots, giving them the perfect camouflage in the dirt-splattered snow.

"These are real reindeer and not cows playing dress up,

right?" Alice asked, clutching her cheeks like a little kid at Disneyland for the first time. I could feel my face matching her excitement. Even though I'd seen reindeer up close many times, I had never experienced it with her before.

"They aren't trying to charge at us; they want nose scratches or treats," I told Alice. "Imagine if a large cow had the personality of a golden retriever. But watch out for the antlers on the big guys. They're awkward and don't understand their size."

We stepped into the pen and slowly approached the first reindeer, a young male named Alf. Alice greeted him in soft whispers and his nose nudged her palm.

"He likes you," I said. "Give him some treats." I handed her a small paper cup with reindeer snacks the staffers had scooped for us when we entered. I poured it into her cupped palm, and she squeezed her eyes shut as the beast inhaled the offering, leaving her in a tickled giggling puddle. Other reindeer got wind of the lady with the snacks and trotted toward us.

It was difficult to believe that the cute, bouncy woman was the same one who gave me the best orgasm of my life hours ago. Mutually beneficial oral sex was not exactly on the itinerary, although I wasn't complaining. I thought I'd be lucky with a grabby make-out session, but as soon as we got inside the warm walls, I was desperate to get her undressed.

"Hello, everybody," she nervously whispered to the herd gathered around her for handouts.

I too am eating out of the palm of her hand.

"I don't care if they're as friendly as a puppy, I'm terrified," she confessed through a tight smile. "I come in peace. I have snacks."

"Don't be scared."

"Easy for you to say. They're looking at me like they want to spear me through the gut."

A laugh rumbled in my chest. I tucked her head against my shoulder, placing a soft kiss in her hair. "I take it they don't have reindeer in Arizona."

"Probably illegal since it's as hot as the surface of the sun."

We held hands and dawdled through the herd, handing out more snacks from paper cups we refilled from old gumball machines. My arm slung casually over her shoulder, and I drummed my fingers across her arm. "Want to know something embarrassing?"

"Besides the excessive sci-fi figurines on your bookshelf?"

I tried to pinch the side of her hip but grabbed a handful of cold-weather layers instead.

She stuck her tongue out at me.

"Oh, you're gonna get it later."

"Counting on it," the little minx winked. I feared I was in over my head with her.

I cleared my throat and pushed away thoughts of her facedown in a pillow. "On my seventh birthday, I wished for a reindeer farm."

"Because... you wanted to be Santa?"

"Nonsense, there is only one Santa," I clarified. "I wanted to host the Reindeer Olympics, like a rodeo, but with reindeer tricks and... stuff."

"And *stuff*," her lips twitched. "I'm trying hard not to make fun of your childhood dream."

"Your face is turning purple. You can let it out."

"It's not too late," she said, fighting for each breath. "To chase your dream."

Alice's lighthearted teasing lifted something heavy

inside me. There was a fondness in her tongue-in-cheek expression, and all I felt was lightness and joy.

She exhaled a boisterous, attention-grabbing laugh. "I'm so..." she breathed intermittently between words, "*so*, sorry. That's really cute."

"For the record, I don't want that *now*," I shrugged, "Reindeer Olympics and stuff."

"You can lie to yourself, but you can't fool me. You know you want it."

"It would be kind of cool... I guess."

Alice led us around the town square, stopping for photos or sneaking in a selfie. I'd been here several times, but knowing it would be my last Solstice Festival made me feel something indulgent, perhaps sentimental.

Alice posed herself in front of a large bonfire. "Silas, come here." I butted up next to her shoulder-to-shoulder. "Smile," she said as she snapped a few shots. I put my lips on her cheek which caught her off guard. She showed me the photo of her beaming with a tinge of pink cheeks. "Thanks for the photo. I wanted to remember the day I gave a blowjob in a yurt."

Across the street, families filled the ice-skating rink. More adventurous folks were on a snowshoeing tour to the top of Moose Hill, where they watched the lights and festivities from high up.

I put my hands behind her head and pulled her in, whispering, "To think no one here knows what we did a few hours ago." The reminder of how it felt to have our mouths on each other sent a thrill of heat coursing through my body.

She stopped in her tracks, gasping at the shock of the scene in front of us. A line of people on horseback waited for their turn at a runway made of snow. It was like water skiing behind a boat, but much colder and set on a smooth, snowy trail. The excitement in the air was palpable as the *skijoring* participants readied to launch into the winter wonderland.

"I know I say every day that nothing here would shock me anymore, but I am speechless."

"Good," I said. "Then we're doing something right."

We watched riders race down the snow-covered runway, gaining speed and momentum by the strength of the horses pulling them until they reached a snow packed jump and released the rope. They did backward flips, twists, and turns you'd see on a gymnastics floor but with laminated strips of waxed wood clipped to their feet. Someone jumped over three barrels of fire.

A bell rang and everyone moved toward the center of the town square. Volunteers handed out unlit candles with a metal disk on the bottom to capture wax. The person at the end of each row had their candle lit first and they shared their flame with their neighbor. And that flame with the next. A light and warmth in the dark cold, shared from one person to another but never diminishing the flame as it's shared.

"This is the corny part of the festival, but everyone cries," I said into her ear.

"I bet you don't."

"No, I never cry."

She reached up to put her mouth on my ear, her breath tickling as she said, "Except for when you're about to come in my mouth." She stared at me down, waiting for me to blink or say something first. "Now who's the speechless one?" she bragged.

I set my jaw on her head and looked around, sneaking

in more words meant only for her. "The things I want to say to you right now would get me arrested."

She blushed and I couldn't help but stroke her rosy cheeks with my gloved thumb.

"Your fire can light the path for yourself, if you know where to point it," the woman on the dais began. "It can warm the space for you and your neighbor, if you share it. It can also be destructive. Each person here has a natural born fire within you. On this Winter Solstice, embrace the warmth and the glow from the flame to remember how to use your fire for good. Whether a flicker in the dark or a roaring fire to draw others near you and find comfort in your goodwill, you have more power within you than you know."

I wrapped my arms around her from behind and let her take whatever moment she needed. When the fires began to die down and there were more silent murmurs than raucous partying, it was time to go.

We went back to my place and as soon as the front door shut us inside the confines of my home, the air immediately shifted. It tightened into something we had to consciously seek out, like taking a breath in the same space was arduous work.

"Allow me." I delicately unwrapped the scarf from her neck, painstakingly slowly. I felt her warm, heavy breath on my hands as it unraveled. I unbuttoned her wool jacket one painful button by one *excruciatingly* painful button at a time, and my hand grazed her thigh when I unhooked the final one.

She peeled off my hat and gloves, stuffing them in the jacket pocket hanging on the rack. Watching her hang her outerwear next to mine felt normal. Like they lived together, and that rack was their home, snug together and relaxed. I started a fire and told her to help herself at the bar cart, fix me one of whatever she made herself.

Alice changed into a pair of yoga pants and a white sweater, one I could tell she favored as much as me, though for probably different reasons. She wore it to stay warm and I loved her wearing it because it made me want to pet her soft fabric, then pull it over her head.

She poured two fingers of caramel-colored bourbon on ice, and we clanked our crystal low-ball glasses in silence. The first sip burned my tongue but found a smooth, even swallow in my throat.

I went to my room and changed into a pair of sweats and an old med school T-shirt. I lingered in my bathroom, debating how I could get her into my bathtub. I never used it, but I wouldn't mind sharing a soak with Alice.

When I walked out into the living room, I was surprised for a moment to find her there, sitting on the floor scratching my dog's ears. I was accustomed to an empty house, except for my dog, who was now gleefully soaking in the belly rubs in front of the fireplace. She gave me dopey eyes, as if to say, *I got her first.* Alice stood up when I walked toward her and brushed some light specks of dirt off her ass. I tilted my head to get a better look.

"You missed a spot," I lied, an excuse to rub her down. "Sorry, I haven't been home much lately to clean and Snøf carries in a pound of dirt every day."

"It's a big house for just you." Snøf groaned at her feet. "I meant you two, Snøfnugg. One human to dust and mop all this wood is a lot of work."

I put my finger under her chin, lifting her eyes to meet mine. "It's nice to have you here." My lips craved the taste of hers. Regularly. Our noses grazed as our lips opened, finding a soft landing against each other. I slid my palms down her lower back, stopping at the dip before her yoga pants curved over her ass.

She ran her hands along my forearms and exhaled slowly. "It's taking tremendous will not to maul you right now."

"Oh, please, maul away." I winked.

"You're the first person I've met who can't be rushed. Shouldn't be rushed," she said. "I want to lay underneath you all night."

I raked my hand up the nape of her neck and pulled her mouth back to mine where it belonged. Our tongues met and I swallowed a moan from her mouth. One hand ran through her hair, the other landed on her breast, thumbing the nipple through her soft sweater. "Your body is so responsive to my touch." I didn't recognize my own gravelly voice at that moment. Dark and breathy.

"Your sexy voice is... diplomatic. You could probably get me to do anything."

"There's one thing I want."

"Hmm?" She etched out between kisses, tempering from hot and desperate to soft and tender.

"I need to hear what you sound like when you beg."

"Silas, what surprises do you have in store for me?"

"Say my fucking name again," I pleaded.

Exhaling softly, I whispered, "You're ready for more... *Silas?*"

In both hands, I gripped her full and pulled her up to my waist. She squeezed her legs, and I could feel my hardness responding to the warmth between her legs. That fucking material was about to get ripped in half.

My phone buzzed on the kitchen counter, disrupting our heated moment like a clap of thunder. I recognized the sound of the ringer that followed the vibrate. I held her close, keeping our foreheads together. "Fuck, *fuck*. I'm sorry. I have to go."

"Work," she stated, her voice flat, as if she already knew the answer. Her quiet certainty gnawed at me. I hated that she was already familiar with my grinding, exhausting, unpredictable life. I was burned out, and the last thing I wanted to do was drag anyone else down with me. Especially Alice.

I chewed the inside of my cheek. "Yeah."

"It's alright."

"Will you stay? Be here when I get home?"

She nodded and I took her hand, leading her my bedroom. I changed into a pair of black scrubs. I added a fleece vest, and grabbed my work bag from the closet floor, double checking that my badge, pager, and stethoscope were all in place.

"This was the worst timing, but they called a code triage. Many casualties from a car accident." I pulled my jacket off the coat rack and ran my fingers through my hair, staring at her face. Her pupils were blown, arousal written all over her face, even as she held a stately smile. "Fuck, fuck. I hate leaving you here like this."

"I'll be okay," she said, tugging my beanie over my head for me. "Go. Save lives and shit."

"Make yourself at home, please." I kissed her on the cheek and locked the door behind me.

CHAPTER 21
ALICE

I stood slack-jawed in Silas' foyer blinking AT the door. One second sparks were flying between us; the next, I was abandoned in his home with his dog. Puttering around his house like a lost child, I kept myself busy washing dishes—one lonely white mug with a coffee stain on the bottom—and wiped down the counter.

Was I allowed to miss him? And if I did, what happened next? He'd come home from work, and we'd pick up where we left off like a normal domestic couple?

I retrieved my phone out of my purse to text him a picture of his dog doing belly flops off the porch into the snow before I bribed her back in with a treat.

Imagining Silas opening that photo after a difficult night, smiling at his goofy dog, did something to me...

My chest fluttered.

Uh-oh.

"Oh, Silas." His name lingered on my tongue, like the last bite of a perfect dish—a flavor I wasn't ready to say goodbye to.

The "Old Alice," desperate and humiliated back in

Arizona, so badly wanted to invade my perfect snow village bubble. It was only mine for a few more weeks.

Imagining Silas, with his sweet eyes and that perfect searing mouth on mine, discovering my back story made my mouth taste tangy and sour.

I quickly dressed, plotting my escape. I knew he'd be disappointed when he got back to an empty house, but I was doing him a favor. This had gotten too serious, too quickly.

Unexpectedly.

He deserved much more than what I offered which was nothing more than a tangled mess of a confused woman without shit to her name.

This needed to end before it went further. I gave myself a mental pat on the back; how unselfish and kind of me, really.

At the sound of the deadlock unlocking, a whimper drew my attention. Snøfnugg sat obediently, staring right at me. I couldn't leave her alone; who knew how long Silas would be gone?

"Ugh." I tossed my beanie and gloves on the floor and my jacket over the couch. Her tail wagged aggressively, her mouth broke into a tiny smile. I scratched the top of her head, looking at those pleading brown eyes. "You got me to stay tonight. But this can't become a regular thing. So who's gonna tell him? Me or you?"

CHAPTER 22

SILAS

What a fucking terrible night. One DOA. Two stabilized in our ER before being life-flighted to the nearest trauma hospital. Two more didn't meet criteria for transfer, but probably should have, which kept us on our toes all night trying to keep them stable.

Before I left the hospital, I dry-heaved on an empty stomach in the staff shower as the hot water and soap washed off the sweat and grime from the worst shift I'd had in a year. I shoved stale crackers and a juice box down my throat around midnight to keep my blood sugar up enough to not pass out.

Physically and emotionally, I was drained. Fumes weren't pushing me anymore. I was stalled in the middle of traffic.

I banged my head on the outside of my front door before going in. My dog was going to be so pissed. She deserved better than me.

When I opened the door, a pile of outerwear tripped me up, and my eyes drifted to the back of the leather chair where a heavy parka was draped.

Alice.

Fuck, fuck, I forgot she was here.

The past two days had been as blurry as an over-shaken snow globe—whirling, dizzying, swallowed up in a frenzy. Yesterday we were touching and sucking each other off at the little cabin. Then we were about to fuck here last night until I got the call for code triage. The thought of her alone in my house, uncertain if she'd stay, gnawed at me all night, even as I tended to injured patients. The rhythm of the ER was automatic, but thoughts of Alice lingered, always right at the edges of my focus.

"Alice?" I softly called her name, stepping over the pile of her stuff strewn across the room. The memory of seeing her jacket on the rack next to mine last night warmed me, and I hated seeing it misplaced. Exhaustion overpowered any other basic need save for tidiness. I picked up her items, placing them right where they belonged. Jacket next to mine on the rack. Gloves and hat on the shelf on the wall.

It wasn't yet dawn, and the stars still twinkled in the dark sky. I hurried up the stairs, careful to quiet my footsteps as I approached my room. I nudged the door open with my foot. The glow from a lamp in the hallway that led to the connecting bathroom illuminated the space, giving a serene glow to what laid in my bed.

Snøf laid at the edge of the bed as she did with me, and Alice was asleep on my side. I froze on the spot, staring at my dog and this woman who looked like she belonged in my bed as much as I did.

I slid down the wall, crouching with my elbows resting on my knees watching Alice's chest rise and fall. Her once sun-kissed bronze skin was fading into a lighter pale, the damning nature of this fucking Arctic zone.

I scrubbed my hand down my face, pained by the peacefulness on her face.

The impending reality of our separation loomed like the darkness around me. I was a mess internally. Exhausted, bitter, burned out.

Leaving Tidings was the only thing that would save me. But losing her would ruin me.

Falling for someone organically didn't reveal itself with an ostentatious display. No big parade or burst of fireworks in the sky. It started as an attraction—of course, anyone would be a moron not to be attracted to Alice. But then, brick by brick, she gently tore down the walls I'd built. Light poured in, bringing with it joy and comfort. She relaxed me, exposing the true feelings I'd hidden from everyone else—the disillusionment I'd kept buried for years.

How many times did I run off because I had to put patients above all else? Yet she stayed. She was fucking here. I bit down on my fist, holding back emotions that wrestled with my voice box.

It'd be comical if it wasn't terrifying how fucking reckless it was to fall in love. *"Here, woman, perfect stranger to me before the last full moon, take all my damn money. My dog, my house, my support, my sanity. You can have it all."*

Of course, leave it to the woman who showed up as I was leaving to have me acting like a stupid idiot. We hadn't even had sex, and I was dumb gone for her.

She had no fucking idea how much I needed her.

"Silas?" Alice's quiet voice called out for me.

"I'm—" I choked back emotion that gathered thick like cement in my throat. My face was hot and tense. "I'm here."

She leaned up, squinting in the dark to make out my

shadow's presence. "What are you doing on the floor? Are you okay?"

My dog snorted at Alice's movement, disturbing her precious sleep. The mutt rolled onto her back and stuck her paws in the air, drooling and dreaming about chasing snow bunnies most likely.

Striding toward me, Alice's bare legs stuck out from underneath one of my T-shirts. She stopped short of our toes touching, a few inches more and I'd see what else was underneath that shirt. My restraint snapped.

"Alice, if you don't want to get fucked right now, you need to back up."

She bent down, her arms wrapping around my folded knees. Gently, she reached out and stroked my face, her thumb rubbing beneath my eyes. "You're not okay," she whispered.

"I'm fine," I said, my tone sharper than she deserved. "And a little bit of patience will go a long way for you with me in the future. But right now, I don't have a patient bone in my body. I'm seconds away from self-combusting."

Her fingers rubbed beneath the V-neck of my scrub top. "As long as it's on me and not in your pants." My mouth went dry and I became the one without words.

"Fuck." We tumbled across the rug until I was straddled on top of her; she was breathless and biting her lip beneath me. "Slow down, slow down," I said more for my benefit than hers.

"You are unexpected, Silas."

"In what way?"

"Every way." She stroked her fingers through the overgrown hair on the back of my neck, and I shivered. "You need a soft touch, don't you?"

She grabbed her shirt by the hem, tugging it over her

head. Her burgundy lace bra hugged her chest tight, giving the most satisfying lift to her breasts. Curved and plump. Mouthwatering. Her chest rose with a palpable thrill. Her body was devastating. Every curve and dip vied for my attention, and I fought with myself over where to start first. My attraction to Alice was insurmountable. I wanted to touch every inch of her, inside and out.

"You need a soft place to land," she whispered, gentle as cotton between my thumbs. A tender touch against my skin.

I put my forehead to hers. "It feels so damn good coming home to your eyes."

"Are you going to touch me, or do you just want to look?" Her voice was laced with teasing.

I pinched a ripe ass cheek that earned me a satisfying squeal. I got the impression that Alice had more layers to her than she herself even knew. That she was more herself in Tidings, and selfishly I hoped with me, than she had ever been before. "I'm taking it in for a second." I pulled my shirt off and loosened my scrub pant strings.

"It's a shame you're not wearing one of those belts I spied in your closet." Her tone dripped arousal that I thought was only possible in my dreams.

Oh, fuck.

I pulled her up to stand. She was in nothing but a dainty pair of underwear and a poor excuse for a bra. It was so sheer her hard nipples flashed like emergency lights, making my brain go haywire. I lifted her legs around my waist and groped every inch of her ass I could find from that position.

"You've got some pants you need to hold up?" I swallowed hard and skimmed the dip of her waistline with my hands. My fingers brushed against her warm skin, ripples of goosebumps beneath my touch.

"I was thinking more along the lines of these wrists," she rotated her hands palm up and the image of what she suggested flashed in my brain like a slot machine in Vegas that hit the million-dollar jackpot.

"You're a kinky little thing, aren't you?"

We fell backward onto the bed, and I ran my hands down her hips, across her legs. My fingers grazed her ankle. I pressed my thumb into the heel of her foot. She groaned with an obscene moan.

"Sorry, my feet still aren't used to carrying the weight of the heavy snow boots."

I kissed the bottom of both feet and her eyes fluttered closed.

With one hand, I held her leg open and nestled my face between her thighs. She squeezed my other hand, linking our fingers together resting on her hip bone.

Hands free, I dove in. Maybe it was only five in the morning by now, but I already knew tasting her would be the highlight of my day. It was certainly making up for the hell I'd been through overnight.

Since Alice arrived in Tidings, my life felt less bleak. Her green eyes added color to my dull life, her scent of warm air and honeysuckle lingered on my skin. When a part of her body was in my hands or my mouth, I wouldn't trade it for anything.

I was so ready to leave this town until she came here. Now, I couldn't imagine her going. Had she fallen under Tidings' spell? Would she stay here forever?

I'd stay in Tidings for you.

"Your eyes are pretty," she said, inhaling a deep breath as her inner thighs quivered, tightening against my face.

Vaginas were complex anatomy, but eating Alice's pussy was so much fucking fun. She was my marionette doll dancing for me as I pulled her strings. A tongue flick on her clit sent her back arching. Suction on her labia had her sighing deep and exasperated. My fingers toyed with her, drawing out little whimpers. I fought against the sleep that threatened to take me under. I wanted to stay awake and do this forever. I never wanted it to end.

When she came, I held on to her hips, not letting her buck away from me as her fingers tugged tightly in my hair.

Stay.

Stay.

Stay.

"I've wanted this for years," I muttered.

Her voice sounded a mile away when she spoke. "I'm supposed to be taking care of you."

It was the last thing I heard before I blacked out.

CHAPTER 23

ALICE

"I'VE WANTED THIS FOR YEARS."

His words hooked themselves into my brain like a pop song's earworm. They basically pulled up a fucking lawn chair and parked themselves in my mind's front yard.

What did that mean?

I laid on the crook of his arm, nestled between his shoulder and chest, drowsy but awake. His soft snores, coupled with the crackling fireplace, made up the quiet soundtrack in the room. Meanwhile, I basked in the afterglow of orgasm.

Memories from this early morning were a hazy, lust-drunk trance. Silas taunted me so well with his languid tongue, slow and measured. Then with a flick of his tongue in the exact place he knew where a million nerves collided, he shocked my system like a polar plunge into the winter's ocean.

God, he did his work between my legs so well.

So fucking well.

I stroked his hair after the orgasm he gave me, peeling

the skin from my bones. Drunk on pleasure, I whispered his name, only to be greeted with little sounds coming from his mouth. I came all over his mouth, and the man was actually snoring between my legs. I chuckled at his cheek pressed on the inside of my thigh.

"You fell asleep?" I said loudly, shocked he didn't even budge. "Oh, this is a fucking story for the books."

I maneuvered my way off the bed, cleaned myself up before waking him to a partial-conscious state by tickling his feet. It was enough to help me turn his big body around so his head could reach a pillow near the headboard. I pulled the covers over him and snuggled his back, listening to his sweet snores until I fell asleep.

His eyes had misted and glowed as he... feasted. Silas was a starving, thirsty man, and I was a bit anxious he might never get his fill before I succumbed to dehydration.

He even winked—playful, devastatingly flirtatious. It was enough to send my body into an uncontrollable spasm. The visceral reaction I had to Silas was almost terrifying. But what frightened me more was how deeply I was drawn to him—not just by the attraction, but by him as a whole person.

When his eyes fixed on mine as he worked all avenues of his tongue between my thighs, I drowned in his irises. I saw beneath layers of repressed thoughts and dark secrets; his eyes pleading, *see me, see me, see me.*

What are you hiding, Silas?

Snøfnugg grunted as she stretched and used her big body to claim her space. I considered how to quietly sneak out of bed to let her outside to keep Silas sleeping for as long as possible.

I loved feeling his breath on me. He deserved to rest,

and I bathed in the glory that it was my body responsible for delivering his deep sleep.

He smiled even when he was tired. His eyes were rimmed in red and purple tints. Compared to my sun-kissed skin—although my golden Arizona glow had faded little by little each day—his pigment was camouflaged in the snow. He was unhappy, miserable even, and potentially causing irreparable harm to his body and mind. UV light bulbs everywhere in his house, heated floors, and cabinets full of vitamins were his lifeline. He scrounged by with scraps.

How did everyone else tolerate this place? Were they as unhappy beneath their exterior? The weekly festivals, nights out with friends, and frequent hook-ups were strategies to help people survive without completely losing their damn minds, since by nature, Tidings should only be habitable for polar bears and moose. It didn't take a doctor to see that human beings were being pushed to their limits mentally and physically living here.

Snøf huffed at me and pawed at my legs. I gingerly released myself from Silas' grip and tip-toed my way out of his room. I waved maniacally at the dog for her to follow. She didn't budge.

"Come on, Snøfnugg," I whispered. She yawned. "What is your command?"

She rolled onto her back, maneuvering across the rug to scratch an impossible itch. I repeated myself, snapping my fingers and waving at her like a flightless bird with a broken wing.

"Don't tell me it's 'snow'?"

She jumped up, shook off her sleep and trotted past me. Her big body bounced off my leg and I backed into the door. "Oh, come on, really?"

The door hinges squeaked but Silas slept through it all. I let her outside where she did acrobatic moves off the porch into the endless piles of snow while I made a pot of coffee. It took me way too long to locate the grounds and the filters. For someone as organized as Silas, he had them scattered about in different cupboards in the kitchen. I stood at the back door watching that dang dog lose her mind in the snow.

As long as she was alive, Silas would have to live here for her happiness.

Silas' phone buzzed on the table. We weren't at any point where I felt like I could check it and see if it was worth waking him up for. It could be the hospital, but the man was as energetic as a corpse; he was in no condition to take care of others. He needed to learn that he couldn't take care of others if he wasn't healthy himself. What kind of masochists were doctors anyway?

As I waited for the coffee to percolate, I tried to wrap my brain around everything that had transpired in the past twenty-four hours.

I never considered myself to have a fire within me, like the woman had said at last night's Solstice event. Never for good, for bad, for power, for warmth. I kept searching for that moment when something would click, and I'd know right then what my purpose was. I'd bellyache about it, but I was envious of my sister who knew what she wanted to do from an early age, made a plan, and followed the appropriate trajectory from college to employment.

Until recently, when things started to make sense. Not a big revelation, but piece by piece. My work routine, my friendship with Ginger and Dagny, seeing familiar faces at the café, and picking up conversations with acquaintances like we never left off.

I scoffed at my ridiculous thoughts and tried to burn them away with too big of a sip of steaming coffee, burning off a dozen taste buds along the way. I wasn't here to make friends or fall for a near-perfect man. I was here to run away and live to tell the tale another day.

But something happened last night. During that corny speech, I looked up at Silas and saw the reflection of the lit candles dancing in his eyes and I knew I was going to leave here more broken than before. This time my heart would be shattered which was worse than a bruised ego.

It was childlike to believe in magic, and yet, undoubtedly whatever was happening here was just that. Pure, glistening, irrefutable magic.

Silas hadn't asked me about last night when I lost control of my emotions in the middle of town square, sobbing uncontrollably. The woman in front of me turned around with a napkin and assured me that it happens to someone every year, the overwhelming beauty of the event. I wanted to shake her and confess everything: *I'm a fraud! Burn me at the stake!*

A hand folded over mine, taking the mug from my hand. Silas brought it to his mouth and took a long, satisfied sip. "You make good coffee," he said in his too sexy sleep voice. Hair mussed, sweatpants, and an old college T-shirt clinging to his boulders for shoulders and tight biceps. I was fucking *into* that.

Silas' soft mouth found the nape of my neck. I leaned into him, and he stroked my covered hip, fingers moving in between my thighs. Reflexively, they tightened to hold him there.

Last night he had worked me unerringly, guiding my body through each orgasm with fingers and tongue. Oh god, I had lost count. That was a man who delivered pleasure like it was his sole purpose on earth. I'd never tell him this for the sake of having one sliver of pride, but I was afraid my future sex life would gravely suffer. I'd never met a man so thorough in his ministrations. And doubted I would ever again.

I craned my neck and kissed his lips. "You fell asleep with your head between my thighs."

"What kind of sleeping drug do you have infused in there?" He pulled me back into him, my ass brushed against the hardness growing beneath his pants.

"I think it's called sleep deprivation."

"I don't want to sleep when you're here. I don't get you long enough," he confessed. He turned me around, setting the mug on a side table, and wrapped me in his arms.

"It's bad for your health," I said into his chest.

"Okay, *Dr. Woods*."

"Ha. Not a doctor."

"You can be whatever you want with me." The words spilled from his mouth like he was wading through chest-high floodwaters: dangerous, determined.

"Can I take care of you?" I asked.

He didn't respond, but I led him back to bed where he held me tight. We stayed like that for a while; his breaths slowed as he fell in and out of sleep. I was perfectly content trapped under his arm for as long as he'd keep me.

My stomach grumbled. Silas opened one eye and smile lines crinkled across his delicate skin.

"The only thing that can get Snøf out of the snow is a pancake. She'll smell it as soon as I crack the door open. Watch."

It was lunchtime, but Silas made pancakes from scratch, despite his exhausted state. He didn't even need a recipe on his phone. He had memorized the exact amount of baking powder (one-quarter teaspoon—he said each ingredient and measurement out loud, walking me through it step by step), and baking soda (one-eighth teaspoon), two ingredients I was always scared of mixing up, even on my best days.

The three of us ate our pancakes around the kitchen island, the dog chowing down from a plate on the floor.

"Spoiled rotten," I muttered.

"Yes, she is," he said. "And so are you when you're with me. I'd do anything for the girls I—" he stopped himself, shook his head, and bit the last of his pancake off his fork before doing the dishes.

Licking syrup off the edge of my hand, I glanced at him while he loaded the dishwasher, his movements deliberate, like he was trying to occupy himself.

What had he almost said? "For the girls I..."

My heart beat a little faster, but I forced myself to push the thought away. It was probably nothing—just a slip, an awkward half-sentence.

I looked down at my plate, absentmindedly pushing a piece of pancake around. The dog had finished her meal and was lying in the corner, eyes half-closed, content. I envied that simplicity—no thoughts of what could have been or might never happen.

I hadn't missed the quiet intensity in Silas' voice when he said, "And so are you when you're with me."

Silas did spoil me—comfort, companionship, safety— but it wasn't with the intent to overwhelm or control. It felt good, in an almost effortless way.

He dried his hands, then shifted, crossing his arms and leaning against the counter. I studied his cocky smile—he pulled it off effortlessly—eyes sparkling with mischief, lips tilted to one side like he was in on a secret I wasn't privy to.

I tried to focus on the moment, but the warmth of the kitchen and the hum of the dishwasher couldn't quite drown out the quiet ache deep within me.

But the question lingered: What was he about to say? And why had he stopped?

CHAPTER 24

SILAS

"What time is it?" Alice asked.

I rubbed my eyes. "What fucking *day* is it?"

The gray sky promised a snowstorm soon. Bluebird days would be hard to come by until around Valentine's Day as it snowed perpetually. Low-hanging fog froze your eyelashes until it warmed up a few more degrees before the precipitation could fall.

Like the storm clouds above, I was rippling on the inside, desperate to burst.

The more time I spent with Alice the more I wanted to bring her in. I hadn't lied directly, but omitting the truth felt just as shitty. I needed to submit my resignation by the end of the year, find a job, and a new community. That would be a different story if I'd responded to the dozen emails I've ignored from hospital recruiters. I was confused and uncommitted... ever since meeting Alice I wasn't sure what the truth was anymore. Did I stay or did I go?

Alice wouldn't be here much longer, either. She had weeks left and after that—who the hell knew?

Many of life's problems could be solved with honest

communication. But asking the hard questions always felt uneasy—sometimes it was more painful to ask than to be the one answering. Waiting for the answer, wondering what someone would say that might shape our next steps or force big decisions, was agonizing. And I wanted to know so much more about her, especially what had brought her to Tidings. A person with nothing to hide didn't relocate to one of the most desolate places in the country.

Why was she in Tidings? Where would she go next? Did she want me?

I was too chicken shit to hear her answers. I needed a bit more time in ignorant bliss. So, fuck it, I'd communicate differently for now.

"Do you want to go somewhere with me?"

She quirked an eyebrow. "Right now?"

"Get dressed and meet me at the front door."

I sent some texts, then bribed my dog to come inside with a bacon-flavored treat. Snow was second nature to her, and she always threw a temper tantrum when she was recalled. Sitting on her rump at my feet, she waited to cash in for her reward. I tossed her the treat and scratched her head. "Aunt Dagny's gonna come get you, okay? I've got business to handle." Her head craned, ears pulled back. "Not work, you judgmental snob. Something else I have to do."

Alice's scent never seemed to wither in my house, and after her morning shower the vanilla and floral combination perforated my sense of smell, like there was an Alice-scented candle lit in every room following me around my house. I knew she was here—omnipresent—but when I walked into my room, the sight of her hit me like a puck to the chest.

She was in my room. I wanted to keep her.

The sky's dim glow carried rays of light through the window, illuminating every inch of her semi-nude body. She'd removed my med school T-shirt and stepped into her thermal leggings, stretching and jumping into them. She twisted as they clung to her perfect ass and when she shimmied, her breasts jiggled. I couldn't decide what I wanted to suck on first, her ass or nipples.

Christ, she was gorgeous. I'd forgotten what I came in to do.

"Enjoying the show?"

My eyes flicked like a student getting caught peeking at a neighbor's test answers. I swallowed loudly. "I'd like it better if you were taking them off instead."

"You're the one making me get dressed."

Right. I had a mission.

As I passed her, my fingers grazed across her stomach. The feel of her hot skin only sent more blood roaring south.

I opened a cedar chest in front of the window and removed an empty, large bag, bigger than the daypack I had carried to the cabin last time. We moved around each other in silence, but I noticed Alice watching as I filled the bag with items from the chest: a packable blanket, a fire-starting kit, a flashlight, and a hunting knife. From the kitchen, I added freeze-dried potato soup. And a thermos of hot cocoa, sans peppermint flavor. I was playing to win.

"I'm ready," Alice said, reaching for her jacket on the coat rack, but I nudged her hand away. I appreciated suiting her up, not as much as removing her clothes, but it brought me pleasure to serve her. I loved watching her pulse flutter in her neck as I zipped the jacket up to her chin.

"Your jacket wasn't on the rack when I got home," I said as I tugged her beanie over her head and ears, then reached for her gloves from the shelf. "Did you take Snøf for a walk?"

We knew the answer. I feared she would panic when she was alone in my house, assuming she got spooked when I told her to wait for me—to be *home* when I got back.

"Yes," she lied.

I'd allow her that for the time being. Soon, I'd share my hopes for a future with her, but she wasn't ready to admit that she nearly walked away from me. From us.

I drove us to the snowmobile station in tethered silence; words sat idle on our tongues we couldn't expel. I recognized her hesitation and short responses as if they were my own placating solutions.

"Going to try to see the lights again?" she asked.

"A requirement before you leave," I said, swiping my credit card through the reader to rent a snowmobile. I looked down and flicked my gaze to her legs covered now in her adorable snow pants. I thought about my hand stroking her thigh during the drive. She wore those fucking suspenders again and my brain was rapid firing solutions to get them off as quickly as possible.

"No horse and carriage this time?"

"Didn't feel like waiting on the hems-and-haws of an animal tonight." That was for the full tourist experience. Today was for us.

I tightened the helmet strap under her chin. "You're okay going out there again? If we want to see the lights, we have to stay the night. Ride out in the morning."

"Hence the blanket."

"There's supplies there, but that's for our comfort."

"Silas," I heard the deep need in her voice when she said my name, "Are we finally going to have sex? You've been alluding to it, and we've had some fun, but I want to be clear where I stand."

I tucked Alice into my side and pressed a kiss to the top of her helmet.

"Whatever you want. Just because we're sharing a bed doesn't mean we have to, and obviously if this is too much pressure you can tell me."

"Definitely not pressured. I'm good."

We trudged through the snow to our ride, lifting our boots through a foot of snow, like wading in thick peanut butter. My hand grazed her lower back before taking a grip of her ass in the suspenders that I wanted to rip at the seam so I could sit her on my lap with my dick inside her. I spent enough time in the shower picturing the straps crisscrossed across Alice's bare back, gripping them with pressure and release as she rode me, a fair balance of control and softness.

"Or do you not have the energy?" She paused, crossing her arms and sassing off. Her stare was so intense I was prepared for her to push me on my ass in the snow. "After all, you did fall asleep with your head between my legs last night."

I rolled my eyes and bossed her around—teasing her was the best foreplay. "Get on the fucking snowmobile, Alice."

The pack was tightened to her back because it was too big to rest between us, and I wanted to feel her closer to me. She gripped my waist with the same force as last time, still terrified to ride on a half-ton diesel machine over feet of snow. I rubbed my gloved hand over hers, giving reassurance.

The clouds cleared out during the ride, garnering an afternoon blue sky perfect for viewing the Northern Lights.

Pulling up in front of the cabin, I paused on the snowmobile, gripping the handlebars. I flicked the visor up and gazed at the cabin. My heart raced erratically, like symptoms of tachycardia, a combination of adrenaline from the ride and portending what was next. I helped Alice carry the bag.

"Thanks for wearing this," I said.

She hummed a response as she took in the sight before her. "Why does it feel different today?"

"Different good or bad?"

"Not bad. Nothing's bad with you."

"Even when you're giving me a hard time about passing out?"

"I'm more concerned about your health than an orgasm, Silas."

We walked together to the door where I let us in. A pile of fresh firewood laid inside next to the fireplace, and on the small dining table was a basket of provisions and a small unit that uses gas cannisters to boil water.

"Nice touch," Alice said, shedding her outer layers, tossing them into a pile in the corner. She must have seen me tightly hold back a grimace because she said, "You don't like messes, do you?"

"It's okay."

"No, Silas," she toed off her boots and flicked them to the corner and I winced, "if you don't like it, you can say something." She glided toward me, almost predatory like.

"I'm trying to get better about it," I admitted. I arranged the firewood in the hearth and placed a ball of tinder on top of the stack before striking a match. My breath quickened as Alice crept next to me. We watched the fire's glow slowly emerge.

"Is this an OCD thing?"

"No, not technically. More of a... control issue."

"You don't like it when you don't have control?"

She studied me and her expression hardened. She removed her shirt and chucked it across the small space into the kitchenette, then her pants overhead. In only a bra, a tiny pair of underwear, and tall wool socks up to her knees, her eyes challenged me. "How aggravated are you at the mess I made?"

With her body on display, I didn't even flinch at the clothes she tossed. How could I possibly care about a mess when that beautiful woman was undressing before my eyes?

I slid my fingers in her hair, digging into the back of her skull with my finger pads. "Okay, Alice. You got me. I don't like messes. I like my space tidy, and objects in their designated places. I can't stand going to sleep with dirty dishes in the sink and I never let a load in the dryer sit overnight."

She swallowed a lump in her throat. Alice was the half-naked one in the room, but I was the one baring myself. I spoke quietly. "It's silly. But it's like the one thing I have control over in my life. Work and the damn snow dictate everything else."

I pulled her mouth to mine and she opened for me, her tongue flicking into my mouth. I rubbed my hands up and down her arms, generating heat and friction as she inclined herself closer, lifting a leg to wrap around my waist. I lifted her other leg and held her by her thighs, never pulling our mouths apart.

The room was charged with silence. I could hear the cracking noises of old wood settle, the delicate collection of snow falling on the roof. I slipped a finger between her thighs and toyed with the material covering her, and she released a moan into my mouth. My middle finger grazed her clit, and she whimpered softly.

"I was about to leave," she said, breaking the spell of

quiet. "Last night. I panicked being alone in your house, waiting for you to come home... to me. I don't want to say anything that will scare you off but I'm trying to figure out how to not be scared myself."

I held her in place around my waist as I carried us across the room, falling backward onto the couch. She straddled me, lowering the zipper on my jacket, and began removing my layers.

We talked as we explored each other's bodies. We *talked* —when we were both dying to fuck.

"When you leave Tidings, where are you going to go?" I asked.

"I don't have a plan. Life is a little bit messy for me," she chuckled. "And we know how you feel about messes."

I wrapped her hair around my fist and tugged gently; her neck collapsed backward, collarbones flaring. Her delicate throat pulsed.

"Don't do that," I said. Alice made a habit out of self-deprecation to deflect, and every time she made a comment at her expense, it was another opportunity to learn who she was hiding behind the veil.

She was immovable, not even flaying like a fish out of water, offering her still body to me. I tugged her bra down and rubbed a thumb over a nipple until it pointed and hardened like an icicle.

"I like you messy with your hair down." I sucked on a nipple and released it with a pop. Its wetness glistened. "The uptight librarian bun doesn't fool me."

"The sleek, tidy hairstyle is my control issue," she said on a breath. Then, just quietly enough for me to hear she added, "It's the one thing in my life I can predict."

I brought our faces back together, licking up her neck to her ear. "Show me your wild side, Alice."

CHAPTER 25

ALICE

Silas' arm tugged at my lower back as his other hand pulled my mouth to his.

I was on top, holding him down between my thighs and I wanted to add pressure to get a feel for him beneath his clothing.

"Did you pack condoms?"

He grinned. "Of course, I did."

"I'm on birth control, too."

I grabbed the hem of his black long-sleeve shirt and pulled it over his head. Silas' body was all-encompassing, welcoming me in with warm skin and aching flesh. He wrapped me in a hug and flipped us on the couch. He caged his elbows around my head and tangled his fingers in my hair as he playfully fluffed it up. "Be right back."

Silas jogged toward the bag, ripping the zipper open to pull out a packet of condoms. He was shirtless, pants unbuttoned, hanging loose on his hips. He unlaced his boots, and with a shrug, tossed them indifferently onto the ground.

I reached for him, fully unzipping his snow pants. His

red-hot erection was one second from burning a hole in his boxer briefs, and when I pulled it out, he groaned as I gripped the crown, already wet. I made no game of it, pulling him toward me and shoving his dick in my mouth. I twirled my tongue around the tip, then spit on it. Silas uttered a plea I couldn't hear through the blood roiling between my ears. My toes curled into the fur rug, clenching my thighs together at the sight and sounds of a man in pleasure courtesy of me.

"Your mouth is so warm," he gritted between teeth.

I pulled him out, and rested his cock on my chin, spitting a slow, long line dangling above him. Sweat formed at his furrowed brows.

"I want to be inside you, Alice," he lowered his voice to almost a whisper, "Please."

His fingers shook as he grabbed me under my arms to stand, rolling us onto the rug in front of the fire—an early inferno on the brink of fierce flames.

Silas kissed the underside of my jaw, working his way down my body and removing delicate pieces of fabric on my skin. He kicked his boxers off and here we were again, naked on a rug in front of a fireplace. Except this time, I was familiar with his body, he with my sounds of pleasure. We had more exploring to do, but I knew exactly what my body needed at that moment.

"I want it, too," I said. To feel him as close as two people could be together. He rolled a condom on and positioned himself between my legs. My knee bent and I dug my heel into the small of his back. I was wet and needy for him, grinding my hips in searching. I couldn't wait to see his face when he buried himself deep inside me; giving Silas pleasure was worth enduring Tidings.

Could I be here forever? With him?

He nudged at my entrance, and I released a tight breath, relaxing enough to get the feel of him inside me. "Of course, you would be tight, too," he sputtered in exertion. "Fucking perfect."

I didn't know what it felt like for a man when they fucked, especially that adrenaline surge in their veins as they entered, but Silas made sure I'd never forget every thought he had. He thrust inside me fully, and moved his hands to my hips, holding me down. He fucked relentlessly, dragging himself across me as he went in and out, hitting my perfect spot. From his force, I would have slid across the rug until my head banged into the wall if he hadn't held me down hard like I was a flight risk. I fucking loved it.

He was a desperate man, fucking me like he had something to prove and everything to lose. His eagerness, like everything else about Silas Hill, launched me into zero-gravity space. My back bowed and my chest arched. My fingernails scraped across the fur rug, searching, searching, searching for something to hold on to.

"Look at you, look at you," he breathed.

Orange shadows danced across my eyelids. I pictured what we looked like from above, his back muscles gliding across the floor, rolling with each thrust, my legs becoming increasingly limp and loose around his slick skin.

"God, how is this so good?" Silas' confessions floated around us. Sounds of wind brushed the windows, the door groaned, and the fire crackled and popped. "Die happy."

An orgasm didn't roar through me—it was a perpetual wave that never peaked or crested. Instead, pleasure poured out of me, rough, chaotic, and undulating. "Holy *hell*," I screamed or cried; I couldn't tell the difference.

Silas leaned back on his knees and pulled my wilted body to his chest. Our heartbeats were irregular and sporadic, pounding against each other's damp skin. His hair was wet above his ears, a bead of sweat drizzled down his jaw that I caught with my tongue. Salty with a hint of sweetness, and not even close to satisfying my parched mouth.

He grunted and threw himself on his back, pulling me up onto his face. "Sit," he commanded. His arms looped through my thighs, holding me in place across his face as he drank from me, piercing me with his tongue and sucking on my clit.

Slippery and wet, I couldn't tell anymore which part was me and which was his tongue. I leaned back on my hands, searching for anything that would bear my weight, giving my whole body to Silas' mouth. He licked and drank ruthlessly, trailing his tongue everywhere, yet nowhere at once.

On a scream of pleasure, I released myself from his grip and slid my way down his body, fucking impaling myself on him. I could handle any girth, any length, any which fucking way he wanted because my body was no longer mine. He could have it. He *did* have all of me.

He adjusted to a sitting position, pressing his forehead against mine, slick and hot. Spit and breath merged on our lips as my lower half lost control, rolling and climbing.

"Don't stop, don't stop," he groaned, kissing my lips, my neck, fingernails digging into the skin on my ass cheeks. "I can feel you getting closer—you're tightening and pulling me in. Fuck, *fuck.*"

"I don't know if I'm going to live through it," I said. It wasn't hyperbole; my heart felt like it was carving itself out of its chest. It wasn't a performance; it was a goddamn exorcism.

Breathless and panting, his fingers tangled in my hair, gripping my scalp. "Look at me."

I bucked, riding him wildly and loudly, wringing every ounce of strength I had left to give him friction and pressure. Our skin slapped. He was so deep he was hitting nerves I'd never felt before, and I couldn't fucking take it anymore.

Limbless and drunk. I was floating.

"Give us a chance," he prayed. He grunted out his orgasm, every hot rope filling the condom, filling me.

We peeled away until my head was on his chest, rising and falling with each breath. The tremors set off a chain reaction, knocking down the last sorry excuse for a wall around my heart.

"Alice," a deep voice woke me. My eyelids opened to Silas hovering over me, fully dressed. I looked down at the so-called bed we slept on, which was more like a generous cot, to find myself naked but covered in the blanket he brought from his house.

I rubbed my eyes, yawning. "Oh shit, we missed the lights again."

"No, we didn't, babe. Strong aurora activity incoming," he said with glee. "Get dressed."

"In my condition?" I flared my hand out. "I'm as solid an overboiled noodle."

His nose nuzzled my neck. "But the lights are almost here. It's dark now."

I summoned strength through the same commitment that helped me work the three-a.m. shift at a coffee shop in college—hardly, and with hostile complaints.

"Here," he said as he pulled my sweater on me.

"I need a restroom."

"It's in the back outside—lace up your boots." He pinched my butt, and I was confident I snarled at him.

He fucked me into a stupor.

Fully dressed but somnolent, I trotted to the latrine and washed my hands. A small gas fire pit lit the pathway where I met Silas on the balcony. Two chairs were placed on either side of the fire pit, but Silas pulled me onto his lap.

I gazed up at the sky, filled with clusters of stars and galaxies, shifting from inky black to a rich navy-blue, as if someone were adjusting a dimmer switch, gradually changing the brightness above me.

"Remind me what you said last time about this being a magical experience?" I asked.

His embrace tightened around my chest, and he rested his chin on my shoulder. "An old folktale from a hundred years ago, probably when they thought the Aurora Borealis was an alien invasion," he said, speaking so quietly I wouldn't be able to hear him if his lips weren't on my ear. "People claimed when they watched the lights from this spot, they... um," he rolled his lips together and leaned back against the chair. "That it brought good luck upon them."

"Well, I'm in need of some good luck that's for sure," I said.

"Troubles got you down?"

I turned my head over my shoulder to face him. He raised an eyebrow. "I don't think people just come to Tidings unless they're running from something."

"Or searching," he added.

"That too," I agreed. I nestled into his body, my lap resting between his strong thighs as I curled up into a small ball, ready for him to hold me close.

The fire helped stave off the bite of the treacherous cold, and combined with Silas' body heat it was surprisingly tolerable to be outside in the dead of night. Flickers of green lit behind the snow-covered mountain peaks, the first hints of the phenomenon to come.

"Watch, it happens so quickly," Silas breathed.

Wisps of light danced like fluttering wings, graceful and majestic.

When I thought it couldn't be more spectacular, with each second the colors deepened. A wave of emotion rolled through my stomach. Perhaps a mix of anxiety and apprehension, but I told myself those emotions were confused for excitement and audacity.

In the stillness of the night, the lights pulsed like a heartbeat of its own. Deep emerald and amethyst. My god, it was beautiful. My heart beat erratically, and I let out a shaky breath.

Silas rubbed my back. "I know," he whispered.

When the sky returned to its dark stillness, I missed it already. The memory of shimmering green silk was a wistful thought.

"It comes back every night," Silas said, eyes shimmering in the afterglow. "I mean, how on earth is that real?" He shook his head in disbelief.

I turned to him, my heart racing. "I didn't just see it," I said, my voice soft and full of awe. "I felt it."

It was a physical experience, like the vibrant colors knit through me, threading an open seam, binding it tightly closed. I wasn't an astrophysicist, so I didn't deign to understand the science behind it. I simply felt it for what it was: the idea that anything was possible.

He nodded. "We felt it together."

Flashes of the night's events burst through my memories like dancing shadows. Silas holding my hips down as his body showed me how much he coveted me, the aggressive jolt of our simultaneous orgasms. Then his gentleness as he held me outside, giving me stillness, and peace as I took in the most incredible sight I'd ever seen.

Tears froze against my cheek. I swallowed whimpers to hide my emotions.

I came to Tidings for a second chance and a fresh start.

But I think I just fell in love.

CHAPTER 26
SILAS

I wasn't the same man I was before mind-boggling sex with Alice. I felt like a shaken snow globe, pieces rearranged, falling anew.

Casual or friends with benefits worked well before, but I took specific steps to be painfully straightforward with women in my past. *I am not looking for a relationship, but I will always be honest and respectful. This is simply to have a good time and release tension, chase endorphins.*

I had never given Alice that speech. And I fucking hoped she didn't want to hear it.

Alice and I spent all night exploring each other's bodies. I found a freckle on that spot right below the ass cheek where it meets the thigh, and some in other places. My curiosity was piqued, and I sought new freckles on her body like a numismatist searching for the most rare and valuable coins to add to my collection.

I laid in the tiny bed remembering last night like it was a movie reel.

My hands moved with a mission of their own, gripping her ass, lifting the cheek to run a steady stream of licks across her heated skin. When I spotted the cute freckle, I paused my unhurried tongue trail, fucking consuming that freckle like it was a nutrient my body depended on.

I was so fucked.

She fell asleep after our late breakfast, now peacefully snoring and drooling. I unhooked myself from the barnacle grip she had over my arm and rolled onto my back. I stared at the ceiling, allowing my thoughts to wander unexplored places. Unleashed and untethered. A precarious position for a man's satiated sex brain to be.

Is this what it means to lose your mind over a woman?

Alice stirred in her sleep, her REM cycle nearing its completion, as my nocturnal self finally started to feel like I could drift off. She scooted into me, and I lifted my arms, placing them behind my head in hopes that her drowsy body would find the perfect spot on my chest to lay her head.

Success.

I grinned as she burrowed into me. Fingertips trailed down the curve and dips of her naked torso. She flinched and released a light, breathy giggle. Although I was beyond familiar with Alice's body, I think I skipped the part where she was ticklish. I lifted her chin, turning her face up toward mine. Her eyelids were closed but her lashes fluttered, and when I put my lips on hers, she indulged me.

A rush of blood bolted to my cock, surprising no one more than me after she drained my life force only hours ago. Alice's tongue flicked in my mouth and my hands found themselves back on her hips, pulling her onto my lap before a second thought crossed my mind. I pulled us up the bed until I was sitting up against the wood headboard and the tips of our noses hugged.

She let out a moan, sucking in her breath once she was

perfectly situated on my lap. My chest puffed at how quickly I could get rock-hard for her. I hadn't even looked at her tits yet and I was fucking ready.

"Sorry," she gritted her teeth, "I didn't realize how sore I'd be."

A smile tore across my face from ear to ear. She playfully swatted my cheek and then she pinched my jaw between her thumb and forefinger as she added, "I shouldn't have said that. Now you'll be insufferable, you peacock."

"If anyone should be cocky here, it's you. You do this to me, Alice." I nipped her ear and fingerprinted her hips, gravitating toward that sweet ass taking up all the headspace in my brain. I skimmed my pinky between her two plump cheeks, and I felt her skin light up with goosebumps. She tensed, holding back another hiss of breath. I relished in that feeling, selfishly. "I'll give you a break. I don't want to hurt you," I said all too proudly.

She rolled her eyes and pinched my nipple. "Ouch!" I yelped but groped her tighter to me. I ached at the closeness of her naked body resting on me without any grip or friction.

"You're an animal. I'm surprised it hasn't fallen off yet," she enunciated between wet kisses along my neck. "Besides, it's going to hurt me enough riding back on that big, heavy machine."

I put space between our faces and looked her square in the eyes. "Alice," I said softly, "I like your descriptor, but you can just say you love my big fat c—"

She flipped herself onto her back and a whoosh of laughter enveloped us. I kissed down her chest making my way farther south. I wiggled my eyebrows. "Want a tongue massage to make it feel better?"

"Flip me around, big guy, and I'll suck you off at the same time."

"Fucking deal."

So, I did.

And then we did.

AFTER THE BEST ORGASM OF MY LIFE—A TEASING, TAUNTING SLOW burn before I heard Alice gulp down my orgasm while she was perched perfectly on my face, wet and sated—I was nearly unconscious. I drifted in and out of sleep as I heard her busy herself in the cabin's little kitchen. The smell of warm vanilla and cinnamon aroused my senses.

"Found some coffee," she said in a tender voice. I appreciated not being awoken by the grueling sounds of my pager or loud screams. We drank in bed in companionable silence, then packed up to go home. I reluctantly dropped her off at the lodge and raced home to get ready for work.

The beginning of my shift was suspiciously quiet, but the nurses and techs knew not to mention it, a known superstition in medicine. We tiptoed around the awkward peace busying ourselves with word games on our phones. I typed a text message to Alice a hundred times before I erased it each time. I couldn't decide what to say to her because I had a hundred thoughts that circulated around things that would likely scare her off: *I'm leaving Tidings; will you come with me? I'm falling for you. I can't stop thinking about you.*

I needed more of her—now. I must have still been coming off my orgasm hangover because she was nestled in my headspace where she set up permanent residence. I wanted to feel her body heat next to mine. She was too far away.

But all I had of her was one photo on my phone I snapped when she was wrapped in a blanket in front of the dwindling fire, somewhere around five in the morning.

On my phone, I pulled up my nearly defunct Instagram account I hadn't used in years, mostly full of poorly lit food pictures, and searched for *Alice Woods*. Social media hadn't crossed my mind since I can't remember when. All I did was work and survive, work and survive. There were far too many options for accounts for me to search and filter her, so I googled her, adding in "Arizona."

A LinkedIn page was the first search option and then a list of news stories that grabbed my attention.

Arizona employee burns career with viral NSFW image

Ten dumb ways to get fired: Arizona state employee sent lewd AI image to colleagues

Vulgar email goes viral – State employee fired after blasting doctored image of boss to 30,000 colleagues

NSFW images goes viral—employee in hot water

"Shit," I muttered, staring at a thumbnail image of Alice next to one of the concerning headlines. It looked like a selfie with a group of friends; all but her face was blurred; it was definitely her. I clicked the story and read the summary paragraph, telling me all I needed to know. I turned my phone off and tossed it on my desk.

I leaned back in my chair and groaned.

That was why she came to Tidings, to run away from that mess. *What the hell were you thinking, Alice?*

I stared at the clock on the wall watching the seconds tick by as the memories from the past twenty-four hours merged into tangled thoughts. Alice's picture on the screen was the same woman who, hours ago, was leaning over my face, hair draped like curtains. I had tucked a tendril behind her ear, and she nuzzled her head into my hand, almost purring like a kitten. I traced her earlobe noting the small gold hoops she never removed; maybe she had forgotten they were there at all, like they were another part of her body. I had thought about asking her if she took them off when she showered but would rather find out for myself.

There were so many things I needed to ask Alice. And in fairness to her, I needed to tell her I found out about her history.

I scrubbed my hands down my face and rubbed my eyes.

Did she think this would go away on its own? Did Ginger know? Of course, Ginger knew; she knew everything, especially when found with a simple Google search. But she was still willing to take a chance on this girl whose reputation preceded her on the internet.

"Dr. Hill?" a man's voice snapped me back to the present.

I pressed the talk button on the hospital's communication device clipped to the V on my scrub top. "Yeah, what's up, Pete?"

He was probably bored off his ass tonight compared to what he'd been through overseas.

"You have a visitor."

"Ms. Morgan isn't due for another day," I replied, referring to the frequent flier who visited the emergency department every eight days with "chest pain." Ms. Morgan was a divorced, middle-aged woman who worked as the receptionist at the only car maintenance shop in town who couldn't get her fill of flirting with me once every ten thousand miles on my truck. So, she came here, like clockwork, every fourth day of my shift.

"If this is Ms. Morgan, then I'm gonna shoot my shot," Pete said in a husky whisper.

I pushed my hands against my desk, forcefully rolling my chair backward, spinning around one-eighty degrees. I nearly tripped over my own damn feet as I hustled with an extravagant sense of urgency. As I ran down the hallway, I pressed the button on the device and growled into the microphone, "Don't hit on her, Pete, I swear to god." The sound of feminine giggles came through the speaker.

Nurse Imelda shouted at me from the door of a patient's room, "Emergency, Dr. Hill?"

I slammed my hands on the double doors exiting the secured area of the emergency department and jogged to the front desk. I came to a halt, screeching my tennis shoes along the white flooring as I took in the sight before me. Pete leaned against the front desk, arm with the sleeve of his scrubs about to burst against his biceps. The asshole was smiling at our beautiful visitor. *Mine.*

She laughed and it took my breath away.

That laugh is for me.

I dabbed at the perspiration on my forehead with the back of my hand and straightened my back. "Alice? Are you okay?"

She appeared completely healthy, not a scratch on her.

Alice looked away from Pete and smiled at me. He winked and skipped back to his desk, opening a bag of pre-popped popcorn from the drawer, and tossing a piece in his mouth.

"I'm fine," Alice said. "How are you?"

Pete's eyes volleyed between us, and he grinned like a stupid motherfucker.

"Good, good. It's been quiet."

"Dr. Hill!" A barrage of indignant voices shouted my name from all corners of the lobby.

Shit, I had broken the cardinal rule. Alice caught me off guard, and she always made me act like an excited, clumsy golden retriever.

I wanted her to pet me.

Imelda poked her head out the doors and glared at me. "Stupid doctors," she said before she traced a cross over her body.

Alice reared back. "Now a bad time? Sorry, I can go."

"It wasn't a bad time until Dr. Hill invoked the call sign of chaos. I better fuel up and get my electrolytes in," Pete stood from the desk and walked toward the staff break room. "Alice, it was such a pleasure to meet you. Come by anytime. I'm here Monday—"

"Electrolytes, Pete," I interrupted and gave him my most menacing stare. He laughed and offered a crooked salute. A man who'd seen far worse on the battlefield wouldn't be threatened by me. It wasn't like nurses feared doctors anyway—an outdated stereotype. They ran the show and everyone within the hospital walls knew it.

Alice stood like a deer in headlights caught at the wrong time.

I shrugged. "We have fun. Gets us through the hard times," I said, trying to break the ice. "What are you doing here?"

She gave me a look that said, *Want to phrase that again?*

"I mean, I'm happy to see you. But shouldn't you be in bed?"

She stepped forward, meeting me toe to toe and tugged on my scrub top at the spot where it tucked into the bottoms. "Are you my daddy now?"

My body shivered from hair to toe like a wet dog shaking off after plunging into an ice-cold lake.

"You look scared shitless, Silas."

I swallowed hard and looked around us. The front desk was empty and there were no patients waiting. Even with no eyes on us, I still felt like my body was on fire.

"Don't worry, I'm not here to live out a *Grey's Anatomy* fantasy in the on-call room."

The thought didn't even cross my mind, because there was nothing sexy about a hospital, especially the emergency room. Communicable diseases and MRSA on every surface—no fucking thank you. I shuddered, but still the idea of being with Alice excited me. I adjusted my crotch, and she laughed, toying with the strings of my scrub pants.

I groaned at her touch. "Stop, please," I managed to say between gritted teeth, each word a struggle against the arousal ripping through me. I tugged her hand and found a dark corner where we had more privacy, away from the nurses' eyes peeking through the glass doors.

"I can go," Alice said, and her eyes lost all the confidence she walked in here with. "I feel like I overstepped."

"No. I'm happy to see you."

I ran my hands through her hair, tucking a strand behind her ear. It was an excuse to touch her. I'd make up a million new ones if it allowed my hands on her.

"Are you okay?" she asked quietly.

I gulped, remembering the webpage on my phone with her beautiful face and all those horrible stories written about her. We needed to talk about it, but now wasn't the right time. I still didn't know what I was going to say, or how to react. The rational, cerebral part of my brain kicked in, reminding me I barely knew this woman. She came into Tidings with her vanilla and floral scent, overflowing tits, and sweet kisses, bewitching me into a certified pussy-whipped fool.

Who was I to judge? I had secrets of my own.

Recruiters reached out to me daily for physician jobs in much sunnier places. I didn't get the job in California I interviewed for because it turned out it was only a legal job posting and they had plans to hire a resident graduating next spring.

It was for the best. Now maybe it was a decision I could make with Alice. I'd rehearsed the casual way I'd ask her if she wanted to be far more than casual... not a temporary fling in the snowiest town in America.

I didn't take for granted the risk and personal sacrifice it would be to her if she followed me across the country for my job. But I was confident I knew how I felt about her, that I'd go anywhere she wanted me to. I hoped she felt the same way about me. Another fucking conversation not meant for our current location. Hospital cameras were probably zoomed in on the sweat pooling at my forehead.

"Hungry," I said. "You?"

She smirked, opening the shoulder bag tucked into her side to reveal take-out containers. "Red curry sound good?"

"Perfect," I said. "We could eat in my office in the back."

"Oh, I brought it for you. I didn't think I'd stay and take up your busy time."

"You came all the way here to bring me dinner?"

She bit her bottom lip, a look of concern dawning. Could she have felt what I did last night, too? "I've never felt so vulnerable with someone," she blurted.

Her abrupt confession softened my rigidity. Tendrils of thread began to unspool, loosening the tight ball of tension.

"Suppose that's normal after your beautiful ass was on

my face—" I flicked my wrist to look at my watch, "—exactly seventeen hours and thirty-three minutes ago."

She slapped me across the chest, a flirtatious tic of hers I'd grown to love. Except here, in the dark corner of a hospital, I couldn't respond with her wrists pinned above her head.

"Want me to pinch your nipple again?" she teased.

"Ow, sorry, okay yes, you're vulnerable. Now, pretty girl, tell me all your dirty little secrets." Her face flinched and I bit my lip. Fuck, I hadn't meant to say that. I decided I was going to play ignorant and confront her about this later when she wasn't a cornered kitten.

I backed her into the corner as far as she could go, her back against the wall and nudged my leg between her knees. I stroked the side of her face with my open palm and softened my voice. "I enjoy teasing you."

"I think you're gonna get fired if you don't stop."

I lifted my hands. "Discretion is key."

She exhaled a long breath and scanned my eyes, searching for... something. "I've been thinking," she said. "My time in Tidings is ending soon... maybe sooner than I'd hoped. Which is hilarious because I have had a countdown app on my phone since day one."

"You've warmed to the place?" I asked.

"No, I'm still forever cold. But the people here have been —" she paused, searching for the right word to say next, "good."

"Unexpected," I stated, using her word again.

With her boot-covered toe, she drew circles on the white linoleum, clumps of snow fell off her shoe. "I got in trouble at my last job. I actually tried to get as far away from Arizona as possible. Looks like that wish came true."

"What kind of trouble?" *This was good, she could tell me herself and I'd be off the hook.*

A *whoosh* from behind me sounded, drawing my attention to the automatic glass doors at the entrance of the emergency department. A terse-looking woman, someone I was willing to bet was a tourist based on her impractical footwear, stomped through the entry. She didn't look like she was having a medical emergency; she looked homicidal.

I stepped away from Alice and approached the woman. "Ma'am, is there an emergency?"

"Damn right there is," she said loud enough to alert the entire hospital. Pete and Imelda were by my side before I paged them. The woman crossed her arms and turned her back to us, watching the doors as a man limped in. "My idiotic husband wanted to try something new."

"Butt stuff," Pete and Imelda whispered.

I turned to Alice who bit her lip, holding her composure. Barely.

"Duty calls," she said as she brushed past me, her pinky finger grazing mine. "I'll see you later."

I fought a hard battle with myself to not reach out and hold her, to kiss her goodbye. I wanted her to go back to my place and wait in my bed until I got off my shift so we could discuss her troubles, brainstorm together how to fix them, and then when all the talking and sorting was finished, sink myself into her.

Instead, I gave her a pathetic wave. "See ya."

CHAPTER 27
ALICE

The benefit of having sex with someone who worked night shifts was that his body was programmed to function all night long. The downside of being part of the diurnal crowd, was that his body will torture you all night long with the most wicked things the two-a.m. hour conjures.

I awoke before ten, which couldn't be said for Silas. His sleep schedule during his work stretches was chaotic and even on his off weeks I didn't know how he made up for it. He'd been putting extra stress on himself trying to make time for me, and while it was endearing, I felt guilty for him wasting so much time on me.

His night schedule was not a consistent strategy for dating, or hooking up, or whatever we were. Fortunately, I had today off so I could indulge in the stillness of the beautiful moment beside him.

The list of items to discuss was growing and the clock was ticking.

Over the side of the bed, I rubbed Snøf's soft head as she lay on the floor snoring blissfully. Waking up to the sounds of dog snores comforted me, and I loved having the excessively fluffy dog trail me around the office once I started watching her to ease Silas' schedule. I suggested Silas leave her with me on his work nights, maybe a slight manipulation for an excuse to see more of him, and the dog of course.

Neither seemed to mind.

I distracted myself by checking updates on my stocks, now that I'd moved everything out of Mark's choices. I still hadn't heard from him which I didn't mind, but I did find it unusual you could be with someone—*live* with them—and go full no-contact immediately. I must have really done a number on his fragile ego... poor reputation dragged through the mud being associated with me.

In the light of day, I felt like an absolute lunatic showing up at the hospital late last night. I was brimming with emotion—anxiety, excitement, infatuation.

Something more.

When I moved to this mysterious snow-drenched town on a whim of panic-induced mania, I was running away from an embarrassing situation, hoping when I came back to the real world I'd be buried in the trenches of the internet.

My employment contract stated three months was the maximum time I'd have this job. Even if I wanted to stay, there weren't any opportunities I'd be interested in. I didn't want to work at the café or the peppermint factory.

But it was a special place with people who genuinely cared about each other, a symbiotic economy that func-tioned like a well-oiled machine. Everyone rooted for the other to succeed. The most cutthroat person in town was Ginger who had bigger brass balls than the town sheriff. She was the glue that held the community together. Elvin and the old-timers gave Tidings the backbone of tradition, always adding an extra sprinkle of magic to flow through the veins directly to the heart of the city.

My worries were a mile away, my focus on the people who surrounded me. The smile lines that formed around Silas' mouth as he laughed at something someone said. The way Ginger's red waves blew delicately against the wind and her eyes rolled before she stuck her tongue out in the direction of Allan. Laughter, taunting, hugging—everyone there belonged.

Silas stirred, pulling me out of my head. I smiled at him, fulfilled and sated in all the right ways. But there was still the topic we avoided, and it was only going to hurt the longer I waited.

I ripped it off like a Band-Aid. I whispered my confession. "I won't have a job waiting for me back in Arizona," I said warily. "I have no idea what the hell I'm going to do next. I'd be embarrassed if I wasn't halfway scared to death."

"It'll work out," he mumbled.

My cheek rested on his chest and his heartbeat pounded in my ear. It was an embarrassing conversation but if I didn't look at him, I could muster the courage. "You're a professional. You have a mortgage. You could do a podcast on how to make your parents proud."

His fingers stroked my hair, fanning it out across his skin.

"Thank you," he said softly.

His breathing labored, in and out of sleep as I rattled my insecurities. "Aimless... thrown away... purposeless."

"I wished I had more time to explore other things when I was in my twenties." He sharpened his gaze at me. "All

I've done is school and work. Moved here for work, not even caring about the experience."

I rested my chin on his bare chest, looking up at his sleepy face. "Something else has been on my mind."

He hummed an exhausted response but didn't open his eyes as he tightened his hold around me.

"Don't get mad or I won't do that thing you like again."

He opened one eye to look at me. "You have a knack for softening me up before you go in for the kill."

"It's about Dagny."

I felt his body flinch and his face screwed up in disgust.

"Gross. Please don't talk about my sister when you're naked next to me."

I slapped him on his chest. "I can go put on clothes."

His arm tightened against me again, pulling me closer. "Or you can stop talking about my sister."

"You're talking about her."

"Because I'm asking you to not talk about her while—oh fuck," he buried his face in his pillow. "Just go on with it at this point."

I stroked my fingers through the hair on his chest. "She wants to teach biology at the local school."

"Dagny is going to medical school. I've told you this."

"*You* have. But she hasn't."

He groaned and pushed himself up, resting his back on the pillows stacked against the headboard. I sat, clutching a pillow against my front.

"She will come around," he said, assuring himself more than me. "She's anxious about the MCAT. Everyone is."

"I don't know, Silas. It sounds like she doesn't even want to go to medical school. To be honest, I think you're the only one who wants her to become a doctor."

When our mouths weren't glued to each other's bodies,

I'd painted my family dynamic with broad strokes, and he returned in kind. I knew Silas more intimately than I'd ever known any other man, yet there was still so much of him he kept tucked away. But I got the impression Dagny's future weighed heavily on him.

We all had a web of issues to sort through before bringing in outsiders—if ever. But I'd observed enough to know his intentions were noble; he simply wanted his sister to succeed in her career. If only it were so *simple* because her career of choice was different than what he wanted. But it wasn't his choice.

My dad expected greatness according to *his* standards, a level I hadn't achieved, nor did I desire to pursue. It may have taken me longer than expected but being in Tidings gave me a new perspective. I enjoyed being a part of a tight-knit community and thinking of ways to help streamline services; maybe I—

My train of thought came to a screeching halt.

It struck me like the crash of a stack of ceramic plates.

Every decision I'd made up until this point, for better or worse—and most of them had been real shit—was meant to happen, to bring me to Tidings.

The silly little hotel front desk job was the change agent. My life would never be the same after Tidings.

I couldn't say it, but it was right there, scratching my brain, and trying to claw itself out of my skull.

What kind of nature-bending shit was sprinkled in this snow-covered village?

I turned my head away, hoping he didn't see the emotion that I felt brimming in my eyes.

"Tidings is a good place for her to hunker down and focus on studying until she takes the test in January," Silas said.

I looked at him. Really looked at him and appreciated the solid man next to me. One who stripped me bare more than in the literal manner and hadn't run away from what he'd seen but adored each piece of me. Pressure built inside me, the sudden urge to shout it from the rooftops, to express myself fully and without shame or fear. To tell him what he had meant to me.

I'd fallen in love with him. But was it real love if it wasn't enough for me to want to stay to be with him?

I ran my tongue across my lips. "Silas." I climbed on his lap and straddled his waist. Logically, not the best position to be in when hoping to have a breakthrough conversation with someone while said someone's morning wood was lined up perfectly between your thighs.

"Good, that conversation is over." His eyes were crowded in sleep and steel, broaching on lust. "Because I'd like to put my mouth to use on something else."

"Maybe you should hear her out."

"Alice, you—" he paused to scan my face in a way that felt like reverence, "—are a very caring person. Thank you for bringing this to my attention and for looking out for her, too. I'll talk to her and try to help her remove any distractions."

"I don't think you're understanding me."

"Oh, I understand clearly." His hands drifted to my lower back, kneading the top of my ass. A collection of his fingerprints collected in that favorite spot of his like a book of stamps. "Now, I'm telling you that we are done discussing this."

The overbearing, overprotective big brother was admirable in small doses, but for their relationship's sake, he needed to drop the interference act.

"I don't appreciate your tone with me," I said.

"And I don't appreciate you getting involved in personal family matters," he replied.

And furthermore, he couldn't be such a brute toward me.

I slumped backward. A forceful blow to the gut. I tore myself from his lap and grabbed my clothes off the floor, bunching my sweater and pants into a ball covering my front. "Right. None of my business."

I walked to the bathroom as I heard an exaggerated sigh behind me, with my name a plea on his lips. I closed the bathroom door and splashed water on my face.

As I dressed alone, Silas knocked gently. "Fuck, Alice. I am sorry."

Some indecipherable sound, nestled deep in my chest, escaped. I tightened my lips. Saying nothing was the best approach because if I opened my mouth the only thing that would come out would be a full-blown sob.

Could I escape out the window in the bathroom? But then I'd get frostbite on my toes because my shoes were by the front door and I'd end up in the hospital being treated by him and truly nothing could be worse than that, right?

"I'm very protective of Dagny," his voice carried through the closed door. It was the most vulnerable he'd been with me about his family. "Sometimes she makes mistakes but she's my little sister, so I help her."

I perched my butt on the edge of the bathroom sink and crossed my arms. "Isn't that for her to find out on her own, Silas? God, you sound like my fucking dad. Is this a man thing?"

"This is not sexism, Alice. It's wisdom. Lessons taught through lived experiences. If I, and I'm assuming this is where your dad is coming from, too, can help Dagny avoid unnecessary consequences then it's my duty to do so."

I opened my mouth but couldn't find the right words. Was he out of his damn mind?

"Alice?"

I pinched the bridge of my nose, nonplussed.

"Take your time," he responded quietly.

"Okay." I leaned against the door and spoke quietly, even though I wanted to rage scream. "From what I've heard, she wants to be a teacher and not spend the next eight or whatever years in school digging herself into more debt. She has a teacher's heart and passion. I'd suggest talking to her sincerely about that and hearing from her directly, okay?"

"Teaching is noble. But it's not an option for her."

"And who are you to say that about her choice?"

"I'm—" Then, silence. A thud smacked the door before Silas dragged himself down to the floor, his toes peeking under the gap. "Would you come somewhere with me?"

"You can't be serious. I'm not going to the sex cabin!"

"No, something else. Sometimes I'm better at showing than telling."

Without making eye contact or saying a word to each other, we got dressed for the elements and met at the front. Silas held the door open and we traipsed through a layer of fresh snow—at what point did it stop being fresh if it never ended?—to his truck. He opened the passenger door. I murmured a wary thank-you.

We drove to the other end of town in painful silence. I kept my gaze on my lap, fiddling with my gloved hands until he parked behind an unremarkable building I didn't recognize. "I shouldn't have gotten involved between you and Dagny."

"No, you're right. I needed to hear those things."

"You don't have to placate me. Just because we're

sleeping together doesn't mean I should insert myself like that."

He gripped the top of the steering wheel with one hand and stuck his tongue in his cheek. "Is that what this is? Sleeping together?"

"I think we are one of those cliches." I looked out the window at the unassuming building. "Right person. Wrong time."

"Half-way right." He pressed his jaw together firmly, a subtle tension playing across his cheek.

"Well, we had the pleasure of meeting in Tidings. But it's not forever."

"No, Tidings is certainly not forever."

He flipped through his console and other hidden storage areas looking for something and coming up short. In a sign of frustration, he removed his beanie and combed his fingers through his hair, until he froze when his gaze fixed on my chest.

"Whatever you're looking for isn't in there," I said, nudging my breasts with a palm.

"Sorry, I thought I had hand warmers in here."

I gasped. "I'm not going out there, it's snowing."

He snapped his fingers. "It's always snowing. Out you go."

With a groan, I reluctantly made my way out of the warm truck into the fucking elements I hated with every fiber of my being. Layers of tech heat and wool were a fortress against the cold, but my face remained exposed, hardened, and cold. A small finger flick could crack my skin like a delicate sheen of ice. "You know, just because I let you tell me what to do when I'm naked doesn't mean you're my boss now."

He grabbed me by the hand and dragged me down a

back street, behind a restaurant where the containers of trash smelled like discarded food and cigars. If he was planning an impassioned farewell fuck in the putrid alley, count me out.

I gagged. "This is disgusting. You've got to stop taking me places where I think bodies are decomposing."

"Almost there," he said with a tight jaw.

At the end of the alley, we stopped in front of two large metal doors displaying a sign marking this entrance for deliveries and loading only. I looked up at all eight stories of it, stained-glass windows stacked row by row.

"I've never been here before."

He hit a string of numbers on the locked keypad and a click sounded before he opened them.

"Because you wouldn't be caught dead coming here otherwise."

He opened the door, and an unmistakable scent wafted directly toward me, assaulting my senses. Oh, sweet hell.

"You broke into the peppermint factory?" I smothered my nose and mouth with my gloved hands.

"I didn't break in. I know a guy."

"And he, what, hands out the entry code in exchange for a free appendectomy?"

He released a low chuckle. "I don't do those."

"This feels illegal. Does Tidings even have a jail?"

He reached for my hand but then thought twice about it. We walked until we reached a set of double doors that automatically opened as we got closer. Sounds of whirring machines and loud voices carried and I froze. "People are here," I whispered.

I crossed my arms and continued following him down a runway bridge that overlooked the night crew, dressed in white overalls, and hairnets.

"There were quite a few workplace accidents that happened over the span of two months. Someone lost a finger, another worker had a chemical burn, a broken toe. I got permission to come by because I wanted to see what was sending people to my ER regularly."

"You moonlight as an OSHA inspector?"

We stood shoulder to shoulder watching the assembly line work flawlessly.

"It helped to see the common cause of injuries."

"And your conclusion?"

"Poor management. Ginger took care of it swiftly."

I snickered. "You help a lot outside of the hospital. That was not your responsibility at all."

"No, it wasn't. But I felt the employees were too scared to report their shitty boss."

"Wouldn't be the worst thing in the world to be forced out of Tidings," I grumbled.

He gave me a sidelong glance. "These are lifers and the peppermint factory is the bedrock of the economy. It started almost a hundred years ago because candy canes were the cheapest and easiest candies to make, giving this desolate area a leg up during the depression." He pointed to different sections of the assembly line, describing in detail the role of each area. "Winter is the peak season for fresh products. I don't see any candies tonight. Looks like they're making vats of lotion or shampoo."

I appreciated the hard work it took to get one peppermint tea bag made, but I'd never drink it again for the rest of my life. Even the scent of rosemary was ruined for me. Too close in the herb family.

"Are you trying to turn me into a peppermint proselytizer? Never gonna happen," I aired my frustration and set my hands on my hips. "You dragged me here and now I want to leave."

He tilted his head, a silent plea for me to follow him across the suspended bridge, and we settled into a seat reserved for official tours. We didn't talk for a while; the hum of the machinery filled the silence. A loud bell rang, signaling break time, and we watched as the employees filed out to the break room.

"I've accommodated everyone my whole life," Silas said. The vulnerability in his expression hinted at an emotional release.

Still upset about our earlier conversation, I pushed that aside temporarily because I could tell he was determined to say something he'd been working his courage toward. I watched the lines on his face twitch as he paused, coalescing his precise words.

"I came to Tidings because it checked all the right boxes. An exceptional career opportunity, a place where I could find a stable place as a community helper. I check in on Elvin and the other old-timers because they're too stubborn to go to their primary care doctor. I'd rather not find them dying in the ER, or already dead, from an untreated heart condition. I was upset about the amount of workplace injuries, so I did my own investigation. But... Alice." He put his elbows between his knees and lowered his head, clearing his throat. "I hate this fucking place."

What I anticipated him to say was nowhere near close to that.

I thought we were headed for a proper soliloquy about why Tidings was meant for him. Us, possibly. Drastic plans scurried through my head like he'd suggest I become the manager at the peppermint factory. Maybe he'd run for mayor and finally start the reindeer Olympics.

He placed one hand delicately on my cheek. "When we first met at the airport, I had just come back from visiting California. I told everyone I was there for a vacation, but I was interviewing for a new job."

Ginger had warned me that he'd be leaving. It didn't feel any better even with the heads-up from her. And I also didn't know why I gave a shit. I wouldn't be in Tidings for much longer either. I'd be gone soon, too. Maybe it was because it was the end of this, of his legacy in this community. The end of us, whatever we were.

He formed his hand on my face, adjusting his grip as if it rocked through turbulence. "The sunshine felt so good. So fucking good, like the first home-cooked meal after eating junk shit at college, you know? But something didn't sit right. I was pissed off. Frustrated. I felt trapped. And then I saw you, and I fucking swear to you Alice, you *glowed*. I felt like I was standing next to the sun next to you. And in the car, you smelled like... like a flower but not a rose, something sweet, plus warm like what I imagined a clear blue sky would smell like. And god, it's hard to explain but you smelled like *life*."

"Silas, I—"

"No, please. I have more to say, okay? Then you can give me your rational rebuttal because I'm sure I sound insane." He put his hands on the side of my face, glanced at the tip of my nose, my chin, then my eyes. "There's this thing about Tidings—you can't explain it. Like the town is halfway sentient or magical or some shit. The day before I left for California, I spent every minute in between seeing patients on the phone with the travel company. They messed up my flight and I had to get a layover instead of a direct flight to LA. I connected in Phoenix. I had no reason to be there, Alice. I had eight hours to kill so I went downtown. I saw *you*. I know it was you. Rolling your broken suitcases down the sidewalk, crying. Your friend ran up to you and gave you a hug and insisted on giving you a ride to the airport instead of you taking the bus."

I couldn't think beyond the sight in front of me. Silas' swollen eyes were glassy, and his mouth was tight holding back. The undereye bags looked heavier suddenly. He was panic-stricken. He put his nose to mine and we stayed like that, consuming each other until our breathing slowed and synched. He added, "I knew you before I met you. And now I'm in love with you."

A snorting wail escaped me.

A decent man told me he loved me. *Me.* Hot mess me. He confessed it on a park bench in the middle of the peppermint factory and now I couldn't ever hate the smell of peppermint because it smelled like invigorating, all-consuming love. "Please take me home."

For hours, until I couldn't tell if my legs were still attached to my body or if I was even on a planet and not floating through space, we devoured each other. I'd never known what it meant to make love, but that's exactly what Silas did to my body. To my heart. He told me over and over, without refutation or concern, how much he loved me.

I had the love of a man who was so desperate for me he was convinced it was fate.

But he didn't know my whole story.

I'd never felt more ashamed.

CHAPTER 28

SILAS

It was the beginning of my extended stretch of paid time off and I'd never been as excited to indulge in every minute. In the four years I'd worked at Saint Lucia, I hadn't asked for more than the standard days off between shifts more than once. I believed my mental health was strumming along fine; I was in great physical shape. I hadn't considered the possibility that nothing about that was true.

Until I found something—someone—who made my time off never feel long enough.

No intense workouts. No peer-reviewed medical journals to skim or CME credits to earn. Instead, my to-do list was simplistic and sensational: Alice, eat, sleep.

I wanted that woman for all five of my scheduled meals and snack breaks. The horny part of my brain, the kind that only came to see the light of day when I was exacted of every part that revolved around my job, was ransacking my brain like a jewel thief breaking glass, tipping over shelves, and stealing whatever they could find. In the hours leading up to taking my small suitcase over to Alice's where I planned to seduce her for seven days straight, my one-track mind placed my dick in the premium showcase section, foregoing any other want or need of mine.

How terribly unfortunate for my inner primal need to rear its head on the only day when my sister needed to talk with me. We didn't have quality one-on-one time; usually we spoke in passing at the restaurant or around our mutual group of friends.

It was time to show my cards and let her secure the winning bid.

As I drove to Dagny's house, a call came through, flashing an unknown number across the screen in my truck that I sent to voicemail. I had a hunch who was calling, and it was an issue for later.

Everything was hitting all at once today.

I knocked three times on Dagny's apartment door before I shot her a text that I was about to lose an ear to frostbite if she didn't answer. The other side of the door proved signs of life with the clatter of whatever three girls did in the privacy of their own home as they did the hair and makeup shit to get ready for a night out.

I peeked through the window to the side of the door and watched a high heel fly across the living room followed by a shimmery piece of fabric. One of Dagny's roommates appeared from the darkened hallway, draped in a towel and gathering the items roommate number two tossed toward her. She looked up with a shoe and dress scrunched in front of her towel and made eye contact with me through the window before I could duck out of the way. She shrieked, a piercing girl sound I heard through the walls straight to my inner ear. Ten seconds later, Dagny came stomping out of her closed door, scowling.

She jerked the front door open. "You're early." She

crossed her arms and looked me up and down, preparing to launch an insult.

"Sorry to interrupt the fashion show." We remained in a defensive stance on either side of the threshold. I looked around her shoulder into the house. "I'm freezing, Dags."

She rolled her eyes and stepped aside. "Laura and Janie, my annoying brother is here so dress appropriately. We'll be in my room."

"Annoyingly *hot*," someone snickered behind a door.

I didn't visit Dagny often. Truthfully, I'd only been over three times and one of those was technically considered breaking and entering, but my mission had been to check her slumped-over body for a pulse. I'd never had wild party days like her, although she did it enough for the both of us to make up for my lost time. Looking at her outfit, I bit my tongue holding back on my suggestion for her to stay in and study instead of going out, but that betrayed the reason for my visit.

This was about forging a new relationship with my sister. One that was better for her. For us—I hoped. The future I dreamed of didn't include keeping eagle eyes on my baby sister, even though it was a sour pill to swallow.

"Thanks for making time for me," I said as I sat at a desk chair spinning in a half circle. I held my appendages in tight, equal parts scared and uncomfortable. The fear of a sex toy walking on its own hind legs out from under her bed kept me on edge. Nope, not my sister. She did not do that. I scrubbed my hand down my jaw and sighed.

"Relax, nothing's going to hurt you in here, Silas." She sat at the edge of her bed cross-legged, and she looked so young. My twelve years her senior felt like a defensible reason to be the know-it-all brother with life lectures I had bored her with for years. Since she was born, I held the belief it was my duty to share wisdom, to help her carve an easier path without the dumb mistakes I made. Not anymore.

"I am sorry," I started. "An apology is long overdue but hopefully not too late. You are smart and spectacular. You deserve a brother who is supportive and helpful, or who shuts up and nods his head, when and if you decide to share parts of your life. I saw the potential in you from an early age and I knew—strongly believed—you were born to be a physician. I wanted you to succeed along with me. But along the way, I misconstrued your success as mine. I see now that I was overbearing. Or, as you put it earlier, annoying."

Dagny stared blankly at me, not even a raise of an eyebrow.

I braced my hands on my thighs. I'd delivered catastrophic news to patients before. But nothing had ever made me feel like I wanted to puke like this conversation.

I was letting go.

The realization that I'd bossed her around for so long was... discomforting. "I want whatever makes you happy. I'm proud of you." I released a huff and refrained from pulling my hair out of its follicles.

She uncrossed her legs and stood in front of me. She was five inches shorter than me, and I had eighty pounds on her, but at that moment I'd never felt smaller. "Now might be a good time to tell you I've taken up stripping at the Reindeer Lodge."

I shuddered. "Is that what they do there?"

Dagny smirked and outstretched her arms, summoning me to stand for a hug. "It's not a big deal, Silas. I appreciate you looking out for me." She gave me slow, intentional pats on the back. Patronizing. I cringed as I suffered through my punishment.

"Sorry for being an overbearing asshole."

"Apology accepted. But your first mistake was thinking you could force me to do anything."

"But you've been studying for the MCAT. Why waste your time?"

"Meh, it was kind of cool knowing I wasn't going to go through with it. I learned a lot and it proved helpful," she said with a shrug and a mysterious glint in her eyes. "You know, since I was hired to be the new science teacher at Tidings High."

I pulled her in for a tight hug, rocking her from side to side. "Dagny, that's incredible. I am so happy for you."

"Thank you. It still feels like a dream."

It felt good to hug my sister without a black cloud hanging over us. And I was relieved how easy the whole thing was to handle. She was less ball-busting than I anticipated. I was prepared to be dressed down and disemboweled.

I wiggled my shoulders out of the hug, but she kept a crocodile grip on me. "Ah, since we're here," she said. "Remember your love for me and your desire for my well-being?"

"You're going to say something that'll ruin my life."

"You stay put and listen to me," she released me from her tight grip and stared daggers at me. She was wholly capable, and I was so wrong to think I could shrink her down into expectations I had neatly carved out for her. "See how easy it was to have a simple conversation about something? Many of the world's greatest problems would be resolved if we listened to one another."

I rubbed my bicep where she had latched. She was

petite but I swear she could bench press twice her weight. "Why do all the women I love and respect the most in my life completely terrify me?"

Dagny craned her head.

"Get on with it," I bemoaned. "What else do you have to tell me?"

"I'm staying here in Tidings."

"Yes, I assumed since you got a new job."

"And I'm moving in with Pete."

"Who?"

Dagny rolled her eyes and huffed. "Pete. Tattoos. Army medic."

"You're moving in with…" I backed my legs up against the bed to catch me before I passed out. I dropped my head between my knees, blood rushing back to my brain. "Pete? The nurse?" The words squeaked out of me. A tunnel crept into my vision.

Oh my god, this is what a panic attack feels like.

"I love him."

I rubbed my temples. "No, this is too much."

"You're not in charge of my life, remember? In fact, he had finally given me the courage to tell you about the job and him, but you beat me to it first with your neurotic heart-to-heart. So, thank you for being the first to go; it made this a lot easier. I was expecting bloodshed. Yours, not mine."

"What do you mean you *love* him? How long?"

"Back off, brother bear."

"I'm having a major medical event, Dagny!"

"Silas?" Dagny's voice drifted somewhere in my periphery. The back of her hand landed on my forehead. "You're taking this exactly as expected. My track record is perfect."

"Dags, this is the worst possible guy for you to be with,"

I swallowed down bubbling vomit. I wheezed. I confessed, "I can't be the intimidating brother—he was in special forces!"

Dagny laughed. "He's definitely not scared of you. Especially since you're leaving Tidings."

"What?"

"Don't play dumb. It's been in the works for a while. Then Ginger got Alice here and it was all but set in stone."

"Ginger did *what?*" It was possible I stroked out and was having delirious hospital visions.

Dagny walked to her dresser, grabbing earrings from a bowl and poked them through her ears. Her reflection in the vanity mirror caught mine. "I think you have news to share with someone else now."

ALICE HAD AIRPODS IN HER EARS AS SHE SWAYED AT THE KITCHEN sink, her back to me, giving me a gloriously indulgent view of her ass clad in shorts so small they could have been bikini bottoms—they were indecent and spectacular. Goddamn, I loved that ass. Like a perfect plush pillow made for my face. I leaned against the wall, bracing myself to get comfortable and enjoy the fucking show for however long I could stand there being a creep before my hands ached from not touching her.

Which lasted all of two minutes before I needed to get my hands on her. I removed my outer layers and placed my phone on the table before walking up behind her.

I drew nearer and slid my hand gently across her hip when she jumped, sending a pot she was scrubbing up over her head, splashing her hair with soap and spewing suds on my cheek.

"Oh my god!" she yelled. "You can't sneak up on people like that."

I laughed at the pile of bubbles on her head and brushed them off. I pulled her AirPods out of her ears and set them on the counter. "Sorry," I said, shutting the faucet off.

"No, you're not. You enjoyed that." She crossed the kitchen to grab a towel and dry her hands and dabbed it at the suds on my cheek. "Perv."

She stepped back, butting against the counter. I cradled her hips in my hands and leaned in, pressing my nose to her neck. "You smell good."

"A mix of dish soap and sweat?"

"Bottle it up and sell it." I licked up the side of her neck. "But what is that floral scent you always have on? Light but earthy."

She hummed. "Must be the last of this lotion I bought back home, scents of the desert. Honeysuckle and sagebrush."

I buried my nose into her. "I'll buy you a lifetime supply."

And for a brief blissful, domestic-feeling moment, I forgot about the difficult conversation I had with Dagny. I went into it thinking the worst thing that would happen was I'd have to walk with my tail between my legs; *never* did I imagine she'd tell me about her and Pete. The thought made my stomach churn.

I kissed Alice on her cheek, her lips, her forehead. I wanted to cover every inch of skin, a task I was eager to begin and never wanted to end. She wiggled out of my touch back to the sink, spraying water around the basin and turning on the disposal to suck debris down the drain. The loud noise broke my musings, and I cleared my throat, reaching for the glass of water she set in front of me, sensing perhaps I needed a minute to gather myself.

"I talked with Dagny." I drained the water in one swallow and refilled it at the fridge dispenser.

She dried her hands on a pale-yellow dishcloth. "Yeah?"

"It sucked."

"But you were such a brave boy," she teased. I appreciated that.

I fumbled my way through her kitchen, opening cabinets until I found the one where she stored glass containers for leftovers, placing the dishes she hand-washed. "Did you know about her and Pete?"

"Pete?" she asked. "The special forces medic?"

"Yes, that would be the one." I banged my head against the cabinet. "They're moving in together."

"Aww, how cute."

"Nope, not cute. Scary."

Alice opened the fridge and pulled out a plate with plastic wrap on top. She peeled it off revealing one piece of pumpkin cheesecake. She waved it in front of me, the aroma of cinnamon and nutmeg wafting through the air. I reached for the drawer behind me to grab a fork, but she stuck her finger in the cheesecake and held it up to my lips.

"Sounds like she has her future all planned out."

I caught the sight of her throat working a swallow. Her mouth parted as she scanned my face. We toddled on that wobbly line between present and future, dodging important conversations that couldn't wait longer if we wanted to avoid a clusterfuck of last-minute adjustments—financially, physically, and everything between.

I had Alice here and now, with her fingers on my lips, I could postpone the inevitable for another hour. I licked the cheesecake off her finger and then fed her with mine. We finished the dessert without exchanging any words.

She linked her fingers with mine and dragged us to the couch. I stroked my thumb on hers, braving myself to mention the unmentionable.

"The sun's out today," she noted.

I was prepared to beg, plead, bribe if it meant having her. I wanted Alice as my future more than anything else. But I stayed frozen in fear with her legs wrapped around my hips and her mouth pressed against my shoulder, kissing and nibbling my skin.

The letdown could wait another day, a lie we told each other in silent understanding.

In the precious moments of sunshine, we clung to each other, yearning for something brighter amidst the melancholy.

Light was a scarce resource in Tidings. If the gloomy look on her face was any indication, she agreed.

CHAPTER 29

ALICE

"I draw the line on moose tongue," Bror said. "I'll never be *that* hungry." He spoke with his arms waving in front of my face amidst the chaos of the rambunctious game of *Would You Rather?*

I looked around the dinner table at my friends, laughing and poking fun at each other. Each person was unique with their own individuality, yet they loved each other unconditionally, and it was hard to imagine I never knew people like this existed almost three months ago.

Tidings itself didn't exist in my real life, even in my wildest dreams.

But I'd made friendships that felt like they could last a lifetime, even out of this bubble, and somewhere under the warm sun.

Most of all, Silas, had been worth every resentful feeling I had toward a snowflake.

Tidings was never my forever plan. Not even a million dollars could coax me here long-term. All that money would be spent on wool layers and building myself a walking insulated bubble. I wasn't built for this climate. It simply did not exist within my abilities as a human to function.

Some people were natural-born leaders, dancers, or even doctors. I was a natural-born lizard, who needed a dry, hot rock in which to lay my body upon or I'd shrivel into nothingness.

Something more settled and defined called on me to move on to the next part of my life.

Tidings was like new age cold therapy, a shock to my system that reset my cells, turning over a newer, better me. A perspective that was the most logical one I'd ever had. A chance to experiment, learn something new, plucked from my comfort zone, and tested my mettle.

I was even looking forward to catching up with my parents and sister. Telling them everything about Tidings.

Well, not everything.

What will I tell them about Silas?

"Is anyone shocked he chose the testicle option?" Ginger asked before she took a delicate sip from her martini glass, a fragrant espresso-and-peppermint concoction I could identify from across the high-top table. She was on her third of the night but was still stitched together tighter than the threads on her custom black blazer. I hadn't figured out if I was more scared of or infatuated by Ginger. Style impeccable, shifty as hell, the emotional strength of a steel beam, and handled her liquor better than anyone else. Either way, she may have started off as my supervisor, but I would consider her a friend.

Everyone at the table was my friend.

Bror waved a middle finger in her face and Ginger grabbed it, playfully chomping down. "For the record, in the event of the apocalypse, I will not hesitate to eat any of you," Ginger said. "Survival of the fittest, fuckers."

The cacophony that insulated us drew to a ruptured silence, except for me who was laughing. The group simultaneously directed their stares to me, as if I were the offender. "Oh, was that not funny? I thought she was making a joke."

"You haven't been here long enough, Alice," said Dagny. "She's deadly serious."

"Oh." I looked away as I finished my drink. "I'm going to get another one."

I walked to the bar to give me a chance to check my phone for an update from Silas without prying eyes and nosy questions. He planned to meet us here after meetings at the hospital. I missed him even though I had seen him this morning leaving my place.

And last night. The day before.

Admitting our relationship was only temporary, when our connection would never fade, stung like a swarm of angry hornets, piercing my skin and leaving permanent pockmarks. Silas was a fling—an exceptional one.

Where his fingers touched, my skin burned with imprints. Everything hurt.

I wanted to tear at my brain. The closer I got to figuring things out, the more tangled the wires became, too. If I stayed here for him, I'd need frequent trips to white sandy beaches and make real investments in more underlayers. But I could make it work. That rowdy group of people perched around the table to my back became my found family faster than I could say "estranged sister."

Tidings' people were warm and hospitable, while the place itself was inhospitable and brutally cold. Some people adapted to that and endured the long, dark days, and polar temperatures. I wouldn't be able to overcome my resistance to that. I'd need to be reprogrammed in a lab with new, adaptable DNA.

Winter Solstice had come and gone, the darkest nights of the season behind us, and Tidings was heading toward brighter days. Sommar was still months away but we were promised sunshine and temperatures warm enough to grow flowers. Wild mountain berries grew like weeds. A surplus of carrots, beets, and leeks stocked pantries. Never-ending fields of tulips, lupines, and peonies covered mountain ridges and yards like free-spreading clover grass. I smiled until I remembered I shouldn't. My throat thickened at the familiar sense of self-loathing I elicited.

Self-sabotage was my personal Olympics.

Silas deserved far better than me. And I'd need to summon the courage to tell him tonight.

I unlocked my phone, disappointed to see that Silas hadn't called, but I had a screen full of messages and missed calls from Patrick. Worried he was in jail or in need of help, I lifted a finger and swiped to his messages.

I pulled up the voicemail but could hardly understand him through the loud commotion in the background.

"Alice... asking about you... Bumper... Tidings..."

Then I opened a stream of unnerved messages from Patrick in full bedlam.

> I'm on the first plane or train or fucking sleigh out there.

> I'm bringing my brass knuckles.

> Wait, are those allowed on planes?

> No, I need the weapon of my mind.

"Hey beautiful," Silas wrapped an arm around my waist

from behind, kissing the side of my neck. His chest rose when he inhaled my scent, torturing myself by giving him more time of blissful ignorance before it all came crashing down. I was about to ruin a good man's life. Or at least, a life he thought he was maybe, possibly building with me.

I didn't turn to look at him, didn't move a muscle. I wasn't sure if I was breathing. A hand on my cheek turned me toward his face.

"Your eyes are bulging out of your head like ping-pong balls," he said.

I turned away, chewing on the tip of my thumbnail, deciphering Patrick's messages. I opened an email from him that explained more. My insides stretched and folded like sourdough. I rubbed my chest, feeling the burn intensify.

"Who's Patrick?" I couldn't fault him for his sensible interest.

I cleared my throat. "Uh—friend back home."

He held my chin, scanning my eyes like he was checking for signs of head trauma. He had the same look on his face when he tended to a child who slipped at the ice rink last week. "Babe, you okay?"

It registered to me I hadn't mentioned Patrick to Silas. My life here in Tidings froze everything from my previous life. Nerves roiled in my stomach and clawed themselves against my skin from the inside. I pulled myself together enough to text Patrick back.

Call me.

I gripped my phone and forced a smile. "He's probably having relationship drama and needs to talk it out." *Liar. Big, fucking liar.*

He nodded and gave me a sheepish smile, anyway.

"Someone I knew from Arizona is here," I said in a hushed tone, a confession.

God, his arm around my shoulder messed with my head. It was so safe and warm, but everything about me was about to come to light, and it'd be over. We'd implode and specks of dust of what was once us will scatter across this bar.

"Do you want to say hi or is this someone you don't want to see?" he asked.

"Oh, trust me. They'll be sure to make a scene first. Silas, I am really sorry you got entangled with me. My life back in Arizona is messy, and this was a temporary thing; I never meant for you to get hurt."

"Temporary?"

"You... were unexpected. My hesitation shouldn't come as a surprise. I've said before you should avoid me like I'm stinging nettles. I burn everything I touch."

Silas grabbed me by the elbow, pulling me into him.

I had deceived him and everyone else in Tidings. The Alice they knew was helpful, competent, and trustworthy. I'd describe myself as silk hiding in steel, but that would be giving myself too much credit. I was an imitation, a cheap knockoff.

Amidst the low hum of chatter and clinking glasses, I took a long sip of my cocktail to soothe my nerves. It didn't work.

Everyone in the bar could see my pulse bulging from my neck as I spotted a man I'd never met before, but who I could easily identify, enter the bar. He wore an Arizona Sun Devils baseball cap and a small black bag on his shoulder. We locked eyes and my executioner strode toward me.

I swallowed hard, bracing myself for what was to come.

"Alice, you're difficult to track down," he said, voice laced with a hint of sarcasm.

"Original," I replied, trying to keep my voice steady despite the rising panic within me.

"But since it led me to this place, I won't complain," he continued, his gaze flickering briefly to Silas before settling back on me. He extended his hand to shake mine. "Bumper Austin."

The date to leave Tidings was within eyesight. By the way that everybody here talked about "fate," I thought it would save me from the ghost of my past mistakes. Instead, it was a reckoning.

"Excuse me," Silas interjected, his voice sharp with indignation. He put his body in front of mine like he was prepared to block a blow. Shoulders pulled back with his relaxed, flirtatious side gone, in its place was a calm-under-pressure assertiveness he carried when he wore his work uniform. "Who the hell are you?"

Bumper dismissed Silas' protest, his focus solely on me. My hands trembled, shaking the glass I held before it dropped to the floor, shattering into a hundred sharp pieces.

"I think you should leave," Silas said, his voice cold and firm.

Our group must have sensed the tension, or Ginger heard everything because she had every square inch of Tidings bugged with listening devices, because each person was out of their chair and gathering in a hacky-sack circle around the stranger.

Ginger appeared more infuriated than ever. Leaning against the bar, I searched for balance as I feared the intensity of her glare might shift the earth's tectonic plates. The fiery intensity in her eyes could ignite a wildfire.

"Who the hell are you and what are you doing here?" Ginger asked.

"I wanted to talk to Alice about a story, but I think I found an even better one. Does Tidings have a mayor?"

Ginger smirked. A glint in her eyes told me she was thrilled to be challenged, hungry like a predator ready to strike with calculated precision. "Finally, someone exciting to harangue."

"What the hell is going on, Ginger?" Silas demanded.

"Is this a mafia stick-up?" Bror asked.

Silas pointed to the door, a degree of heat in his eyes like his insides were boiling over. He called for Ginger, a commanding voice she might make him pay for later, but one that left no question. He was done fucking around with these people.

An entourage of people stood up for me. Ginger was a finger tap away from activating the Tidings cavalry. I imagined a group of Krav Maga experts riding in on caribou or pulled by sled dogs surrounding the invader.

I gripped the skin covering Silas' ribs from behind and placed a kiss on his shoulder blades.

Goodbye, Silas.

Once I confessed, understandably, he couldn't be associated with me, a viral embarrassment. It was precisely for this reason why I'd omitted this from him.

I pulled Silas' body to the side and inserted myself in front of him. He said my name, low in a warning. I looked at him with a grim smile to say, *It's okay, I've got this now.*

"I was fired from my last job. I made a stupid AI image of my boss that was... gross... and I was a total idiot who emailed it to everyone who works for the state of Arizona instead of texting it to my friend." I released a shaky breath, fighting for composure. "I went viral. And this guy wanted me to do an interview about my national embarrassment. A redemption project of sorts."

The doors burst open, and I heard him before I saw him —panting, swearing through broken breaths, followed by a shrieking, "Oh my god!"

The room's collective gaze shifted toward Patrick, eyeing him up and down ascertaining the level of threat of the latest newcomer. He held his back against the door, wingspan spread, bracing against each side.

"Um," he searched the room, panicked. "There's a *fucking moose* charging down the street."

It was quiet enough to hear Bror swallow the last of his beer, walking toward Patrick. "Oh, hello."

For his credit, Patrick looked appropriately confused at the nonchalance of the room. People here were used to Marshmallow.

Outsiders, not so much.

Silas eyed me. "Patrick?"

"Yup."

He chuckled. "Your friend came all the way to Tidings to warn you about this knob?"

Bror had Patrick cornered before he could get to me. He hadn't even had a chance to pull off his hat and jacket. He eyed me then typed on his phone. I reached for mine in my pocket as it buzzed.

> Patrick: Girl, what the fuck? There's a moose on the run. I thought he was going to eat me.

> Alice: He's harmless, I think. His name is Marshmallow.

> Patrick: They named him Marshmallow?

Alice: Looks like you met Bror.

Patrick: And looks like you met someone who's preparing fire darts to throw.

With quiet confidence, Silas squared his shoulders toward the intruders. He didn't need to say a word for his looming presence to be clear: *You're done here; get out.*

"I'm not surprised you haven't told him about your past. I don't blame you; it *is* quite humiliating." Bumper turned to address Silas. I felt like I was going to throw up. "But if you do an interview with me, we can humanize you. Reshape your public image with internet forgiveness."

"Don't," I said to Silas whose lips curled into a snarl. "He's trying to bait you into fighting him, so you could be the next hit piece on his website."

Patrick gently walked toward me, uneasy.

"How did you find me?" I asked both men.

"Google," they said simultaneously.

Ginger huffed. "They were supposed to fix that."

Patrick glared at Bumper and crossed his arms. "He seduced me."

Bror wrinkled his nose. "You were seduced by a man named Bumper?"

"I had a bad day," Patrick protested, then turned to face me. "Bethany was being exceptionally annoying. I was hungover."

I gave him a pity face. "You and him? Oh, Patrick."

Bumper stepped forward, pulling a small notebook out of his bag. "So, since I'm here, let's talk."

"Could we do this somewhere else?"

"Sure, anywhere you want to go, Alice."

"You're not going anywhere with him," Silas said.

"Chill bro, she's not my type." Bumper winked.

"I don't give a shit—she's not going to talk to you alone. She's not going to talk to you here. She has nothing to say."

I felt the gaze of everyone on me. My skin inflamed, and I knew my neck was red and itchy.

"Why don't you let her be the judge of that?" Bumper argued. "And my article will help you control the narrative. Own the mistake publicly and people will move on."

"This seems pretty dramatic for a stupid email," Ginger said, examining her cherry red nails. "Alice is moving on without your interference. Right, Alice?"

I looked at Silas whose expression was difficult to read. Pity, maybe. Judgment, more likely.

As I stood in the crowded bar, the walls seemed to close in around me, each whispered conversation and curious glance amplifying the weight of my anxiety. The air felt thick, heavy with expectation, like everyone was dissecting my every move waiting for me to say something. I wanted to escape—to find a quiet corner where I could breathe without the weight of everyone's scrutiny.

"I don't know what else to say." I let my chin fall to my chest. My blurred gaze narrowed on my shoes. "But I am sorry for bringing this spectacle to Tidings."

"Can someone clue me in?" Bror asked.

Silas shot him a furious look. "Let it go."

Ginger stepped toward me, eyes widening. "Everything works out in the end, doesn't it?"

A loud thud hit the closed front doors and suddenly I wasn't the center of attention. The bartender reached below the counter for a small canister labeled "bear spray."

Bumper and Patrick paled as everyone else calmly filed toward the back of the bar.

Silas grabbed my hand and walked me toward the back, gripping me in reassurance. "Stay calm—it'll be okay."

"Tourists," the bartender raised his voice. "We have a visitor. Stay calm, don't make sudden movements or loud noises."

Erratic thuds and scrapes continued at the door until it finally gave way with the sound of wood splintering, and cracking open just as a large, pointy antler pushed through. All air in the room was sucked out and the burly bartender stood between the patrons huddled in the back of the room and the giant beast.

Its massive frame was so much bigger than I ever imagined, knocking over chairs as it padded through, each step echoing in the silence. He snorted and sniffed as he stuck out a large velvet tongue and licked the plates of uneaten bar food, knocking some over onto the ground. He was unfazed by the crash, but each time a plate shattered I gasped. Large antlers twisted like gnarled branches, ready to stab any moving threat.

I held my trembling fingers against my mouth. Silas linked our fingers together and kissed the back of my palm. "It'll be alright," he said.

"I heard the warnings—" I froze mid-sentence as the massive animal crept closer, "—but I never imagined how big it was."

Patrick chuckled behind me.

"Now's not the time for juvenile jokes," I shouted in a whisper.

"Dick jokes always help," Bror added.

"I would know, my fucking name is Bumper," the reporter added. The three men laughed together.

I glared at them with an expression that asked, *Are you kidding?*

Bumper removed a handkerchief from his shirt pocket and dotted his head. Bror and Patrick rubbed his back. "It's okay, Marshmallow never hurts anyone," Bror said.

Silas snickered behind me at the events transpiring before us.

Marshmallow stopped mid-bite on a cheeseburger to crane his head at the entrance. A second set of loud hooves stomped through the door, revealing a cow moose.

"She's getting his drunk ass out of the bar and taking him home," Ginger said. "Get it, girl."

"Who's that?" I asked no one in particular.

"Wasabi," whispers answered around me.

"The female is Wasabi and the male is Marshmallow," I clarified. "Sure, nothing else makes sense in this town; why not?"

"He's a big softie," Silas said.

"And she packs a punch," Ginger added.

Wasabi groaned and bellowed, lowering her head and assuming a charging position. Her hooves scraped at the wood floor, and I stepped back in horror, looking for a place to hide. Silas stood in front of me, arms out wide.

"Just so you know, I'm not at all impressed by this strongman act."

"You're right," he cocked his head and leaned down close to my ear, "I should just charge at them and sacrifice myself so you can make a break for it." He pinched my ass cheek, squeezing tight between his fingers. "Stay calm."

"What are you doing?" I whispered.

Silas whistled like he was hailing a taxi not drawing the attention of two fur-covered killing machines who trapped us in a room. The bartender made a mad dash toward the entrance drawing the moose's attention. They followed him outside where he sprayed the canister before slamming the door shut.

"Holy shit, *holy shit,*" Bumper was one word away from a panic attack.

"Take a deep breath," Silas said. "They're gone."

"You live *here* with those things?" Patrick shouted.

"They're the town pets. Very friendly," Bror added.

"If your version of friendly is getting reamed in the ass by those things then sure," Patrick added.

And then the entire bar burst into laughter.

Silas pulled me toward the exit, propping the door open with his hip. He followed me from behind, a shadowy presence guiding me toward the parking lot.

Our boots crunched on the layers of ice topping old snow. It hadn't snowed for four days, the first time there was a break in precipitation since I arrived, but the temperatures crept above freezing enough for snow to melt then froze overnight creating a slick ice rink.

I could have been selling solar panels in the desert.

Silas unlocked his truck with the key fob and opened the passenger door for me to get in. Like a prisoner following her guard, I obeyed. He walked around the front, pausing to let loose a long exhale visible by a large plume of warm mist in the freezing air.

He turned the engine on and adjusted the settings, turning the passenger heat warmer to high.

"Just so you know, I'd rather Humpty Dumpty myself onto that sheet of ice than have this conversation," I said. We got through the awkwardness in the bar thanks to the moose invasion, but now there was no avoiding it. Him, me, and all the secrets about to be aired out trapped in the truck. He pulled his beanie off and ran his hands through this tousled hair, pulling it back over his ears with a grunt, mumbling about hating the itchy wool.

"What?" His tone surprised me, sharp with agitation.

"Nothing." I fiddled with my thumb in my lap, willing myself to hold back the shivers as we waited for the heater to kick on. "You said yourself, there was nothing simple about me."

I expected Ginger to dismiss me, kicking me out of their precious Tidings, leaving it as nothing but a confusing fever dream for me. I sat on my hands, burning them against the heat of the seat.

"Stop with the pity party before you're too far gone."

The drive to the lodge was only a few minutes in dry weather and sparse traffic. After he parked along the curb, we stared silently out the windshield. We arrived quicker than I prepared for, leaving me with nothing to say for myself. I went for it, like a free fall over a cliff.

"Sometimes I cry when I look at baby pictures of myself," I said to Silas, but maybe it was a confession to myself. "I think about the promise and optimism my parents had for that new child. And I've done nothing but let them down."

"That is not true." From my periphery, he turned toward me. His hand lifted like he was going to reach out, but he pulled back, gripping the steering wheel.

"It's okay, I don't need you to try to preserve my feelings with the nice guy thing. You can be mad or confused or whatever. But allow me to get this out, please. And then I'll be out of your hair."

"Let me ask you something," he said. I nodded, giving

him the go-ahead as I kept my mouth shut. "What will make you happy in life?"

I scoffed.

"Have you been happy here?"

That was the most difficult question to answer. Every reason that led me to this moment was shrouded in a web of lies. Emotion burned my eyes.

"Besides the ever-looming threat of frostbite? Although my body has not adapted, surprisingly, yes. I've found more joy here in Tidings than I've admitted."

Silas hummed as he opened the driver's door, coming around the front of his truck to my door, where the familiar and painful cold air stole my breath. He reached his hand up to help me out.

"Careful," he said quietly. The sidewalk was caked in ice.

"I'm not trying to disguise what's happening by choosing careful words. I want to tell you everything honestly."

"Oh, we'll talk. I'll get it all out of you one way or another." He spoke with authority, but also with a tone that felt like he... cared.

Of course he cared; he was Silas.

"Come on," he walked me toward my suite, a well-known route from regularly visiting the lodge to visit me with morning coffee or to sneak in my bed after his shift. I had become accustomed to his sensual, lazy touch, and the smell of his post-shift decaf and fresh shower scent. I was going to miss that.

What I left behind was a life full of snags and barriers of my own making. It wasn't honest to blame my life choices on anyone else or any past events when I was the sole decision-maker. A glorious, sweetly simple life here felt unworthy.

The door creaked open and shut with such force the sound was still there when he pinned my back against the wall, his arms on either side of my shoulders. He looked me over like he was scanning for cuts or bruises. He sighed, with relief or hesitation, I couldn't tell.

"Let's do this softly." He kissed my cheek, and his breath lingered on my skin. I curled my neck around like a cat purring, seeking chin scratches. "I'm not making any judgments."

He led with gentleness, a common trait of his that made my spine stiffen.

Unworthy. Unworthy. Unworthy.

He unbuttoned my jacket, a routine task he had become intimately familiar with, as if it was his own coat, then unwound my scarf and removed my gloves.

I moved to the kitchen to boil water for tea. The evening's cold pricked my bones sharper than before, like it was a dagger lodged in my marrow. I shivered from the brutal cold and the heightened heat pumping through my body. Silas covered me from behind, wrapping his arms around my waist and holding me. Just held me.

"You don't have to tell me what you're not comfortable with." He whispered into the delicate piece of skin behind my ear and a rush of blurry shadows danced behind my eyes. He made me so dizzy. "But I hope that you are comfortable with me."

He was *so* serious. My vocal cords felt thready, and I knew if I spoke my brittle voice would betray me. I forced a smile.

"If being a doctor doesn't work out, you could join the CIA. I hear they need honey pots to seduce."

He slung his thumbs through my belt loops and placed a kiss on my shoulder. I felt his warm breath through my sweater as his mouth lingered.

"Why are you so nice to me?" I whispered.

"It's not obvious?" He placed his chin on my head. And I could have melted into a puddle so deep it'd be confused for a lake. My heart rate beat faster, giving away my anxiety. He put his fingers on my throat's pulse point, whispering consoling shushes. "It's all okay," he repeated.

Silas was the epitome of a man in control, not a controlling man. He was going to get me to talk on my own accord, guided by his careful ministrations. I'd give anything to be like him: collected, open-minded, a step ahead of everyone else, always with the right decisions.

He deserved to know the full story without any embellishments or convenient lies of omission.

"Back home, I have nothing left. I was fired for a really stupid AI image I made. I meant to send it to Patrick from my phone, but it blasted out as an email to every state employee. Then, my ex-boyfriend dumped me and kicked me out of his house the same day. And stupid me, prior to all that I trusted him with all my money for investments. I lost my savings to trendy stocks, real estate flips and—" I removed my hands from the counter and placed them on top of his, giving them a squeeze, "—this is so embarrassing. God, I can't believe I have to say this out loud. Cryptocurrency."

He turned me around and hugged me tight.

"I can literally feel you laughing," I said.

"It's just the way you say *cryptocurrency,* like in pure disgust of gory horror." He cleared his throat and rubbed his palm down the side of my head, giving a gentle tug on my hair. "Fortunately, I think you're young enough to bounce back. You took a risk, and you learned, right?"

"No, I'm stupid."

"Don't talk about my girlfriend like that."

I reared back. "Girlfriend?"

"We—well, *I*, anyway—feel like this has moved in that direction."

I couldn't allow him to say anything I knew he'd one day regret. His feelings for me were so pure... yet devastatingly misplaced.

He tucked a flyaway strand of hair behind my ear. I made a lame attempt to smooth down his cowlick that always flew up in the front when he'd take his beanie off. Perhaps the only part of him left untamed.

"When you tell the whole story, you were right. It's easy to judge."

My heart sank. "I—"

He put his fingers to my mouth to shush me.

"But I also know you're intelligent enough to know that you made the best choice for you at that time. So what? You took a risk at a young age. You have plenty of time to save up for retirement, to course correct." His nonchalance was startling. This was much bigger than a silly, dumb risk. It was thousands of dollars, not a *teehee oops!*

"I was stupid. And gullible."

"Or, optimistic and searching for the good in others?"

"Don't push it."

"What can I say to help you feel better?"

"It would be helpful if you had an equally dumb and embarrassing story." His eyes searched my face, the look of disappointment flowed in his eyes as he came up empty. "And that's the sound of crickets, isn't it?"

"Look, maybe I didn't make bad decisions that affected

my career or financial situation, but I've been an obnoxious brother who put a wedge between my relationship with my sister and refused to accept that for years. You helped me see that."

"My sister doesn't even talk to me. She's a famous geologist and I'm the reason why my parents' life expectancy is shrinking."

Silas gave me a chaste kiss on the lips and rubbed his knuckles down my cheek.

"Give yourself more credit."

I rolled my eyes. "Oh, come on. Be serious."

I pushed him aside, but he grabbed me by the crook of my arm, gripping me tight. Opening up to him felt too natural. Before I could get another word out, he kissed me. Hard. His tongue pushed my lips open, and it danced against mine.

Our breaths merged as I pulled back. "Tongue flicking was one way to shut me up."

"I'll flick it wherever you want me to." A mischievous grin lit up his face. He chuckled and gripped my sweater by the hem, pulling it over my head. His shirt came off next, setting the skin on our chests together.

"You heard everything I confessed, right?"

"Yup." He peppered my shoulder with kisses.

My nipples hardened at his seduction. My neck lost the gravity battle to his seductive kisses. "And none of that bothers you?"

"Nope." He shrugged, looking inordinately content with the whole mess.

"Why the hell not? I wouldn't want to be with you if you were a viral embarrassment."

"I don't care. It makes for a fun story."

All this time I was preparing to adapt to my new identity and this man shrugs it off as... a fun story?

"Look," he said, hesitating, then pulling back. Immediately, I missed the feeling of his warm breath on my skin, instead, a painful chill came over me. He stuttered. "I was curious about you. One day I—"

"—you found the stories online?" I interrupted, knowing what he was struggling to confess. I felt defeated.

"I apologize for the invasion of privacy."

I shook my head. "It's public knowledge. You didn't know what you were going to find."

"Not that for sure. But I knew it was best to hear it directly from you. I read one paragraph and tossed my phone."

"Do you want to hear everything now?"

"No." He leaned into my neck again, bringing his breath back where I needed it, where I ached for him. "I know enough, darling."

Silas put his hands under my ass cheeks—a part I learned his hands must touch once a day or he'd have withdrawal shakes—and lifted me up over his hips. A moan escaped my mouth, caught blindsided by the hardness of him pressing into me.

He carried me to the sofa across from the fireplace, laying me out beneath him. He must have started the fire while I was preparing the tea. The kettle eventually stopped bubbling as the sensor paused and I forgot all about that boiling water. My mouth brushed his, setting him off like a bucking bull let out of his pen.

Either Silas was crossing an item off his bucket list to fuck a girl-gone-viral, or he was doing something much worse: showing me how much he cared. That none of this mattered and that he was going to stick by me. It wasn't fair to let him make this mistake when I could see it so clearly. He deserved better than me. He was distracted by the mist of lust, and after he came he'd regret it all.

I ground my hips into his, feeling the full strength of his hardness.

The look in his eyes was somewhere between hunger and hunting. Starving and glazed. He dug his fingertips into my hips, matching his to meet me harder. He surprised me when he flipped me over, face down on the couch. He told me to scoot back. "Ass in the air."

He leaned into me firmly, and I felt all his pressure against me. A million endless nerves eviscerated across my body. Every limb felt like it was on fire. I inhaled and gripped the cushion as he unbuckled my belt and loosened my pants with such ease, air blew across my ass before I realized he had my pants down to my knees. His hands smacked both cheeks, spreading them apart. I became drunk as hell on the idea of taking unprecedented steps toward pleasure.

"You like this?" His voice was strained and scarce.

He sensed my wanting, maybe from the arch and press of myself back into him. Maybe I said it out loud; everything is such a blur of hazy lust. "Is this what you want?" He leaned down over my back, tilting his head to bring his chin to meet mine. Our hot, heavy breaths filled the air. "I can fuck you hard. I can give you bruising grips and take your breath away when you roll your orgasms all over me."

Fuck. His dirty talk sent my heart rate skyrocketing. I always wanted Silas to fuck me, and either hard or sensual, he did it with reverence. God, my body craved him, but I couldn't let him treat me like a woman who deserved respect. Maybe if I let him live out a debauched fantasy, it'd be easier for him to move on after this.

"Come on," I rasped. "Give it to me."

As he gripped my hips, I felt dizzy. But then I felt a breeze glide across my skin, and his melting touch was gone.

Silas plopped on the opposite side of the couch and pulled me on top of him with a spider web snug embrace. His pants were still on, and his eyes looked like melted glaciers, watered down with emotion and tension. "I know what that was," he said.

"What do you mean?" I sat up and tried to play dumb in a pathetic, clueless attempt.

Then he kissed me deep and hard. His tongue flicked in my mouth. "Don't pretend."

"Pretend what?" I sneaked through slow strokes of his tongue.

"I can read your body language. And I can read *this* between us."

My delusion was under a spotlight; rough sex would cover real emotions bubbling at the brim.

He brought my palm down, steady and secure between his two hands. He spoke quietly, "And if you need it, I want to help you heal."

"Why?" I asked.

"Why do you think so?"

My body was suspended in time, frozen in ice, hovering over the couch. I wasn't steady on earth.

Our foreheads touched and he kicked my jeans off all the way. His fingers slipped through me with reverence. He removed a condom from his wallet. "Help me take my pants off."

He never took his eyes off me as I kneeled on the floor between his legs, tugging his pants over the rolling muscles weaved from his thighs down to his tight calves. I bit down on his knee and swiped my tongue over the imprint. My nails left red imprints in his skin.

"Come here," he said softly. He helped me ease up to my feet before he pulled me into his lap, guiding my hips across his. I let him have me this way.

This time, I allowed myself to feel all of this between us. I'd never felt a man be so tender, yet possessive as he fucked me.

He groaned as he filled me entirely. Leisurely and languidly, he rolled into me to feel every grip of flesh as I rode him. "Why did you want to avoid a moment like this after the day you had?"

I didn't answer his question, probably because I couldn't remember how to speak; he showed me how he felt about me. About us. My toes curled into the leather, making scratching sounds each time I lifted and dropped down. Silas' hand rolled up my spine holding me as I rode a wave of pleasure so intense I couldn't hang on without assistance. My desperation flooded our senses as I begged for more from him. He held me firm, gripping the skin that hung over in the seated position, never loosening his grip.

"We're going to come together. Like this." He rolled his hips, our bones ground and our flesh melted together. The tension inside me built higher and higher, like climbing a ladder with no end in sight. I had never felt such a buildup before and the fear of falling escalated.

What would it feel like when I finally reached the top?
When I fall, will I live?

Our releases met like two war-torn lovers finding their embrace at last. A flood of endorphins encapsulated my body. Between shallow breaths, I knew what I needed to say; there was no other option. I pleaded with him to tell me what I was most afraid of, but it was compulsory. Damnit. "Say it, Silas."

He held the back of my head and slowed the roll of his hips as his lips grazed mine. Our noses brushed before he dragged his across my cheek, planting a kiss on my ear. Warm breath tickled my earlobe, and his scruff ignited that delicate spot behind my ear. Before he said it, I knew what was coming. And I braced myself like a gentle parachute landing in a field of soft grasses.

"I'm very much in love with you, Alice."

ALICE

I slapped my hand around on the nightstand to hit the magic red button sending my mom to voicemail. I recognized her personal ringtone, the loud, annoying alarm that sent most people running when they heard it. Instead, I was met with Silas' outstretched palm, phone in hand.

He mouthed as if she could hear through the phone, "Do you want to talk to her?"

"You know she can't hear, right?" I said an octave louder than normal.

He blushed and toddled two options for me to choose. Phone in one hand, mug in the other. I took both, opting to hit the red button and then take a scalding sip.

"Shit." I sputtered, and the coffee dripped from my mouth back into the cup.

"Too hot?"

"Too *something*." I wiped my mouth with the back of my hand, scrunching my nose. "You made this?"

"I uh—" he scratched his neck and looked down, clearly embarrassed. "Usually order my coffee or get it at the hospital."

"But at your house you'd bring me coffee in the morning."

"Mmhm."

"Hold on, hold on." I kicked my legs out from under the blankets, careful not to spill hot coffee on my bare legs. As I inched closer to the truth, a thrill overwhelmed me. This was madness. I could never let him live this down. "You... what? Had it delivered to your house and poured it into a personal mug?"

Between my obscene laughter I heard a few words in his response, namely: *why, talk, mom.* I cackled and gasped for air. "I can't believe you can save someone's life, but also kill them with your coffee."

Silas resisted my contagious laughter in impressive strength. "You're deflecting," he said.

"You're shit at making coffee! And you tried to hide it." I tugged at the waistband of his sweatpants to pull him closer to me. I ran my hand up his stomach. "It's adorable, really."

He linked his fingers with mine. "And you avoid talking to your parents."

"It's nothing," I arched an eyebrow and flicked my wrist at my phone. "I don't want to talk to my mother when you're standing here half naked with coffee. Priorities."

He crouched on his knees, setting my phone and mug on the bedside table. He rubbed his hands up and down my bare thighs and laid his chin on my knee. "I'll work on it. I'll learn how to make a whole damn cappuccino if that's what you want."

My voice dropped to a near whisper. "I'm leaving in two weeks."

The words hit me like a wild pitch to the jaw. And I still

didn't have an exit plan. I looked for jobs online, but I hadn't submitted my application to any. I hesitated each time I stared down at the submit button, never understanding why. I was qualified for them, and they seemed far more interesting than travel writing from a cubicle. I chose locations known for moderate to warm seasonal weather. Exciting adventures awaited. Blah. Fucking. Blah.

Except, I had no one waiting there for me. I'd arrive alone in a new city. A fresh start. With no one. Wasn't that what I always wanted?

I swallowed a lump in my throat.

Silas shrugged his shoulder and ran his hand down my cheek. "Then I want to be all in for as long as we've got. All hands on deck."

"Wrong metaphor. But I do like you using your all hands on me."

"Baby, I know your body better than you do." He tucked an invisible piece of hair behind my ear and nipped my earlobe. He whispered, "Do you know you have a freckle on your perineum?"

I pulled back, nose scrunched. "What?"

"That delicate spot between your—" he rolled his lips and said in a cringy, clinical tone, "vagina and anus."

"You absolutely must stop. Right now. That is so unsexy."

"I know you like my testicles in your—"

I covered his mouth with the palm of my hand. "Do not bring anatomically accurate terminology into the bedroom with me."

He licked the palm of my hand, and I gave him a displeased look. He was having the time of his life.

Everything with Silas was... easy.

Talking. Laughing. Being.

Easy to fall for.

He could make me laugh in the middle of an existential crisis. But that deep-rooted achy feeling inside me mounted. I couldn't find a comfortable breath, lodged somewhere between tangled branches made from anxiety and leaves of panic.

In a broken breath I said, "This has been the best time of my life."

Silas sat next to me, the edge of the mattress squeaking under his weight. He rested his chin on my shoulder. I felt the heat of his gaze on the side of my face. "Imagine how much better we can be together where it's warmer," he said, sincerity and pleading in his eyes.

"We—"

"—go together," he finished, eyes shifted nervously.

"Where?"

"Wherever you want." He lifted me onto his lap. I adjusted to straddle him, meeting his eyes. "Everyone needs ER doctors. It'll be a cinch."

"Don't be cocky, it's unbecoming of you."

His lips arched up into a satisfied smile then he kissed me on my neck, rubbing his nose down my sensitive skin.

"You're saying you will... go where I go?" Silas had been nothing but trustworthy with enough references to support his character. But the last time I put all my eggs in one basket with a man, so to speak, I ended up broke and one big fat joke.

He nodded his head, flaunting a roguish grin. "I've got a dozen emails of job offers waiting for me to pick one."

"That easy, huh?" I crinkled my nose then curled my body in, shrinking myself. "What if you get there and change your mind?"

I'd taken enough risks. What I needed now was security —not in a job, a man, a town, but within me. Holistically. Silas was someone I could trust, quite easily I might add. But he'd never gone out on a whim on anything in his life before. I couldn't stomach being his test subject. A theory that later he'd look back on and think, *Yeah that was stupid.*

He cupped my face. "I've never changed my mind about anything. I set a goal and met it. I'm not wishy-washy."

"Now you're bragging."

"I can be really boring."

I bit back a smile, and he slid a finger between my lips, plucking at them like a guitar pick.

"Sales pitch could use some work."

"I'm also stable, reliable, and predictable. Let me be that for you."

"How do I know you haven't found what you're looking for yet?"

"Because, Alice," he said, speaking into my chest where he nuzzled his face, "I believe you were meant for me."

And I believed the hell out of him, in a way I felt inside my bones. Like a rib snapped and a piece of his integrity slipped between it inside of me. "And if you need healing, I can give that to you," he added.

"It's literally your job to heal people. I remember a little old man saying that exact thing to you when I arrived here three months ago."

"Not like this, baby." He kissed my cheek, inching his way across my face and down my neck. He nibbled on my collarbone, and I swallowed back a moan. "Not like this." His tender words faded across my skin.

I had spent so much time hiding my failures and my silly little dreams, and now here I was, nude in all ways literal and metaphorical, in front of a man who offered me

not simply blanket security, but pieces of himself so vulnerable that if I squeezed them in my palm they'd crack like
an egg.

He could help me heal. I could help him find a life-
saving balance.

CHAPTER 31

SILAS

"I did it. I went all in with her," I said, slicing a medium-rare filet mignon. It rested for ten minutes and was a perfect pink. I spooned a mushroom glaze on top, pairing it with mashed potatoes. "I think it could work out. *Will* work," I added. "You might like where we go, too. It won't be as snowy, but you'll love the water."

I filled a glass of wine and carried it with my plate to the dining room table. "This one's mine," I said, looking directly into her pleading, hungry eyes.

I cut an unseasoned filet into chunky pieces, tossing it into a bowl with cooled chunks of potatoes and carrots.

"Snøfnugg, get down! Yours is right here." My damn dog was on her hind legs, sniffing my plate. "Off!" I commanded.

She dropped back to all fours and gave her body a vigorous shake, adding a displeased grunt.

"Bow down, bow down, royalty is here," a sharp female voice called from the front door.

Another woman piped up. "We brought upside-down pineapple cake!"

Dagny and Ginger met me in the kitchen, unloading their contribution and chucking their jackets on the floor. I tried to hold back a shudder. "Just make yourself right at home," I said.

"Thanks, I will. Since this will be mine soon," my sister said. I agreed to let her move into my house and rent it to her and Pete with no family discount, specifically for that last reason. "Alice here?"

"Working," I said, plating their dishes, licking a bit of spilled sauce off my thumb. I looked over to Ginger. "Find Elvin's new hire yet?"

Ginger eyed her phone, sliding her thumbs around the screen. "About two hours of downtime between."

I nodded, handing the women a glass of wine each. A knock at the door had Snøfnugg look up from her gourmet dinner bowl and let out a quiet bark.

"We're not expecting anyone else, are we?" I asked. Dagny took a sip of wine and Ginger hid a smile behind her fist.

"I'll get it," Dagny said, walking in quick strides toward the door. When she opened it, a tall, shadowy presence entered, wrapping his hand around the side of her neck and pulling her in for a kiss. She whispered something and laughed, nudging him away with an open palm on his chest. He stomped his old, weathered Army boots on the doormat, and his smile dropped when he looked at me. Shoulders back, he stepped forward with an arm wrapped around my sister's back.

Ginger held her wine glass to her mouth, muttering before a sip. "This ought to be good."

"Sup, man," Pete said, grinning like a cheesy mother-fucker and extending his hand.

I looked at his open palm, an invitation to accept him in

my life not as a colleague, but as my sister's boyfriend. He was a good guy, probably the best kind of person someone would want to protect and love their sister, but I had to tuck away a shred of disappointment that lingered.

Three months ago, my life was in disarray. I thought I'd had it all planned out: I'd leave Tidings, Dagny would go to med school, and I'd be happy wherever I ended up. I was so focused on the future, that I overlooked how Dagny was busy crafting her own beautiful, independent life while I worked myself to death. If I'd spent half the time worrying about me as I did her, perhaps I wouldn't have been a glum asshole.

The ladies studied me, Dagny with bated breath while Ginger wore an exasperated expression. Pete maintained his charming smile, but the corner of his lips twitched slightly.

"Yeah," I brushed my hand across my pants, then extended it forward. Pete's shoulders dropped as we shook. "Yeah, welcome, Pete. Want a beer or wine?"

"Whatever you have open," he said. Dagny beamed up at him with a bright smile.

I emptied the bottle of red by topping off my glass and reached for another to uncork, giving Pete the first glass from a very expensive bottle. *Better appreciate it.*

"How can I help? It smells delicious," Pete asked.

"All good. Didn't know we had another guest coming but I had an extra plate prepared anyways."

"I don't need to take Alice's dinner," Pete chuckled awkwardly.

"It was for the dog," Ginger said as she swiped a finger through the mushroom sauce out of the pan.

"Not that one unless Pete likes his steak unseasoned," I said.

I rocked on my heels, searching for more conversation. At work, Pete and I had no problem finding things to talk about: music, patients, the weather. But at my house, as my sister's guest, it was going to take more effort to find common ground.

"Well, thanks for letting us rent your place," he said, tucking his hands in his front pockets.

"So much for the family discount," Dagny groaned, and Pete gave her a look that said be nice.

"I probably can't cook as good as you, though." He was putting in the work to butter me up. Maybe he was just as nervous about this new situation as I was uneasy.

"No, I'm sure you can't," I grinned.

"He's being polite, Silas," Dagny interjected, holding a finger in the air. "Pete trained with a French chef during deployment."

"Weren't you busy doing other things at war?" I asked.

"Less austere bases had decent amenities, especially from our allies. French troops brought a chef in for morale, and it was a good opportunity to learn a new skill."

I grabbed a seat at the table and tried to ignore the awkward dick-measuring contest with... him.

Everyone dove into their dinner, talking and laughing. I reminisced about my first year in Tidings when I was new and unknown to the townspeople. Ginger was the first person I met, and even though she stuck her nose in my business like she was my mother, I would forever be grateful for her friendship and for bringing Alice to Tidings.

I'd miss Elvin and the other old-timers, hoping they would take care of their health without me having to barge into their lives with a house call like I was a fucking primary care physician. And seeing how happy Dagny was made me regret all those days being a miserable ass, when we could have enjoyed each other.

"Will you visit us?" I asked Dagny abruptly.

She nodded and turned her head, hiding her emotions as Pete tried to soothe her with a hand over hers on the table. Pete and Dagny made corny lovey-dovey faces at each other, and I must have wrinkled my nose because Ginger tapped my foot with hers.

"Stop," she pulled my attention away from them. "You have the same lovesick look on your face when you're with Alice."

"I do not."

Snøfnugg stood to spin around in the same spot then laid down with a loud thud.

"Even your dog knows you're full of shit," she added.

"Okay, so what?"

"I knew it!" Ginger clapped her hands together.

"It shouldn't come as a shock to you since I'm following her across the country," I added.

"But you've never actually said it."

"I've said it to the person who needs to know," I said, twirling my wine glass at the stem.

"When you know, you know, right?" Pete stroked a hand over his beard, thicker than the last time I saw him a week ago.

"Growing that out?" I asked.

"Yeah, Dagny likes it."

"Bro, please." My dining table was starting to feel too small for my guests. I was ready to kick them out before dessert.

"Silas, shut up," Dagny said. "I had to watch you putter around like a big dumb caveman every time Alice talked to another guy. And don't get me started on that time I saw you handsy as shit in front of the café."

We frowned at each other. Dagny tossed me a middle finger.

"Siblings," Pete and Ginger grumbled simultaneously.

"There is something I wanted to ask Pete," I said. "How did you hear about Tidings anyway? You know what they say: 'Only those who are meant to find it will,'" Dagny and Ginger joined me in a chorus.

Pete took the fork with a piece of meat Dagny offered, took a bite, and cleared his throat. "Got an email as soon as I turned in my discharge papers. It was weird, when I opened it, 'Jingle Bells' played, but there was no attachment or video."

"Alice said that, too," I said.

Slowly, Pete, Dagny and I turned our heads toward Ginger, waiting for her response.

She only shrugged.

My phone buzzed in my pocket, and Pete tensed across the table waiting to see if I was being called in. I had two more weeks of answering pages on my days off. I'd negotiate fair days off into my next employment contract, wherever I ended up.

Alice: Did you know Elvin got hearing aids?

Silas: I didn't! That's great.

Alice: He's also going to tell the new me to use the software I downloaded. He said it's better for the environment than printing out unnecessary papers.

Silas: There's no 'new you.' You're irreplaceable.

Alice: Awww. How's dinner?

Silas: Pete's here.

Alice: But did you die?

"Hey!" Ginger shouted. She must have been trying to get my attention for a while because she looked irritated—more so than usual. "You find a job yet?"

Silas: I miss you.

I set my phone down on the table and watched Alice's name pop up with a message of simply a heart emoji.

"I'm looking. I want to make sure it's the perfect fit."

"What's Alice doing exactly? Dagny said something about old houses?" Pete asked.

Shit. It wasn't common knowledge. I didn't think Alice wanted me to tell anyone yet. She was waiting for it to be "official official," she had cautioned when I congratulated her.

"Uh, yeah. Ginger has some friends in Charleston who helped her make some connections. She's still waiting on the final confirmation since she did a video interview yesterday, but I'm sure she's going to get this internship."

"Finally putting that degree in anthropology to use?" he asked.

"She wants to work with historical societies, but she doesn't have experience yet, so this is just the beginning," Ginger added.

"Of what will be a very successful career, I'm sure," Pete said.

We tossed grins at each other, and I tipped my glass toward his. "Absolutely."

CHAPTER 32
ALICE

I was packing up the gently used clothes I bought from Bror's boutique, which would be picked up and delivered by the sled dogs. I was relieved to be reselling my heavy goose feather-stuffed parka, never to be used again. Bror reminded me I was required to come back and visit, especially since Silas' sister would be calling Tidings her home permanently. I'd worry about that damn jacket when the time came around—hopefully years later once my bones had thawed.

"Knock knock," said a female voice who let herself in through the front door I kept propped open. I turned around to see Dagny with Ginger who was carrying a large gift basket. "Hope you saved room."

My nose wrinkled, knowing damn well what she was gifting me with. I nudged my chin toward my zipped-up suitcases. "All full. Bummer."

"We will make room," Ginger said, lifting her black sunglasses off her eyes up on top of her head. She crouched down to my suitcases on the floor, unzipped and rifled through them like she had the right. "Think how good your luggage will smell when you're traveling."

"Great, everyone will be looking around for the walking candy cane," I replied. The girls tore through my suitcase, folding and scrunching up clothes, cramming in peppermint-flavored tea, chocolate, candies, and God knows what else. "I held my ground for three months; I'm not suddenly going to start craving Tidings' finest," I said that last word with a punch.

"You won't, but Silas will be homesick for peppermint tea," Dagny said. My heart rate picked up at the reminder that Silas was leaving, too. With me.

I swallowed a thick lump in my throat, and my face tightened. I looked at my two friends, each who helped me find the new me—the happy, confident me—when I had been at my lowest. They were honest to a fault, but loyal as hell.

"I'll miss you both," I said, pressing my fingers to my eyes. "Promise you'll visit all the time?"

We embraced in a sandwich hug. Dagny pulled away first, gently smacking me over the head. "I'm not going anywhere. We're practically family now."

"Sisters-in-law!" Ginger shouted and threw her arms in the air.

"Whoa, whoa, whoa. Silas and I aren't married. We aren't even engaged. That's a long time away," I stated. "If I don't fuck it up first."

"Shut up," they said in unison.

"I can't thank you both enough, and Ginger, for hiring me here and helping me with the Charleston job."

Ginger had recommended me to a friend of hers from college, who managed the historical home society in Charleston. She offered me an apprenticeship for three months, and if it all went well, I'd be hired on to a full-time position. Silas—ever the adorable nerd—was so excited for me that he bought a dozen books on historic preservation, principles, and practice.

Only minutes before I got the phone call offering me the job, I received a pleasant email from my old boss—who I'd accepted had rightfully fired me. What I did was stupid. Devin told me he had forgiven me months ago for my "reckless mistake," and assured me he had said only nice things when the hiring manager called him. He acknowledged to her that I had been fired but was assured I learned my lesson after suffering my penance in the nation's coldest place. According to my new boss, Tiffany, Devin had rambled on and on about my spreadsheet wizardry.

As it turned out, the viral picture was an embarrassment for me, but it put Devin on the map... in all the right ways, it seemed. According to Bethany, he couldn't keep the ladies away. She texted me that Devin was on a new date every night of the week, and had lightened up enough that he forgot how to micromanage. She and Patrick were able to work remotely, having never hired my replacement. She emailed me from a ranch in Texas where she was visiting a rodeo superstar.

And Patrick was on a beach somewhere with Bumper... and Bror.

"Hey, before I leave, I have questions," I said. "What's the deal with the jingle bells in the email? And when you said you worked hard to get me here, what did that mean? And how did you know Silas was leaving before he told anyone?"

Ginger and Dagny exchanged indifferent looks. "Did you wiretap my phone? Are there strippers at The Reindeer Lodge?" I had a dozen more questions that needed answering. They hugged me and walked out the door. "I'm not done!"

Tidings was full of unanswered questions, mysteries buried beneath its layers of snow. There was always more to explore—more explanations that needed to be uncovered.

But not from me. My time here was done.

HAD I LEARNED MY LESSON FROM MAKING IMPULSIVE DECISIONS? Not exactly. Moving to a new city with a man I only recently met and fell in love with didn't reassure my parents I would be in a better position next Christmas.

I completed my research and set boundaries to protect myself in case shit went sideways: a secure employment opportunity referred to by a trusted friend, a city that came highly recommended, and a man that, should he do anything stupid, would have his sister and Ginger's wrath to face.

Pete was a nice addition to the intimidation squad.

Truthfully, I wasn't worried about getting my heart broken. Silas was honest and sincere. When he said he'd come with me, he wasn't bullshitting for any nefarious or selfish reasons. I was the missing piece to his puzzle, he told me.

Silas was the companion on my road less traveled. He'd hold me close, but not hold me back. We were in it together, side-by-side.

A familiar hand caressed my elbow. "Want a coffee?" Silas asked.

I turned from the window on the train and smiled back at the man seated next to me. The last time I was on this train, we had been on it together as strangers. He looked lighter, like he left his baggage back on the train platform. We stared at each other with stupid, loving grins like two love-struck fools, and hell, we probably were.

"Yes, please."

He leaned over the armrest and gave me a peck on the cheek. "I'll be right back."

We chugged along through the windy mountains, glimpses of patchy grass beneath the glistening snow on the side of the tracks emerged. Spring was on the horizon and soon a sturdy, warm breeze would carry into Tidings, waking up dormant perennials and hardened souls. We wouldn't be there to see it.

I'd miss the serenity of Tidings. Outside, the snow continued to fall in soft, thick layers, blanketing Tidings in its quiet, persistent embrace, as if it existed in a world of its own, disconnected from the chaos of everywhere else. And for some reason, I gave it a farewell wave, relieved yet grateful.

Glimmers of snow winked at me. I flipped them off.

Silas handed me a hot paper cup of coffee as he sat next to me, taking a sip of his own beverage. He wrapped his arm around my shoulder. "Not having second thoughts?

"God, no. I gave the snow my middle finger."

He chuckled. We sat in companionable silence, feeling the rumble of the train beneath us as we watched out the window the trail of snow and pines morph into speckled dogs as we rode down the tracks.

"You?" I asked, finding the courage in anticipation of his response. He hummed in response, lost wherever his mind had taken him. "Second thoughts?"

Silas rubbed a hand over my knee, giving a reassuring squeeze. "No. And it'll be no again in an hour. Tomorrow.

Next year." He tilted my chin toward him and leaned in for a chaste kiss. Children and families were around and if I tasted his tongue deeper between my lips my want for him would overpower any sense of public decency. I was over-whelmed with desire for that damn man. "I'll never tell you to stop asking. If you must ask for your own peace of mind, I'm happy to oblige. But I hope there is one day where you unequivocally trust me."

"I trust you." I leaned my head on his shoulder. "But I wouldn't mind you coming up with creative ways to keep reassuring me."

"You never miss an opportunity for an innuendo."

"Excuse me, I was talking about more of your restau-rant-quality dinners."

The conductor announced our impending arrival to the station at the municipal airport. One more step until I was back on what I remembered fondly as Earth One. Tidings was another planet.

"Silas?"

"Yeah, babe?"

"Was this a fever dream? How will I know this was real?"

"Well, I could give you the poetic response Ginger or Elvin would dish out: *You'll always feel Tidings in your cold, cold, heart.* Or if you ever want to believe again, we can come back to visit."

I feigned a disgusted look on my face. "Too soon."

Ginger and Dagny had set plans to visit us soon, much to Silas' chagrin. His face turned a shade of green at the mention of it, since Pete would be joining Dagny.

The train whistle carried through the valley as it approached its stop, the jerky motion from the brake swaying our bodies closer in the seat. We gathered our bags, Silas insisting on carrying my tote purse over his shoulder. I trailed him down the aisle, pausing when I felt a hiccup in my heart. I ducked out of the aisle for one last parting glance. I breathed on the window, fogging a section of glass before I drew a heart. "Thank you," I said aloud to no one person or thing in particular... but somehow to all of it.

Silas extended his hand at the bottom of the stairs, and we stepped on the platform together, walking together into the airport. We passed by a young woman with a stricken look on her face as she walked in circles like she was in a foreign country and didn't speak the language. I released Silas' grip and walked toward her, pulling out my wool mittens from my jacket pocket.

"Excuse me, would you like these? I'm leaving and won't be needing them anymore." She was apprehensive, her tan cheeks flushing with a deep shade of pink. "There's a great boutique called Needle & Wool. Bror will take care of you—tell him Alice sent you."

She pinched her brows together, anxiously looking around at the passersby. "Do I look lost?" she asked.

"You look like me," I leaned in, "Good luck."

CHAPTER 33
SILAS
FOUR MONTHS LATER

"No, that's not the right one," Alice said.

I groaned. Again. "Babe, this is the eleventh blue shade we've tried. Eventually you're going to have to pick one."

We laid on the floor of our bedroom staring at the blank wall with eleven paint strokes in varying shades of blue. I didn't learn until now that there were dozens and dozens of blue-ish.

We had been in our new house in Charleston for a little over four months and Alice was committed to "taking her time to do it right." I wasn't in any rush. I was sure she'd be redecorating and changing her mind with the seasons for the next fifty years.

The living room in our century-old Colonial-style home was exquisite, but it was the only space fully decorated. Halfway complete projects lined the hallways, scattered art pieces lay against the walls in the spare bedrooms.

She found super deals in vintage shops on wood furniture, but I insisted on purchasing a new sofa, a whisky-brown leather wrapped in an L-shape. Enough room for Snøfnugg's to stretch her big, furry body out. I liked how comfortable it was to hold Alice against my body while watching the news or golf or Netflix. I never knew whatever the fuck was on when she laid next to me. I usually had a hand up her shirt in the first five minutes, and she lost her focus quickly, too.

I learned early on that there wasn't a boring day to be found when living with a girlfriend, especially one as eccentric as Alice. If I wasn't nodding along to her endless scrolling on Pinterest for ideas, I was looking for new places in the house to fuck her. Funnily, the two went hand-in-hand. Like last night, when I had her bent over a small table in the foyer, she was designing. "It collects a bunch of junk —think how nice it'll be to be organized," she said as she came down from her climax. Her fingertips made rivulets in the fogged-up window.

"If you're thinking about home projects then I'm not doing my job right." Still leaning over her, I was panting and nipped her earlobe.

"You bring out the creativity in me," she said, encouragingly patting me on my thigh.

Next to me, Alice let out an exasperated groan, and I brought my focus back to the present. I couldn't help but daydream and reminisce about her body. That was my full-time job.

"I want to put this project behind us before I start my new job next week. One less thing to worry about."

"If we don't, we don't," I said. I stroked her hair. "It's a simple problem, nothing to worry about."

"I can't sleep like this. There are all these colors on the wall looking at me; it's giving me anxiety."

I rolled over and put my hands around her face, holding her in like a picture frame. I leaned down for a kiss and she put her hands on my arms holding me back.

"Silas, you can't distract me with your body. I need to decide."

"We are in no rush. We can go slow."

"Are you talking about sex or the paint?"

I captured her lips and bit down, holding her to me. "Both."

She grunted and squirmed around. I let her crumble her fists on my chest.

Her apprenticeship with the Department of Tourism ended two weeks ago and she accepted a full-time coordinator role. It's an entry level position because she's only getting started, but I could tell she was more excited and nervous than she let on. I was ecstatic for her.

I pouted. "You can't wait to get away from me."

"Someone has to pay the bills around here," she said and rolled on top of me. I spanked her ass and let her rile herself up more. She was cute and fun and light.

"My sugar mama," I said with a kiss, grinning.

"You only want me for my stocks," she teased, sticking out her tongue.

"Keep that tongue out and see what I do with it next." I pulled her up to stand. "Let's take a break. Snøf needs a walk, and you could use a fresh perspective. Maybe you'll find another shade of blue on a colorful building on the walk. Get those creative juices flowing."

"Ew, don't say juices."

My ER job wouldn't start for another month. The whole onboarding and credentialing process for new physicians took forever, so technically I was unemployed, but my savings were holding us over. I found a position at a smaller hospital and have already gotten to know some of my future colleagues. They seem like a great team. The pay is lower than at Tidings, but the hours are fewer and the case-work is lighter. Most importantly, I'm starting to get my health and well-being back.

Meanwhile, Alice was working her minimum wage job at the local paint store—something she insisted on, even though we both knew it wasn't necessary. She'd pulled herself out of the hole left by her dipshit ex, who'd wasted her money like water through a sieve. Last she heard, the Securities and Exchange Commission was very interested in talking to him and his business partners.

Alice's investments didn't make her a millionaire—not even close—but damn, she was proud of getting every cent back, plus a little extra.

Of course, I never let her live down her crypto trading.

I leaned toward her, kissing her cheek. "I love you, darlin'"

"Did you just say that with a Southern accent?" Alice asked, grabbing the dog leash from the mudroom. Hooking the leash on Snøfnugg, she gave her indulgent belly scratches. "Summer in the South is going to be a special kind of hell for you, girl."

"We'll be at the beach as much as possible," I said. Our snow dog seemed as happy splashing in the cold Atlantic Ocean and hunting for clams as she did jumping into piles of snow. Except for that time when a crab pinched her nose, it was a painful lesson to avoid the snapping crustaceans.

I held Alice's hand as we walked along the path from our neighborhood toward a dead-end street with an obscure walking path that dropped onto the beach. Southern hospitality wasn't a myth. We'd already discovered our usual spots for grabbing a coffee and pastry along the way, and Mrs. Myrtle asked me every day if I'd made an honest woman out of the pretty lady yet. Alice rolled her eyes at the old-fashioned sentiment, but we were on the same page.

When the timing was right, we'd know.

She picked up a shell in the sand, examining the purples and pinks reflecting off the sun. She pocketed it, a new one to add to her collection. I watched her suck in a breath as she zipped her windbreaker up and took a sip of the steaming coffee.

"Cold?" I asked.

"You'll be happy to know my tolerance is improving daily," she quipped. "But the Atlantic beach in April, tropical it is not."

"We can go back to Hawaii whenever you want."

I'd take Alice anywhere she desired. At thirty-five years old, I'd finally found the person I wanted to endure everything with from the dark, dreary days to the sunny, carefree times.

Alice's phone buzzed in her pocket and she hesitated when she saw the name flash across her phone. She handed me her coffee, and surprisingly, instead of hitting ignore, she pressed the green button. "Hi, sis."

She walked along the beach, Snøf's leash in one hand and her phone in the other pressed against her ear. I watched her laugh as she drew circles in the sand with the toe of her tall green Hunter boots. Green was my favorite color on her, just like the emerald gemstone ring I kept hidden—for when the timing was right.

I'd propose right now if it were only up to me. But I wanted us to enjoy some time together without any added pressure of wedding planning. I was certain I'd spend the rest of my life with her, and I knew she felt the same way. As they say, when you know, you know. And I fucking *knew* it with my whole chest.

The emerald reminded me of the Northern Lights. It reminded me of us falling in love in the most unexpected place. Through *fate.*

"Hey," she said, holding my cheek with her cold hand. I tossed our empty cups in a trash can, and wrapped both of my hands around hers blowing hot air.

"All good?"

"Yes, actually," she said. "Turns out, there's some cool fossils to dig for along the Carolina coast. Looks like we might get another visitor this summer."

"Same time as your parents?"

"Overlapping by a few days. Ready to give up our privacy this summer?"

"It's not like they'll be in our bedroom."

She mimed a vomit reaction, mouth hanging open. "Thanks for being so great with all that. I love you."

My smile could be seen from the highest peak in Tidings. I picked her up, dropping the dog leash in the sand, and swung her over my back. "I love hearing that."

She giggled as I ran down the beach, the dog chasing after us, tongue hanging out, and slobber flying in the wind.

"What're you doing?" She giggled as she feigned displeasure.

"Better get to work before the house is full of guests." I was sputtering as I picked up pace.

"Painting?"

"Sure, if that's what you want to call it."

I felt her smile buried in the back of my neck.

It took me a lot of time to remember how to be

genuinely happy. I went through many difficult life lessons to learn how to prioritize my needs.

But I'd endure it all over again to have her wrapped around me like this.

THE END

Acknowledgments

First, to you, reader.

Writing a book is extremely vulnerable. It's kind of like getting your body cut open, allowing anyone to see your guts. How big your heart is. What kind of dark thoughts and deep desires live inside your brain. I'm grateful that you trusted me with your valuable time. Thank you for reading this story and coming along with me to Tidings — I hope you enjoyed your stay! Reach out to me on social media and let me know if you'd live there. If you liked this story, please leave a review on Amazon, Goodreads or StoryGraph.

To my husband, Alex, whose unwavering support has meant the world to me from the moment I shared my dream of telling stories and creating characters. Thank you for your endless patience and for all the sacrifices we've made as a family to give me the time and space to bring this vision to life.

I chose to make Silas a physician because, as a beginner author, I felt more comfortable writing what I was familiar with. Since being married to medicine for 11 years, and working in healthcare myself (as a writer and marketing strategist), I drew on the nuances and real-life experiences I've encountered to help shape this character. If you know my husband in real life, please don't think this was some sort of fan fiction moment. I don't even think he knows how to drive a snowmobile. Full transparency, the USMLE scene in chapter 15 did happen when we were dating. A piece of my heart lives in that scene.

To my children, Josephine and Oliver—someday, you might read this, and I won't be able to stop you because you'll be 18+. Josephine, you've been my North Star. When you ask me how the book is going, when you proudly tell your friends that your mommy is an author, when you cheer me on, and when you cry tears of joy for me, please know that I chased this dream because of you and your brother. Even though he can't talk yet and doesn't know what's going on, I want to make you both proud. You can do anything, my incredible girl. I love you.

To my in-laws and extended family who think it's amazing that I wrote a book—remember I warned you to be cool with a few things. Jocelyn, my mother-in-law, helped tremendously with the baby while I worked on deadlines, and I'll forever be grateful for your support.

To my alma mater, The University of Nevada. Go Pack!

To the village: Thank you for always asking how the book is going, listening to me ramble about ideas, and entertaining my sometimes-absurd jokes—thank you: Annie, Rachael, Kiersten, Johnny, Matt, and Mike.

Big hugs and many thanks for you encouragement and excitement each step of the way: Kristen & Diana (Sister Wives!), Sara, Telisha, Misha, Melody, Becky, and Louise. To early readers Susan and Erin. And many, many more who have sent me messages checking in on the status of this project. Thank you for being with me!

To my writer friends, Emi Turner and Katy Townes, who volunteered to beta read and have become immersed into my life now. I'm excited to have you as a new part of my inner circle.

To Luna Literary Management who created space for Alice & Silas to come alive across social media and in reader inboxes. Thank you for your creative PR and Marketing efforts for my debut. I am so excited to continue my author career with you on my team. Lauren, thank you for your tremendous amount of hard work and creativity managing ARCs and giving your entire heart to your authors.

Thank you Ashley Warren of Scribemind Studios, for your fantastic editing! And for being such a wonderful friend. I feel so blessed that we've stayed in touch since college and are now working together as fellow writers. Your natural talent, years of education and practice in writing, and sharp sense, added the right amount of flourish and clarity to bring my vision forward. I will always trust you.

To my first editor, Ashley Harmon, who saw this story when it was a much different draft. You met Silas first! From its early stages, you helped shape it into what it is today, and gave me the encouragement to keep going through revisions.

To my proofreader, Charity Chimni, thank you for your

sharp eye and attention to detail. Alice will forever appreciate knowing how many suitcases she had.

Thank you to Lindsey at Lily Bear Design Co., for the beautiful cover. The image of Alice in those suspender snow pants made all my dreams come true. The Northern Lights are gorgeous and give this book life.

THANK YOU to all of my ARC readers! It is surreal, and to be honest, it makes me emotional to think about all of you who signed up for a chance to read this before it was published. I am so grateful for you.

This story wouldn't exist without my author bestie, Tobie Carter. She pushed me and would never let me give up. We found each other years ago, and over time, we've become more than just colleagues—we've become lifelong friends. Thank you for your tough love (I mean it!), your constant support, and for bringing me into your heart. I'll always feel like I have a seat at your table.

And special shout out to all the authors and writers across platforms from Threads to IG to Smutfest 2.0. Writing can be lonely and isolating, but with this community it doesn't have to be. We are in this together and I'm rooting for all of you!

My step mom Sherri (who passed away before I published this book) read an early draft and couldn't believe I'd used the "F-word." Surprise! When I told my dad that I was going to write a book he said, "Well, alright. That's what we think you should have been doing this whole time." That's my daily affirmation. I know you purchased a copy and it's totally fine if you didn't read it except for this page. Love you.

Finally, I have to believe that somehow this message reaches my mom in her final resting place. She passed away before I started seriously writing. In fact, her death cracked me open and allowed creativity to flow in a way it never had before.

Mom, since you've passed, I've published one book and given birth to your only grandson. I can see you reading this now, getting through parts of the book where you'd have gasped and chuckled, "Marysa Callie! I can't believe you wrote that!" But still, you'd tell me how proud you are of me. I know.

ABOUT THE AUTHOR

Photo by: Josephine Stevens

Marysa Stevens studied journalism at the University of Nevada and worked in healthcare public relations before pursuing creative writing and learning to appreciate the Oxford comma. She lives in Washington State with her husband and two children. This is Marysa's first book. Follow her and reach out on Instagram @marysastevens.writer and marysastevensauthor.com

Also by Marysa Stevens

Thanks for reading *If The Fates Allow*. Stay tuned for more information about Marysa's next novel, *Behind Enemy Vines*, coming spring 2025.